SUCKERS

A HORROR NOVEL

SUCKERS

A HORROR NOVEL

Z. RIDER

A **free** eBook edition is available
with the purchase of this print book.

CLEARLY PRINT YOUR NAME ABOVE IN UPPER CASE

Instructions to claim your free eBook edition:

1. Download the BitLit app for Android or iOS
2. Write your name in **UPPER CASE** on the line
3. Use the BitLit app to submit a photo
4. Download your eBook to any device

Dark Ride Publishing
PO Box 63
Erwin, TN 37650

This is a work of fiction. Names, characters, places, and incidents either are the product of the author's imagination or are used fictitiously.

Editing: Ashley Davis
Cover design: DamonZa.com
Illustration: Nate Olson
Interior layout: Heather Lackey

ISBN: 978-1-942234-00-5

Robert A. Wells
1941–2001

PART ONE

Why 'Two Tons of Dirt?' 'Cause that's how much they throw on your grave, you know?

— Ray Ford

CHAPTER ONE

DANNY FERRY slipped out of interest.

It had a way of happening, leaving him with one hand pushed into his jeans pocket, a bottle of beer in his other, and a vacant smile on his face.

A guy with a Two Tons of Dirt tattoo told him how their song "Light It Up" had gotten him through a shitty breakup. A girl with raccoon eyes gripped his hoodie sleeve with enameled nails as she talked about the other three shows she'd caught this tour—"But *this one* was *epic*." Which wasn't quite the way he remembered it, but they'd done their best, given the circumstances.

The split skin over his knuckles stung when he gripped the beer a little tighter.

Another guy, looming like a yeti in wire-framed glasses, asked if he had a sponsor deal with Epiphone, and were they working on a new album yet?

No one asked about his knuckles, the drying blood still bright, the scab moist and fragile. The bruise pulsed off rhythm with the Dead Confederate album piping through the club's PA system. And the rest of him…was just a body, a placeholder. Keeping his spot while his brain stepped into limbo. Fans fed him, literally and spiritually, and for that he was grateful, but tonight… tonight was just one of those nights.

The bottle of half-warm beer wasn't helping. He dragged himself back to the moment, rubbed at his eye, and tried to listen to a skinny guy with cut-off sleeves telling him about his own band—well, sort of a band. They had a bass player, and his cousin had picked up a guitar at a pawnshop, but the neck was loose. It would go out of tune halfway through a song. Or maybe it was his cousin's playing. Anyway, Two Tons was a huge inspiration, and he wished his cousin could have gotten off work to come to the show, see how it was done—hey, what effects pedals did Ray Ford use?

The skinny guy's eyes widened as he spoke, looking past Dan's shoulder.

A hand clasped him from behind. Ray said in his ear, "Ready to go?"

"Seen Jamie?"

"He said don't worry about him."

Which was cause to worry. Jamie and his up-and-down drug problem—up more than down, or down more than up, depending on how you looked at it.

Ray tugged him by the back of his hoodie.

"Thanks for coming," Dan said as he let Ray pull him along. "Thanks for being there for us." The raccoon-eyed girl reached out. He clasped her fingers, a split-second physical connection with another human being before he turned away for good.

"He was in the green room," Ray was saying. "Hanging out with a couple chicks. I think he'll be okay. Us, on the other hand—you want to catch a cab or walk it?"

The club hoarded heat from the earlier show, the ceiling fans in the rafters swirling it around. The sink bath he'd taken between their set and coming out for the after-party hadn't held up for long.

"How far?" he asked.

"Just a few blocks, right?"

Fresh air. Peace and quiet. "I'm game if you are."

Ray pushed through the crowd, a half-weary smile on his face as fans reached out. He had a knack for not letting people stop him to talk. Dan followed, giving a thanks here, a couple of "See you again soons," though he had no idea when they'd be coming through again. After two years on the road, he was starting to wake up forgetting he actually had an apartment and his own bed, a bathroom he didn't have to share with anyone.

Somewhere.

They went through to the back, leaving the crowd behind. Ray pushed the exit open. A gust whirled in, skimming Dan's cheeks. His face relaxed. His shoulders loosened. As he went down the concrete steps, his strides became easier. And, miraculously, nobody was out there.

"*Much* better," he said from the sidewalk.

"You ain't whistlin' Dixie." Ray already had a pack of cigarettes out of his pocket.

Sweat cooled the back of Dan's neck as he sucked in a lungful of air. He rolled his shoulders and looked at the sky, yellow lit and dense, the city's lights reflecting off the clouds.

A lighter rasped. Ray cupped his hand around the flame, his cheeks hollowing as he sucked the cigarette to life.

They headed up the incline side by side, Ray's shoulder hitching when his weight fell on his right foot.

"Gonna see someone about that?" Dan asked. During the set, Ray'd managed to play down the limp he'd gotten from the pedal board that had landed on his foot, but out here with just the two of them, there was no need to put on a show.

"It'll be fine." He'd sworn nothing was broken, but knowing how Ray felt about doctors, Dan was skeptical.

Ray whistled a bit of a song they'd been working on, one they'd started in Cincinnati or St. Louis, or maybe it was the one from Kuala Lumpur. They reached an intersection, and Ray jerked his head to the right, still whistling, no cars passing as they made their way up a street fronted by two- and three-story brick buildings, the shop windows in the lower floors dark. It could have been Any Small City, USA. Might as well have been. Dan slowed to look up the side of a gray stone building to its gargoyle-guarded roof ledges. "Where are we?"

"I dunno. Three, four blocks away."

"I meant—"

"Bet that alley cuts it down to two." Ray nodded at a dark mouth between a bookshop and an art gallery. "And I'm pretty sure we're in North Carolina. Asheville, because I remember mountains when it was light out, but I've been known to be wrong." The blacktop where the alley met the street crumbled in under the glow of a streetlamp. Beyond that, shadows.

They looked at the alley with their elbows poking out, their hands in their jacket pockets. A breeze lifted Dan's hair at the back of his neck.

"It's dark," he said.

"Mmhm." The cigarette bobbed between Ray's teeth. "Other option is walking up to those lights up there, over a block, then back down."

Dan stifled a yawn and blinked back the exhaustion prickling his eyes.

"Straight across is looking like a pretty sweet option right now," Ray said.

"Okay, but if the boogeyman jumps out, I'm shoving you in its direction. What with your handicap, I should be able to get away clean."

"You're a pal." They stepped off the curb and crossed the empty street, traffic lights at the end of the block blinking yellow.

"Kinda smells," he said as they crossed into a darkness that made shapes float in front of Dan's tired eyes as they tried to adjust, like shadows moving at the edges of his vision. The alley smelled like rotting food.

His boots scuffed the pavement. Ray's had a crisper click, but not by much.

"How's your hand?" Ray asked.

Dan flexed it. The scab shifted over the raw scrape and the duller bruise beneath. "No real damage."

"Tell that to the wall," Ray said.

"He's lucky it was the fucking wall."

Ray ground his cigarette on the asphalt without comment. "So what do you want to do?" he asked.

"Finish the tour." They had a handful of dates left. A *handful.* So close to the end.

"And then?"

"Take a fucking break." He shrugged out of his hoodie, clutching it in his fist as they walked. "After that, I'll let you know."

"He needs to get into rehab," Ray said.

"He needs to be someone else's problem for a change." His shoulder bumped Ray's. He hadn't realized he'd been veering. The soft nudge set him back toward the middle of the alley, like a pinball in molasses. A yawn rose through him. He tipped his head back and stumbled toward Ray again.

Ray gave him a one-handed push back.

Exhaustion weighed on his muscles, made his eyes want to shut—his tiredness didn't care that he was still walking. But at least he was going to undress soon, stand under a spray of hot water, and climb between clean sheets, where he could black the fuck out until it was time to haul himself on the bus for another round.

He gave Ray a half-hearted shove.

"Hey now," Ray said. "Watch my toe."

The sharp flap of wings sounded—papery, fast.

Dan canted his chin upward. A dark shape hurtled at the edge of his vision. He moved to dodge it, but his head was whipped aside, hard, before he could get out of the way. He stumbled, the dull *thump* of impact replaying in his head. He brought a hand to his cheekbone. "Shit. What the fuck?"

Ray glanced toward the sky as he walked back toward Dan. "Are you okay?" He tipped Dan's chin toward the light.

Blinking away water at the corner of his eye, Dan said, "Did you see it?"

"Just a blur. Heard it more than anything. You all right?"

His cheek throbbed in time with his bruised knuckles. Ray touched it, and he winced.

"Bad?" Ray asked.

"No. Well, like someone with a boxing mitt punched me in the face, but I'm okay." Except for his heart racing at a hundred and eighty beats per minute.

"That was fucked up," Ray said.

"Fucking bird or bat or something must have been drunk. Let's get out of here?"

"Hey, I'm right with you."

They took a few steps, and the sound came again—wings flapping, fast. They picked up their pace, Ray's left boot coming down harder than his right. Adrenaline prickled Dan's skin, made his stomach do the kind of flip you got when you crested a hill too fast. A *thud* hit off to his left. Ray stumbled forward with a grunt.

Dan spun, walking backward fast. "Are you all right?"

"What the *fuck*?" Ray looked over his shoulder, still moving. "Fucking thing dive-bombed my back."

Dan turned back around. The alley outlet grew near, the street beyond deserted but wide open. He threw a look over his shoulder.

Nothing but alley.

Nothing but the clap of their footfalls.

Then the beat of wings.

The signal to move the fuck faster left his brain on a slow train to his legs. He ducked as the flapping overtook his hearing. The thing smacked into the back of his neck like a softball, pitching him forward. His hand opened in surprise, his hoodie spilling to the ground. His boots stumbled over broken asphalt. His knee connected hard with the ground.

He let out a sharp cry at a needle-prick of pain in his neck. He reached over his shoulders, trying to get a hand under the thing to protect his neck. Hot and rubbery and *writhing*—not the thing itself, but underneath its skin, like it was a coarse leather pouch dug from a hot riverbank and full of squirming things.

Ray's shin banged his sides. His fingernails scraped Dan's fingers as he scrabbled for purchase on the rubbery mass. Coated with something like sweat, the thing was slick and slippery, and Dan's mouth flooded with saliva at its texture, the thought of it clinging to his skin.

The thin, sharp pain in his neck grew hot, like a needle sterilized in fire. He cried out again. His vision grained. The asphalt in front of his knees swelled and heaved. His stomach bucked, and everything he'd had to drink after the show shot back up.

Through the pounding in his eardrums, he heard Ray yell, felt Ray's foot hard against his back. A surprised yelp followed, a confusion of feet over pavement. Wings flapped, and the needle pulled free of his neck.

Ray spilled to the ground behind him.

Clamping his hand against his nape, Dan looked upward, acid burning the back of his throat. The creature—whatever the fuck it was—grew small against the yellow-tinged night.

His fingers slipped in a warm slickness. Imagining blood, he clenched his teeth.

The thing pierced the underbelly of the clouds and disappeared.

CHAPTER TWO

RAY scuttled across the pavement. "Are you all right?" He grasped Dan's wrist. "We've gotta get the fuck out of here. Are you okay?"

Am I okay? Can I move? I can't move. A dark spot swooped across the gray clouds behind his eyelids. His hand slipped a little. He clutched harder.

"We've got to get out of here." Ray dragged him to his feet.

Once he discovered he *could* move, moving was easy. With Ray clutching a fistful of his shirt, they took off, their boots pounding the final twenty feet of alleyway. They spilled onto a wide, desolate street. Ray yanked him to the right, and there was their hotel, a yellow glow casting across the dark carpet beneath a blue-and-gold awning. Their boots slipped on the mat as they threw themselves at the door, hoping the damned thing wasn't locked.

A cool blast of A/C stole Dan's breath as he stumbled into the lobby. Far to the left was the front desk, elbow-high polished wood with a narrow alcove behind it for the desk clerks, none of who were present at the moment.

"Nice," Ray said. He tugged Dan toward the elevators.

A thin, wet trickle licked the inside of Dan's wrist. He squeezed his eyes shut as his footsteps sank into the lobby's thick rug, letting Ray lead him by the elbow. He imagined blood oozing between his fingers. He didn't want to look at how much. As Ray punched an elevator button, lightheadedness washed over him. He braced himself against the cool wall. "How bad is it?" he managed, his voice like a wire stretched between poles.

"It'll be okay," Ray said.

"Should we call an ambulance?" His face was clammy. The floors dinged off. His knees felt like hinges, about to fold.

"Do you need to go to the hospital?" Ray asked.

The door glided open.

"How bad is it?" He lifted his hand, turning so Ray could see.

Ray's fingers, feather-light and a little raspy, sent a shiver down his spine. He wondered what Ray was seeing. How bad *was* it? His face went cold at the memory of that thing on him. Bile flooded the back of his throat. He swallowed it back.

"Did it get you?" Ray said.

"What?" He clamped his hand over his neck. "It fucking *bit* me."

"All you've got back there is a mosquito bite."

The elevator doors slid shut with them still standing outside it.

He felt the wetness with the tips of his fingers. "But I'm bleeding."

Ray shook his head.

"Are you sure?" He let Ray look again, and Ray's touch did it again—a light vibration going right through his vertebrae.

"I don't see anything. It just looks like you've been scratching an itch. Which, if you got bit as much as I did while we were in Florida, is no fucking surprise."

"I haven't been scratching." His insides churned again. He braced his shoulder against the wall. "It *bit* me." He looked at his hand. Whatever was wet on it was colorless. He'd imagined a virtual glove of blood, dripping down his wrist, up his forearm. Instead, a tinge of pink colored the crook of his thumb.

"Your cheek's bleeding a little." Ray touched it, and Dan wanted to bat his hand away. That tingle again.

Movement from the lobby drew their eyes—the desk clerk, still on her goddamned cell phone. "I'm not bleeding," he said, his voice flat.

"Your cheek is. Do you still want to go to the hospital?"

"There's nothing back there?" He rubbed it.

"I didn't see anything."

"Holy shit." He pressed the elevator button. If he didn't have to go to the hospital, he wasn't going to the hospital. Two things they didn't need: news all over the internet about the bass player for Two Tons of Dirt getting attacked, and some doctor deciding to keep him around for testing. They were so fucking close to the end of this—the last thing he wanted was to come back for rescheduled dates. "That was *fucked up*," he said.

Ray huffed a laugh.

"What the fuck was that out there?" Dan asked as they stepped into the elevator.

"Your guess is as good as mine."

The doors slid closed. That felt safe. That felt good. They were in a box, solid walls on four sides, solid floor under his feet. A small box with no shadows for anything to hide in.

"What'd it look like?" he asked.

Ray held his hands apart. A small cat could fit between them. Jesus. The doors opened. Dan put a hand out to keep them open as Ray said, "I never felt anything like it. Fucking… I can't even describe it."

"You think it was a bat?" Dan said.

"Not any fucking bat I've seen. Man, it had a hold on you."

"No shit." He massaged his neck as they stepped out of the elevator.

"I'm surprised you *don't* have marks," Ray said. Which made Dan think of his hoodie, still out there on the ground. He should have been wearing it; maybe it would've saved his neck.

The hotel's silent hallway felt safe. It felt real, and what had happened out there—out in the alley at the far side of the hotel—felt like something your subconscious dredged up as you fell off the edge of sleep.

His cheekbone stung. The knuckles he'd busted against the wall in the club earlier throbbed like a distant beat. And the nape of his neck felt…strange. Not tender, but something. He scratched it.

"You're a mess," Ray said, cocking a little smile at him as he ran his keycard through the door lock. The green light flashed. They spilled into the room. A couple lamps burned as if Ray hadn't wanted to come back to darkness. Or, more likely, he hadn't thought to switch them off when they'd left for the club.

"Let's get you cleaned up." Ray flipped on the bathroom light.

"Let's get a drink," Dan said.

"Raid the minibar?"

"If there was ever a time to pay six bucks for a bottle of beer."

"How about we splurge on something harder?" He winced at himself in the mirror. His cheek had a split in it to match his knuckles.

"I'm not gonna argue with you," Ray said from the other room, bottles rattling as he yanked the minibar's door open.

Dan turned his shoulder toward the mirror and cranked his neck, one hand pulling at the collar of his t-shirt. His skin shone with the wetness the thing had left on him, but Ray was right—there was just a stray mosquito bite back there, barely a bump. He cranked on the faucet, his stomach turning at the thought of having that thing's slobber on him. Grimacing, he grabbed the sliver of hotel soap and scrubbed all the way up his forearms.

Ray came through the door with a tiny bottle of Wild Turkey for him.

He bent over the sink and scrubbed his neck, pushing his wet hand under the collar of his shirt. He closed his eyes—*What a fucking night*—before cranking the faucets off. He straightened, water dribbling down the middle of his back, under his shirt. He took the Wild Turkey and threw it back, the burn rolling down his throat like fire, heat spreading like a hand through his belly.

What a fucking night.

Ray cranked the water back on and took hold of Dan's chin, turning it toward him. He dabbed his cheek with a wet facecloth, making Dan wince. Another dab, another flinch. Every time Dan's eyelid jumped, Ray's squinted in empathy.

He set the Wild Turkey on the sink by feel. His hands trembled. He jerked his face away from the washcloth. His chin tingled where Ray's fingers had held it. He splashed his face. Gripped the tap and turned it back off. Blinked water from his lashes as he watched the last of it spin down the drain.

When he straightened, Ray had a dry towel for him.

He left a dab of blood from his cheek on it, a watery tinge of pink.

His fingers thrummed with the aftershock of adrenaline.

"That was some scary fucked-up shit," Dan said.

"What about the others?"

Dan's stomach tensed. Their crew was out there, probably as tempted as they were to walk it to the hotel. People they were responsible for. People they needed in one piece if they were going to finish this tour.

Dragging his phone out of his pocket, Ray said, "I'll get a hold of Moss." Of their crew, Moss was the Reliable One. Not to take anything away from Stick or Josh, because their drum tech knew his shit and Josh could work a merch table like nobody else, but when an *adult* was required…it fell on Moss.

Dan swept the empty bottle of Wild Turkey into the trash bin. He winced at his cheek in the mirror. Turning his head, he stretched his neck to see it, exploring with his fingers where he'd felt the stab of pain.

Ray was in the other room, his voice low and fast.

Dan came out of the bathroom to find Ray on the end of the bed clicking through TV channels: infomercials, late-late-night talk shows, public access, soft-core porn.

"No answer," Ray said. "I left a voicemail. Looking for the news to see if there's anything about other people being attacked.

Here." He handed Dan the remote and brought up the contacts on his phone again. Put the phone to his ear.

Dan clicked to another channel and landed on CNN. Nothing but talking heads and scrolling headlines about the Gaza Strip, the latest jobs report. A NASA flight engineer who'd killed her kids then taken her own life while she was in custody. Arson was suspected in the recent California fires. A bombing killed seventeen in the Balkans. Dan's gaze moved to the window, its sheer curtains lit from the back by the street, the blackout drapes wide open. As Ray left a voicemail for someone else who might still be out there, Dan dragged the drapes shut. "Try Jamie," he said, though that was probably useless.

"Just did."

"Stick?"

"Pissed off at being woken up while you were in the bathroom." Stick had been fighting a cold for the past week. No surprise he'd jumped on the opportunity to crawl into a bed.

"Any more whiskey?" Dan asked. Carey, their tour manager, was likely in bed too. That just left their errant drummer, plus Moss and Josh, and their sound guy, Greg.

"Hey," Ray was saying as he fished through the contents of the minibar. "Where are you? Speak up. I can't hear you." He tossed Dan another airplane bottle. "Who else is still there? What about Greg? Okay, do me a favor. Tell everyone to grab a cab or get a ride from someone. Do not walk back to the hotel. And don't take a ride if it means you have to walk three blocks to get to the car. Got it?"

Dan torqued the cap off and drank half of it down, closing his eyes as the warmth spread through his insides.

"Don't even stand around outside waiting for the cab to show up if you call one. Watch from inside the door. I'm serious. This fucking bat or something attacked Dan and me. No, I'm not kidding. Yeah, we're good. Just be safe, okay?"

At the club, surrounded by people, the only part of Dan that'd felt anything was his knuckles, their dull throb like a heartbeat—and him drinking beer to try to forget it. He closed his fist to feel it again. The memory of sheetrock buckling under it came visceral, right alongside the anger that had led him to do it. *You've got one job to do for two fucking hours—sit behind the fucking drum kit and play what you're supposed to* when *you're supposed to. Is that too much to fucking ask?*

"Grab Jamie," Ray was saying. "Make sure he gets in the car with you, whatever it takes. If he has to bring people back to the hotel with him, stuff them in too. Whatever it takes, just get his ass here. We can't afford to lose our drummer with a few dates left. Yeah, call me when you all make it here. Thanks, man." He hung up.

Dan said, "Moss?"

"Josh. Stick and Moss went back to the hotel as soon as they finished load out. Carey too. Since Moss isn't answering, we'll just hope he turned his ringer off before he turned in."

"Yeah." He looked at the plastic bottle of whiskey in his hand before closing his eyes and finishing it.

"You doing all right?" Ray asked.

"Yeah." He scrubbed a hand through his hair. "Yeah, I'm okay. You?" He dropped his empty bottle in the trash. Headlines scrolled across the bottom of CNN.

"What do you think it was?" Ray asked.

"The only thing I can think of is a bat."

"I'm no expert, but…"

"Yeah." Taking a seat on the end of his bed, he put his head in his hands.

Ray said, "I'm not going to be able to fucking sleep," and Dan felt the same. What was going to do it—knowing where everyone was? The sun coming up? Getting drunk enough to pass out?

Ray cracked a mini of vodka. His phone rang. "Greg," he said as he lifted it to his ear. "Yeah?"

Dan studied the pattern of the hotel carpet while Ray talked to their sound tech.

"Nah, we're shook up, and Dan's got a bruise on his cheek that'll make him look tough on stage, but we're fine." He fumbled a cigarette from his shirt pocket. "Yeah, do me a favor—if Jamie's still around, grab him by the collar and drag him along." He listened for a minute, drawing smoke into his lungs, streaming it back out his nostrils. A half-smile—no humor, but a smile nonetheless—came onto his face. "Yeah, if you could do that, that'd be awesome. Thanks, man." He tossed the phone on his own bed.

"What's he gonna do?"

"Collar Jamie and drag him in the cab with the rest of them."

"Nice." At least their sound engineer was big enough to get it done. He could stick Jamie and Ray under each arm and run them up a field like footballs.

"Better him than me," Ray said. "That's not a job I'd want." The smile had turned wry. Dan dropped back on the bed.

Ray unloaded his pockets—phone, wallet, lighter. He headed for the bed, the limp back—exaggerated now—his cigarette clamped between his teeth.

They'd had the tour all planned and budgeted out so that everyone got their own room when they had a hotel night. But legs got added, opportunities came up that they couldn't afford but couldn't resist—Kuala Lumpur, for instance—and at some point they always wound up cutting corners to make it work. It was that or get off the road. As exhausting as touring was, staying in one place was harder.

"I'm gonna take a leak," Dan said, "then give sleep a try at least."

A few minutes later he came back out, pulling his shirt over his head. Ray sat with his back against the headboard, his ankles crossed on top of the bedspread, an ashtray in his lap. He had the remote in his hand again. "Why is there never anything fucking on this time of night?"

Dan worked his boots off. He was exhausted all over again, his limbs heavy. He managed to get out of his shirt and jeans and crawl under the covers.

Ray turned off the lamp, still clicking through the channels. Smoke filled the air. It felt almost comfortable. Familiar. Dan rubbed the back of his neck, then let his hand rest on his shoulder. He closed his eyes and hoped sleep didn't hold off for too long.

The roll-spark of a lighter, the sibilance of burning paper. A stifled cough, a clearing of the throat. The seals around the minibar's door gave. A second later, a plastic cap skittered across the dresser top.

Ray dropped a boot on the floor, then the other. His phone trilled. He put it to his ear with a mumbled, "Yeah," as he headed toward the bathroom.

Dan listened to him say, "Awesome. Good to hear," as the door shut, then it was just murmurs.

He listened harder, but couldn't make anything out. After a while, the toilet flushed, the door opened, the lighter did another rasp-spark. The TV clicked through channels. Dan's thoughts stopped making sense, bleeding into each other, images rising before slipping into dark waters. He realized he was drifting off. He blinked in the bluish darkness. The TV was on, but he couldn't make out what was playing.

The springs in the next bed complained softly as Ray shifted.

Dan turned over and buried his head under the blanket.

When he woke a few hours later, in the flickering glow of the muted TV, in a room smelling of stale cigarettes, Ray was asleep on his back, on top of the covers.

Dan knocked over an empty beer bottle on his way to the bathroom. On his way back, he made out another beer on the nightstand with what looked like a tiny bottle of vodka toppled against it. Ray's cigarette pack lay on the floor, crumpled. Everything had a not-quite-real feel to it, like he was dreaming. He touched the drapes over the window. They felt real enough. He eased one aside, squinting out to see the sky, dark purple in the distance. Already the street below seemed less dead; a delivery truck rumbled by, followed by a car with a bike rack mounted to its roof.

He touched the glass.

He didn't feel real, but the glass did—cool and smooth and hard against his fingertips.

Ray mumbled in his sleep. Dan looked over his shoulder. Then he crossed the room, came around Ray's bed, and found the remote sticking out from under Ray's hip.

When he eased it free, it seemed to buzz a little, both as a feeling against his fingers and a distant sound in his ears. This was the unreal feeling he'd been having since he'd woken: everything a little electrified yet at the same time indistinct. Even Ray was a little electrified. Dan's fingernails vibrated where they'd brushed his side.

Thrumming.

He turned the TV off.

Somehow he managed to miss any turned-over bottles on his way around the bed. He climbed under the covers and lay in the dark—thrumming—until it was only semi-dark. And then not so dark at all.

And there he was, still thrumming.

CHAPTER THREE

A HAND clamped Dan's shoulder as he was about to shove his bag under the bus.

"Let's see that rabid bat damage," Moss said.

Dan pushed his bag inside before straightening.

Moss, a paramedic before he'd become their guitar tech, stepped closer and palpated the bruise on Dan's cheekbone, making Dan's eye twitch.

"Everything feel okay?" Moss asked.

"Feels fine—you know, for being hit in the face."

"Did you see what hit you?"

"It was dark. Whatever it was was dark too. It latched on to my back."

"Turn around."

"Ray had to pry the fucking thing off." Moss's fingers sent a shiver down his neck.

"I don't see anything."

"Yeah, I don't know what the fuck was going on." He shrugged into his jacket as Josh hopped off the bus, grinning. "Bat boy."

"Funny." He dragged a hand through his hair. "You guys didn't see anything on your way back?"

"Nope. The most vicious thing we came across was Jamie, when we told him we were taking him back to the hotel."

"How bad'd he take it?"

"Put it this way," Josh said. "It was a good thing I had my jacket with me. We bundled him in it so he'd stop trying to scratch us and got into some chicks' car. Me and Greg stuffed ourselves in after him and made the chicks drive us here. When we told him we were dragging him inside by the shorthairs if we had to, he said fuck it and invited them up to his room. That was the last I saw of him."

Dan glanced toward the hotel. "How much you want to bet he didn't stay at the hotel after you guys took off to your own rooms?"

The door opened. Ray strolled out, placing a cigarette between his lips as a breeze lifted his hair.

"Well, we did what we could," Josh said.

"That's all you can do." He nodded at Ray. "Seen our methhead this morning?"

"Yep." Smoke streamed from his nostrils. "He's a little worse for wear, but I'd blame it on a night on pills more than freaky creature attacks." He flipped the collar of his jacket up. "He should be down soon."

As the others got ready to go, Dan stared toward the alley they'd run out of last night. It looked nothing but dingy in the late-morning light. A moving van bounced past its entrance.

By the time Jamie sauntered out, Ray was at the end of his second cigarette, getting in as much nicotine as he could before climbing on the bus where, for the sake of the nonsmokers, smoking wasn't allowed. Jamie had a cigarette going too, half smoked, no concern for whether or not he should be smoking down the hallways of the hotel. He took a drag as he stopped to look at Dan. As smoke curled out his nostrils, he said, "I heard what happened. You okay?"

"Yeah, I'll live. Ready to get out of here, though."

"You don't have to tell me." He clapped Dan on the back and headed for the bus.

No matter how well they tried to air it out, the bus always smelled like farts and old socks. Dan had a theory that socks crawled behind the panels to die, which was why they never managed to end a tour with more than six socks between the eight of them.

When Dan came up the steps, coffee was already going in the galley, covering the staleness with a richer smell that made Dan's stomach growl and tighten at the same time.

Stick yawned with his hands braced on the edge of the counter, watching the pot fill, his mouth still open when he turned his head and caught sight of Dan's face. "Shit. Who'd you get in a fight with?"

"A creature of the night," Dan said. "Feeling any better?"

"A hooker hit you?"

Dan laughed. "Yeah, that's it."

"Man, that's rough. Were you trying to gyp her?"

Dan patted his shoulder as he passed by. "Something like that."

"You can't gyp the ladies, man."

He headed for the back lounge, where he found Jamie and Greg sprawled on the wrap-around couch, the TV blaring cartoons.

"Get any sleep?" Dan asked.

"Shit," Greg said, while Jamie said, "I passed out for a while. Does that count?"

Dan gave a shrug. His fingers found their way into the front pockets of his jeans. He slouched down to make more room for them.

"I think I threw up on Josh's coat," Jamie said.

"He didn't mention it," Dan said.

"Maybe it wasn't his, then. In which case..." He sat back and rubbed an eye with two knuckles. "I'm glad I was up and out before the girls I was with woke up."

"They're still in your room?"

"Yeah."

Dan closed his eyes and let his head fall back. All he could do was hope they didn't charge a huge breakfast to the room and steal the lamps.

No, he could do more than hope. He got to his feet and strode back off the bus, looking for their tour manager. He found him at the front desk, getting receipts.

"Ouch," Carey said, seeing his cheek.

Dan dismissed it. Talking about the 'bat' was getting tiring. "Jamie left some girls up in his room."

Carey sighed. "I'll take care of it."

"Thanks." The money would come out of Jamie's end if they trashed the place, but it never seemed to work out that Jamie was the only one his shit flew back on. It tended to splatter everyone in the vicinity.

"Hey," Carey said as Dan started away.

He turned.

"It was really a bat that hit you?"

"Your guess is as good as mine. Oh, but don't come stumbling in here in the middle of the night after getting smacked by something around the corner, 'cause the desk clerks disappear like roaches when a light comes on."

"Great." Another road-worn sigh.

Dan spun back and headed for the exit.

On the bus again, he slumped on a couch in the front lounge, his chin tipped up toward the TV mounted on the ceiling. Ray had it on a news channel again, but if anyone was getting attacked by bat-like creatures, it wasn't getting national coverage. Trust them to run into the one fucked up bat in the country.

"Where's next?" Dan asked, watching without taking in the B-roll footage of the astronauts returning from their international cooperative space mission. He wondered if it had been the vastness of space that had gotten to the astronaut who'd killed her kids—what had she seen up there? Maybe it'd been being cooped up in a tin can for months on end. That he could relate to.

"Somewhere north of here," Ray said without looking away from the TV.

"Someplace without bats, I hope." With Jamie safe on board and the pull of gravity as the bus started away from the hotel, his thoughts turned back to the night before. What he wouldn't give to shut off *that* instant replay. The quick flap of wings rushed his ears. He could taste the acid of his stomach all over again.

Ray flashed him a quick smile.

Dan massaged the back of his neck.

"How are you doing?" Ray asked.

"Fine." His voice was flat. He shifted to get more comfortable on a couch that'd had all its comfortable spots worn out of it months ago. He tried to focus on the television.

What he did instead was rub his neck, remembering how that thing's body had felt when he'd tried to grab hold: writhing and rubbery and slick. Like a pulsing, thick-skinned organ outside of its host body. A shudder jerked down his spine.

The television wasn't doing anything for him. His gaze dropped to Ray's upturned profile, his nose and chin like an outcropping of rock in the face of a cliff. If he had to be attacked in a dark alley with anyone, he guessed Ray was about as reliable as they came. He hated to think if it had been Jamie.

"Hey," he said.

Ray looked over.

"Thanks. For last night."

"No problem." He tilted his chin back toward the TV.

The bathroom door shuddered open, sticking in its tracks. Josh called it colorful names under his breath it as he tried to close it back up.

When this tour was over, one thing Dan wasn't going to miss was this bus. "How many more shows?" he asked Ray.

"Three. No, hold up. Four."

Four. The shows didn't exhaust him, but all the hours in between… He scrubbed his face.

"Day off today, though," Ray said.

Shit. He'd take shows over downtime any fucking day.

CHAPTER FOUR

IT WAS a day off only if you counted sitting on a bus for seven hours a "day off."

Because they had all afternoon and evening to travel, they could afford to stop for a sit-down meal at least. After some discussion about the road signs on the highway and what everyone was in the mood for—everyone except Jamie, who was crashed in his bunk—they rumbled off the interstate.

Jamie managed to haul his ass out of the bunk to join them, sulking in a half-stupefied state until he was on his third drink.

After two weeks on the road, you ran out of things to talk about. Got irritable. Pulled into yourself. By the time you got up close to two years, you were like a big family crammed in a three-room trailer—and sometimes there was still nothing to talk about. You ate to the sounds of forks, ice cubes against glass, an occasional fart. Maybe a story from Stick about the chick he banged the night before...because he could pick 'em.

As they made their way through lunch, Jamie, bristling against the quiet, began dropping silverware for the hell of it. He'd call the waitress over to get another replacement—and another drink, thanks. Drumming his spoon against his water glass while he waited. Laughing to himself: sudden short hiccoughs over nothing.

It was a spike hammering into Dan's forehead. The anger that had ebbed since the night before came scrabbling back on claws. *Jesus fucking Christ.* Had it always been like this, this much of a pain in the fucking ass? Jamie'd been worse, a lot worse—there was the time he'd gone missing for three days in the middle of laying drum tracks, running up the bill on the studio for no fucking reason. Or when he'd moved himself into their rehearsal space, a twenty-by-twenty room with no windows, and they had no idea he was living there until the building owner to let them know they were violating the rental agreement.

Or the time he pawned his drum kit because a dealer he owed money to was going to "kill" him. He still owed them for buying it back for him.

Dan wondered if he was getting too old for this. He was barely thirty. They'd been doing this ten years, the three of them. At some point it had to get better, right?

He wrenched the spoon from Jamie's hand.

Jamie said, "What?"

Ray wiped his hands on a napkin, dropped it on his plate, came out of his chair without a word. He ambled toward the doors, pulling a cigarette pack from his shirt pocket.

Dan was wary of thinking Ray felt the same as he did. Whenever he assumed something like that, it usually came back to slap him in the face.

Ray had *infinite* patience—and a little panic at the edges of his eyes at the mention of replacing their drummer. Maybe it was superstition more than patience. They'd gotten where they were because of the configuration they had, each of them an important piece of the talisman. Change something in that and maybe it was like spilling salt, breaking a mirror, going to a black cat convention.

That, and Ray just didn't give up on people. Not after what happened with his mother.

Jamie beat a rhythm against the floor with his sneakers.

Without looking up from the baked potato he was working his way through, Carey said, "Knock it off for a few, huh?"

Which got an edge of a laugh from Jamie, who crumpled his napkin and headed for the bathroom.

The time it took to suck down a butt passed, and Ray didn't return. The bill came. It got paid. Jamie'd made a detour at the bar instead of coming back. He was leaning on it, chatting up the cute bartender when it was time to leave. Trying to get a free drink, knowing him. Chances were he didn't have the cash in his wallet to pony up for one himself.

Dan corralled him with an arm around his shoulder, pulling him close as he walked him out the doors. "Just a few more days, huh?"

"Fucking finally."

They stopped to let a car pass. The bus was at the far end of the lot, because that's where you parked buses, far away. "Think you'll be able to hold it together for that long?" Dan asked.

"What? Yeah?" He seemed surprised.

"Looking forward to getting back home for a while?"

"Uh, yeah. As soon as I figure out where that is."

Dan held back a sigh, stifling also the urge to say, *Well, you know, if you need to…* Nope. No way. He had an apartment all to himself, and after two years of not spending more than two weeks at a stretch in it, he was going to enjoy the fuck out of the space and solitude. *Without* Jamie's bullshit tromping in and out day and night.

"You could always check into rehab," he said. "You know, get a breath of fresh air for a bit? If nothing else, it gives you someplace to stay for a month or two."

"Uh. Yeah. Sounds like a blast." Jamie dug in his jacket for a cigarette, using it as an excuse to pull free of Dan's arm, and for a second it felt like the past pulling free. It wasn't always this shitty, the Jamie thing. They used to have fun.

Ray and Moss waited outside the bus, watching traffic pass in companionable silence, Ray with a cigarette dangling between his fingers. Moss, who didn't have a tobacco habit but could drink all of them under the table and still wake up ready to go at the crack of dawn, had his hands in his jacket pockets, no doubt enjoying the leg stretch.

Jamie, lit up by now, leaned his shoulder against the bus. He smiled, to himself it seemed like, and blew smoke into the air.

Dan had the irritable beginnings of a headache, a holdover from Jamie's silverware concert. He hauled himself up the bus steps, mourning the fact that fresh air hadn't made its way inside while they were eating. Someone had brought boxed leftovers in. Garlic pasta mixed with the stale funk of their tin can home. He got a water from the fridge and headed to his bunk with the morning's *USA Today*, compliments of last night's hotel stay.

It was more of the same—everything he'd learned from CNN Headline News, only in print. He folded it up and tossed it by his feet. With lunch heavy in his stomach and his skull feeling like a vise was cranking closed on it, he couldn't summon the motivation to even pull off his boots. Closing his eyes, he hoped for a little sleep.

A while later, the bus downshifted, then downshifted again. He rubbed his tongue against the roof of his mouth, trying to work up some spit. He pushed himself up, then dropped again. Sleep had been thin and sweaty, and now he had that same unsteady feeling he'd woken up with in Ray's room. He fumbled for his warm bottle of water, that hyper-real sensation coming over him again: he was foggy and indistinct while everything else was overly real.

He unscrewed the cap, marveling at its ridges, and propped himself up enough to take down a few gulps.

Warm or not, it was what he needed.

The bus lurched, turned, and slowed yet more. The brakes hissed.

He rolled out of the bunk and made for the bathroom as the others gathered their shit—laptops, phones, Ray with his cigarettes and a beat-up paperback folded around his thumb.

When Dan dropped to the ground from the bus's steps, they were closing up the luggage area in the bus's belly. His bag sat on the pavement. Yawning and shrugging off another few layers of sleep, he grabbed it and headed for the hotel behind everyone except Ray, who'd stopped to light a cigarette.

A lot of times on the road there was nothing to say, and he appreciated that, for the most part, the guys they traveled with didn't need to fill up the silences. As he and Ray stepped in behind the rest of the crew, waiting for Carey to get their room keys from the desk, Ray lifted an eyebrow to ask how Dan was doing, and Dan answered with a half-hearted shrug. He could use some real sleep, for one thing.

"I'm gonna stretch my legs," Ray said after dumping his stuff in front of his bed. "Might get something to eat, too. You want me to give you a call if I find someplace decent?"

"Nah. I'm good."

Two nights in a row in an actual bed was a luxury. It was after ten by the time he'd unpacked and hung the Do Not Disturb sign. His nap had left him wide-awake but scattered. He touched the window before pulling the thick drapes closed, ran his hand over the upholstery of the chair in the corner, grasped the edge of the dresser, feeling its hyper-real solidity, wondering when that weird effect was going to wear off.

He worked his laptop out of his bag, plugged it in, and set it up. While it booted, he lay back and massaged his temples. The thin shell of a headache hadn't cracked away yet. He found a travel bottle of ibuprofen in his bag. After washing two down, he sat cross-legged in front of the computer.

An image search for "black bat" returned a shitload of clip art and comic book character Cassandra Cain. His headache said, *Fuck it man, give up. Have a drink. Get some sleep.* He squeezed his eyes shut for a moment before scrolling down the page—row after row of cartoon bats, the Black Bat, the Batmobile. He growled under his breath and deleted the word "black."

Bats.

He cupped the back of his neck as he looked at a bat cocooned in its own wings. He opened an image of one in flight. Watched videos of them flying.

No way was what had gotten him a bat. What he'd felt under his fingers had been rubbery, clammy, but something else too, something that made his gut go loose every time he thought about it. He rubbed his eyes, drank more water, and tried searching on the city they'd just left for "bat-like things." Nothing. He tried "attacked." A car hijacking, an elderly woman mauled by a neighbor's dog, a man robbing a 7-Eleven with a crowbar. He expanded his search beyond the city. Even with tweaking, the best he could do on "humans attacked by animals" was monkeys in Thailand stealing food out of tourists' hands. He dropped back on the bed, his brain skittering from one thing he didn't want to think about—Jamie—to another—bats—to another and another. Eventually he gave up and sat against the headboard, staring at the TV. Everything was in the middle of itself. *Click*—a movie he'd already seen. *Click*—news. *Click*—an SUV commercial. He dropped the remote, leaving the commercial and whatever would come on after it to play out. He rubbed circles into his temples.

*M*A*S*H* came on after the break, late into the plot. After that came *Hogan's Heroes*. *F Troop*. All of it shit. He'd hoped the TV would shut down his thoughts, but no: bats, Jamie, what the *fuck* had attacked him?

Halfway through *F Troop* he took a piss, got out of his clothes, turned everything off.

He pulled the blankets up and closed his eyes.

He thought for sure he was going to lie awake all night, but after a few ticks of silence, he was gone.

Something squirmed in the back of his neck. Some *things*. He had no idea where the band had gone, the crew. He tried to flip the hood of his sweatshirt up to cover his neck, but he remembered he'd left it in the alley. He clamped his hand over it, the skin there stretched tight, about to split like a tomato in the sun. Things wriggled underneath, hot and alive.

He woke in the dark, unsure whether this was real or the dream was, and he rubbed the back of his neck, feeling the ghost of tiny insect legs creeping over it, but nothing was there.

He got out of bed, pissed, gulped down more water. Looked at the other bed, its covers untouched, Ray's bag right where he'd left it. His shoulders felt like someone had stuck a key in his back and wound them tight. He rolled them to loosen them, then texted Ray, chewing a fingernail while he waited for a response. The tension in his muscles was giving him a killer headache. His phone lit up. He let out a breath of relief. The text said, "Hotel bar. Wanna come down?"

He passed on the offer, took some more ibuprofen, and stood under a spray of hot water for a while, trying not to think. North Carolina was four hundred and fifty miles behind them. They'd gotten away. The alley attack was just a bad dream.

He burrowed under the sheets. Sleep came in fits and starts. As it came over him one time, his body began to vibrate. He heard bees. He snapped his eyes open. A soft rustle of clothes came, a light step on the floor. The bathroom door closed. He slipped under again.

And felt more dragged down when he forced his eyes open in the morning than he had when he'd closed them.

Breakfast ended up being more like lunch, then they were back on the bus, heading to the club for soundcheck—which Jamie made it to, and which went off without a hitch, so thank you higher power for *something* going right. They jammed for a while at the end of it—their support hadn't arrived yet, no one was breathing down their necks. Playing eased the headache he couldn't completely shake.

After soundcheck, Carey herded him and Ray to a picnic table in a fenced-off smoking area, where a freelance journalist with hair the color of candy apples introduced herself as Prism.

He tried to focus on the interview, but his thoughts were muddled and muddied. He wanted to be back in the dimness of the club, his bass in his hands. Or in bed again, in the dark. Prism had Ray talking about how their songs evolved on the road, how they never really considered a song finished when they put it on an album.

"We'd do a live album for every tour if we could," Ray said. "But even then…you know, six, seven years after we put out a song, we pull it back out, and it's all new again, it's changing again. There's always more to do with it."

Sunlight glinted off the thin hook in Prism's nose as she nodded.

"Nothing's ever finished," Ray said. "Not until you're, you know, fucking dead." He gave a wheezy laugh as he raised his cigarette to his mouth.

Dan cupped the nape of his neck. The mosquito bite had gone down, but it felt weird back there, under his skin, in his vertebrae. Tingly.

Prism laughed at whatever Ray'd just said, Ray saying now, "Well, you know." And then the thank-yous went around, Prism stopping the recorder on her phone, gathering her stuff.

Dan rose, his hand out. "I hope you got what you needed."

When she grasped his fingers, a sting pinched the back of his neck. He jerked away from her touch.

Her mouth opened.

"Sorry. Static shock." A hive of bees swarmed hotly at the back of his neck, under his palm.

"I hate those," she said. "I didn't feel that one, though."

"Sometimes they just getcha one way," Ray said. When he offered his own hand, she said, "Are you sure you want to do this?"

"I could probably use the jump," Ray said. She laughed.

As she headed off, Ray raised an eyebrow at him.

"I don't know what the fuck happened." He rubbed his neck again, where the bees hummed distantly.

He grasped Dan's shoulder. "You been feeling all right?"

The bees swarmed at the touch—a vibration crawling through the top of his spine. "Headachy," he said.

"Need something for it?"

"I've got ibuprofen."

Ray nodded and removed his hand to light his cigarette.

The hive of bees flew apart, and the headache pushed tighter against his temples. Between soundcheck and showtime, there weren't many places to hang out—the bus or the back of the club, or the smoking area, which would be packed with fans soon. He retreated to the bus's bathroom—the smell of disinfectant intensified by the fact that it didn't get as much air conditioning as the rest of the tin can—and leaned a shoulder against the wall and let his mind wander, mostly through empty fields, which was what he was after. On the road, you had so much downtime you started to feel like you were stuck in your head. You got sick of yourself, sick to the roots of your teeth of your thoughts chasing after each other. Sometimes you could take off, walk around an unfamiliar city, crowd out your thoughts with sights and sounds and smells. Other times you were trapped, and you had to take that walk in your head. Empty fields. The woods after a warm rain. Scuttling over rocks at the top of Mount Chocorua in the bright morning sunshine.

He closed his eyes, letting the noise from outside the bathroom—voices, feet, traffic—settle and slip away. The buzzing at the base of his skull was so soft he had to settle into himself to hear it. Staying inside himself, he rested his back against the wall. He wished the bus were moving so he could have that rocking feel, that vibration under his boots.

He stayed there until Carey gave a quick knock and a "Dan? Almost time."

He was ready. He took a leak, then went out and played. All the tension and frustration and the sound of his own thoughts plowed down his arms, through his fingers, and out into the noise he was making. He attacked the bass with his eyes closed, with a pick pinched between his fingers, with his lips bumping the mic as he sang words without having to think them first.

After the show, they talked with fans behind the venue, stood for pictures. He dropped an arm around a girl's shoulders, and the bees swarmed and buzzed. His arm tightened. He dragged it off her—it felt filled with lead until contact was broken and the bees died back a little.

"You all right?" Stick asked, passing by with a crate of t-shirts.

Dan gave a short nod. The next photo, he just stood near the guy. Their shoulders bumped. He shook his head to clear the bees when the guy moved away. It was dark behind the club, just a security light and a standard bulb at the back entrance. A flash went off in his face, and he thought he saw grains in it. He needed something solid to grab on to—solid and inanimate. He shoved his hands in his jacket pockets and blinked through another flash.

"Sorry to break it up," Carey said, "but we've got a schedule."

Josh had a couple bottles of water in his hands. He flipped one toward Dan. Dan caught it against his chest. The fans drew back a little, disappointed but understanding, and he thanked them as he backed toward the bus, turning around to make real headway toward it while Carey said, "You too," as he grabbed Ray in the middle of a laugh, dragging him away from a small crowd.

As the bus started away from the sidewalk, Josh grabbed a can of beer from the fridge. Jamie was sober. Everyone seemed to be feeling decent. They pulled through a twenty-four-hour Taco Bell for something to eat.

"You feeling okay?" Stick asked again from the couch in the front lounge.

"I'm gonna go lie down." In the bunk area, he shucked everything but his shorts and crawled into bed with a Michael Connelly novel he'd gotten halfway through last month and forgotten about until it resurfaced in his bag earlier today. He half expected the others to turn in early too, but it sounded pretty lively out there. Maybe a card game going on. The laughter sounded good; it was enough just to hear everyone getting along—no snarking, no short fuses. He laid the book on his chest. After a minute, he turned off the reading light.

He was still awake when people dragged themselves to their bunks. It sounded like Moss had been the big winner, but that was about usual.

With the bunk area full, the bees vibrated inside him. He pressed his hands over his eyes.

He was still awake when the only noise was the road passing under the bus's tires.

He was still awake—and pacing the front lounge with a bottle of orange juice—when sunlight made its way through the cracks between the blinds.

Standing in front of the window in only his shorts, he watched flat acres of land spool by like a film reel.

CHAPTER FIVE

By the time the others stirred, he was back in his bunk, his head under the pillow. He'd swallowed three ibuprofens. The headache thrummed under the surface of his skull—more tension than anything. But he was tired of it, not to mention just plain tired. Tired and wired. His brain wouldn't shut up and let him drift off.

The bus slowed. In a few minutes they'd be gassing up, and Ray would be sucking down smokes, a sight so familiar by now it was almost iconic. Freshman year in high school, Dan had been in the marching band and Ray on the football team—smoking even then. Dan didn't bother with marching band sophomore year, and Ray wasn't any good at football, but during that first autumn of high school, when they'd both spent time on the field, Ray had singled him out somehow, calling him names with the kind of lazy smile that made you not take it too hard. They jabbed each other through the fall semester, passing in the hallways, the cafeteria, out on the field.

He had no idea why. Even Ray shrugged if you asked him about it: "You looked like you knew what you were doing." On the field, he'd meant, in the marching band. How it looked like he knew what he was doing with a fucking tuba, Dan had no idea.

"And you had that Stooges shirt," Ray would add.

One day, in line at the cafeteria, Ray'd said, "If you want to hear some *real* music instead of that marching band shit…"

Real music turned out to be Ray and a pockmarked kid named Steve, one on guitar and vocals, one on drums, making nothing but noise. Painful, set-your-teeth-on-edge noise. *Loud* noise. The noise drew Dan, though, and there was something else there too, if you ignored Steve's dropping the beat to push his glasses up and Ray's inability to decide whether he'd rather be Jimi Hendrix or Greg Ginn. There was something about what Ray was trying to do when he wasn't trying to be someone else, and it clicked with Dan.

Around the same time, Dan happened to see an old Global bass at a flea market. Cost him twenty bucks. Getting an amp to go with it cleaned out the cash in his sock drawer.

Bass turned out to be a lot more fun than tuba.

They went at it every day—after school, weekends, school holidays. Steve got tired of their relentless practices, the hours of jamming and writing—especially the writing, Dan and Ray with their heads together, talking in half-sentences they didn't need to finish, and Steve bored, flipping drumsticks. He'd been uncomfortable with original music, stuff he couldn't pop into a CD player and mimic. After a while, he'd begun complaining about being the third wheel.

Dan wondered if Jamie was also a third wheel. If he was, he *had* been—for like a decade now.

Unlike Steve, Jamie was usually happy to let them do their thing. Not to take anything away from him; he could play his ass off, and he had no problem working with all-new songs. It was just…it was the way they worked, he and Ray holed up for days or weeks, a month or two even, with or without Jamie over in the corner, building tiny cities out of stubbed-out cigarette butts. Then they'd bring Jamie in on it. Jamie'd put his touches on what they told him they wanted, and they'd be ready to go.

It worked really fucking well, actually…when he wasn't wanting to wrap his hands around Jamie's neck and shake his eyeballs out of their sockets.

But if the band could get by without a drummer, he'd be all for it. After all these years, he couldn't conceive of finding a third member for the band who gelled the way he and Ray did. If they thought of themselves as brothers, Jamie was the one who'd come along too late to be coming at things from the same point of view Ray and Dan had.

When Dan finally wandered out of his bunk, rain was pelting the bus's roof, fast and hard. What light came through the windows was bleak and dismal. The weather subdued the whole crew: Stick and Josh stared slack-jawed at the TV, with Jamie between them snoring softly, his head tipped back. Carey hunched over the table, going through papers and receipts, checking his calendar, answering emails. Moss read; Greg played a game on his Nintendo 3DS.

Scrubbing the back of his hair with his hand, yawning, Dan headed to the back lounge.

Ray had his head hung back, his eyes closed, his hands laid one over the other on his stomach. He cracked open an eye as Dan pushed the door shut. "It lives."

Dan dropped onto the couch cross-legged, as far from Ray as possible. "Just fucking barely." He propped his elbows on his knees and massaged his temples.

"Another headache?"

"Yeah," Dan said. "You got anything stronger than ibuprofen?"

"I like Excedrin. Mostly for the caffeine hit. Want some?"

"Yeah, I'll try that."

As Ray got to his feet, Dan said, "You want to play for a while?"

"Are you up to it?"

"It beats sitting here doing fucking nothing."

During the few minutes it took for Ray to come back, Dan stared at the thin carpet, the bits of grit in it. He rubbed circles into his skull, and straightened when Ray walked in with a bottle of water and a couple pills.

He held the pills over Dan's palm. Dan thought they were going to drop right in, but Ray's hand dipped. Skin touched skin. An electric zap shot up Dan's neck. He clutched the pills, jerking his hand away.

"Are you sure you're okay?" Ray asked.

"Yeah." He popped them in his mouth—"Get my guitar"—and chased them with a swig of water as Ray opened the cabinet over the couch.

Dan squeezed his eyes shut, rubbing one with the heel of the hand that still held the bottle cap. Trying to get the slight graininess in his vision to go away. When Ray stood in front of him, holding out the guitar, he looked a little blurry from the eye rubbing. Dan pulled the acoustic into his lap with one hand and took another long pull off the bottle.

CHAPTER SIX

PACING the bunk area, Dan rubbed his hands to distract himself from the queasiness rising in him.

Something is wrong with me.

Step, step, turn.

Something is seriously fucking wrong. By the end of jamming with Ray, he'd had to get out of there, shut himself in the bathroom, and pull at his hair to get a hold on the bees.

He was losing it.

Step, step turn. The curtains along the empty bunks brushed his arms.

Stick leaned in the doorway from the front lounge, bracing his hands on either side of the frame. "Hey, you all right?"

"Yeah. Edgy. I'll be fine. Just one of those nights when I can't wait for the show to start." Step, turn.

"Burn off some of that agitation, huh?"

"Yeah."

"Won't be too much longer. Plasticine Stars'll be finishing up their set soon."

"Thanks."

Stick headed back through the lounge toward the exit, Dan turned and pushed his hands against his face. Fuuuuuck.

When they finally got on stage, Dan snapped two strings in the middle of a breakdown. He kept going, his fingers racing to keep up with fretting the whole thing on the bass's remaining strings. Anything to keep his mind off the buzz at the back of his neck, like a black cloud growing expectant with electricity. He stayed away from the edge of the stage, out of reach of grasping hands. Their fans were used to having the chance to get a hand around his ankle, touch his guitar. But he was too off-kilter as it was, too overwhelmed. Too drowning in whatever the fuck was wrong with his head.

He changed basses between songs, grabbing the new one from Moss without letting Moss come in contact with him.

He fielded a glance from Ray, nothing from Jamie, who kept up but had a vacant look on his face. Vacant enough that Ray strolled over to the drum kit between songs, standing there to get his attention, making eye contact, making sure Jamie was aware he was still on stage, in the middle of a show. It worked, babysitting him. All the songs kicked off the way they were supposed to. But man, what a pain in the ass.

During an intro where the bass line didn't come in for the first forty-two seconds, Dan crouched on one knee, head bowed over his pedals, eyes closed. Teeth gritted. The legs of a thousand bees crawled over each other at the base of his skull. When it was time for him to come in, he shot to his feet, turning his back to the audience. He attacked the strings with everything he had.

Afterward, everyone was subdued. The weather hadn't improved since morning, and they were all one more night road-worn than they had been. Jamie was irritable, his mood a spiral of frustration: he first couldn't find his jacket, then couldn't find the drink he'd set down. He went off on Josh, accusing him of throwing it away—when it was sitting right where he'd left it. He broke a cigarette trying to get it out of the pack. Someone handed him an intact one, heading off a fit.

Brittle. Everyone seemed brittle tonight.

Dan hung at the edges, his hands in his jacket pockets. Wanting to head out to the bus but not wanting to feel guilt twist like a hook in his stomach as he walked by fans with barely a nod.

"Hey." An unlit cigarette bobbed between Ray's teeth. "What's going on with you?"

He clenched his fists in his pockets. "Coming down with something, I guess. Figures, right? At the end of the tour. I get to go home sick."

Ray reached like he was going to check Dan for a fever.

Dan ducked out of the way. "I'll be okay."

"Drink some water. Get some sleep."

"Do me a favor?" Dan asked.

"Sure."

Dan nodded toward the club's back door. "Grab Jamie so we can get out of here, and distract whoever's out there so I can get on the bus."

Ray's posture relaxed: something he could do to help. Sometimes that was all he needed. "Sure. No problem."

"Thanks."

"I'll do you one better, even," Ray said. "Hold on." He came back with Carey in tow. "Me and Jamie'll head out first to give them someone to talk to. You guys come out after, deep in conversation. Just walk straight to the bus, talking."

"What are you coming down with?" Carey asked.

"I don't know. The flu. Maybe nothing. I just feel like shit tonight."

"All right. Come on." He started to reach for Dan's arm, and Dan pulled ahead, saying, "Yeah, let's go."

He kept his head down. Carey rambled about tomorrow's timetable: "We should be pulling in at ten. We've got a day room, you guys can get showers. Load-in's at…" And up the bus steps they went.

Carey stopped at the top, one hand on the back of the driver's seat. "All set?" he asked.

"Yeah," Dan said. "Thanks."

"Get some sleep."

"Yeah."

Actually, he was hungry. He dug a Hot Pocket out of the stash in the bus's tiny freezer. BBQ beef. By the time the microwave dinged, the smell had soured his stomach. He forced a bite down, the pastry dry on the outside, sickeningly sweet on the in. It stuck in his throat, and he folded the rest in a paper towel and threw it away.

It was the perfect kind of night for getting blind drunk. A few years ago, he'd have been well on his way. Instead he dragged himself to his bunk—better to get in before the others boarded. The bees were not his friends tonight.

He pushed his buds in his ears and pulled up music on his phone. That too-real/unreal feeling was back, the plastic casing on the earbuds almost too smooth in his ears. He cranked up Bass Drum of Death to block out everything beyond his bunk. To block out the fucking bees. He buried himself in the noise of John Barrett's guitar while the bus pulled out of the lot.

In the silence after the last note of "(You'll Never Be) So Wrong" dipped out, Dan studied the darkness. He was genuinely worried—afraid he was going to snap. Afraid, too, that if he didn't do something (what?) he was going to snap soon. (But what?)

Two more. He had to make it through two more shows—just hang on for two days and one last drive.

The road whistled beneath them, on and on.

He slipped out of his bunk. His feet hitting the floor jarred the pain in his skull. He grabbed hold of the bunk to steady himself. A dim light flickered from the front lounge—whoever was still up had a movie going. The door to the back lounge was shut. After using the bathroom, he came back through the bunk area and slid the door open.

The lights were on, music from the TV almost lost in the rush of wind coming in through the cracked-open window. Wind tousled Jamie's hair as he passed the cigarette they were sharing toward Ray.

"Hey." Ray took a drag, squinting at Dan. "I thought you'd crashed. Feeling any better?" He blew the stream of smoke out the side of his mouth, toward the window.

Dan's head, heavy as concrete, felt like someone was trying to hammer it open. The buzzing didn't take concentration to hear anymore. It was as loud as the rush of road from the window.

Ray took a last drag before flicking the cigarette out.

Jamie got up with a stretch. "I'm hitting it."

"'Night." Ray pulled the window shut. The TV got louder, not having to compete with the wind. The lounge smelled like cigarettes.

The bees hovered at the base of his skull, making his teeth vibrate. He flattened his shoulders against the wall as Jamie pushed by. His head turned, like it was being pulled by a wire, his eyes pegged on Jamie as he slipped through the doorway. He didn't know what it meant exactly. He had something building in him, something restless. He dug his fingers against the paneling behind him.

"You really don't look good." Ray's voice sounded like it was coming from the bottom of a well.

Dan dragged his head forward. His eye twitched. The restlessness crowded his chest, making it hard to breathe. His vision started to disintegrate.

Ray moved his pack of cigarettes from his thigh to the couch to get up.

It was like watching him through a TV with bad reception. Dan's heart thudded, hard enough that he put a hand over his chest. He swallowed, trying to calm down. He didn't know what was happening, only that he felt like he was going to explode out of his own skin.

"Jesus." Ray ducked his head a little to look into Dan's face, lifting a hand toward Dan's jaw. "What the—"

A muscle in the side of Dan's jaw pulled tight. His shoulder clenched. His fist came up, fast. Throwing the punch was like watching someone else doing it. The contact of knuckles to the soft area under Ray's cheek barely registered. The force knocked

Ray's head aside, made him stumble back, spilling over the front of the couch. Ray tried to get out of the way, but Dan grabbed him by the shirtfront and shoved him back, climbing onto him. Ray tried to sit up, push him off. Dan knocked him back hard enough to make Ray's head thud on the cabinet over the couch. The magnetic catch tripped, the door popping open as Dan dragged Ray forward by the shirt.

Gritting his teeth, Ray tried to wrestle his arm off him.

Dan lunged. His teeth snapped. Ray dodged, just missing getting a hole in his cheek. As he shoved his hand up to protect himself, Dan's teeth found purchase in the fleshy heel of it. Ray yelled out and kicked him from below. Dan felt it distantly, but his jaws loosened reflexively.

Ripping his hand free, Ray shoved him aside, palm against the side of Dan's face as he struggled to get himself out from under him. Dan snapped his teeth again, got an elbow hard in the jaw for it. He didn't give a fuck because his teeth scraped along the skin there, and he dove forward to try to bite it, pushed by the need to feel his teeth break through skin, feel blood burst into his mouth. He tore at Ray's hair, but Ray had leverage now. With his forearm braced against Dan's neck, he managed to steamroll him backward, tripping over his own feet on the patch of carpet between couch and wall.

The wall shuddered as Dan's shoulders hit.

His vision swarmed. He tried to get at Ray with his teeth again, and Ray heaved him back with both hands on his chest.

His skull banged the edge of the audio system, pain rattling dully through bone. His knees went loose, like someone had pulled the pin out of a hinge. He clasped his head. He was hyperventilating, or close to it, breaths coming fast and shallow and panicked. He had Ray's shirt bunched in his hand, hanging on.

"Dan."

"Stop..."

"Dan, what the fuck?"

"Bees…" Ray's heart thudded under his knuckles. They spread like a swarming flower through his brain. His vision muddied. Ray's mouth, saying who knew what, became a gaping hole of darkness.

The last sensation he had was of dropping, fast.

Darkness. Confusion. He swung out at something, connected hard. A smell, bright like new pennies, filled his head with a roar like a jet taking off in his skull. He threw himself toward it, mouth first.

Darkness.

Silence.

Peace.

A familiar cough.

He peeled his eyes open to the kind of brightness you only see in the morning. He looked to one side: a window with a curtain half pulled across it. Ugly fucking curtain, textured with muted multicolors, the kind of pattern that didn't want to be anything in particular, like it would offend someone if it were flowers or checks or stripes, so it was a bland blur.

"Hey." Ray's voice.

He moved his eyes to catch Ray stepping up to the side of the bed. Behind Ray was another ugly curtain, this one sectioning them off from the rest of the room.

"Hospital?"

"Yeah." He curled his hands around the bedrail.

Movement at the end of the bed—Jamie getting up from a chair.

"Go grab a nurse," Ray said.

"Right." Jamie gaped at Dan, wide-eyed.

Ray turned his head, and Jamie snapped out of it. He ducked through the ugly curtain, leaving it waving in his wake.

"What happened?" Dan asked.

"You fucking tell me. How're you feeling?"

His mouth was dry. He made a face and tried to work up some spit. He pushed down against the mattress, trying to sit up. Pain stabbed his knuckles—a lot like right after he'd hit that wall when Jamie'd pissed him off. Was this right after that? What about all that stuff that'd happened in between—the bat, had he dreamed that?

Carey came through the curtain, a can of Coke in each hand.

"He's awake," Ray said.

"Can I have some of that?" Dan croaked.

"How about some water?" Carey said.

"Whatever. Anything. Where are we?"

"New York," Carey said. "How are you feeling?"

"Thirsty." He glanced down at his hand, still throbbing like he'd been in a fight. It was swaddled in white bandages. He looked at Ray for the first time—really looked at him. His breath caught as sensations came rushing back, noises—the congestion in his chest and the black static in his vision.

Carey opened his mouth to say something, and Jamie and Moss came charging through the curtain. "Nurse is coming," Jamie said, and on the heels of his words, the curtain flared.

"Good morning, Mr. Ferry. How are we feeling?" The nurse clamped something that looked like a bulky clothespin to his finger, and while that did whatever it was supposed to do, she popped a cone onto the end of a thermometer and held it to his ear.

His headache was gone, he realized. In fact, he felt pretty good for a change. When he said so—cautiously, with last night leaning hard on his thoughts—the nurse said, "That's what we like to hear. I'll let the doctor know you're awake, and we'll get you something to eat as soon as she clears it. Sound good?"

"Can I get some water?"

"Got some right here." She lifted a pitcher, ice thumping plastic. She filled a cup halfway and handed it to him.

He downed it in three gulps, the best thing he'd ever tasted.

Jamie stepped aside to let her out, then they were alone again, the five of them.

"Any idea what happened?" Carey said.

Dan shook his head.

Ray leaned against a wall, his arms crossed, watching him.

"All right. I've still gotta get in touch with the promoter." Carey ran a hand over the shine of his head, though, instead of reaching for his phone.

"I don't want to stay here," Dan said.

"Yeah, we don't want that either. I'm just waiting to see if we have to reschedule the rest of the dates and get you home."

He closed his eyes and leaned back, swallowing hard. He did *not* want to reschedule fucking dates.

As the curtain rolled back, he turned his head. A woman in a doctor's coat strode in, her dark hair fraying from what had probably started the shift as a tidy ponytail. A line of blue ink marred the white over her breast pocket. She looked like she'd spent the night popping Adderall.

"Mr. Ferry," she said.

"I wish people would stop calling me that."

"I'm Doctor Shue."

"I'm Dan, actually."

"How are you feeling?" she asked, drawing a penlight out of her pocket.

"What's wrong with me?"

She clicked the light on and shined it in his eyes. "Your blood work looks good, vitals look good. CT scan. How's your hand?"

He flexed it. "A little sore. Did I—"

"Any history of seizures?" She moved to the other eye.

"No."

"Any history of it in the family?"

"Not that I know of. Did I have a seizure?"

The flashlight clicked off. "Has this ever happened before?"

"What? Waking up in the hospital with no idea what's going on?" He rubbed the blanket, his knuckles itching under the gauze bandage.

She scanned his chart. "Any history of violent episodes?"

"No."

"Do you remember coming to the hospital?"

"No."

"How about the CT scan?"

He gave a short, frustrated shake of his head.

"Well," she said, "we have a tech who's not going to forget you anytime soon."

He didn't know what to say.

She pointed the end of the penlight at his bandaged knuckles. "You popped him a good one in the nose. We had to pull you off and sedate you."

Jamie said, "You were trying to bite him," his eyes wide.

That was unsettling as fuck. "I totally don't remember that."

"I thought something might show up on the tox screen to explain it," the doctor said, "but it came back clean. Did you take anything last night?"

"Not unless you count a few bites of a shitty Hot Pocket."

"What about you?" she asked Ray.

"Me?"

"I'm just hunting around for an explanation for what you thought you saw."

Dan shot his gaze toward Ray. "What'd you see?"

"Worms in your eyes," Carey said.

"What?"

"Thin little squiggly things." Ray held up his thumb and finger, pinched close together.

Dan looked toward the doctor, who said nothing.

"Moss didn't see it," Ray said, "and neither did anyone by the time we got you here, but before you crashed, I thought I saw… things in your eyes."

A sick, wet heat crawled up Dan's face. He clutched the sheet with his good hand.

"What I think"—Dr. Shue lowered the tablet with his info on it—"is that the both of you have been on the road a lot, under a lot of stress, with not enough sleep and a fair amount of alcohol, if nothing else." She lifted an eyebrow. "You're probably suffering from stress and exhaustion, and once you get some rest you'll find the symptoms don't repeat themselves." She slipped the flashlight into her pocket. "But if you *do* have an experience like this again, you need to make an appointment with your doctor."

"Does that mean I can go?" *Exhaustion*. He liked that diagnosis. "What about the things in my eyes?"

"If you have any vision problems, you should come back or see your own doctor."

"I had headaches," he said. "And buzzing…"

"With some rest, exercise, and a healthy diet, I think you'll be feeling a lot more yourself. More fruits and vegetables, less caffeine and alcohol, okay? Any other questions?"

"Well," Carey said once she was gone, "I guess that's good news."

Jamie stretched his arms toward the ceiling, the hem of his t-shirt hiking up to expose a slice of belly. "Are we getting a hotel?"

"Yeah, I've gotta arrange that and cancel the show still."

Dan turned his head. "Hey."

Ray lifted his chin, acknowledging him.

"Are you okay?"

"Yeah, just a few bruises. I'm more worried about you."

"I actually feel pretty good." The sun was shining, the headache was finally fucking gone. So were the… Holy shit. Were they? "Come here."

Ray stepped closer, curling his fingers on the bedrail again.

Dan laid a hand over one.

Holy shit. The fucking bees were gone.

Ray's hand shifted under his, turning over. Dan let his own slip away. And saw the purplish bruise on the heel of Ray's hand, the faint tooth-shaped dents in it. "Shit. I'm…*really* fucking sorry. Can you still play?"

He closed his fist, opened it back up. "Yeah, it's nothing."

"Do you *want* to play?"

"Ain't that what we're on this crazy ride for?"

Dan shoved the sheets down. "Where are my clothes?" He swung his legs over the side of the bed. Ray backpedaled a few steps, knocking into a rolling bedside table.

"Whoa." Carey put his hands up. "You might want to wait till they take your plug out at least."

The line coming out of the back of Dan's hand rattled against the IV pole.

He looked at Ray again for a long second. Couldn't say he blamed him for the reticence to get too close when he was on his feet. Ray put his hands up a little, a gesture to say he was okay, keep going. "I can get my fucking pants on at least. Are you gonna drink that soda?" He was still dying of thirst. "What time is it?"

Ray crouched and dragged a bulky plastic bag from underneath the bed while Carey said, "Almost noon."

"How far's the venue?" Dan asked.

"An hour and half, two with traffic."

"That works." He grabbed the pair of jeans Ray'd pulled out of the bag. "We can make that work."

"You're not thinking of playing, are you?" Carey asked.

"I feel great. Seriously. And if we get the fuck out of here fast enough, maybe no one will realize we were ever here." Just get this fucking tour over with. And stay out of the news. That was all he asked. They needed to go home and get their heads back together. *He* needed to go home and get his head back together. What they didn't need was to have to get back on the fucking road two weeks from now for a rescheduled show. Unless someone in the band was fucking *dead*, they had a policy of no cancellations, only reschedules. Even the time they'd been a no-show at a festival thanks to canceled flights, they'd managed to get another date booked in the same city a few months later—with a liquor manufacturer sponsoring it, allowing them to let five hundred fans exchange their old festival tickets for entrance to the show.

"Well, at least one of us got a good night's sleep," Ray said. "Are you sure you're okay?"

Dan stopped.

Ray looked like he'd been wadded up and shoved in a duffle bag, then shook out and stood on his feet. Five o'clock shadow, dark smudges under his eyes. He could use a shower and a comb through his hair. They all could. "Shit," Dan said. "We were getting a day room today."

"Fuck it. We'll be in our own homes in a couple days. I just want to make sure you're doing the right thing. I mean, last night was pretty fucking crazy."

"If you think we should take a night off," Dan said, "I'm cool with it. I mean, I'd rather not." He felt good, and there was no better place to be when he was feeling good than on stage in front of a crowd of fans singing their words back at them. "But I'm the one who got some sleep."

"Nah, man," Ray said. "People are at work, thinking about the show they're gonna see tonight. Or getting on the road from four hours away to come see us. We've got a crew that's gotta work for a living. Besides, what the fuck else are we gonna do all night if we don't play? Tiddlywinks?"

"Jamie?" Dan asked.

"Tiddlywinks, drums, whatever you guys want. I'm cool." He'd sprawled out in a vinyl-upholstered chair, one leg hanging over a wooden arm. Waiting—they were used to waiting.

"If you're sure you're okay," Ray said.

"This is insane," Carey said.

Ray glanced over his shoulder. "Noted." Because if there was one thing Dan could count on with Ray and Ray could count on with him, it was they both wanted to be on stage more than they wanted to be anywhere else.

Especially if 'anywhere else' was a fucking hospital.

"We've gotta get out of here." Dan looked at the IV in his hand. Fuck it. With a groan from Carey, he slid it out and used the tape that had held it there to stem the bleeding.

"Oh that's sanitary," Moss said.

"Fuck it. Let me get my boots on and let's go."

The women at the nurses' station looked up at the crowd of them coming out of the room.

"Just a sec," Dan said before veering toward the station. "Hey. How's that CT scan guy?"

"Oh," said an older lady with her red hair tucked under her cap, "not happy, I don't suppose. But he'll live."

"I'm really sorry about that. Can you get me his name?"

He handed the slip of paper to Carey, who didn't need to be told to make sure the guy got something for it.

CHAPTER SEVEN

THEY got to the club after three hours in traffic. Some of the crew—and Ray and Jamie—got in short naps during the ride. They loaded in as fast as they could, with the band lugging and connecting equipment alongside Stick and Moss. Soundcheck was short. Dinner came off sandwich trays backstage.

The show went well. Not the best on the tour, not even the best in the past month, but it went off without a hitch, despite everyone on the crew side-eyeing Dan, looking for him to start acting strange again. By the end of the show, he still felt as good as he had in the hospital, only with a layer of satisfying tiredness on top of it, the kind you got after good, hard work.

They pulled out on time, the bunch of them hanging out in the front lounge, drinking beer they'd gotten when they'd convinced the bus driver to pull in at a truck stop just before the interstate on-ramp. The show had gone well, and whatever'd happened the night before was a hundred miles behind them.

Now they were talking about the zombie apocalypse, what they would do if one happened.

"I'd stop at a library," Moss said, "grab a bunch of books—foraging, hunting, trapping. I'd head out to the middle of nowhere with Deb and Penny, the middle of the woods somewhere. Up to Canada, maybe. Take a machete with me, bow and arrows, shovel and hoe."

"There you go," Stick said. "That's what I'd grab me. A couple a' hos. Maybe four or five of them."

"And birth control pills?" Carey asked, his nose not buried in schedules and receipts for a change.

"Well, yeah, obviously," Stick said. "But you know why I'd do it?"

"Because your pecker is your favorite thing?" Ray said.

"Pussy's my favorite thing. But the way I see it, you've gotta have something to live for. These girls, I'd be their protector. I'd keep them safe from the zombies. As long as they had me, they'd be okay. And that's what'd keep me going, taking care of the ladies."

"What about you, Ray-Ray?" Moss asked.

"I'd shoot myself in the head."

"Come on. Seriously."

"Seriously. Who wants to live through that? Living in a bus is as primitive as I want to get."

Moss tipped his head to look at him. "What if it was something real? Climate change, the honey bees all died, whatever."

"Food shortages everywhere? Oil shortages, power going out?"

"Yeah."

"And this is a worldwide thing?"

"Yeah."

"Shoot myself in the head," Ray said. "I can't hack the worst of humanity, especially my own."

"There you go," Stick said. "He sacrifices himself so the rest of us can eat a few more days."

"You're not eating me," Ray said. "The rest of them, okay, but you—stay away from me. I'm worried you'd go straight for my dick."

"Nah, not a fan of tube steak."

"Brraaaains," Jamie said.

But Dan sat up. "What if the situation improved, though? What if smart people figured out a solution, and things turned around?"

"You mean what if in a week or a month or half a year later the world is saved?" Ray said. "I guess I'm shit out of luck then. But what are the odds, once everything starts falling apart? Our support system is just a line of dominos. I think if someone can catch that first one before it goes over, we're fine. But once that first one hits the next…we're fucked. They're all going down. Give me a gun and a bullet. You guys can watch the world end without me." He leaned back and closed his eyes, a can of Natty Ice propped on his knee.

The lounge got quiet.

Dan finally said, "I'd kinda miss you."

Ray cracked his eyes open, and part of the night before came sliding back to Dan, putting him off kilter. The bees buzzing, the *thud* of skull against cabinet, the give of the fleshy part of Ray's hand. He took a pull off the last of his beer to drag himself away from it.

Ray said, "Well, I'd kind of miss you too." He closed his eyes again. "If my brains weren't splattered all over the dirt."

"Jesus," Stick said. "What if you missed?"

"Missed?" asked Josh.

"Yeah, you know, like those people who try to commit suicide," Stick said, "only the bullet goes through their jaw instead, or just nicks their brain—you know, leaving them simple the rest of their lives."

"We picked up a girl once when I was with the rescue squad," Moss said. "Fifteen years old. Terrible home life. Her father'd been forcing himself on her since she was three. Her mother cut out of the picture when she was eight, leaving her behind with this asshole. She bought a gun from someone at school one day, kept it under her pillow for three months, couldn't bring herself to shoot the cocksucker. She was afraid he'd get it from her and beat the crap out of her for it. One day, she couldn't take it anymore. She put it to her head." He pantomimed it. "*Bam.*

Only she flinched when she pulled the trigger. She'll be blind the rest of her life. Big chunk of her face right here, gone. Last I heard she was living in a home for the blind. Got her away from that asshole at least, but that's about the only good thing you can say about it."

"Shit," Stick said.

Ray said, "Dan'll finish it. Right?"

If it meant not having to watch Ray die slowly, or scream in agony, or live the rest of his life drooling down his chin, unable to even pick out "My Dog Has Fleas" on a guitar… "Sure," he said quietly. "If you fuck it up, I'll finish it off."

Ray smiled. "You're a pal. I'm holding you to it."

"Pussy," Stick said. "I could never do myself in as long as there was pussy out there."

The lounge was quiet for a moment, until Josh busted out laughing, and everyone else followed, except Ray, who smiled distantly and took a pull off his beer.

"Okay," Jamie said, "forget the zombie apocalypse. What if aliens landed and tried to colonize us?"

CHAPTER EIGHT

THEIR last show was in Massachusetts. Two hours after loading out, they rolled over the New Hampshire line. By the time they pulled into Dan's mother's driveway in Deerfield, it was edging on four a.m.

Seeing his car sitting there—his mom had been taking it out weekly to keep it running—gave him a rush. Freedom, independence, the ability to go wherever the fuck he wanted whenever the fuck he wanted without relying on anyone or making arrangements.

It was good to see all the familiar things—the old split-level, the barn, the gas station down at the bottom of the hill.

By the time they finished unloading equipment into the barn, Dan's mom was up, standing on the front steps in her bathrobe, calling out that she had a big pot of coffee and plenty of eggs and bacon on. More than enough for everyone, as long as they didn't mind scrambled. The band and crew trotting to the door, saying, "Don't put yourself out, Mrs. Ferry."

"Hey, Mom." Dan gave her a hug.

"Everything go okay?"

"Yep."

"And this one was it for a while?"

"Yep."

She smiled. "It'll be good to have you around again."

"I don't know. I might freak out when I wake up a few days from now and I'm still in the same place."

Moss, Carey, and Stick were on the phone with families and girlfriends, arranging pick-ups. Josh was going to have Stick drop him off. The bus driver'd be on his way to a hotel after breakfast, then to Atlanta to return the bus to the leasing company. And Dan would get the band home.

Once they had full bellies, everyone was antsy to be on their way. He gave his mother another hug and a promise to come by for dinner soon before hopping in his car with Ray and Jamie.

"So where are we taking you?" Dan asked as he pulled out of the driveway.

Jamie sighed. "My parents'."

To Ray, Dan said, "Do you want me to drop you off first?"

"Nah, don't go out of your way." He slouched in the seat, getting his head comfortable. "I'm good. It's nice to see some familiar stretches of road again." He propped his foot against the dash.

"I don't know; all those other stretches of road are starting to look pretty familiar now, too. It's nice to see some road from behind a steering wheel for a change, though."

"Hey, Joe would've let you take over the wheel of the bus any time." He would have: Ray'd slid into Joe's seat a time or two, letting the driver grab a piss, stretch his legs. Dan just didn't think he could drive a bus without a little road training first.

"Glad to be home?" Dan asked him as they merged onto I-93.

"Yeah, well. It'll be nice to see the old shithole again." Ray had an apartment at the back of a multi-family building his brother and sister-in-law owned. It was the darkest and smallest of the building's units, but the rent was hard to beat, and with Buddy and his family in the next building over, he had the peace of mind of someone looking out for break-ins while he was gone.

"I hate this fucking place," Jamie said as they got off the interstate.

Jamie'd been in marching band in high school too, but in Merrimack. Drums, not tuba. He'd hung out in Manchester Friday and Saturday nights, usually at the arcade on Valley Street, where the video games got shoved against the walls to make room for shows by local bands, but Dan and Ray had made a game of trying to get into real clubs, driving halfway into Maine if they had to, chasing one garage band or another they'd heard about through word of mouth. They didn't cross paths with Jamie till they found him playing for a shitty ska band in a club in Concord. After they heckled him into quitting that band to join theirs—which they were calling Aces & Eights at the time—practices moved out of Dan's parents' basement into Jamie's parents' garage, which gave them a lot more space.

Jamie's parents made good money and put his two sisters through college. Jamie was supposed to go, but he never got around to writing the application essays. His dad got pissed off, wrote one up for him, and sent the applications out. Jamie carried the only acceptance letter he'd gotten in his back pocket for a while, probably until he lost it. Never told his parents about it. It would've meant leaving the band, and being in a band had sounded a whole lot better to all of them than sitting through another four years of school.

Dan dropped him off in front of the garage they practiced in when they were teenagers before getting himself and Ray back on Route 3 to Manchester. The car was quiet—what'd he and Ray have to say to each other after sharing the same few hundred square feet of space for the better part of two years?

In the light of morning, Ray looked like he'd been living on the street. He hadn't shaved since before the hospital, his shirt rumpled like he'd wadded it up at the bottom of his bunk then pulled it back on three or four days in a row. He just might have.

He was gnawing at his lip, looking out the window, when Dan pulled up to the sidewalk in front of his building, a three-story, asphalt-sided, diarrhea-tan box with no appreciable architectural detail. A crumbling driveway led to a tenant parking area around back, where Ray's car likely sat. His brother, Buddy, and Buddy's wife, Sarah, used it as their second when Ray was on the road, and paid half the insurance for the privilege.

"Well, give me a ring in a few days, man," Ray said. He offered his hand. Dan went to shake it, and Ray pulled back at the last second, his fingers brushing Dan's palm. He smoothed his hair with a smirk.

"Some things just never change," Dan said.

"Some boys just never grow up." With that, he was out of the car, his boots crunching on road debris.

In that split second before Ray'd slid his hand away, Dan thought he'd heard the bees again. Far, far away. He listened for them now, but all he heard was the ticking of the engine.

Exhaustion. He hadn't slept in thirty-something hours. He was hepped up on two cups of his mother's high-octane coffee. No surprise he was a little shaky. He opened his hand and looked at it. Either his eyes or his fingers were trembling a little.

A soft *thump* came from the back of the car.

Oh yeah. He yanked the trunk lever. As he waited for Ray to slam it closed, he tapped the steering wheel. As if the distraction of percussion could keep the bees away.

Ray rapped on the side window, gave Dan a last nod, and walked off with two bags over his shoulder and a guitar case in each hand. Dan pulled away.

Dan's apartment was on the third floor of a boxy white building that dominated the corner it sat on—just five blocks from the apartment where Ray and Buddy had grown up. Sometimes he drove by there for old time's sake, the place still looking like it was waiting for Mr. Ford to come home at the end of another shift, but it'd been six or seven years since Mr. Ford had come home, not since that final heart attack.

It was strange walking up the back steps of his building with the early-morning sun on his back. The place was at once familiar and surreal. He felt superimposed on it, like it was a

ViewMaster slide. *Click-click*: here was his porch. *Click-click*: here was his back door.

He set his bags down and fished for the right key.

"Home" was a strange concept after all that traveling.

He let himself into the kitchen. Four rooms opened right off it: bathroom around the corner, living room straight ahead, two bedrooms through doors at the other end. The place was clean, not a spot of dust. Of course: the price you paid for leaving your house keys with your mother. He wheeled his suitcase against the kitchen table, glanced at the mail sorted into neat piles: bills, personal, business, magazines, junk. A Pappy's Pizza magnet clipped a note to the fridge door, pale blue paper with handwriting he identified from across the room. He slipped it free, reading off the list of ready-to-heat meals his mom had put in the fridge so he wouldn't have to worry about cooking. She'd also had the landlord fix the flickering light fixture in the bathroom, and his great-aunt Cathy had had cataract surgery—maybe he could drop by and see her Sunday.

"Thanks, Mom." He folded the note.

The junk mail went right into the trash, the magazines into the bathroom. The business stuff he didn't even want to think about, and the personal mail amounted to a reminder to schedule a dental cleaning and a late birthday card from a girl he'd gone to high school with who managed to remember him on two or three card-giving occasions throughout the year. He sent her postcards from the road sometimes. She was married now, two kids and managing a restaurant in North Conway. Everybody was married now, it seemed like.

With the mail processed, he headed into the bathroom, which was so vacant that his footfalls echoed off the porcelain tub. When he was finished there, he wandered across the kitchen and into his bedroom, looking it over—everything neat and dust free. In the living room, he dropped onto his couch.

Three stories below, cars crept up the street. Someone in the building had their daytime TV turned up. A guy down on the sidewalk called to someone else out there and laughed, and up the street, probably at the auto body shop, metal clanked to no particular rhythm.

What he didn't hear was buzzing in his head.

He lifted his hand in front of him.

Still a little trembly. Thirty-some hours without sleep, two cups of Ma's coffee. No surprise there.

And no fucking buzzing. In the car with Ray, that had just been a fluke. His imagination.

He dropped his hand and sat there with no idea what to do with himself, outside of the obvious: unpack, take a shower, crawl into bed. He was too beat to unpack, too wired to sleep.

This was how it was, coming off the road, like you've been on a roller coaster, up, down, around and upside-down, and it's crazy for three, four, six months at a stretch—then it comes to a stop.

Dust motes hung in the air. Even they'd come to a stop.

The apartment felt empty.

It felt *huge*.

Ray'd been the first to get his own place, a decade ago now, itching to get out on his own, live the glamorous flophouse life while he worked at a machine shop to fund his lifestyle of take-out food and beer, which he paid the old guys in the building to buy for him. The place, over on Pine Street, had had one bathroom per floor, no hot-plates allowed in the rooms, and each room came with a bed, a dresser, and a clothes bar mounted between two walls.

Ray was happy as shit, going home to his own place at the end of every night. That was back when his dad was still alive and Buddy, who was going to college in town and working full time to pay for it, was living at home to save on expenses.

Dan had thought Buddy had the right idea—his parents' place was a little out of the way, out in Deerfield, but it was cheap, the food was free, and his mom made plenty of it. He had a car, he could get around. Why give up a good thing?

Jamie'd wanted out of his parents' house, but he turned his nose up at the flophouse. It took a while, but eventually he talked Dan into getting a "real apartment" with him. That lasted four months before Jamie moved back to his parents'—it was that or get a job to cover his share of the rent.

The real apartment was where Dan still lived—since he was there so little, it was hard to justify moving.

Whenever they got off the road and he found himself sitting on the couch in the empty living room listening to the neighborhood below, he kind of wished Jamie was still there. Just a little. Just so there'd be someone there he could say, "Well shit. What do we do now?" to, and maybe get an answer. Jamie, for all his lack of responsibility, had actually been fun to hang out with, way back when.

He dragged himself off the couch, intending to start unpacking. Instead he said, "Shit," and put a hand to his head, closing his eyes against the dull pain there.

People get headaches.

He'd been awake way too long. The tour was finally fucking over. A little tension headache wasn't unusual.

CHAPTER NINE

HE DREAMED of the buzzing two nights in a row, and woke the morning of his third day home with the skin at the back of his neck prickly and hot. A scalding shower—followed by a blast from the cold tap—took care of that, but not the cleaver-like headache he was getting from sleeping so much. His gut wasn't buying that explanation for it, but he didn't want to listen to his gut.

He was out of coffee, and just about out of socks, thanks to the tour. He pulled on yesterday's pair, trying to think what else he needed. Keeping busy was key, he decided. Give himself stuff to do, have a good meal, play for a while, sit out on the back porch and watch the neighborhood—maybe even write something. Then a good night's sleep—no sweaty fucking dreams.

He added sleep aids to the mental shopping list.

A couple blocks from the apartment, he pulled into the Dunkin' Donuts parking lot to take care of his immediate and future needs for caffeine. It was an off-hour of the morning. The place was empty. He grabbed a bag of ground coffee off a rack, plopped it on the counter, and asked a woman in a brown visor for a large regular—up this way that was how you ordered cream and sugar, and it was one of the things he looked forward to getting back to when he was on the road. The little bits of familiarity.

"That'll be eleven twenty-seven," she said.

He slid his card through the machine with her staring like she was trying to get a look at his face. He wondered if it showed something—the headache, maybe squirmy things in his eyes. A bitter taste washed his mouth. He had a sudden feeling like he needed to sit down.

What you need to do is relax.

"Do you want your receipt?" she asked.

"Nah."

While she went to get his coffee, he tapped the counter, reading the advertisement in front of the cash register. As she made her way back, he lifted his head.

"You look so familiar," she said, handing the Styrofoam cup to him. Her fingers bumped his.

The bees lurched from their half-sleep.

The cup slipped right through his hand.

"Shit," she said. "I mean shoot! Shoot. I'm so sorry. I let go before you had it."

"It's okay." He lifted his bag of coffee from the counter, its bottom dripping.

"Let me get that." She had a towel out, reaching for the bag.

Afraid she was going to touch him again, he let it fall into the mess. "Shit. Sorry." He scrubbed the side of his face.

"Are *you* okay?" she asked.

"Yeah, it was just…a static shock. Sorry. I'm really sorry about this."

"That must have been a bad one," she said as her towel sopped up the mess. "And I didn't feel a thing." A wave of cream-colored coffee splashed over the front edge of the counter, pattering at his feet, making him step back. He was glad to step back. As his breath rushed out, he realized he'd had a tight hold on it.

"Sorry," she said. "Did I get you?"

"No. I'm just…I'm gonna go," Dan said.

"Let me get you another coffee. A doughnut too, if you want it. On the house, because I am *so* sorry about this."

"No, it's okay. I'm just gonna…" He took another step back, his thumb pointing behind him, to the doors.

"Grab a fresh pack of ground off the shelf at least. You paid for it. Grab two. Please. I feel wicked bad about this."

"It wasn't your fault."

"Oh!" Her eyebrows popped up. "I got it! You went to Central, didn't you?"

Road noise got loud behind him as someone opened the front door. More people, just what he needed. His heart slammed in his chest. He turned and lurched through the vestibule, swinging a wide berth around the truck driver coming in.

He dug in his pocket for his keys. When he got in the car, he dropped his forehead against the steering wheel.

He wanted those sleeping pills a whole lot more than he had twenty minutes ago. If it weren't for those, he'd drive right back up the two blocks to his apartment building and lock himself in. But he didn't want to do that and sit there, wide-awake.

Just give me the chance to knock myself out again for a while.

A rap on his window brought his head up, fast.

The girl from the shop had two bags of coffee. As he rolled his window down, she fed them through, her apron soaked with the coffee he'd spilled.

"Thanks." He held them by the bottoms, careful not to make contact with her.

"Are you sure you're all right?"

"Yeah. Yeah, I'm…I'm okay. And yeah, I went to Central."

"Class of 2003?"

"'02."

"Ah. I was a year behind you. I knew you looked familiar. You hung out with Ray Ford, didn't you?"

"Yeah."

"I had a wicked crush on him. Not that I ever got up the courage to say more than two words to his face. Do you ever hear from him?"

"Yeah," he said, detached from himself. Trapped by the need to be polite to someone who'd cleaned up after him. "We still hang out."

"Gosh. I'd ask you to say hi, but there's no way he'd remember who I was."

"Hey, you never know."

She started to open her mouth. "No, no, never mind. I've gotta get back in before George has a shit fit. Take care of yourself, okay?"

"You too."

As she hurried to the front doors, he put the car in drive. Wal-Mart was the closest everything-store he could think of. He hoped he didn't run into any more old classmates.

The place was more crowded than Dunkin' Donuts. Older folks mostly, pushing carts up the aisles. He skipped the socks, which were in the middle of the store, and headed straight to the pharmacy section, right past the registers. Cold and flu, allergy, motion sickness. NoDoz. Where were the fucking—*a-ha*. He grabbed three packs off the shelf and headed for the checkout. The nicest thing about Wal-Mart was its self-checkout. No human contact. He scanned his ZzzQuil, dropped it in the plastic bag, pressed the pay button.

A cart with a sticking wheel bumped toward him.

He slid his card through the reader.

The old man with the cart started unloading stuff onto the shelf at the side of the checkout.

Dan tapped his foot, waiting for the card to process. Waiting for the go-ahead to grab his shopping bag and get the fuck out of there.

The man dipped into the cart, struggled to heave up a case of canned dog food.

The receipt finally printed. Dan yanked the bag off the carousel.

And as the man turned with the case of dog food, he bumped Dan in the arm.

Dan barely heard the "Excuse me" over the roar of bees. Like a jet taking off in his head.

He jerked aside, his arm up, saying, "God fucking damn it."

The old man stepped back, blinking. "I *said* excuse me."

"Sorry. I'm sorry. Just…it's a bad day." He sidestepped past the cashier stand and fast-walked it out of the store with his head down, the bees staying with him, crawling all over each other at the top of his spine. He swerved around a pair of older women heading for the front doors and crossed the parking lot, squeezing his keys so hard the jagged edges dug impressions into his palm.

Goddamnit.

It was back. Whatever it was, it was definitely, absolutely, no question about it *back*. He had the sleeping pills, though. He could knock himself out, wake up hours from now just like he had in the hospital. Wake up feeling fine. Right?

And if he weren't fine, he'd see the doctor.

He hoped he'd be fucking fine.

*God*damn*it.*

He wanted to hit things. Pick shit up and hurl it at the asphalt. Instead he yanked open his door and threw the bag inside.

"Fuck!" He slammed the roof of the car with his hand. Propping his elbow against it, he covered his eyes. *Fuck.* The bees buzzed restlessly. Hotly. He gritted his teeth, his lips pulling back.

Fuck!

He drew back and hit the car again, hard, and just off enough to slice the edge of his palm open on the wind deflector. "Fuck." He shoved the cut in his mouth, sucking on it to stem the bleeding. *Fuck.* He closed his eyes.

And opened them.

It was quiet.

Completely quiet. Oh, there were motors running, the crash of one of the Wal-Mart guys shoving two lines of carts together. A pair of high heels clicked efficiently across the pavement. But inside him, total peace and quiet.

He dropped his hand from his mouth. Let his breath out.

Peace and quiet.

His phone rang.

He looked at the side of his hand, slick with spit, blood beading from the cut. He licked it.

His phone continued to ring.

But the bees were gone. The *headache* was gone, just like that.

Just like that, everything felt all right again.

He reached across himself to pull the phone from his pocket with his good hand.

"Hello," he said to Ray.

"Hey. What are you up to?"

"Fucking shopping. Remind me to do it online next time."

Ray gave a wheezy laugh.

"What's up with you?" Dan slid into the driver's seat.

"Jamie just called."

"Uh-oh."

"He wants a ride to this detox place in Rhode Island. I told him I'd do it."

"You want some company?" The bees were *gone*. It gave him confidence. He was suddenly not so keen to go home—wander around his empty place, waiting for the bees to come back? No thanks.

"Only if you're not busy," Ray said.

"No plans for the day. Swing by and pick me up."

"All right. I just got on 293. I'll be there in a couple."

"You'll probably beat me." He had a lot more lights between himself and his place than Ray did.

When he rolled around the corner, Ray's beat-up Fury idled alongside the sidewalk. He left his stuff in his car, locked up, and jumped in with Ray.

"It's strangely clean in here." Usually he had to kick trash around to make room for his feet.

"Yeah, Sarah cleaned up when she was using it."

"I'm in favor of that. Still smells like an ashtray, though."

"What can you do?" Ray said around a cigarette. They headed back to the interstate with their windows down, wind blowing their hair.

"So why's he want to go to detox all of the sudden?" Dan said.

"'I don't want to talk about it' is all he said."

"Ah shit. That always means 'There's something I don't want to tell you about.'"

"'That I *should* tell you about,'" Ray added.

"Yep."

"Well." Ray glanced in the rearview before sliding around a car going fifty. "Don't look a gift horse in the mouth is how I see it. Whatever his reasons, he's going to detox."

"And it's far enough away that he might not hitchhike home after a day," Dan said. "Maybe."

"Maybe."

Jamie was sitting on his parents' steps when they pulled in. He jumped to his feet, a duffle bag in his fist, and strode to the driveway. The bag went in first. Jamie climbed in behind it, all knees and elbows.

Dan waited till they were back on the interstate—too far for Jamie to spring out and walk home—before he turned in his seat, grabbing hold of its headrest. "So is it just detox, or are you going to do rehab too?"

"I'm taking things one at a time, trying not to get too far ahead of myself. Detox, then see where I am." He shoved his hair back from his face and blew a stream of air out as he looked out the side window.

So detox only then. Dan wanted to ask whether they should expect the cops or a pissed-off chick to come knocking at their doors looking for him, but Ray was right: the guy was going to detox, whatever the sketchy reason behind it. Best to look on that bright side.

"So what's this place in Rhode Island?" he asked instead.

"They do medical detox. No one around here does that, at least not that I could find on the internet."

"And medical detox is…?"

"They give you drugs to get you off drugs," Ray said.

"Whatever works." Dan turned back around and settled in for the two-hour ride.

The two hours stretched to nearly three when Jamie wanted to grab lunch before checking in. If Dan hadn't been feeling so much better, he'd have been edgy by the time Ray flagged down the waitress and begged her to bring their check. He looked at the side of his hand, the cut stiffening with a delicate layer of scab. So was it…?

Had he gotten rid of the bees by sucking his own blood?

"Let's go." Ray dropped a couple twenties on the table.

"Don't be in a rush to get rid of me or anything." Jamie slid out of the booth.

"I'm just in a rush to get a smoke," Ray said. "Come on."

"Can I get one off you?"

"You can get a whole pack."

"Can you smoke in detox?" Dan asked, following behind.

"Yeah," Jamie said. "They don't make you quit *everything*."

In the car, Ray leaned across Dan to pop the glovebox. He grabbed two packs and tossed them over the seat. His elbow brushed Dan's arm, and…

Nothing.

With a sigh of relief, Dan sank down in his seat.

Absolutely fucking beautifully nothing.

"So HOW'RE you doing?" Ray said as they drove back through Massachusetts.

"Oh, you know." He studied the trees whipping by. "I'll live. You?"

"Adjusting." Ray smiled. He actually did better on the road. Being in one place too long started to itch at him almost as soon as his bags were unpacked.

"Get unpacked yet?" Dan asked.

"Nah. I'm thinking of having HazMat come pick it all up and dispose of it. Except for the guitars."

"Of course."

"Probably be doing my neighbors a favor. I don't even want to unzip those bags. How've you been feeling, though? Any repeats of the other night?"

Dan chose his words carefully. He didn't want to lie to his best friend—but he didn't want Ray pulling up to the ER doors instead of his apartment, either. "I think I'm still catching up on sleep. And, you know, non-fast food."

"Mom stock the fridge?"

"You know it."

"Nice," Ray said. "The only thing in mine when I got back was condiments and beer."

"And now it's down to the condiments, right?"

"You know it." Ray grinned.

The album Ray had going on the car's stereo—the only update the car had had since it rolled off the factory line in 1978—ended, leaving a restless silence. Dan scrolled Ray's phone for something else to put on, decided on Louisiana Red—dark enough to fit the shit in his head. When it started up, he turned up the volume before settling back in his seat to watch Wellesley pass by the windows.

The sky turned the gray of engine exhaust.

His body still felt good, but he chewed on the edge of his thumbnail as Red sang about feeling the sweet blood call. He pressed his eyes shut for a moment, thinking of his hand. Thinking about the silence the moment blood had touched his tongue.

"Looks like we're in for a storm," Ray said.

"Yeah. Hey."

"Mmhm?"

"I'm sorry about what happened on the bus."

"Yeah. Just don't let it happen again, we'll be fine." Ray squeezed the steering wheel with the hand Dan had tried to gnaw on, and Dan dragged his eyes away. Thinking about the give of flesh under his teeth. About the CT tech and the dark shadows of that memory.

Was it blood he'd been after?

Jesus, he was becoming a fucking vampire. He'd have laughed if he weren't so freaked out.

"When do you want to get started back to writing?" Ray asked.

"Any time's fine with me. How's the foot?"

"Better since I'm not walking on it so much. I'll give you a few more days to catch up on sleep. Lord knows I could use it."

Fair enough: once they started writing, they'd be up till sunup, hardly noticing time spinning past.

"I've got a few ideas on the one we started in Dallas," Ray said.

"Cool."

"That breakdown problem we kept running into." He hummed a bit, like a question mark, and when Dan said, "Right," he said, "I think I've got that smoothed out. I'll show you when we get together. Thursday good?"

"What day is it today?"

"Monday. I think." He tapped a beat on the steering wheel. "Yeah, pretty sure it's Monday."

"Thursday's good," Dan said. "I've gotta have dinner with Mom soon. This weekend, maybe. Wanna come?"

"If I'm free. Buddy's throwing a thing for Sarah's birthday this weekend."

"There's always next time if you don't." He stretched, pushing his hands against the car's ceiling.

They fell into a familiar silence that took them up into New Hampshire. Salem, Pelham, Windham, Derry. The gray sky darkened the farther north they went. By Londonderry it felt hours later than it was.

Dan said, "How are Buddy and the family?"

"Good. Jane started school and has no front teeth. Sarah wants another one. Buddy's wanted another one anyway, so he's happy about that." He tapped the wheel again, the rhythm of the Dallas song. One of them was going to need to put words to it.

"You ever want kids?" Ray asked.

"I get exhausted thinking about having a goldfish."

Ray laughed.

"What about you?" Dan asked.

"The idea of it's pretty amazing, you know? You bring someone into this world that's part of you, that looks up to you, thinks you're the best guy in the world. Then I think, *When would I see them?* 'Cause I can't imagine taking kids on the road. Around Jamie? Around Stick?"

"Stick's actually great with kids."

"Yeah, but you don't want kids underfoot, you know? *I* don't want kids underfoot. So instead of being this guy they looked up to, I'd be this guy they'd see a couple weeks at a time, in and out of their lives like a stranger. My memories of them would be snapshots. *Their* memories would be snapshots."

"I think everybody's memories are snapshots."

"You know what I mean. Anyway, it's just making excuses. The reality of the situation is if I wanted kids, I'd find a way to make it work, so I probably don't want them that much."

"You've given it a fuckload more thought than I have."

Ray shrugged. "It's just 'cause of Jane. That's the first kid I've had in my life. But while I'm the cool uncle who disappears for months at a time, the way she looks at her dad... Sometimes I think, I *want that.* I want to be someone's whole world. But... you know, at the same time, I don't want to give up any of my own world." They slowed for traffic, and Ray said, "That night we took you to the hospital, what do you remember?"

Dan sighed, looking out the window again. The first fat drops of rain hit the glass. "I don't know. Everything after blacking out was black. I vaguely remember a struggle. I guess that was the tech, before they sedated me. Actually I vaguely remember trying to bite someone's face off. Were you there for that?"

Ray twisted his hands on the wheel. "They wheeled you away for the CT scan."

"Was I awake then?"

"Sort of sleep-mumbling."

"It's all fucked up in my head. I don't know if I was hallucinating or just losing my mind. You said you saw things squirming in my eyes?"

"Yeah. I thought so at the time, but it seems kind of crazy now, right? I was probably just freaking out."

Dan bit his lip. When he let it slide free, it was to say, "I didn't mention it at the hospital, but when I was all fucked up,

I couldn't see straight. It was like when you're dreaming and you're trying to read something, and the harder you try, the less you're able to see."

"Fuckhead," Ray said.

"What?"

"You should have told them that at the hospital. Because if I did see what I thought, and *you* saw what I saw from the other side—that's seriously fucked up. They'd have checked you harder if you'd said something."

Dan shook his head, not denying it, just not wanting to talk about should-have-dones. It hadn't come back, the eye thing. Who was to say they didn't both hallucinate it? Who was to say he wasn't having trouble seeing *because* he was losing it, and Ray just thought he saw something in a flash that wasn't there? A week past the events, the edges could have softened enough to let them jimmy their two pieces of memory together and call it a match, but what if it was just coincidence?

And it hadn't happened again, the eye thing.

"It hasn't happened again," he said.

"That's good to hear. Because, man, that was fucked up."

"Yeah. It was."

Ray hit his blinker and eased onto I-293, the road black with rain. They rode in silence till Dan's exit came up, his apartment just around the corner. Ray pulled up behind the building, engine running, windshield wipers sweeping water off the glass.

"Well. Thanks for coming."

"Anytime. Hope it sticks for him."

"That'd be nice."

"See you Thursday."

"Yep."

He shut the door, ducked his head against the rain, and hurried toward the building. The parking area smelled like fresh dirt, all the grit in the asphalt getting stirred up in the rain. Ray's car pulled away from the sidewalk just before Dan's feet hit the wooden steps. As he hauled himself up the two flights, all he wanted was to swallow a couple ibuprofens for the headache that had come back with the storm clouds.

CHAPTER TEN

A FEW hours later, he picked the scab off the cut on his hand and squeezed it until blood welled.

He put his mouth on it and closed his eyes, and the headache went away, taking with it the tension in his shoulders.

Okay, so it is *blood.*

Which was fucked up as hell.

He stood in front of his freezer, the door wide open, looking for meat. Red meat. All he had were TV dinners and single-serving casseroles his mom had frozen. Plus some ice cream that'd be freezer-burned into tastelessness and a cut-open bag of ice from the gas station across from Dunkin'.

Fuck it. The headache was gone; there'd be no buzzing. He pulled his jacket back on and headed down to his car.

It coughed a little before the engine caught. Great. Another problem he needed like an extra hole in his ass. He backed out and headed to Market Basket. Bought the rawest, juiciest steak he could find at the meat counter. Up in his apartment, he unwrapped the Styrofoam tray and set it on the table.

He took a seat in front of it.

People ate steak raw all the time, right?

He did an internal check while he stared at the glistening slab.

Actually, he felt okay. A little grumpy, a little twitchy, but on the whole okay. If he wanted to see if this worked, he needed to wait till he was having symptoms.

He stashed the steak in the fridge and went to waste time on the internet instead.

He typed in "Urge to drink blood." The top result gave him a little checklist of all things: "Are you drawn by the sight of blood? Do you have an attraction to the sight or smell of blood? Do you fantasize about drinking blood or rubbing it on yourself?"

"How about, 'Do I get headaches and bees in my head until I drink blood?'"

"Do you fantasize about vampires? About being a vampire? Do you watch vampire movies or read vampire fiction? Do you dress like a vampire? Do you wear prosthetic fangs?"

"If so," Dan muttered, "you need to get out more." He scrolled to the next group of questions.

"Do you cut yourself to drink blood?"

He ran a hand through his hair.

"Have you drank or thought about drinking animal blood? Have you drank or thought about drinking human blood? Have you injured someone or thought about injuring someone to get their blood?

"Do you believe you need to ingest blood to survive?

"Do you believe you obtain health or special powers from drinking blood?"

"Well, you know, if you consider feeling fucking *normal* a special power…" But his face was clammy. He wiped his palm on the leg of his jeans.

The end of the questionnaire was a single paragraph: "If you answered 'yes' to these questions, you should seek help from a qualified psychiatrist, doctor, or therapist. There are many conditions that could be causing your urges and impulses, and they are treatable." It contained a list of some of these conditions. The words blurred together. Dan put the heels of his hands against his eyes. Great. He was just fucked in the head.

After a few minutes, he sat forward to read up on the first possible condition: Renfield's syndrome, which it turned out was attributed to a traumatic childhood event, not to being attacked by a rubbery bat in a dark alley. He ran a search on his symptoms and found that if he took blood out of the equation, he might have high blood pressure. That at least he could test at a drugstore, except that when the symptoms were occurring, the last place he needed to be was a crowded drugstore—or any other place people were likely to be.

Finding no answers—no cancers, viruses, or bacteria to explain what was going on—he switched over to Netflix and spent the rest of the evening skimming vampire movies, less for inspiration than the mindless occupation of his brain.

After that, he got another serving of the shepherd's pie his mother had left in the fridge—eying the steak as he took the container out—and ate without tasting it much.

When it got late enough, he swallowed a couple sleeping pills and got in bed, in the dark, with his iPhone plugged into the speaker by his bed, Chelsea Wolfe drowning out the cars passing in the street below.

After a while, he thought the headache was coming on again, so he rolled over and resettled his head till he didn't feel it as much anymore.

When he woke, it was black as night in his room, his bottom sheet soggy with sweat. Grogginess crowded his head. He tried to get comfortable over to the left and fall back to sleep, but the headache pressed on the backs of his eyes.

He put a hand to his neck.

The skin back there was on fire. He touched his forehead, his cheeks. What if he was just coming down with post-tour crud?

He slipped out of bed and padded through the kitchen. If nothing else, he had to piss.

He rubbed his hand over the low hum of bees.

After the bathroom, he returned to the kitchen and pulled the steak out. Standing in the light of the fridge, he peeled back the plastic wrap. The absorbent pad was a purple bruise. Syrupy blood dribbled toward the corner of the tray when he tilted it.

Here goes nothing.

He tipped it into his mouth.

It was cold, and tasted like beef.

And it didn't do shit for his headache.

Tentatively he took a bite of the meat, wrenching it free with his teeth.

It just tasted like cold, raw meat. He'd eaten grosser. He managed to swallow it down.

The bees were uninterested.

Fuck them then. He dropped the steak in the fridge. As he headed back to the bedroom, he tore yesterday's scab off again. With the side of his hand jammed in his mouth, he worked up fresh blood. Copper pennies blossomed over his tongue.

Feeling marginally better, he crawled between the sheets on the dry side of the bed, sucking his hand. When he had silence again, when the headache had eased away, he rolled over and fell asleep with his hand in front of his face.

He woke up groggy, pushed himself up, and looked around. The hyper-real sensation was back. He had an urge to struggle awake, like he was caught in one of those dreams where you only *think* you're awake. Instead he crawled off the bed and padded to the kitchen to get a knife.

The scab came up easily, if painfully. Underneath, pink skin tried to heal. He pinched it hard, but all that brought up was more pain. So he dug the knife in.

The bees hummed as he lifted his hand toward his mouth, and they quieted as he closed his eyes and sucked.

When he'd gotten everything he could get out of the wound, his kitchen looked like his kitchen again, nothing hyper-real or dreamlike about it. Pale morning light filtered through the window.

He sat on the floor and put his head in his hands.

He didn't feel great, the way he had when he'd woken in the hospital. The headache had left, but his muscles were tired, like he was coming down with post-tour crud after all.

He could become a hermit—was this what happened with agoraphobics? They hid in their houses because they couldn't trust themselves anymore beyond their own doors?

He made half a pot of Dunkin' Donuts coffee and took a piss while it brewed.

He got through two mugs and a shower before the headache threatened to come back.

Below him, the second-floor tenant was letting herself into her apartment. With his third cup of Joe in hand, he felt himself drawn to his own door, listening. She made it inside and stopped, probably to pick up grocery bags she'd set down.

As she crossed her kitchen, he crossed his, the bees vibrating distantly at the base of his neck. He followed her from counter to refrigerator to cabinet, then into the bathroom, sitting on the toilet lid as she relieved herself below him. She had a daughter—Lily—three or four years old, who must be at a sitter's, or her father's. Janice—that was the downstairs neighbor's name. He followed Janice to her bedroom, just beneath his. Back to her kitchen. He sat on the floor while she fixed herself something to eat.

This is insane.

She was still in the kitchen when he forced himself to his feet. His muscles resisted; it was like trying to get up with a piano leaning on his back. He hauled himself to his bedroom, shut the door, and climbed into his bed, in the darkness: the shades drawn, the blackout curtains pinned shut. He pulled the blankets over his head and breathed his own heavy air.

After a few hours, Janice left.

Dan pushed back the covers and ate the leftover steak raw, standing in front of the kitchen sink, staring through the window. The only thing it did was give him the shivers, which was enough reason to go back to the warm cocoon of his bed. He left the knife he'd used earlier on the nightstand, in case he needed more. He probably needed more. How long could he hole up here, fending for himself?

What was the alternative?

The fucking hospital?

Maybe if he'd found information on anything remotely like he was dealing with on the internet, but he wasn't keen on the idea of walking in there with something entirely unknown.

In fact, the idea scared the fuck out of him—more, even, than what he was going through did.

When Janice returned—with Lily running into the apartment ahead of her—he fought the urge to get up and follow them around. Instead he slid the knife under the blankets and made a new cut. Fresh blood skated down the side of his hand. He licked it, sucked on the cut, and both the headache and the urge to stalk his prey receded.

CHAPTER ELEVEN

Somehow he made it to Wednesday. He smoothed the last Band-Aid he had in the medicine cabinet over the latest cut before he started a pot of coffee. If this kept on, he was either going to have to brave Wal-Mart or level up to gauze bandages. The razor blade he'd used sat on the side of the sink, licked clean. The safest place for him was in the bed, under the covers, and when he got sick of hiding there, he'd swallow sleeping pills with a tall glass of water and returned to it, shoving his laptop back onto the nightstand—it hadn't given him any more answers today than yesterday. He'd crossed more things off the possibilities list: spinal meningitis, Lyme disease, Meniere's disease, peripheral neuropathy, stroke. They were easy because none of them came with an urge to drink blood.

A text message came in from a friend: "Just saw Ray. Didn't realize you were back in town. Call me when you get a chance." He turned the screen off after reading it.

Somehow he was going to have to get past this.

The cut on his arm itched. He rubbed it through the Band-Aid. The headache was out there, waiting to come back. The sense of hyper-realness. The bees. With luck, the pills would kick in before it all did come back, buying him time before he had to make another cut.

The phone rang. His mom. He let it go to voicemail, listened to the message later. Dinner Sunday. Call her if he couldn't make it.

He'd feel better by then, he hoped. It had to end eventually, right? Work its way out of his system, like a bad bug. Maybe he needed to stop feeding it—not that licking his own wounds was helping much anyway.

He turned off the ringer and pushed the phone under his pillow.

THURSDAY MORNING. Janice was getting ready for work. He was on all fours over her head, tracking her movements.

The bees wanted to go out the door, down the stairs, and in through her door. Grab her by the neck and tear at her face with his teeth until blood gushed, hot and delicious and sanity rescuing. He dug his fingernails against the hardwood and held himself on his hands and knees with all the strength he could muster.

She crossed into the kitchen, with him right above her. His knees banged linoleum. His nostrils flared. She was heading toward the door, thank god. All he had to do was keep himself from opening his.

He pushed his forehead against the painted wood, his teeth gritting, sweat trickling along his temple.

Her car door creaked open in the small parking area. It groaned on its way to thunking shut. He dug his head against the door and breathed easier. For now.

If the bees would shut up for two fucking minutes, he could at least *think*.

He pressed a hand to the door, tried to pull himself to his feet. And dropped back down, his vision swarming.

The light through the windows crept over the linoleum, laid its warm hand over his calves. He was shaking, and everything was going black.

CHAPTER TWELVE

THE bees the bees the bees the bees. They were going crazy about something, but all he could see was darkness. Tiny feet, the beat of wings—his body vibrated with bees, and he couldn't get up. He thought he was on the kitchen floor. It felt hard under his cheek, his hips. And the bees the bees.

In a split second, all his muscles jumped. He was as mindless as the bees: clawing, grappling, hitting. *Tasting*.

Sweet relief, the bees humming as one: *Hallelujah*.

Peace.

His elbow thudded against linoleum.

Every breath he took was difficult, his chest slammed hard against the floor.

His finger twitched.

Someone panted, close to the back of his head.

He twitched his finger again. Dragged in a long, shallow breath.

"Dan?" Ray whispered behind his ear.

Dan shifted—hard to do under Ray's weight.

"Yeah?" he said back, quietly. A little scared. The twitching finger, he saw, had a streak of red on it. Panic scurried on little feet through his scalp.

"Jesus, Dan," Ray said.

He stared at the streak of red. "What'd I do?"

"You were passed out," Ray said.

The bees were gone. "*What did I do?*"

"Shh. Are you okay now? Can I let go?"

He didn't know. He knew he probably wasn't going to do anything he'd regret—but he didn't know if he was okay.

He sure as fuck was *not* okay.

"Are you okay?" Dan asked back. He felt trembly, his skin cold. He ground his temple against the floor. *Jesus what the fuck?*

"I haven't had a chance to check that yet," Ray said.

Ray moved on top of him.

"I think I'm okay," Dan said.

"Think?"

"I'm okay."

"Don't fucking move." He shifted again, moving off him a little but holding him down. "Okay? Don't fucking move till I get out of the way."

"Okay," Dan breathed.

The weight came off. Boots scrabbled across the linoleum, away from him. When they stopped, Dan planted his hands against the floor and pushed onto his knees. He hung his head for a moment, afraid to look.

Ray cursed quietly.

Dan sat back, hands on thighs. That smear of blood on the inside of his finger. *Shit.*

And that's what Ray said too, looking at his own arm, his lip curled as he squeezed his wrist. Blood dribbling between his fingers.

Ray's bangs hung down, hiding his eyes until he lifted his head, looking at Dan.

Dan put a hand to his mouth, an old copper aftertaste there.

"What the fuck?" Ray pulled back against the wall, wedging his shoulder against the kitchen door. Blood oozed from the marks Dan's teeth had made. "What the *fuck* is wrong with you?"

"I'm sorry. I didn't mean to…" Dan looked around the kitchen. His kitchen. Normal kitchen, except for the mail splayed across the floor, the knocked-over chair. Otherwise completely fucking normal.

"You should clean that," Dan said. He closed his eyes. *Peace. Quiet. So fucking good.* But he was shaking—what the fuck had he done?

"What the fuck is going on?" Ray asked.

He opened his eyes and looked around again. The door hung open, the traffic from the street louder than it should have been. "I forgot you were coming by today." What would have happened if Ray hadn't? How long had he been lying comatose? He remembered Janice leaving. Remembered pacing his apartment, the bees urging him toward the door, toward people, toward blood. Remembered even considering tying himself down to keep from running outside, scared of being that crazy person on the news: *He just grabbed the woman pushing her child in a stroller and started eating her face!*

"I think I have a problem."

"No shit?" Ray said.

"You should clean that out. I won't come after you. I'm good right now."

"I'll stay over on this side of the room anyway, if that's okay."

They watched each other for a long stretch of seconds, until Dan said, "I don't blame you."

"What are you, a fucking vampire now?"

Dan pulled himself back, hugging his chest. "Vampires get cool side benefits. All I've got is bees." He squeezed his eyes shut for a moment. Jesus—he didn't remember anything. "Did you see them again? The squirmy things in my eyes?"

"I didn't have time to examine you. As soon as I put my knee on the floor, you were coming at me. Barreled right into my chest. Fuck, man. Is it the same thing as before? On the bus?"

"Yeah. The same thing. It wants blood." He pressed his hands against his eyes. "Blood shuts it up."

"What the fuck's 'it'?"

"The bees. The buzzing. The headache. That fucking thing did something to me when it was on my neck. I knew I'd felt it bite me. It did something, and now everything's all fucked up." He slid his hands down his face. "I was stalking my neighbor this morning. I was going crazy, wanting to go down there and get blood from her. Jesus, she has this little girl...can you imagine if I had? This little girl watching her mother be attacked?"

"Much better you saved it for me. If we get in my car, could you ride the two minutes to the hospital without trying to kill me?" He pushed against the wall, getting to his feet, one hand still clutching his arm.

Dan gave his head a violent shake. He could absolutely make it two minutes to the hospital—if that first time he'd lost his mind was any indication, he could make it almost a week. That tech's blood had kept the bees at bay awhile, unlike his own. But what would happen when he got to the hospital? What would they do with someone who attacked people to suck their blood? "I'm not going to the hospital."

"Danny..."

They could feed him blood, there was that. Or they could refuse him blood, lock him in a psych ward, stuff him with pills. Strap him down to keep him from attacking the staff. Dope him up. Declare him violently insane, and he'd never see freedom again. Now there's a life. As Ray tore paper towels off the dispenser bolted under one of the cabinets, Dan said, "There's nothing about this on the internet except crazy people."

"When they see what happens to your eyes—"

"Yeah, then they can say, 'He's not crazy, he's just got some insane thing wrong with him. We'll pin him to a board like a bug and study him. I'm good now. I just needed, what—a *teaspoon* of blood?" He couldn't have gotten much more than that off Ray before Ray got him pinned down. "I'm *good* now." His face prickled. He knew he was being an idiot, but Jesus. He did not want to go to the hospital. First they'd run tests, then they'd call in the shrink, then when they realized they had something real on their hands, he'd never see the fucking light of day again.

Ray crouched a good six feet from him, bleeding through the paper towel clamped over his arm, and Dan said, "What about the band? If I check into the hospital, what happens then? 'Two Tons of Dirt Bass Player Afflicted with Mysterious Blood-Drinking Disease.'"

"What happens when you attack someone on the street and *that* makes the headlines instead?"

"Help me," Dan said. "Keep that from happening."

Ray clutched the bloodstained towel in his fist.

"I can't go to the hospital." That scared him more than the bees. The memory of stalking Janice through the floor was detached—ridiculous in retrospect. A dream he'd lived. He could keep this under control. There was no need to let it get this bad again, not if he had help.

"I don't know what the fucking alternative is," Ray said.

"It's just a little blood. Just a taste is enough to shut them up."

"*Today*," Ray said.

"If it gets worse, I'll go to the hospital."

"You say now. You know who you sound like?"

Anger flashed. "I'm not fucking Jamie."

Ray watched him a while longer, Dan feeling like that bug pinned to a board after all, until Ray finally stood and dropped the towels into the trashcan. "I don't know, man." He ripped a few fresh ones free, dampened them under the tap.

"*You* wouldn't go," Dan said. Ray hadn't been to a hospital in his life, not as a patient. Wouldn't even go to the doctor unless he was sure he'd just get a script for antibiotics and be sent home.

"Yeah, well," Ray said, on his way to the door with the wet towels held to his arm. "I mind losing myself a lot less than I mind losing you. Give me a call if you need a ride to CMC."

"Thanks for nothing," Dan said as Ray popped the screen door open.

"Thanks for the hole in the arm." Ray let the door slam shut behind him.

HE HAD a week to figure it out, he figured. Less if he didn't want to reach the point of stalking the neighbor again. Maybe he could pay for it—find a hooker, a druggie, give them some cash and a razor blade. Teenage girls cut themselves all the time. How big a deal could it be, aside from the risk of AIDS? It would be an awkward conversation, but if you were talking to hookers… surely they'd had more awkward conversations.

And with the bees gone and his head cleared, he felt like he could do it. He felt like he could do *anything*.

He searched the apartment for his phone, finding it, finally, shoved between his mattress and the wall. A couple new texts, including one from Ray saying he'd be over soon. He shoved it in his pocket, texts unanswered, and got his shoes on. He needed groceries—pig's blood, chicken blood, actual food to eat. Maybe cow blood didn't have whatever it was that shut the bees up. It was worth a try before he had that awkward conversation with a few prostitutes.

It was too bad Jamie was in detox. He could have worked something out with him—drug money for blood. All the addicts win.

He passed his guitar on his way through the living room. *Shit*. They were going to work on songs today. He would have liked to do that. Later. He'd figure his problem out, then go to Ray and tell him it was taken care of, and they could get back to what they do.

He jingled his keys on the way to the car. There were options, damn it. People lived on medication, dialysis, all kinds of medical interventions. That's all this was. A condition to be managed.

CHAPTER THIRTEEN

SATURDAY RAY called. Dan said, "I'm good. I'm fine. Really." He hadn't tried the chicken or pig blood, but they were both sitting in his fridge, the meat laid on top of butter knives on plates so the blood would collect below them—you know, because…raw chicken. He'd rather just drink the blood. "How are you?"

"Hoping I don't turn into a vampire myself is how I am."

"How do you feel?" Dan asked, worried that what he had might be passed through bites.

"Annoyed," Ray said.

He pushed a hand into his hair. "I'm sorry."

"Forget it. What's done is done. I just want to know why it's always gotta be me you're beating on."

"There's the CT guy too."

"Great. We'll start a club. I wonder how he's doing."

Dan hadn't thought to wonder, but now he crawled with it. Did he dare call the hospital and ask? He didn't even know which fucking hospital it was, he'd been in such a hurry to get out of there. Carey'd know.

"Any bees?" Ray asked.

"No. You?"

"No."

"You want to get together?" Dan asked. "Work on that problem with the Dallas bridge?"

"Is it safe?"

"I'm *fine.* If it's like last time, I probably have close to a week before it gets bad."

He listened to silence on the other end, picturing Ray leaned back in the armchair he'd rescued from the side of the road, with its brown plaid cushions and nicked wooden arms. In the image, Ray had a hand over his face, the way he did when he was wrestling with something.

"I wish you'd go get checked out," Ray said finally. "We can both get checked out. I don't think the bite's infected, but hey. Better safe right?"

Well that was monumental, Ray offering to go to a doctor. Monumental, but not enough to move Dan into going. He said, "If it gets bad enough I'll go."

And got nothing but silence from the other end.

"Have you heard from Jamie?" Dan asked, thinking about that trade: blood for drug money.

"Nope."

"Maybe he's doing rehab after all." How he'd *get* the blood from Jamie—or anyone else—he hadn't worked out yet.

"That'd be smart." The tone of Ray's voice implied Dan wasn't.

People cut themselves, he thought. On purpose. Maybe he just needed to find a cutter...somehow.

The silence from Ray's end grew heavy as a lead weight.

"Call me when you want to get together," Dan said.

"Yeah."

"Everything's going to be okay," Dan said. "Really. I'm working it out." One way or another.

SATURDAY NIGHT, a light band of pressure slipped around his head. The pig blood had no effect, and the chicken blood had made him heave. Dan was unsure whether it was that the blood wasn't "alive" anymore, or that it wasn't human. Or maybe he just had a *headache* like a normal person. He drew a razor blade across his skin, wincing as he watched the thin red line appear in its wake.

He sat up all night, cross-legged on the bed in the glow of his computer, trying to work out his options—all of them shitty. For a while, around four a.m., the hospital started to look attractive, but when he woke from a few hours of sleep on Sunday morning, he was back to thinking he could manage it himself, somehow.

After he was dressed, he made a cut with a razor blade, had a little taste, and felt fine, except for the lingering headache. Since it didn't go away, he assumed it was a real headache—and no fucking wonder. He tossed back ibuprofen then grabbed his jacket and keys. He'd just had Ray's blood the other day. He could do this.

When his great-aunt had broken her hip a few years ago, his mom had moved her into an assisted living facility. Aunt Cathy's furniture, the pieces she'd insisted on taking from her home when his mother sold it, crowded the small room at Elder Haven: towering armoire, poster bed. Two wingback chairs sat angled in front of the window, a claw-footed table between them.

The place was spotless, but only one person could move around in it at a time.

Despite the blinds levered shut at the window, Aunt Cathy wore enormous post-surgery sunglasses. The little peak of her nose stuck out below them. He waited until she'd shuffled to her favorite of the wing chairs before kissing the top of her white hair.

No bees, no buzzing. He smiled a little in relief and took the other seat.

Her thin fingers, the joints swollen with arthritis, felt around the chair arm as she said, "So what's new with you, Danny boy?"

"Not a thing. We just got back from the road. Time to make another record next, then do it all over again."

"You get that from your great-grandfather, you know, wandering all over the place. He was a Bible salesman, though if you ask me, he did more than sell Bibles house to house."

Dan smiled. This was not new news. Aunt Cathy had always been of the opinion—and not shy of voicing it—that his great-grandfather had left children all over the Northeast, several of who she insisted had been in attendance at his funeral, strangers who'd hung at the back and left before anyone could say anything to them. His mother, who'd been a girl at the time, had no recollection of this. Aunt Cathy's answer to that was that she'd been too short to see over people's heads.

Not that at four-foot-ten Cathy had had much more of an advantage. "I was taller then!" she'd say, her back stooped.

Now she said, "I hope you didn't inherit his other proclivities."

"They make better birth control these days."

"Oh, you." She swatted his arm, her head still facing forward in those dark glasses, like she'd gone blind.

"How'd the surgery go?"

"Great, they say."

"And you say?"

"It beats a bypass. If your next question is going to be about my blood sugar and whether they've changed my meds yet, I'm going to start calling you Faye and kick you out. They want to replace my bed, did you know? With one of those ugly hospital beds. Laziness is all it is. Makes less work for them. Tell me something interesting. All anyone ever talks about around here is what hurts and what's for dinner."

"I got attacked by a bat in an alley down in North Carolina," Dan said.

"I hate those things. They get in your hair. Did it bite you?"

"I don't know. It felt like it did something, but there was nothing there."

"Maybe you just got a pinch. Was it during the day? That's a sure sign of rabies, in which case you are damned lucky if it didn't break the skin."

"It was at night, after a show."

"I knew a girl who got rabies once," she said. "Silly thing thought she was saving a mouse from a cat. Should've let the cat have it."

"What happened to her?"

"She died."

He felt clammy suddenly. "She didn't happen to have a thirst for blood first, did she?"

"I don't think it was a vampire mouse."

A *ding* went off on the nightstand, and Cathy said, "Poop. Pill time. Hand me that plastic box, will you?"

It rattled as he carried it to her. Three compartments were already flipped open. He popped the lid on the next in line, and she let him dump pills into her shaky palm.

"Water?" he asked.

"Would you?"

She had a glass turned over beside the bathroom sink. He let the water run, the way she liked it. The bathroom smelled like Jean Naté and old lady, the way her bathrooms always had. He filled the glass and brought it to her. While he waited for her to take the handful of pills, one at a time, he itched to pull his phone from his pocket and look up rabies symptoms.

"You'll bring me a copy of the new album, won't you?" she asked as he replaced the pillbox on the dresser.

"Always."

He made it to his car before giving in. Rabies: discomfort, general weakness, headaches. A prickling or itching sensation at the site of the bite. He rubbed the back of his neck, queasy suddenly. *There's no fucking bite, though.* Cerebral dysfunction, anxiety, confusion, agitation, delirium, hallucinations, insomnia. *There's no fucking bite.* And no mention on the CDC's web page of a taste for blood.

It did say that by the time the symptoms showed up, it was fatal.

He leaned back, closed his eyes, and swallowed bile.

There is no fucking bite. And if he had it anyway, there was no fucking help.

He opened the car door and threw up on the pavement.

CHAPTER FOURTEEN

"LOOK who's here!" His mother gave him a hug at the top of the split-level's stairs.

"Who are you talking to?" With her arms around his neck, the bees murmured, their faint buzz tickling his vertebrae. *The day gets better and better.*

"Myself," she said with a laugh, oblivious. "That's what you get used to doing when you rattle around a house all by yourself." She pulled back, holding him at arm's length. "Are you sleeping enough?"

"Too much."

"You look as ragged as you did when you dropped the equipment off."

"I stopped by to see Aunt Cathy."

"Oh good. I'm sure she appreciated it. Hope you're hungry—I have a lasagna in the oven. We can split the leftovers."

"Sounds good."

In the kitchen, she gathered scattered sections of the Sunday edition of *The Boston Globe* and dropped them in a box.

"How're things?" he asked.

"Well, you know, the usual." She smiled as she went around the counter. "Work, upkeep, a little television and reading in the evenings. Set the table while I start the salad, would you? When are you starting work on the next album?"

"Soon. We have seven or eight songs half ready to go. Or at least we think so, till we hear them again."

"Are you feeling all right?" She took his arm as he gathered silverware from the drawer, turning him. She touched the cool back of her hand to his forehead. Far away, the bees hummed.

He ducked, forks and knives in hand. "I'm all right. Just coming down with a bug, I think." He rounded the counter and started setting out the napkins and flatware.

"Do you have a scratchy throat? I hear that's going around."

"No, I'm good. Just a little tired, a little headachy."

"You probably just need to eat." She touched his forehead again as he passed on his way to the dishes cabinet.

"Are we having garlic bread?" he said.

"Of course. Get out of your coat already. No wonder you look flushed."

After laying out the plates, he shrugged out of his jacket and hung it over the back of a chair.

"What do you want to drink?"

"Water's fine." The buzzing, right at the base of his skull, welled and ebbed like a thick heartbeat. He pulled out the chair and sat, rubbing his palm against the edge of the table to distract himself.

Rabies.

Untreatable once the symptoms start.

"Here's some orange juice." She set a glass in front of him.

"I said water's—"

"Just drink it and be quiet." She headed back to the cutting board to work on a cucumber. "How's Ray?" The knife went *chop-chop* on the cutting board.

"Fine."

"And Jamie?"

"Ray and I took him to detox a few days ago."

"Oh? How's he doing?"

"I don't know. Good, I hope."

"Can he get letters?"

Dan rubbed his nape. *I'm going to die from rabies if that's what I have.* "I don't know. I didn't think to ask." He took a swallow of orange juice, sweet on his tongue, cool in his throat.

"I got this new jalapeño ranch dressing." She ruffled his hair as she set the jar on the table. The bees kicked up a storm at the touch.

"Excuse me." He pushed back his chair, knocking his fork to the floor. The pressure around his skull swelled as he bent down.

"I'll get you a new one. Are you sure you're all right?"

He caught the fork between his thumb and finger and stood. "Yeah. Just need to use the restroom." He made his way to it, where he shut the door and leaned against it. *Shit. Shit. Shit.* He had a twenty-five-minute drive back to Manchester, and he was losing it. Not completely. Not collapse-into-unconsciousness losing it, not yet. But still.

Shit.

Not that getting home was going to solve anything, but the last thing he needed was to attack his own mother.

He wasn't stalking her yet—and he needed to get it the fuck under control before he started.

He pushed away from the door and looked in the mirror, leaning against the counter, pulling his eyelids down with his fingers.

He didn't see anything in there.

But how long?

He slid open one of the vanity drawers, pushed through its contents, opened another. *Bingo.* He withdrew a small box, half full of razor blades, cardboard slips covering the sharp edges. He pulled the paper free of one, laid the razor on the counter, and put the box back in the drawer. A box of Band-Aids sat in the medicine chest. He slipped one out, tore it open, and laid it on the counter, ready to go. He turned his arm palm up and hiked his sleeve up.

He pressed the blade against his arm, squinting so he'd only have to half watch what he was doing. With a wince, he drew it across his skin. A line of red chased the blade.

He set it down and pinched the cut, bringing more bright blood to the surface.

The sight flooded his mouth with saliva. He swallowed and pinched again.

When a fat drop started to roll down the curve of his arm, he bent his head and closed his eyes. His tongue flicked, his teeth scraped, his mouth sucked. It was—

It was hardly anything. Not even a teaspoon, just enough to take the edge off, maybe enough to get all the way the fuck home without his vision going out.

He washed up, applied the Band-Aid, slipped the blade back into its cardboard sleeve, and pocketed both it and the trash from the bandage. Mom wasn't going to find anything incriminating in her bathroom.

"Dinner's served." She set a steaming casserole dish on the table as he walked in. A towel-covered basket gave off the smell of garlic. He went up to her as she cut through the lasagna and gave her a light kiss on her hair.

The bees were reasonably quiet.

She smiled, and he sat down at his plate.

As she cleared the table after dinner, she said, "Want some ice cream?"

"No, thanks. I actually—I think I'm gonna head out. Get some sleep."

"That sounds like a good idea. You don't want to be getting sick."

"Nope." He pulled his jacket off the chair and shrugged into it as she dished lasagna onto a plate and wrapped it with foil.

"Here you go." She smiled. A foil of garlic bread sat on top of the lasagna mound.

"Thanks." He put an arm around her as he took the plate, the bees buzzing lightly.

"Thank you for going to see Cathy," she said.

"Yep. Take care of yourself."

"You too. I mean it, Dan."

He tromped down the steps and out the front door, into air that had turned crisp with fall. His shoulders relaxed. He could get through this, if he could get away from people. He climbed in and pulled onto the dark road, hunching over the steering wheel, as if he could outdrive it.

101 was deserted, I-93 only marginally busier. His neck buzzed. A rush of air cut through the window he'd cracked open. He chewed his lip till he merged onto 293. In another few miles, he hit his turn signal and coasted to the end of the off-ramp. Another few hundred feet, and he was pulling into his parking space behind the apartment building.

He opened the door, climbed out, then stood, holding on to the doorframe. He put his forehead against the backs of his hands. The cool air felt good. Maybe he *was* feverish. It just felt good, fresh. It didn't stop the buzz or ease the headache clamped around his skull, but it felt good. He reached in for the plate of leftovers, then pushed the lock down and closed the door.

When he did, something scampered over the garbage cans at the back of the lot.

He looked in the direction of the noise, trying to pick it out in the dark. He took a step forward, then another.

A trashcan lid clattered to the ground as a cat jumped off and sped, stiff-legged, past the front of Dan's car.

"Hey kitty."

He wasn't thinking it. Absolutely not.

"Here kitty, kitty."

The cat watched him, its body low and stiff, one front paw forward like it was ready to dart at the first too-quick movement. Dan set the plate on the roof of the car. Taking the garlic bread off the top, he sank to a crouch. The foil rustled as he eased an edge open. The cat's ears twitched. He pinched a corner of bread off and held it out. "Here kitty, kitty."

What other options were there? Roll a bum in an alleyway? Trawl for hookers? The buzzing was edging toward irrational already. Could he get through the matter-of-fact hooker negotiation he'd imagined? How many no's would he have to get before he just wrote his own yes and wound up in jail?

The bees buzzed like mad. He'd gotten out of his mom's in the nick of time.

"Here kitty, kitty." He pursed his lips and made soft noises. "Come on, kitty." He took a slow duck-step forward. "Here kitty, kitty, kitty. I have milk in the house. And tuna. Maybe. I think. Here kitty." He duck-walked another two steps. "I definitely have chicken in the house, and yummy raw pork." Neither of which he wanted to look at again, ever. "Here kitty."

The cat, a thin, lanky thing, flicked the end of its tail.

"Nice kitty," Dan said, another duck-step closer. He lifted his other hand in front of him.

The cat stretched its neck, its tail flicking.

Dan waited, and the cat took a step, leading with its nose, whiskers twitching.

Another step. The muscles in Dan's thighs started to tire, but he didn't move.

"Good kitty," he whispered as its thin tongue tasted the morsel between his fingers. It tried to ease it from his grasp, delicately, but he drew it back slowly. "Come on, kitty. There's more where this came from." The cat licked it again, then lapped in earnest, stopping every few licks to try to take it from his fingers.

He stroked slowly down on the cat's rear haunches. When it didn't bolt, he nudged it toward him, then closer yet—close enough to scoop it into his arms and trap it against his stomach.

It wriggled, letting out a cranky *meorrw*.

He rose, jogging toward the stairs, the cat fighting in his grip. Its low complaining trailed them as up the stairs, the cat twisting like a fish, trying to lunge free. He caught it, whispering, "Fuck!" Wrestled it back down against his jacket.

Getting his house keys out was a trick. He used the wall of the building to hold the cat against him, tipping his chin out of the way of its claws. He got the door open, got them both inside, shoved the door shut with his hip, and let the cat drop.

"Goddamnit," he said as the cat shot into his bedroom.

He followed, sweating, his hands shaky.

It wasn't under the bed or backed into any corner. He'd left his closet door ajar, and he pulled it wider now, looking into the shadows. These old buildings didn't have lights in the closet. He'd thought, a time or two, about getting one of those stick-on lights, but he hadn't, so he got on his hands and knees and tried to stay out of the way of the light coming from the bedroom's ceiling fixture. "Here kitty." He'd left the lasagna on his car, the foil of bread in the parking lot. He probably had something in the fridge, though. He got up to check.

Half a minute later, he came back with a splash of milk in a cereal bowl. He crouched by the closet again, setting the bowl just inside, next to a scuffed Converse. "Here kitty. Look what I brought you."

A tickle at the back of his brain, his mother's voice, told him not to feed cats milk. It gave them the runs.

Not that it mattered now.

The bees buzzed.

"Come on, cat." He dropped his butt on the floor and sat back.

After another minute, a glistening eye appeared from the shadows. The cat sniffed toward the milk, its striped tail swishing against a box in his closet.

He chewed his cheek and waited. The cat tiptoed another step forward. It gave him one last considering look before dipping its pink tongue into the bowl.

As it drank, it purred like a small motor.

He let it get nearly to the bottom before he shifted closer. "Want more?" He reached for the bowl.

The cat backed away.

Fine. He took it—the cat flinched at his movement but didn't run off—and got more milk from the fridge.

It waited for him in the shadows of the closet.

"Here you go." He put the bowl down and sat, a little closer this time, his chin on one knee.

The cat seemed to relax halfway through the second bowl.

Dan tried to turn off his brain, just not think about what he was doing as he scooped the cat up. It was a little less irritable this time, and a small piece of his heart broke at that. He turned to the bed, shoved the animal under a pillow, and held it there, one hand gripping its body, the other clamping the pillow hard over its head.

The cat struggled and *mrowwwed*, slicing into his arm with its pinprick claws. It squirmed from his grip. He leaned his body against the pillow. A hot tear pushed its way free, sliding down his cheek. A low noise climbed his throat, pain pushing up from the heat and tightness of his chest. He leaned his body against the pillow.

By the time the cat was quiet, he was huffing into the blankets, his face wet. He felt like the world's biggest asshole. But the bees were buzzing, and the worms were going to crawl across his vision. It was him or the cat.

Its soft, hot sides no longer heaved.

He didn't want to look at it.

With a last breathy curse of frustration, of pain, he pushed the pillow away and grabbed the cat up—limp and heavy—without looking at it.

He laid it on the kitchen counter, its head lolling over the edge of the sink. He closed his eyes, and the sight didn't go away. He grasped the counter. "Fuck," he whispered. "Fuck, fuck, fuck."

He straightened. A hot tear dripped off his jaw.

Swiping his cat-scratched hand across his face, he wandered the kitchen looking for things—a bowl or a wide-mouthed jar. He found a Tupperware container his mother had sent food over in. He dropped it in the sink, below the cat's head. Stopped to lick the pinpricks of blood welling from the scratches in the back of his hand. Did the bees care? Not fucking much. His own blood wasn't cutting it anymore—already. He opened a drawer, felt around for something sharp, and came up with a paring knife. No memory of why he had one, but he wouldn't look a gift horse in the mouth. He pulled off his jacket and pushed up his sleeves.

Wiped his face again with the side of his arm.

Sniffed snot up the back of his nose.

He looked at what he had before him: one cat, dead. One paring knife. He put a hand on the cat's head and turned it so its neck faced him. He pressed the edge of the knife against the gray fur. Already it felt like roadkill, like something that had always existed in a dead state. He gritted his teeth and dragged the small knife across its throat. It slid smoothly over the fur. He dug in harder. A thin cut split the cat's skin. Blood welled, slowly. He sawed harder, cutting into muscle, into veins. Blood trickled out, running along the knife, smearing his fingers. Then more. He turned the cut into a gash, opening the cat's throat. Choking back a gag. Trying not to look. He wiped his face against his sleeve as thick blood trudged between his thumb and finger. He lifted the back of the cat, turning it so its throat hung over the bowl, letting gravity do its thing.

Blood chugged slowly, nothing as spectacular as if he'd done it while the cat's heart still pumped, but no way could he have done that.

No fucking way.

The bees buzzed and hummed, and the vise tightened against his head.

He dropped the knife and lifted the Tupperware container—"Here's to nothing." He brought it to his lips, the tang more foul than inviting. He sniffed it, his lip curling back, his head turning away. He closed his eyes. The bees did not dance and writhe at this smell.

If it bought him till morning, though, it would be worth something. A way to push the edge back so he could make other arrangements. Somehow.

Still, his stomach revolted at the idea of drinking it down. He balanced the bowl on a hand and dragged a finger through it, drawing his lip back again, wrinkling his nose. The blood, still warm, congealed around his finger.

He made a face, then closed his eyes and put it in his mouth.

His face crumpled. His lip drew back. He wiped saliva and blood on his jeans, fast little strokes.

Did the bees go a little quieter? Did the headache let up, just a little?

He wasn't sure. It—maybe? Maybe not? But…maybe?

Fuck.

He had to go through with it to be sure.

He touched the container to his lips, his nostrils flaring at the smell, his stomach twisting sickly. He sipped through gritted teeth. Clamped his eyes tighter shut as his throat clenched. He had to fight his urge to retch in order to swallow down the—what, teaspoon's worth, if that?—he'd gotten in his mouth.

With shaking hands, he set the bowl on the counter, nearly dumping it over, somehow managing to steady it.

He put his elbows beside it and buried his face in his hands, swallowing and swallowing, trying to flood the taste away with his own spit.

The bees, they did not give a shit.

They were not into this blood.

"Fuck," he said, straightening. "Fuck!" His eyes closed against hot tears again, his fists tight balls at his sides. He was hopeless. The situation was hopeless.

A sob broke in his chest.

He sank to the floor, pressing his forehead against the cupboard. Big, jerking sobs without much noise hitched his shoulders. The fucking bees milled at the nape of his neck, wondering what the fuck he was going to do for them.

He thought he could smell the cat rotting already, and that broke another sob from him. He hit the cupboard with the flat of his hand.

He was so fucking fucked. And what he'd just done—a fucking waste. His soul felt ripped through at the utter pointlessness.

He crawled across the linoleum to his jacket, where he dug his phone out of his pocket. He wiped his arm under his nose, sniffed, sniffed again, then called Ray's number.

Pushing his back against the wall, he listened to it ring: *three, four...*

"Hey," Ray said.

Dan squeezed his eyes shut, hard.

"Danny? Are you there?"

It came out a whisper: "Yeah."

"Are you okay?"

Fuck.

"Dan?"

He slid down the wall, curling up against it. "No."

"Shit. I'll be right there. Are you home?"

He was on the brink of saying *yeah* when a sob caught him, coming sharp and sideways. He clamped his hand over his mouth.

"Dan...I'm pulling my boots on... I'm getting my jacket. I'm gonna be right there. Dan?"

Another sob hiccoughed out. Dan turned the phone away from his mouth.

"I'm going to the door right now. Hang on. I'll be there before you know it."

"I can't do it," Dan whispered, not sure he was going to get any of it out, but once he started, it all came up: "I can't... This isn't... I'm gonna die..."

"No, you're not. I'm opening the car door right now."

"There's nothing... It's too late..."

"Don't fucking talk like that. You're scaring the shit out of me." The door thudded shut. "How bad is it?"

"Bad."

"Can you still see?"

He blinked at the kitchen—the bottoms of chairs, bases of cabinets, the dust under the fridge. "Yeah." He hocked back more snot. "I can see for now." He watched the legs of the chair closest to him, ready to let Ray know if spots started crawling over it. He closed his eyes for a second, then stared at the chair legs again.

"Did it get bad all of a sudden?"

"Kind of. No. I don't know. It's just…bad."

"How long has it been getting bad?"

He squeezed his eyes shut. "Since this afternoon."

"And before that?"

"Fine. Everything was fine."

"Jesus, Dan. It's only been two days."

He pressed his forehead against the wall. "I've been using my own blood too. It doesn't work."

"Shit."

When he opened his eyes, dark spots floated in front of the white wall. "Fuck," he whispered.

"What?"

He blinked a few times, quickly. The spots careened across his vision. "It's the eye thing," he said quietly.

"Shit. Not you—the light turned red." A second or two of silence, then the gunning of an engine. "No cops in sight. I think we're good. I'm coming over the bridge."

Dan had his eyes shut and wasn't opening them for anything. He couldn't see floating dots if everything was black. He thought he could *feel* them, though, and he clutched the phone harder—for its glass and plastic and solidity. The bees swarmed. They could smell Janice, downstairs, walking around her kitchen. *Janice, Janice, Janice.*

"Door's unlocked," he whispered, grinding his forehead against his knee. *Get here soon.* Janice had stopped at the fridge. His free hand felt for the floor, right above her head.

"Coming off the bridge right now. Running a yellow light. Try not to fucking jump me when I get there."

"Yeah." Lily ran into the room below him, her voice excited as she babbled something to her mom.

"Hear me pulling up?" Ray said.

"I'm in the kitchen."

"Be there before you know it."

It seemed an endless stretch of seconds before boots pounded up the back stairs. The storm door banged open, the kitchen door. Dan tried to pull into himself, shoving his hands into his armpits. Trying to keep from lunging at Ray as boots clomped across the floor to him.

"All right, can you ride to the hospital?" Ray dropped to a crouch.

The bees swarmed. Ray put a hand on his shoulder, and the headache sharpened like a cleaver. Dan grabbed him, out of his mind with the need and the bees and the pain in his head. He held on with everything he had, resisting the impulse shooting through his muscles. Shaking with the effort. He clamped his mouth on his own arm, biting, making the pain break through the ruckus in his head.

Nothing stopped it.

Everything made it worse.

Especially Ray. Especially Ray's blood pumping just beneath his skin, the smell mixed with leather and cigarettes.

Copper rushed over his tongue—his own blood. His nerves screamed with the pain of his teeth sinking into his own flesh.

"Shit," Ray whispered, clutching him. "All right." His body shifted as he looked around. "All right. We can fix this."

Dan shook his head, Ray's heart *tha-thumping* against his cheek.

"Yeah. We can. We'll fix it." Ray pulled free of him, saying, "I need to get a knife. Okay? I'm just gonna—"

Oh God, the cat. He clutched Ray's jacket with the hand that could still reach, afraid to take his other arm out of his mouth. Ray dislodged him, strode across the room.

"Got it."

He dropped back to the floor, and Dan scrabbled for his jacket again. His jaws wanted to clamp down harder, rip his own flesh out, now that whatever was in him had had a taste of blood.

Fingers on his forehead, Ray was trying to look at how bad what he was doing to himself was. Bad enough make Ray hiss. "All right. Let's fix this."

As soon as he made the cut down his palm, the bees went nuts. Dan's jaws let go of his arm. He dove onto Ray's hand, gripping it in two hands like a bowl.

The knife clattered to the floor.

Dan lapped the cut, panting as he swallowed, going back for more.

Ray said, "Careful." He pushed his fingers through Dan's hair.

Not a lot of blood welled from the cut. He backed off enough to pinch it, trying to draw more. He sucked that up too.

Ray held the back of his neck. He felt Ray's eyes on him. He gripped Ray's arm hard enough to make white marks. The cut in Ray's hand was a slice of open skin. With Ray still holding on to his neck, he sat up, wiping his chin—of spit, he saw when he looked at his knuckles. Not a drop wasted.

His head cleared. The volume of the humming went down. Ray held his palm out, a thin line of red seeping into the cut again. He lifted it toward Dan, and Dan pulled it to his face and tongued it until it was done, until *he* was done, his chest bursting with gratitude, relief.

He sank back against the wall, his arm throbbing with fire. He didn't want to look at how bad *that* was. He tipped his head back and covered his face.

"All right now?" Ray asked.

He felt better, definitely better. But—"Shit."

"What?"

His stomach churned at the thought. He got it out, though, his voice cracking: "Rabies."

"What?"

"What if that thing gave me rabies?"

"Then thanks for giving it to me, man." He wiped his hand on his jeans.

"Shit," Dan said.

"I didn't see 'thirst for blood' listened as a symptom when I looked it up," Ray said.

"Abnormal behavior," Dan said. "Wouldn't that count? You looked up rabies?"

"I'll give you that you've been acting fucking abnormal. Have you been drooling? Painful swallowing?"

"There's prickling and itching at the bite site." Dan pushed his hand behind his neck.

"There is no bite site," Ray said. "Let me look."

Dan turned a little.

Ray felt his neck. "Where is it exactly?"

Dan pointed.

"There's nothing there. Not even redness, except from you pressing on it."

"I'm having auditory hallucinations. It sounds like bees buzzing, until it gets real loud. Then it sounds like a jet engine taking off between my ears."

Ray dragged his phone out. "Hold on."

Dan leaned in long enough to watch him pull a web browser up, then dropped back against the wall.

"General weakness?" Ray asked.

"No."

"Fever?"

"My mom said I felt a little warm tonight, but she didn't make a big deal about it, so I'll go with no."

"Headache."

"*Yes*. It goes away after…you know."

"Right. Prickling and itching at the site of the bite you have, theoretically. Cerebral dysfunction…" He looked at Dan. For all he knew, that could mean 'so fucked in the head you thought you needed to drink people's blood,' so he shrugged.

"Anxiety?" Ray asked.

"I think, considering the situation, that goes without saying."

"Yeah, but taking out the situation. Anxiety?"

"No." He rubbed the leg of his jeans. Caught site of the gouge in his arm and grimaced, turning it up to take a better look.

"Confusion? Do you have bandages?"

"No confusion." He tried to think what they could use for the damage.

"Agitation?"

"Only over the situation."

"Delirium? I guess we've covered abnormal behavior and hallucinations. Insomnia?"

"I wouldn't be able to tell you. I've been taking sleeping pills and spending entire days and nights in bed to avoid the situation."

"And you feel fine now?" Ray said.

"Perfect. Again. For who knows how long. If it *is* rabies, I'm fucked anyway." He clamped his hand over the bite, which both hurt sharply where the nerve endings were screaming and calmed some of the deeper throbbing.

"If it *is* rabies, you wouldn't feel better after a little blood."

Dan felt a hot tear welling at the corner of his eye. He turned his gaze to the ceiling.

"Hey." Ray clasped his shoulder. "We'll work it out. I think we can cross rabies off the list, so we're narrowing it down, all right?"

He let out a desperate laugh.

"Is the hospital still a no-go?"

He wrestled with the fact that the hospital had plenty of blood, but panic stomped all over that. The worse his fucking situation got, the bigger his fear grew. "Yeah. Maybe… Shit, I want to say maybe if it gets really bad, but Jesus, this is already really fucking bad."

"Can I call Moss at least?" Ray said.

"Why?"

"He used to be a paramedic and all, so."

Half of him was relieved at the idea of someone who might have some ideas knowing about this but… "You have to promise me—*promise* me—you two aren't going to pick me up and carry me to the hospital."

"Hey, we never did that to Jamie. Much as we'd fucking wanted to."

No. They hadn't.

"I have an idea anyway," Ray said. "I want to run it by him, see if it's doable."

"Okay."

"Okay?"

"Yeah. Call him." He dropped his head against the wall. Ray stood and turned toward the sink.

The cat. The bowl of blood. Shit. Dan brought his arms over his head, wanting to disappear. And doing that, all he smelled was blood, earthy and sharp, from the mess he'd made of his arm. It wasn't even funny that he and Ray were a matched set now.

"We need to get that cleaned up," Ray said.

"It's getting worse, isn't it? After the hospital tech, how many good days did I have? And now..."

"Is it coming back already?"

"No. I was just thinking I only had two good days this time. *Two*."

Ray glanced his way before heading for the trashcan. He carried it to the sink.

"I'm going to have to go to the hospital, aren't I?" He said it lifelessly as Ray's boots moved around the linoleum. Ray dumped the cat with a *thump*, poured its blood down the drain, ran water after it. He washed the bowl, the sink, the knife. Ray didn't even do his *own* dishes if he could help it—that's what take-out and paper plates were for—and here he was cleaning up Dan's.

Dan stared at the ceiling as he went through the drawers, looking for a dishtowel.

He was going to have to go to the hospital. He thumped the wall behind him with his skull.

Ray leaned a hip against the counter, pulling a cigarette from the pack in his pocket. "I had an idea this morning. Maybe it'll work. Maybe it won't."

"What?"

"Tell you in a minute." With the cigarette between his teeth and the lighter curled in his hand, he pulled up Moss's number, walking right by Dan on his way to the back door.

Dan climbed to his feet. With Ray having taken care of the kitchen, the least he could do was take care of himself. In the bathroom, where the window had been strategically placed so that anyone walking past on the porch could look in at the tub, he could hear Ray saying, "Hey, Moss. Sorry to bother you." He turned on the taps, and the rush of water drowned the voices out. He washed his arm, wincing at the sting. Splashed his face, the water cool. Fresh. As he cranked the taps off, he heard, "Thanks a lot, man. See you in a bit." He pressed his face into a towel. The screen door at the kitchen knocked shut. Ray's boots clunked across the floor.

Dan looked over the towel.

"Feeling better?" Ray asked.

"Yeah."

"Moss is on his way. Do you know you have something sitting on the roof of your car?"

"Shit. Lasagna. Want some?"

"Faye's?"

Dan nodded.

"Maybe later. You got some gauze?"

While Ray helped him get his arm wrapped, Dan became aware of the stink of the cat, its blood feral and secret.

Turning his head aside, he tied the neck of the garbage bag and lifted it from the bin, the gauze flashing white on his forearm. Ray watching him. He hated how Ray looked right now—dark hollows under bloodshot eyes, too-pale skin. Thinner than he'd been on tour. Dan was getting too much sleep; Ray looked like he was getting none.

The crisp night air was a welcome wake-up. He went down the steps with the bag in front of him. When he approached the cans, the memory of the cat leapt back to him. *Here kitty, kitty.*

He walked stiffly up, grabbed a lid off the nearest can, and stuffed the bag inside.

As he replaced the lid, he said a silent prayer that no one would go through the garbage, and that if they did they would find nothing there that tied him to the cat with the slit throat. All he needed was cops showing up thinking he was some serial killer in the making, his name in all the papers: "Musician Slashes Cat's Throat for Satanic Orgy Ceremony." That'd be fucking fantastic.

He clamped the lid on tightly.

The aluminum foil on the plate shone under the streetlight. He grabbed it off his car roof and headed upstairs. He hoped Ray would eat it, because there was no way he could sit down in front of the plate and not think about that cat.

If whatever it was he had killed him tomorrow, he hoped God would understand he'd felt he'd had no other options when it came to that cat. Well, none that didn't involve going after humans.

Ray had a new bag in the can by the time he got back upstairs. He shook his head when Dan offered the foil-wrapped plate, so Dan shoved it in the fridge.

"So what's—" A knock came at the apartment's front door.

"Must be Moss," Ray said, the both of them heading into the living room, Dan making sure his sleeve was pulled down to cover the gauze. When Dan opened the door, Moss said, "What's up?" His gaze moved from Dan to Ray, at which point he furrowed his brow and said, "Jesus, are you all right?"

"It's not me you've gotta worry about," Ray said. Rubbing his cut palm against his jeans, he added, "I hope."

Dan wondered if what they'd done was going to turn Ray into a blood-thirsting machine too.

Moss looked at Dan, who closed the door behind him. "What's going on?"

Dan had no idea what Ray's plan was. He headed for the couch. Ray could do the talking.

CHAPTER FIFTEEN

"So do we need some kind of medical license to get it?" Ray asked. He sat on the couch beside Dan, leaning forward with his elbows on his knees. His frayed shirt cuffs matched how the rest of him looked.

"Nah, you shouldn't," Moss said. "If you walk into a medical supply store, they might ask questions, especially after they get a look at you—when's the last time you slept anyway? But you should be able to order it all online no problem."

"I really look that bad?"

"Kinda wrung out there, buddy. They're gonna think junkie right off the bat."

"We'll get overnight shipping." To Dan he said, "Think you can make it till Tuesday?"

"Jesus, I hope so. If this starts coming back in just a day… I'm *fucked*."

"And when we get the stuff, you can do it?" Ray said to Moss. "You know how to draw blood?"

"It's been a few years, but if you don't mind a bruise or two the first time…"

"Yeah, I'll live."

Dan said, "Does it sound like *anything* you've heard of before?"

"Honestly, it sounds delusional. In my inexpert medical opinion," Moss said.

"He's not delusional," Ray said. "Trust me. I've seen the shit in his eyes when he's caught up in it, and I've seen the shit go away after he's had some blood."

"Can I see that?"

Ray looked at Dan. The thing Ray was proposing was supposed to keep him from *getting* to that point. Ray said, "What do you think? Just the once, and then no more."

Dan looked at Moss, who said, "Ray's the only one who's claimed seeing anything, and *both* of you were the only ones in the alley that night. I'd like to know you're not both delusional. Because from where I'm sitting, you guys both seem a little fucked up."

Dan dragged a hand through his hair, then shook his head. "It's too fucking dangerous. I don't ever want to get to that point again."

Moss regarded him before nodding.

"Okay," Ray said. "We'll order the stuff, hang on to it. When Dan needs it, but before it gets out of hand, we'll call you."

Dan nodded. That would be okay. It would be even more okay if they found out they could store the blood. He wouldn't have to rely on getting two other people together when he needed it. What would be *not* okay was if they found the time it took for the blood to get drawn and handed to him was too fucking long. "What if doesn't work if the blood goes from you to the syringe to me, what if the time involved there is long enough to kill whatever it is I need?" he said. "I mean, I killed the cat and dicked around with the blood before I tried it, so maybe the cat *would* have worked, if I'd—" He swallowed. Jesus, he did not want to do another cat.

"I guess we'll find out, won't we?" Moss said. "Also, I have to say it's creepy as fuck you killed a cat and drank its blood."

"Tell me about it," Dan said.

"If I didn't know you guys as well as I do..." Moss shook his head. "Christ. Do you have any idea how crazy you fucking sound?"

"Kinda, yeah," Dan said.

"Anyway," Ray said, scratching his face, giving Dan a view of the angry red cut down the middle of his palm. "Can you find out how much blood a person can give on a regular basis? We don't know how far this thing's gonna go."

The frayed cuff of his shirt slipped a little, revealing the edge of a strip of medical tape. Last week's bite. Dan dragged his eyes away. Jesus, he needed this to work. He couldn't live with himself if he seriously hurt someone.

"Anemia's going to be your big worry," Moss said, "unless this thing goes so far it's taking all your blood. Then you've got bigger problems."

"Yeah, no shit."

"If he's just licking up blood from a cut like you showed me, though," Moss said, "you won't have to worry much. *My* big fear is that this delusion gets out of hand, he starts ingesting more than he'd get out of a little cut like that, and then we have real health problems on our hands—for him more than you. You know blood is toxic, right? There's a reason it makes people puke their guts out if they drink any real quantity of it."

"We'll worry about that bridge when it comes into sight," Ray said.

"Well, you've got me curious at least. If you're both out of your minds, *something* happened in that alley."

"And if we're not out of our minds?" Dan asked.

"That's even more interesting. And fucked up. Either way, I'm putting my collar up at night and staying out of alleys."

"I'LL BE interested to see if it works," Dan said after Moss left. "Blood from a syringe, I mean, because I keep thinking maybe if I'd taken blood from the cat while it was still alive... I mean, like, right off the cat, instead of—"

Ray scrubbed his eyes. "If there's one thing I never want to talk about again, it's that cat."

"Yeah." He rubbed his hands together, hunched over at the other end of the couch. Trying to block the cat back out of his mind. Pretend it had been someone else who'd done that. Because he sure didn't recognize it as himself. He said, "I'm just wondering how fresh it has to be to work."

"I guess we'll find out."

"Yeah."

Ray fumbled in his jacket pocket, his cheeks dark with stubble.

"So why do you look like shit?" Dan said.

"Spent the past I don't know how many days on the internet." He found his cigarette pack, half crushed in an inside jacket pocket. "Every time I lie down, my brain's running around going, *What if you searched on* this*? What if you searched on* that*?*"

"Did you find anything?"

Ray popped one unlit into his mouth. "I didn't see the connection till the *second* time you attacked me, but…there's that astronaut who killed her two kids. Picked them up from their grandmother's, acting a little weird—agitated and distracted—but not weird enough to not let her take the kids. So she goes home and kills one with her teeth, then the other by suffocating him. Two and four years old. Probably would have killed herself then, too, but the kids' screaming had brought the cops."

Dan fidgeted while Ray hunted for his lighter.

"But that could just be coincidence," Ray said. "So there was this woman who was taking out the trash one night in Spindale, North Carolina, when something flew at her, attacking her."

Dan's heart picked up speed. He leaned forward, wanting to hear—finally—about someone else.

"Scared the shit out of her. They called animal control, but no one found anything. Three nights later, she went nuts on husband while he was asleep. Then a homeless guy attacked a woman at a bus stop in Charlotte."

"This is not comforting," Dan said.

"Now you know why I look like shit." He clutched the lighter and cigarette. "The Spindale woman and homeless guy died in jail after attacking a few more people, but what they died of—the woman and the homeless guy—was blood loss."

Dan's scalp crawled. He stood quickly, pacing to keep from throwing up.

"And then there are the rest of the astronauts," Ray said.

Dan turned. "Shit."

"Yeah. Gone for eight months on a space mission, they come back, pass all the medical tests, go home to their families…dead within weeks, leaving a bloodbath behind."

"Wait—all of them?"

"Have you not been watching the news?"

He didn't have a TV, and he'd been wasting his internet time on fucking rabies and *You Know You're a Vampire When…* "I knew it was that one woman…"

"Dobbs was the only one from the U.S. It took a while for Russia to admit their people weren't appearing in public because they'd fucking gone nuts and died."

"And it happened just like these other people?"

"At least you're alive still," Ray said.

He paced faster, trying to keep the contents of his stomach in his stomach. "What do doctors think?"

Ray shrugged. "They don't know. They haven't found anything. They're still looking into it. The media's blaming it on that space mission. My guess is they're probably right." He put the cigarette back in his mouth and stood. "The only one we know for sure was even attacked by anything first was the Spindale woman."

"Where was the astronaut from?" The news had said, he was sure, but he had so many place names in his memory bank, he couldn't pull that one out.

"Montreat. Not too far from Asheville. I'm gonna go smoke."

"Yeah." Asheville. Where the fucking alley'd been.

"Fresh air might do you good too."

Dan rubbed his neck, looking toward the back door. "Don't you worry?" he asked. "About going out there?"

"I worry about everything. Like if my best friend is going to be okay." He was on his way across the kitchen. "If I'm still going to have a band tomorrow. If all this smoking is going to give me lung cancer. I worry all the fucking time."

CHAPTER SIXTEEN

"All right," Moss said without looking up from the medic bag he was unpacking onto Dan's kitchen table. "Roll up your sleeve."

Ray raised his eyebrows; he'd already pushed it toward his shoulder and laid his arm out.

"Sorry," Moss said. "Nerves." He tied a rubber strap around Ray's upper arm, making it look easy. "Are you watching?" he asked Dan.

Dan paced the floor, trying *not* to watch. He rubbed his palms on his jeans and said, "Yeah." He put his hands on the cool stove, leaned against it. Even with his back turned, all he could see was Ray's pale arm on the table.

"Make a fist," Moss said, then, "Dan."

"Yeah." He turned again and came back, his hands shoved in his back pockets.

Moss found and tapped a vein in Ray's arm.

Dan looked at the ceiling.

"For someone who has no problem drinking blood," Ray said, "you're awfully squeamish."

"Yeah, go figure."

Moss tore open an alcohol wipe, swabbed Ray's skin with it. "Little pinch," he said with the syringe in his hand.

Ray looked away. A flinch passed over his face.

After a few seconds, with the needle still in Ray's arm, Moss undid the tourniquet one-handed, and Ray watched his blood spill into the collection tube.

Dan's nostrils flared. He turned away again—not squeamishness this time. The bees hummed in his neck. His mouth, which had gotten a good taste of blood the other night, ran with saliva.

"Open your hand," Moss said. "Hold that there for ten minutes or so." To Dan he said, "All right. Normally there's no way I'd want to see this, but...I want to see you do this." He held the collection tube in the air and shook it slowly.

"Go on." Ray held a cotton ball at the crook of his arm with two fingers.

With a nod, Dan took the tube. He couldn't manage anything more than a nod because his throat muscles clenched, wanting that blood. It splashed the sides of the tube, streaking the plastic a thick, deep red.

Buzzing filled his ears. Everything around him looked too real. The collection tube felt realer than real against the pads of his fingers.

He closed his eyes and tossed it back like a shot. And kept his head back, savoring the taste.

Savoring the near-immediate silence.

When he opened his eyes, the room was normal again.

Moss lifted his eyebrows.

"I need a cigarette." Ray kicked back his chair as he got up, still with his fingers on the cotton ball. With his other hand, he tried to reach in his pocket.

"Well?" Moss asked.

"That's the stuff," Dan said.

"How long you think that'll last?" Ray said.

As he stepped up to help him get his cigarettes out, Dan said, "I wish I fucking knew. But that's definitely the stuff."

Moss shook his head, and Ray said, "Are you okay with that? Can we do that again if we need to?"

"You know where to find me." Moss shoved the tourniquet back in the orange medic bag. He peeled off his gloves, wrapped the used needle in them, then sealed them up with medical tape. "I suppose I'm going to have to drop in and visit my buddies at the rescue squad. Dispose of this needle properly. Hopefully without having to answer any questions."

"Sorry." Dan watched Ray through the screen door, lighting his cigarette with his free hand, the other still holding the cotton down.

"Don't worry about it. Listen, call me if you feel sick or anything freaky happens. Not that I can do much about it."

"Will do."

He stopped to talk to Ray on his way out. Dan turned the collection tube upside-down over his mouth, getting any last drops.

It fucking worked. The blood didn't need to be so fresh that he had to drink it directly off a person. That was something. That was progress. They could work with that. He shoved open the screen door. "Hey."

Ray and Moss looked over.

"Next time can we do two? I want to stick one in the fridge and see if it still works after it's sat."

Ray shrugged. "Fine by me."

"We should tell someone what works," Ray said after Moss left.

Dan's back prickled. He agreed, but he didn't want to become a lab experiment—especially not if they wanted to test what worked by withholding it to see what happened. "Can we just send an anonymous note?"

Ray studied the buildings across the way as he dragged on his cigarette. Finally, he butted it out against the railing. "Okay."

CHAPTER SEVENTEEN

"WHAT?" Ray said the second night they spent hunched over their guitars, scraps of paper scattered around them, empty beer cans. A greasy pizza box on the floor, cheese congealing on the slice neither of them had bothered to eat.

Dan shook his head, as if to get the distant buzz of the bees out of it. He didn't have any bees, though. Hadn't since he'd dumped Ray's blood down his throat. But there was a sense that they waited at the edges, ready to come back. He strummed his Cortez, a chord progression from the song they were working on—"Low Road" they were calling it. He liked it for an album title too, but Ray had thrown in *Bad Things*. It was premature to be considering album titles anyway. Way premature. "I think if we change this up—" He played the part between the chorus and the second verse, only this time he went to D with it before going back down.

Ray said, "Yeah, that could work." Nodding. Giving him a cautious eye. Dan felt like a bug under a microscope. And his neck itched. It was hot up on the third floor. Ray was in long sleeves—didn't he feel it?

He dragged a hand through his hair, the other clutching his pick. "I think we'll need to do it again soon."

And Ray didn't ask, "What, the song?" No, he got it: "All right. Tomorrow? Or sooner?"

"Tomorrow. We could probably hold off till Friday…" Damn the fucking itch. He scratched his neck, quickly, and pulled his hand away.

"But we probably shouldn't push it," Ray finished for him, setting his beat-up archtop aside, its familiar sunburst looking like it'd been dragged over cement sometime in the '50s. "The whole idea is to keep you on an even keel, not let you get where it's crazy."

"Right."

"Because I'd like to not get fucking bitten again." He leaned against the front of the couch, letting a leg slide out across the floor. He tapped a cigarette from his pack and put it between his teeth before searching his pockets for a lighter.

"Next to the ashtray."

"Thanks."

"I wanted to thank you," Dan said. "For doing this. If it hadn't been for you…"

"You'd be in a holding cell for butchering people's pets, or worse?"

"I wouldn't doubt it. Anyway, I know how you feel about doctors, so giving blood like that…"

"Nah, don't worry about it. It's different when I know no one's going to be putting it under a microscope to find shit wrong with me. Don't get me wrong—I'm not chomping at the bit to have Moss prick me again. But it beats the alternative."

"So." Dan pressed his hand to the back of his neck.

"So tomorrow. I'll let Moss know."

"Okay."

"We'll do the two tubes," Ray said.

"You don't mind?"

"Mind being stuck fewer times?" He smiled as he rolled the cigarette between his fingers.

"I guess there's that." Dan rested his chin on his knee. "What if it gets to be every day? What if it gets to be more than a tube every day?"

"Bridges we'll cross." Ray tipped his head back, blowing smoke toward the ceiling. "Actually, I think that might work, your idea for 'Low Road.'" He grabbed the Gibson, stuck the cigarette between the strings. "Let's see." And he started into it, from the beginning. Dan joined in as soon as he had his own guitar back in his lap.

"Yeah," Ray said as they moved smoothly into the second verse. "Yeah, this'll work."

PART TWO

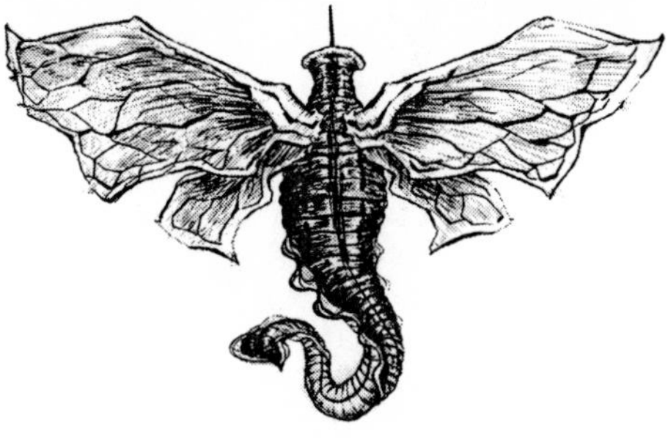

CHAPTER EIGHTEEN

THEY were quiet as they waited in Dan's kitchen for Moss to show up. Almost a month they'd been doing this, and Ray, who'd gone from haggard to gaunt over the course of it, looked like a sack of sticks hunched at the table.

The bees were a brown hive, deep inside Dan now. No more insect feet crawling over his neck. It was the hum of a generator at the core of him. "We can't keep doing this," he said. Moss was going to say the same thing when he walked in and got a look at Ray. This was needing too much blood, too fucking often. And Moss didn't even know about the secret crisscross of razor blade lines on Ray's back, the things they were doing to stretch the days between Moss's visits.

"I was thinking." Ray's hands rested on the table, blue veins crossing the backs like starved worms.

"What?"

"Maybe it makes a difference if it's from the same donor all the time." He caught a papery cough in a hand. His beer sat off to the side—he'd taken two sips and pulled his jacket back on. Dan had felt his hand earlier—it was like he'd been out in the cold.

Dan pulled a chair out and sat, though he didn't know how long that would last. The bees made him restless. "Explain." Because he knew Ray wasn't about to suggest taking him to the hospital. Despite the letters they'd mailed, hospitals weren't doing a great job with this. They'd tried transfusions, which was only working in the sense that people weren't dying from blood loss, but they were still going fucking crazy. Ray'd sent a new letter, but as far as they could tell from the news, no one was trying it. So people were going nuts. People were getting hurt. People were *dying*, and no one was fixing it yet.

And if the acceleration of Dan's need for blood was any indication…maybe it wasn't fixable. Maybe they were just putting off the inevitable. It made his guts clench.

"Maybe the effect lasts longer," Ray said, "if it's different blood. Whatever it is, it doesn't do good with your blood, right? Now it's getting my blood over and over, maybe it's started thinking it's yours. So it isn't satisfied. It wants you to get someone else's, so it knows for sure it's not eating itself out of house and home. Does that make any fucking sense? Because my shit *used to* fucking work, right? At least for a few days, you know? Now we're feeding you twice a day, and you're still on edge."

"Well, that would be a great thing to try if we *had* different blood. I don't see Moss letting you stick a needle in him anytime soon."

"No, he wants you to go to the hospital."

Dan rubbed his palms on his jeans. "I'm worried he's going to put his foot down about it today. One look at you…"

Ray's reached into his shirt pocket with two not-so-steady fingers. "If he does, we'll do it ourselves."

"Come on. You know as well as I do this is spiraling right down the fucking toilet."

"What I know is we haven't tried changing up the blood, and I'm not giving up till we've tried everything I can fucking think of." He pushed up the top of the pack. A single cigarette slid to the corner. "Shit." He pulled it out and stuck it behind his ear. "Anyway, I have an idea."

CHAPTER NINETEEN

IT WAS coming up on five p.m.—four days after Moss had flipped out over Ray's stubborn descent into anemia—when they pulled up to the curb in front of Moss's place, Ray driving. Before Dan could get his door open, Moss came out of the house, looking up the street and then down as he walked quickly toward them with a duffle bag clutched in his hand.

Dan reached back and unlocked the door.

"Everything cool, man?" Ray asked.

"Yeah. Yeah, I just don't like lying to Debbie," Moss said.

Dan shifted around in his seat. "Sorry we had to ask you to."

"It's all right." Moss looked out the window as they pulled away.

"Did you get the shirt?" Ray asked, flicking his eyes toward the rearview.

"Scrubs. Yeah."

"How much?" Dan worked his wallet out of his pocket.

"Nine dollars."

"That's it?" He pulled out a ten. "Don't worry about the change."

Moss pocketed it, saying, "You guys have the rest of the stuff?"

"In the trunk," Ray said. All the needles, tubing, alcohol wipes, sterilized glass bottles. Moss had said upfront he wasn't keeping that stuff at his house, not where Debbie would run across it and start wondering if he was using or something. That's all he needed: his wife suspicious about shit he wasn't even doing.

Dan pulled up some music on his phone, and they merged onto I-293 for their second two-and-something-hour drive to Rhode Island since getting home, the opening track on Black Rebel Motorcycle Club's *Baby 81 Sessions* taking them out of the city.

"Heard from Jamie?" Moss asked.

"Got a call last night, actually," Ray said.

"How's he doing?"

"He sounded pretty good."

"So he stayed for rehab?"

"That or he's crashing with some chick he met at detox and just pretending he's still in rehab."

"That wouldn't surprise me," Dan said.

"You think that's what he did?" Moss said.

"Nah. He sounded like he was really there." Ray tapped the side of his head. "And there."

Dan threw his voice toward the back. "How're Debbie and the baby?"

"Good," Moss said. "Penny's getting to be a real pro at walking. Every time we turn around, she's into something else."

"Did Deb freak out about you going back on the road so soon?" Ray asked.

"She wasn't happy, but, you know, I told her with the holidays coming up… I told her you guys were paying extra for this." Moss was getting what amounted to time and a half. The downside was the three of them would be sharing fifty-dollar hotel rooms, and of course they were stuck in a car instead of a bus, or even a van—something people could stretch out in. Moss's knees pressed against the back of Dan's seat.

"What if this guy doesn't show up?" Moss asked.

Dan watched the road. It was the same question looping through his head, that and a whole stream of other what-ifs:

What if it's actually a cop? What if the guy's got AIDS or something? What if it's a setup to get robbed?

"We move on to the next one," Ray said. "And the next one. Somebody's gonna show up."

"I hope you're right." Moss's voice wasn't full of confidence. They were finding people online, on message boards where vampire fetishists hung out and through some ads Ray had put up on craigslist.

They coasted off I-95 into Warwick a little past dark.

"Should be not too far down this road," Ray said as he eased onto Jefferson Boulevard.

"Up there." Dan pointed at a squat building at the side of a parking lot. As Ray put on his turn signal, Dan realized he still wanted to be on the interstate, still traveling with all the potential of the world ahead of them. A dull lump sat in his stomach, a certainty that no one was going to show up at the diner looking for an oversized male nurse and a vampire, and that if they did, it wasn't going to go well.

They scoped the place from the outside, discussed where to put the car. Went over the plan again, making sure the pieces fit with the reality of the location. They hadn't for a second entertained the idea of having people come to their motel room—if years on the road had taught them anything, it was that a surprising number of people didn't know when to leave.

Ray shut off the engine. "Let's case the men's room first."

"You don't think that's strange?" Moss pulled himself forward by Dan's headrest. "We walk in the door and head straight for the restroom?"

"I've gotta piss anyway. If you don't, just go grab a seat."

Dan was coming in separately, so he wouldn't look like he was with them. He rubbed the door handle with his thumb, anxious to get this going, to sit at a table with a coffee and wait for nothing.

Another car pulled in, headlights splashing their hood. It swept into a spot closer to the restaurant. Dan rubbed the door handle.

"All right," Ray said. "You want to go first or should we?"

"Go ahead."

"Don't forget the shirt," Ray said to Moss as they got out. Ray put an unlit cigarette between his lips, stopping to light it before pushing his door closed. They walked around to the trunk, the trunk lid came up. After half a minute, it slammed shut. Ray and Moss headed toward the restaurant, the cigarette dangling from Ray's lips. Moss had pulled the scrubs on over his t-shirt, then slipped his jacket on over that. The light blue tail hung below his jacket.

Dan rested his head back and closed his eyes. The buzzing was there, his old nemesis, humming away. A headache tightened his skull. This so wasn't going to fucking work. He was going to end up in a hospital by the end of the week.

That frightened the shit out of him.

The more they put it off, the less he wanted to end up there. He was having nightmares about it—strapped to a bed with those tan restraints, never allowed to see anyone he knew. They'd put a mask over his face, like Hannibal's, turn him into a freak.

He hummed under his breath, marking time, tapping the armrest. If the tune had words, they'd have been "I'm fucked, I'm fucked, we're all fucked. We're fucked."

Dan stepped out of the car and slid his sunglasses on, despite the dark. When he came through the door, the hostess was already pulling a menu out. "One?"

He scanned the seating area, spotted the back of Moss's head—hard to miss. "Someplace over there." He nodded in their direction.

She seated him two tables away. He risked one look, met Moss's eyes, then languidly flipped open the menu.

Nothing looked good.

When the waitress came, he ordered coffee and pie.

When she delivered the slice of pie on a plate, he waited until she turned away before pushing it to the side. The sight made his guts twist, cherry filling oozing out like horror show gore. The coffee was tolerable, if a little bitter. It kept him focused.

Everything was already hyper-reality for him; the coffee just gave it that little extra edge.

He cupped his hands around the mug and stared at nothing from behind his sunglasses.

Ray and Moss weren't talking. The waitress brought them food—burgers, fries, Cokes. Dan checked his watch. The meeting wasn't for another twenty minutes. He put down another swallow of coffee.

Time dragged on.

Every time the door opened, he flicked his gaze toward it. An older couple came in. A trio of teenage girls. Another old guy, by himself, a rolled-up newspaper under his arm. He unrolled it as soon as the hostess left him.

A rivulet of sweat trickled down Dan's ribs. It wasn't the jacket but the discomfort. The bees taking interest in the people around him. The buzzing and waiting. He took down another swallow of coffee.

The doors opened.

Two guys in their early twenties shuffled in, glances darting toward the dining room. The tall, round-shouldered one nodded at the hostess, not meeting her eye. His face turned, gaze passing over Dan seated alone at a table—wasn't what he was looking for. The shock of black-dyed hair over his puffy face made him look like he'd been drained of blood already. His friend, a skinny guy with a sharp nose and a black trench coat that fit his shoulders like they would a hanger, stepped on the back of the other guy's beat-up sneaker as the hostess led them to a table.

Dan slid his gaze toward Moss in his light blue smock, the orange paramedic bag on the seat beside him. He could pass for a nurse just off work—Dan hoped. Ray still had his jacket on, his hair, as usual, unkempt. He caught Dan's eye with a nod before sliding a look back at the newcomers.

The guys slid into a booth, flipped open menus on the table.

As soon as the hostess walked off, they started glancing around again, trying to be casual about it. The taller one, catching sight of Moss, nodded. The skinny guy looked, then they looked at each other.

Ray and Moss ignored them.

The guys leaned toward each other, talking, eyeing his guys. One slanted his head toward the booth, as if saying, *Go on. Go see.*

The skinny guy flattened his hands on the table and started to get up. A waitress headed their way. He sat back down. As far as Dan could tell, they ordered sodas, nothing else. As she walked off, the skinny guy got up and grabbed the shoulder of the other guy's jacket. Dan could only imagine the expression on his face. Maybe he was mouthing, *Come on*. His eyes bulging a little. *Come on, come on.*

They crossed the dining area.

Ray, though he'd made no sign he'd seen them coming, moved closer to the wall as they approached. Moss looked over, picked up his bag, and slid over too.

"Sit down. Relax." Ray dipped a French fry in a puddle of ketchup. "Try not to make this look like a fucking drug deal, all right?"

The skinny guy slid in beside Moss, the round-shouldered one next to Ray.

Dan tuned out the rest of the restaurant.

"So which one of you's the vampire?"

Moss pointed in his direction, Dan half watching the table, half watching the cup of coffee between his hands. The guy who'd spoken turned in his seat to get a look.

"You could just be saying that," he said. "How do we know you even know that guy?"

Ray said, "Yo, Freddy."

Dan pointed the dark lenses of his sunglasses at Ray.

"Shit," the big guy said, his voice edgy with excitement.

"Is he okay?" the other one asked.

"He's feeling a little low at the moment," Ray said. "That's why you guys are here."

"Nu-uh," the skinny guy said. "Not me, just him."

"Where are we gonna do it?" the other guy asked.

"Here," Ray said. "There." He nodded at the restrooms. "After I finish my Coke. That okay? You guys want anything to eat? Or maybe you should wait till after."

"How—how much are you going to take?"

Ray let Moss field that one. "Less than the Red Cross does." They were aiming for half that, but the bottles were marked all the way to Red Cross levels, in case after this first time they felt like they could get away with that.

"So, what, like half a pint or something?" the big guy said.

Moss nodded.

"And he's really…?"

"In bad shape," Ray said. "Let's get it done." He ushered the guy out of the booth. The little guy and Moss slid out their side. As Ray pulled bills out of his wallet, he said to the little guy, "Maybe you should hang back here—it might be suspicious, all of us walking in there together."

"I'm his back-up man. He's not going in there without me."

Dan looked back down at his coffee, listened to Ray saying, "Let's get it done, then." They brushed past him, Ray knocking his knuckles on Dan's table on his way by. He turned his eyes up to watch them head past the hostess station and into the restroom alcove.

"Top that off for you?" his waitress asked, coming up from behind with a carafe of coffee.

"No, I'm done. Thanks."

She set the pot down to fish his check out of her apron. "I'll just leave this with you then."

"Thanks."

He stood and left a ten on top of the check before making his way to the men's room.

At the door, he stopped, made sure no one was watching, and rapped quickly. It opened, and Ray pulled him in.

"I can't watch," the skinny guy was saying, pacing away from the stall where his friend was seated on the toilet, the needle already in his arm, blood running down the tube into the glass bottle.

Dan's head swam.

"You all right?" Ray asked, right behind him.

He nodded, up and down jerks. He closed his eyes and turned away, arms crossed, fingers pushed into his armpits. Just a few minutes. Just a few fucking minutes. Then they'd know if this "fresh blood" idea had any merit, though if nothing else, it'd at least take some pressure off Ray as the single donor.

"What if someone comes in?" the big guy asked.

Moss shifted closer in the stall and swung the door shut.

"Yeah, 'cause nobody's gonna notice four size-fourteen feet in there." Ray leaned against the restroom's main door, holding it closed.

Dan grasped a sink and bent his head. Holding himself together. It was worse, being in this small room with the blood *right there.*

"Hey, I can see you in the mirror," the little guy said.

"You watch too many fucking movies," Ray said. "And I need a fucking cigarette." He rummaged in his pocket for his pack.

Dan kept his head down, concentrating on keeping hold of himself. Something was coiled inside him, ready to burst right through his guts, take him over. It was still being patient, but for how much longer?

"You okay in there, Vin?" the skinny guy asked.

"Yeah."

"Are you gonna drink it right in front of us?"

"Watch it," Ray said. "He'll drink it right out of where your head used to be if you get any closer."

"I want to watch," Vin called from the stall.

"I don't," said the skinny guy.

The bathroom door bumped Ray's shoulder. Dan turned the faucet on and pushed his hands under the stream as Ray stepped away, saying, "Oh, hey, sorry about that," louder than he needed to.

The skinny guy whipped toward the urinals with his hands on his belt buckle like he'd just finished.

Dan turned his hands under the water, listening to the newcomer move past, unzip his fly.

Ray said, "Yeah, so like I was saying, we should be in Chicopee in, what, another hour? Hour and a half?"

"Something like that," Dan said slowly.

The skinny guy snuck a look at him, probably thinking, *He talks*. Personally, Dan liked this whole thing better when he didn't talk. He withdrew his hands and turned the tap off. Shook them out. Stepped over to the nearest blow dryer and punched the button with his elbow.

Moss and Vin were being admirably quiet in the stall.

A public restroom was a stupid place to do this. They needed ten minutes of privacy to get the fucking blood.

The door bumped open again. Now there were two strangers in the restroom, one stepping up to the urinals and the other walking away from them, heading for the door without bothering to wash his hands.

"Almost done," Moss said, probably thinking the door opening had been their visitor leaving.

Dan caught white flashing in Ray's eyes, but Ray's voice didn't betray it: "Take your time. No rush. We can wait."

"Y-yeah," said the skinny guy. "We can wait. Really."

Ray's gaze traveled sideways to the skinny guy.

The second stranger stopped to not wash but *scrub* his hands. Time ticked by. Dan shifted his feet. Finally the guy moved to the hand dryer.

"So you guys are going to Chicopee?" the skinny guy asked. He didn't seem to know where to put his hands—front pockets, back pockets, coat pockets.

"No," Dan said.

"Oh."

The second stranger finally headed out the door.

Ray pushed it shut behind him, shoved his foot against the bottom. "Coast's clear, but let's make it quick."

The stall door swung open. Moss handed the bottle to Dan, full to the one-cup mark, its sides hot where the blood was. His face was passive but tight, like he wanted to say something, and Dan was sure he would once he got the chance.

Vin had one pasty arm out of his coat, his elbow crooked to keep pressure on the cotton ball. Moss gave a small shake of his head and started putting everything back in his kit.

Dan swung away from the stall, putting the opening of the bottle against his lips and tipping his head back, swallowing and swallowing with his eyes closed. Silencing the fucking nervousness, feeding the engine-hum of bees in his belly.

"Holy shit," the skinny guy said in an awed voice.

With two-thirds gone, Dan lowered the bottle and wiped his mouth with the back of his hand. "Cap," he said.

Ray got it from Moss. As Dan passed him the bottle, Ray's eyes searched for something, some confirmation that it had worked—not the blood, but the *plan*. Dan gave a ghost of a nod. The corners of Ray's mouth creased upward as he capped the bottle. He handed it to Moss, who tucked in in the bag.

"That's off the fucking hook," the skinny guy said. "Completely off the fucking hook. Can I try some?"

Moss zipped the bag shut. "If you want to end up on a slab with the coroner scratching his head over how someone else's blood got in your stomach."

"Really?"

"Really."

Probably not really, Dan thought, but the reality wouldn't be a whole lot of fun either.

"Ready?" Ray asked Dan.

Wiping his mouth again, he nodded. His hand came back clean. He took a quick look in the mirror, making sure he didn't have blood smeared on his face. "Yeah, let's get out of here."

"Thanks, guy." Ray unfolded his wallet, handed Vin some bills. "Get yourself something to eat. The fries here are good."

"So that's it?" the skinny guy asked.

"Unless you want to donate to the cause too."

"Unh-uh. I'm not good with needles."

"Well that's it, then. Thanks again."

"Thanks," Dan said before following Moss out the restroom door. They headed straight out the front doors and into the parking lot while Vin and his friend lingered inside, probably debating whether to stay and eat.

On the way to the car, Dan said, "I'll drive."

"You sure?"

"I feel good."

"What I like to hear." Ray tossed him the keys.

As he cranked the engine, Dan said, "How about you, Moss?" He flicked his gaze to the rearview. "You doing okay?"

"A restaurant bathroom is a stupid fucking place to do this."

Dan nodded. "Exactly what I was thinking."

CHAPTER TWENTY

IN THE morning, with the motel room's curtains blocking the sunlight and Moss snoring on one of the two double beds, Dan fished the bottle of blood out of the bag and cranked the cap off.

"Already?" Ray asked, coming out of the bathroom.

"I don't need it, but I wouldn't mind bringing myself back up to normal levels again." The hum in the base of his skull was a mosquito, almost not worth worrying about. The hangover from the cheap wine they'd killed after leaving Vin and his friend, however, ramped down his tolerance for even mosquitos. Sniffing at the opening, he wrinkled his nose and turned his face away. "Maybe it's too early for this shit." After another quick sniff, he fastened the cap back on.

The smell of stale cigarettes lingered. Had Ray lit a few while they were toasted? He couldn't remember for sure.

Maybe.

Maybe he remembered Ray leaning against the wall beside the window. Maybe the window'd been cracked a couple inches.

The smell made him kind of green. "I think I just need to spend some time with my head between my knees." He shuffled past Ray, into the bathroom, where the tile floor was cool under his toes. Brushing his teeth, he decided the headache was just a hangover, not the usual harbinger of hell. He pulled himself upright and got into the shower to let steaming water pound the back of his neck.

When he came back out with wet hair and yesterday's jeans hanging from his hips, Ray had the laptop they'd brought open on the bed, rubbing his mouth while he read the screen. Already he looked a little better. Pinker-cheeked. More fleshed out. Maybe it was the light.

When Dan fished a t-shirt from the floor, Ray looked up. "Got a few more possibilities in the works."

"Yeah? Where'd Moss go?" Dan asked.

"Out in the parking lot calling Deb."

Dan pulled the shirt on. "Anything look good?"

"I don't know yet. Maybe." He hunched and typed, one finger from each hand. "Maybe."

They got back on the road after lunch—soup, crackers, and ginger ale for Dan. He felt marginally better after eating.

Moss tried his wife again from the back seat; he'd missed her earlier. Dan let his eyes slip shut and gave in to the drone of the road as Moss made things up about their so-called acoustic tour of indie record stores, just the three of them. "Uneventful," Moss said. "Not a big crowd, but a good one at least."

Dan felt like shit, but it was an existential shit feeling, not a physical one.

From Providence they headed west. The next stop was just over the New York border, a town on the Hudson. The three-and-a-half-hour drive put them there a little past four in the afternoon. Nothing to do but check into the motel and sit around.

Moss turned on the TV.

Ray said, "Fuck this," around an unlit cigarette, pocketed one of the keycards, and went outside to smoke.

Dan, sitting on the end of one of the beds, dropped backward, laying his hands one on top of the other on his chest.

"You hear that?" Moss said.

"Huh?"

"Gonna rain tonight."

Dan stared at the ceiling.

A *thump* against the windows brought him up quickly.

Moss said, "What the—?" He swept open the curtain.

Ray grinned from the other side before turning and dropping his back against the window.

"Don't open it," Dan said. "It'll just let smoke in."

Moss rapped with two knuckles and raised his voice to say, "Gonna rain tonight."

Ray shrugged, made an *And?* face.

The talk show on TV had a celebrity doctor going on about fatty acids. Her voice made the bones in Dan's head hurt. He massaged his temples.

Moss checked his kit, setting aside what they'd need this evening and repacking it so those items were on top—alcohol swab, disposable needle, the rubber tourniquet.

Dan uncapped the bottle from the night before and chugged the last of it down before rinsing it out and leaving it on the bathroom counter.

The three of them headed out to find pizza. This time dinner and donations would be in separate locations, which Dan was a-okay with. When they slid into a booth at a Frank's Pizza, he could relax and actually eat something.

"I hope this goes better than last night," Moss said around a wad of his veggie slice.

"I don't think it went so badly," Ray said.

Moss raised his eyebrows.

Ray shrugged. "We got what we came for, didn't get caught."

"What's the deal with this one again?" Dan asked, already wearing his sunglasses, enjoying the anonymity of them. Of knowing no one was going to look in his eyes and see he had a problem. That he was coming apart.

"How are you doing?" Ray nudged a wadded-up, sauce-stained napkin under the edge of his plate.

"All right." The low-key humming was staying low key. The last vestiges of his hangover was gone too.

Ray nodded.

They paid their bill and went out into the dark, Moss getting behind the wheel this time. Ray rode shotgun with Google Maps, his face lit by the glow of its screen.

Twenty minutes later they pulled up in front of a consignment shop called Skeletons from the Closet.

"Used clothes for goths," Ray said.

Black and purple crowded the window, lace and velvet, crosses and crystals. A foghorn announced their arrival. Three young women hung around a sticker-covered counter at the back, turning their attention toward the front as Moss, Ray, and Dan made their way through the racks of clothes.

"Which of you's Esmerelda?" Ray said.

The corner of a scarlet mouth twitched. A thin black eyebrow rose slowly upward. One of the other girls laughed, her cheeks flushing as she turned her face away.

"Well, Esmy," said the third girl, sizing the men up. "What do you make of this?"

Esmy tilted her head, looking Ray up and down, then Dan, that eyebrow holding its arch. She seemed to have dismissed Moss in his nurse's smock with barely a glance—not even the battered Doc Martens or the dice tattooed on his knuckles made her question whether he might be the vampire.

It didn't take her long to rule Ray out too.

Fastening her gaze on Dan's sunglasses, she said, "So you're the so-called blood-sucker."

He lifted his eyebrows. Her lips twitched at the corner again.

"What do you think, girls?" she said.

The one in front of the counter had regained her composure enough to size them up, with a little less pizazz than Esmy had. "You know who you look like?" she said to Ray.

"Not that fucking guy from Two Tons of Dirt," Ray said. "If I hear that one more—"

Fuck. *Ray.*

"Who? No. That guy from The Dead Weather." To her friends she said, "Delia has posters of him *all over* her walls. What's that guy's name from Dead Weather, Leigh?"

Leigh shrugged.

Moss raised the orange bag in the air. "Do you have a place in the back where we can do this?"

Esmy nodded. "He's coming back there too, right?" Crooking a finger in Dan's direction.

"Yep," Moss said. "This way?"

"I'll hang back out here," Ray said. "Yell if you need anything. You girls ever seen a vampire in real life before?"

"No," the Dead Weather girl said, "and I'm not convinced I have now, either."

The desk in the back of the store was piled under with paperwork and slips of clothing. A cheap, hollow door sat ajar just next to it, leading to a bathroom. Esmy swiveled the desk chair around and said to Moss, "Will this do?"

Moss looked at the dim bulb in the ceiling. "Can you get more light back here? I kind of need to see."

Esmy pushed open the bathroom door and turned on the light inside. "How about this?" The walls, toilet, sink, and even the linoleum floor were white, the latter flecked with charcoal. It was miles brighter than the office.

"That'll work." Moss set his bag on the sink and unzipped it.

"I'm not sure I want money for this." Esmy floated closer to Dan, just outside the bathroom door. Her glossy dark hair was parted in the middle, the ends curling toward her jaw. She lifted a slender hand to brush her thumb over Dan's lower lip. A bracelet made of lace and antique beads slipped down her arm. Her skin was paler than his by several shades.

He felt she was doing a much better job of exuding a vampiric air than he had so far managed.

She said, "You're warm."

"Sorry."

"No, it's okay."

"Ready?" Moss asked, leaning in the doorway.

"Well." She smoothed her short skirt. "I guess I am." She started to turn away, then swung back. "I definitely do not want *money* for this. I want you, in there"—she pointed a scarlet fingernail toward the bathroom—"after this is done. Or I'm not doing it."

She was so close. He traced his thumb slowly along her lower lip. The pink tip of a tongue tasted his skin. She pulled back and smiled.

After some fortifying blood, he thought he could manage that.

"All right," she said to Moss. "Let's get this over with. You've done this before, yeah?"

"You bet. Sorry about making you sit on a toilet."

"No, it's fine."

Moss grasped the edge of the door and raised his eyebrow at Dan.

Dan nodded.

Quietly, he pushed it shut.

Dan's jeans were a little tight in the crotch. He turned away, studying the floor, or what he could see of it through the dark glasses. Seconds accumulated into minutes. Ray's voice and the voices of the other girls filtered through the wall. He paced, slowly, stopping every now and then to read a paper on the desk or touch a clipping pinned to the wall. Tucked under an invoice might be a hand-penned poem. Tacked behind a labor notice might be a charcoal sketch of a willowy gothic lady whose curve-hugging gown ended in tentacles where her feet should have been.

The shop, from what he gathered, actually belonged to Esmerelda.

Every now and then a laugh—Ray's—or a giggle (the girl in front of the counter, Dan thought) made its way into the back. He wondered if Ray was going to get lucky tonight too. Be a shame if he didn't; on the other hand, Moss was straight up about being faithful to his wife, so there'd be a twinge of guilt, the two of them having a great time while Moss sighed, watching the news, wishing Ray and Dan would go to hell.

Dan leaned toward the bathroom door. A murmur from Moss filtered through. He pictured Esmy sitting on the toilet, watching the blood run from her vein down the tube, into the bottle. Moss was probably staring at the one-pint mark. As quickly as Dan had downed Vin's blood, they'd decided they needed to up their take to Red Cross levels—though he still hoped Ray's theory was right, that switching up donors would make the blood last longer. He pictured Moss lifting his gaze every so often to make sure everything was going as planned, then sliding the needle out of her arm, pressing a cotton ball over the puncture wound.

"Hold that there awhile," Moss said.

Dan stepped back.

"How long's 'a while'?" Esmy said.

He took a few deep breaths, actually looking forward to this as Moss said, "Ten minutes," and Esmy said, "Can I use a Band-Aid?"

"Sure."

A few swallows—top himself off—and he'd be good to go. He was horny as fuck. How long had it been? He couldn't remember the last time. The tour was a whole other life.

The door swung open. Moss emerged with his bag. "All yours."

A bottle of blood sat on the sink, cap on. Esmy was on her feet, applying a Band-Aid to the crook of her elbow, over the cotton. She glanced his way.

Moss, behind him, said, "Get what you need, and I'll put the rest on ice."

Dan's nerves hummed. He licked his dry lips. As he unscrewed the cap, his hand trembled, like a junkie's. He took two swallows before recapping it.

Moss shoved it in his bag.

"Tell Ray I'll be out in a few," he said before he stepped into the bathroom and pulled the door shut.

"You all right?" he asked Esmy.

Smiling, she nodded.

The tiny room smelled like blood. It got to his head—the contentedness of the bees, the satiation. He drew his gaze from the red of her mouth to the alabaster skin above her heart-shaped top, then over to her red fingernails, still pressed against the Band-Aid.

As he touched it, her fingers moved out of the way. He picked at the edge with his thumbnail, peeling it up, revealing the tiny hole and the vague purple of bruising to come.

He brushed his lips against the hole. Touched it with the tip of his tongue. Then kissed higher on her arm. Her shoulder. Her neck, flicking his tongue over her pulse.

"You've tasted my blood." She turned her face, bumping his jaw. "Can I taste yours?"

He looked in her eyes. What *about* his blood? Maybe it was contaminated with whatever was forcing him to drink blood. His saliva seemed to be safe—at least Ray seemed to be unaffected, despite Dan sucking on his arm. But blood was the core of it all. If anything was infected, it was that. "I don't think that's a good idea."

She pouted. "Just a teeny taste?"

He kissed the lower lip she'd pushed out, and her mouth stretched into a smile as he backed her against the sink. Her tongue was more brazen than his, pushing into his mouth as she clasped the back of his neck with both hands.

She pulled back after a taste of her blood on him, saying, "Rust," as he kissed her cheek, her temple.

"I'm sorry," he murmured. "I should have rinsed."

"Shh." She tipped her face up and slipped his sunglasses off. "It's mine anyway. You don't look like what I was expecting."

"Too well fed?"

She laughed. "Too tragically all-American."

When he raised an eyebrow, she dropped the sunglasses into the sink behind her. "You look like a college guy who's too normal to be goth and too goth to be a jock. Woe-is-me middle class."

He decided to take 'college guy' as a compliment. The rest, he had no idea what she was talking about.

"But you're cute," she said, "and a little broody-looking, and the blood drinking is hot, so kiss me again."

In a moment, he had her balanced on the edge of the sink, one of her platform boots pressed against the opposite wall. Silky purple panties lay between his feet.

"Shit," he said against her neck. "Condom."

She produced one like magic, presenting it between two fingers. No smiles now. All seriousness. She leaned back and closed her eyes as he tore the packet open.

Glancing up, he realized she was studying him through her lashes.

He guided himself inside, making her chin tilt up. She grasped his shoulders and drew her lip beneath her teeth. As he started moving, she pulled herself up and wound her arms around his neck. She whispered something against his cheekbone, then whispered it again: "Bite me."

"Bite me," she said.

Her fingernails dug into his back.

"Come on, vampire. Bite me."

He turned his lips against her face and kissed her temple, her ear.

"You know you want to," she whispered, clutching him tighter. "Bite me." She wrapped a leg around his waist, trapping him against her—not that she needed to. He was into this, the fucking at least. Scared shitless about the biting stuff, though. He could do it, playfully...but what if he couldn't stop at playfully?

The bees hummed as he fucked her, reacting to the closeness of her, her scent, the heat of her blood surging around his cock.

"Fucking bite me, vampire," she said against his teeth, fucking him back as much as her position on the edge of the sink allowed.

He grabbed her ass in both hands and plunged his tongue back into her mouth, pulling her against him, thrusting as deep into her as he could get.

His mouth was on her neck. He rubbed the pulsing of blood just beneath her skin.

"Yessss, yessss…"

He fucked her and sucked her neck, his teeth buried behind his lips.

"Do it. Bite me. Fucking bite me." She jerked at his hair.

He closed his mouth around a patch of throat, right over the pulse. Pressed his tongue against it. The beat coursing through the artery turned him on like nothing else. He could smell it. Almost taste it. He bit harder.

"Yes! Yes! Yes!"

He dug his fingers into her ass and slammed her against him, biting and licking, giving her nothing more dangerous than a hickey, but it felt good. It *smelled* good. He bit and she squealed, clamping down on his neck, trapping him with her legs wound around his. He picked her up, turned her, and fucked her against the wall, grunting, denting her with his fingers. He found her neck and bit, making her moan, making her clutch him with her fingernails and say, "Yes! Fuck, yes!"

After he came, his teeth slipped over her skin. He made himself kiss her pulse, softly. Kiss behind her ear. She loosened her grip on his thighs, letting one leg then the other drop. He kept her pinned against the wall until he'd had another kiss from her lips, another long, messy kiss. Then he eased her to the floor.

She smoothed her skirt as he slipped the condom into the toilet. She crouched to retrieve her panties, balling them in her fist.

He didn't know what he was supposed to say, so he said, "Sorry."

She flashed him a look—and he didn't know what *that* was supposed to say, either.

He put his sunglasses back on. The room got darker. She seemed to shrink, as though he was looking through the wrong end of binoculars.

"Thanks," he said. "For…you know." He was a disappointing vampire. But the sex had been fucking good.

"Are you going to come back again? For more?" Looking in the mirror, she rubbed at her smeared lipstick with the edge of her thumb. She raised her eyes toward him.

"Uh, if you're willing to donate again…"

She nodded. Serious about it, though.

"It'd…it wouldn't be more often than every three weeks. You know. So you have time to replace the lost blood."

She returned her attention to fixing herself up.

"You might want to take some supplements too. You know, if you're interested in doing it as a regular thing."

"I'll do that." She straightened to her full height, gave him a raised eyebrow and a glance toward the door. He moved aside. Caught a glimpse of himself in the mirror. So that's what tragically all-American looked like.

He followed her out to the shop, where Moss had an elbow propped on a clothing rack, the side of his face in his hand. His eyelids were at half-mast.

Ray lifted his chin to Dan. They locked eyes. And Dan said, "Ready?"

"Turn the sign around when you go." Esmy made a circling motion with her hand.

The foghorn sounded, and then they were walking across a rain-slick sidewalk. Moss got behind the wheel, Ray riding shotgun. Dan slouched in the back seat, his head back, eyes shut behind his sunglasses.

"How was it?" Ray asked. He half turned in his seat, the side of his chin against the headrest. An unlit cigarette jutted between two fingers.

"Fine." He let his eyes slip closed again. He pushed his hands inside his open jacket, into his armpits, hugging himself.

"Funny how the one girl—what was her name, Moss?"

Moss didn't say anything; Dan imagined he'd shaken his head.

"Anyway, as that Esmerelda chick got louder and louder, the girl with the red extensions—or maybe it was black extensions and her hair was red? Anyway, she just kept talking, louder and faster, like she was trying to cover up the noises."

"You heard that, huh?" Dan kept his eyes closed.

"Vin and his little shit friend in Rhode Island heard that."

The seat creaked as Ray turned and settled into it.

"You all right, Moss?" Ray asked.

Moss sighed. "Yeah. I'm fine. It's starting to come down again."

Dan glanced out the window. Raindrops smacked hard against it, sliding down the glass, blurring the lights they passed.

"Is this the street we turn on?" Moss said. "Do you remember?"

"Uh, I think so," Ray said.

Dan was spent, but not like he could sleep. "You guys hungry?"

Ray turned around again. "I could eat."

"I wouldn't turn down some pie," Moss said.

"Danny's already had that," Ray said. "Lucky asshole."

Dan laughed.

"You had two chances to get some yourself. Not my fault you can't pick up women."

"Maybe you should have said you *were* Jack White," Moss said.

"You, shut the fuck up." To Dan, Ray said, "Can you believe she didn't know who Two Tons of Dirt was?"

"She was like fourteen," Moss said.

"You could have educated her." Dan smiled a little.

"I wouldn't have touched her with your dick. Fucking Dead Weather. Seriously?"

"Esmy wants us to come back. She said she'd donate again. I told her it'd have to be three weeks—"

"We can't go back," Moss said.

"Why not?" Ray asked.

"Let's suppose"—Moss put his turn signal on, a Denny's coming up on their right.—"one of those girls decides to look up that guy from Dead Weather. And let's say while they're at it, they Google this Two Tons of Dirt band you mentioned—twice."

"Twice?" Dan said.

"It was a sore spot," Ray mumbled.

"And then," Moss continued, gliding the car into a parking space, "they see that, holy shit, you look *exactly* like that guy from Two Tons, and holy *fucking* shit, the guy who drinks blood is also in the band."

Rain pelted the roof.

"Fuck it," Ray said. "Nobody's going to buy that some rock band is going around buying blood." He shoved his door open, unlit cigarette clamped in his teeth. "I'm gonna have a smoke before I go in. Order me some coffee. Strong." He slammed the door.

Moss shook his head and pulled the key from the ignition.

"We'll be okay," Dan said. He reached for the door handle.

"We can't come back here."

"I know."

As they approached the restaurant, Dan told Moss to grab a table inside before he veered toward Ray, who stood with his back to the parking lot, a cigarette cupped in the curve of his hand. He was hunched into his jacket against the rain.

"I fucked up," Ray said. He laughed that on-the-edge-of-crazy laugh of his as Dan came around him. "I just wanted to throw her off track, you know? In case she was about to say—you know."

"Yeah, I know."

"She'd never heard of us."

Dan, with his hands in his pockets and the rain running rivulets through his hair, smiled cheerlessly.

"Fucking Dead Weather." Ray sucked a quick drag off his cigarette. "I couldn't fucking stop myself. 'Two Tons,' 'Two Tons.' Fuck."

"Don't sweat it. Live and learn, right? It's not like we're pros at this."

"Ha." Smoke billowed with the syllable.

Dan dragged his attention away. "Come on. Let's get some pie."

"Hold on."

"Come on." He grabbed Ray by the wet shoulder of his wet jacket.

Ray came, but not quickly, getting in two last drags before dropping the butt in a puddle and ducking through the door Dan held open.

Later that night, Dan lay on the bed in the motel room, his arms crossed behind his head, while Ray hunched beside him, typing on the laptop, little staccato beats—he hit the keys harder than he needed to, Dan thought. Moss had a book cracked open, some secondhand paperback thriller, reading while he sat on his bed in stocking feet and shorts, a paper coffee cup at his elbow.

The TV jabbered—SUV commercials, Jimmy Kimmel jokes.

Dan felt good. Relaxed. Going on the road like this was like going on the road on tour, which was where—despite how frustrating and exhausting it could be—he preferred to be, and Ray even more so, staying a step ahead of the mundaneness of sedentary life. Being on the road was mundane too, maybe more mundane, but when they were on the road they were moving at least.

When they weren't, he worried he'd fall still and stay that way.

The tip of Ray's tongue poked from the side of his mouth. He finished what he was typing and straightened. "I need a smoke." He batted the laptop shut.

"Neither sleet nor rain nor dark of night..."

Smirking, Ray flipped him the bird.

After he was gone, Dan reached for the remote control. "You watching this?" he asked Moss.

Moss looked at the screen, then back at his book. "Nope."

Dan flicked through the channels. The news was showing a fire on one station, a neighbor dispute gone violent on another. CNN was talking about Hamas. He didn't want to hear about any attacks here in the States, wanted to pretend they didn't exist—just for a few hours. He clicked the TV off.

CHAPTER TWENTY-ONE

UNLESS they could find a decent pool of people not more than a thirty- or forty-minute drive from Manchester, they were going to have a problem. Moss wasn't going to keep agreeing to these impromptu trips, and if they happened frequently enough, Debbie would figure out that there were no Dan-and-Ray acoustic shows going on. It didn't take more than a quick check of the band's website or social media accounts to work that out.

Jesus, they didn't even have their guitars with them.

The last stop was Brattleboro, Vermont, another three-hour-and-some drive, but after this one they were driving straight home. Back in their own beds tonight.

In the car, Moss said to Ray, "What do you do for a living?"

"What do you mean what the fuck do I do for a living?"

"If someone asks you what you do for a living, what are you going to tell them?"

"Fuck, whatever."

"I'm trying to avoid what happened last night at the goth shop."

"So when someone says, 'You know who you look like?' in the future I should say, 'I'm a mechanic'?"

"Mechanic's good," Moss said. "Unless they're having a car problem."

"Shit." Ray propped his elbow on the edge of the passenger window.

Dan pulled himself between the seats. "Do something boring. Fix copy machines or something." Getting that close to the other guys made his head swim—something he'd been trying to tell himself was his imagination. He gripped the back of the seat to ground himself.

"Yeah?" Ray said. "What do you do?"

"I'm a vampire. He's a nurse."

"Well, I guess I'm the vampire wrangler then." Ray rubbed his mouth. Dan knew he was itching for a smoke.

He took another deep breath, got another prickly rush in his head, and dropped back in his seat. The medic bag was right by his foot. All he had to do was crank open the bottle. He closed his eyes. This couldn't be happening this quickly. They didn't have another donor lined up after this one. "Any new responses on the ads?"

"Just a sec."

A second came and went, then a whole string of them. Finally Ray said, "One that I might be able to work into something."

One.

Might.

They got into Brattleboro too early, nothing but time to kill. Dan stayed in the car while Moss and Ray stretched their legs. He nudged the medic bag with his toe. Closed his eyes again and recalled how much was left of Esmy's blood. A lot, but Vin's was completely fucking gone already.

He took a sip—one sip—and got out of the car for some fresh air. The rain was gone, leaving a bracing wind behind. Dan zipped his jacket. Ray's cheeks turned a roughened red. Moss, unaffected, had his jacket hanging open, his hands tucked in his pockets.

There wasn't much to do downtown if you weren't into galleries and bookshops.

Ray slipped his cell phone out every few minutes to see if it had gotten much later yet.

They ended up back in the car too soon, Ray huddling beside it to finish one last cigarette.

"I guess we'll go find the place," Moss said as Ray dropped into his seat, bringing a whip of frigid air with him.

"Might as well." Dan slouched. He tapped his fingers to the song banging in his head—METZ's "Negative Space." Stuck there all morning. More appropriate to how he felt than anything Two Tons had written. He had a feeling that when they got back to songwriting, their catalog was going to take a turn for the fucked up.

Another five minutes, and Moss was saying, "That's it."

Dan straightened. Dunkin' Donuts. He hung an arm on the back of Ray's seat, chewing the side of his thumb while the light turned green and Moss eased them into the lot.

Two cop cars were nosed up to the side of the store.

"I don't have a good feeling about this," Dan said.

"What? It's a doughnut shop. Of course there's cops," Ray said.

Through the plate glass, between posters for the latest coffee concoctions and doughnut deals, Dan made out three officers—two at the counter along the inside of the window and a third by the cash register.

"I've still got a bad feeling." He checked the car's clock. "We've got ten minutes. Let's park and wait. Maybe they'll leave." *Please fucking leave*. He needed this donation. *They* needed this donation—without it, he'd back to relying on Ray again.

Ray shrugged. "Whatever you want."

Moss found a spot far enough away, Dan hoped, for the cops to not notice they were sitting there, waiting.

"You think they have Wi-Fi?" Ray asked.

"Dunno," Moss said.

Ray beat a rhythm on the dash, watching the windows.

Dan rubbed his temples. Why the *fuck* they agreed to meet at a doughnut shop…

When he looked again, the cops were still inside. He propped his elbows on the front seats and stared—as if by staring hard enough, he might get them to stuff their doughnuts in their faces faster, or maybe they'd get a call to go out and arrest somebody. *Somebody* had to be out there committing a crime.

All his sitting up near the front did was bring back that unsteady feeling. An ache at the base of his skull. His throat tightened. *Please do not let this be happening.*

A minute ticked by.

Another.

"Shit," he whispered.

"I'm telling you," Ray said, "the place is just a cop magnet. They're getting their sugar on. They don't give a shit about us."

This felt off. *He* felt off. He grabbed the paramedic bag off the floor.

Ray glanced back.

Dan uncapped his bottle and chugged three swallows. He put it away and sat forward again, between the seats, feeling much better in the head and much worse in the gut, knowing what he'd just done, how much he'd just drank.

"It's a minute till," Moss said.

Dan chewed the inside of his cheek.

"How about this? We go in there, go up to the counter. Order some coffee. Act like everyday normal citizens. See how it goes." Moss looked back. "We don't have to do anything if you're still not good with it."

Dan nodded, eyes on the cops. "Okay. But leave the bag here." It was how they'd told people to recognize them: the nurse's smock and the orange medic bag.

"Okay. Ready?"

"I've *been* fucking ready." Ray popped his door open and stepped out.

The wind hit Dan in the face as he climbed out. He slammed his door and shoved his hands into his pockets.

The three of them strode stiff-legged across the parking lot. Dan ducked his head, as though he could go unnoticed if he didn't look up.

He and Ray came to a stop at the counter, Moss right behind. A girl who looked like she was still in high school asked what she could get them, her smile cheery and bright.

Ray ordered a large black. Dan said, "Regular," and leaned away to let Moss give his order.

As she went to get their drinks, Dan drummed his fingers on the counter, his back tense from the three pairs of cop eyes he was sure were staring at them.

He made a fist and coughed into it.

The door opened behind them, lashing the back of his neck with a whip of cold. His shoulders itched: he wanted to turn and look. He read the labels on the doughnut trays instead. Bear claws, glazed, old fashioned—

"Hey," said a guy behind them. "Are you the guys I'm looking for?"

The tips of Dan's ears flushed with heat. He fought to keep from turning his head.

"Excuse me?" Moss said.

The girl set two of their coffees on the counter. Dan reached for his, pulling it close, peeling back the tab in the plastic lid. Trying to keep his hands steady.

"I'm supposed to be meeting some guys here," the guy said. "I thought you might be them. You a nurse?"

Moss didn't say anything.

"Which hospital you work at?"

The third coffee came, and the girl turned to put Ray's jelly doughnut in a paper bag.

"I work at a nursing home," Moss said. "Excuse me." He got his coffee from the counter.

"I was supposed to be meeting a nurse and another guy here tonight," the guy said, "right about now. You sure you ain't them?"

Ray had his wallet open, swiping his credit card.

"Sorry, I can't help you," Moss said.

"Ready?" Dan said.

Ray grabbed his coffee and the doughnut bag. "Yep."

"Let's go."

The guy who'd been talking up Moss had short, dark hair, an unsettling smile as he nodded at Dan and Ray.

The cops' eyes followed them as they walked out, the weight of their gaze on the back of Dan's neck.

"Fuuuuuck me." Ray dropped into the driver's seat and yanked the door shut. "If the cops *weren't* there for a sting—and I still don't think they were—that guy I'm sure got their attention."

"That went not so well," Moss said. He fitted his coffee into the cup holder hanging from the window. "Are they still watching? Or are they talking to that douche?"

Dan flicked a look toward the lighted windows. "Yeah, they're watching us. God that sucked." He pressed his forehead against Ray's seat.

The car rolled forward, and they put Dunkin' Donuts behind them.

"I came this close"—Ray held up his thumb and forefinger—"to turning around and saying, 'Do you see a fucking orange bag here, moron?'"

"You did not," Moss said.

"I was thinking it. I need a smoke."

"You'll have to wait," Dan said. "It's only an hour and half, an hour forty tops."

"Fuck."

"We need to figure out the next donor." He curled his fingers until his fingernails bit his palm. And that wasn't enough either.

"We're getting some others lined up," Ray said. "It'll work out."

"Yeah. Like this one did," Moss said. "This one went fucking fantastic."

"It'll work out," Ray said.

Dan shut his eyes.

The drive seemed the longest on their trip, all three of them quiet—no music playing, nothing but the rhythm of the windshield wipers. Southwestern New Hampshire slipped by, unremarkable in the dark. Dan's thoughts tumbled over themselves: How long would Esmerelda's donation last? What if he didn't get any more? What if Moss said he wouldn't do this anymore? What if they got caught next time? Or the time after that? What if their faces were in all the papers? "Rock Musicians Drink Fans' Blood," alongside their mug shots. "Former Paramedic Assists in Procurement."

He pressed his hands against his eyes, grabbed hold of his hair, and tried to force his brain to shut up, because panicking wasn't going to help.

After an eternity, the car glided to a stop in front of Moss's house. Dan got out to offer his hand. "Thanks a lot for doing this."

Moss nodded.

"It really means a lot."

"I'll see you," Moss said.

"Sure."

HE SLID into the passenger seat.

Ray put the car in gear.

Dan wanted to ask, "What if we lose Moss?" but at the same time didn't want to tip the balance into making it a reality. He also wanted to say, "I think we're in big trouble," but his throat clenched around a hard ache every time he worked up the courage for it.

As they turned up Dan's street, Ray said, "I'm gonna get right on it, okay? As soon as I get in the door."

Dan nodded.

"I mean it." He slipped an unlit cigarette from his mouth.

Dan nodded again and picked up the medic bag. He pushed his door open. A blast of cold air swept in. He pulled up his collar, his insides roiling as Ray pulled away.

At first he'd gotten by on a teaspoon. Now he was taking it in gulps—and that was just to take the edge off.

He collected three days' of mail from the row of mailboxes on the first landing and headed up the stairs. The apartment was as he'd left it: a little lived in, a little abandoned. He hadn't told his mother he was going out of town, so she hadn't snuck in to straighten up and stock his fridge.

He set the medic bag on the table and took out the last of Esmy's blood. Fighting an urge to top off, he stuck it in the fridge. He'd let that need get to the edge of bad before tapping into his supply. A half-gone six-pack of Dos Equis looked like a reasonable alternative.

With a cold beer in hand, he shrugged out of his jacket and booted up his laptop.

The first thing he checked was their ads. Responses were going to Ray, not him, but at least he could make sure they were still there.

"Vampire in search of sustenance. Donate to the cause. This is a unique experience. Respond to learn more."

Or: "I vant to dvink your BLOOD! Safe, sane, consensual NONSEXUAL blood play." That one they might have to edit a bit.

"Do you believe in vampires? Here is your chance to come to the aid of one. Serious inquiries only. All blood types accepted."

Dan chugged half the beer, then leaned back. Hoping one of these fucking ads would work, and soon.

The bees buzzed somewhere near the base of his spine.

He drowned them with the rest of the beer from his fridge, then got in bed and lay awake, making music in his head that he had no motivation to get up and play.

CHAPTER TWENTY-TWO

THE phone rang as he was coming out of the bathroom. Sunlight cut angular through the kitchen window. He fished his phone from his jacket. "Yeah."

"Did I wake you?" Ray said.

"Nah. I'm up."

"Wanna come over? I'm working on some leads."

"Yeah. Sure." He yawned and blinked at the sunlight. "You want me to pick up some breakfast?"

"Anything but Dunkin'."

Smiling at that, he said, "Sure."

The slight headache was there, and the buzzing. Far away but not going away. He sat with Esmy's bottle on the couch in his living room and contemplated it, trying to get a hold of himself so he'd take only what he absolutely needed, and not one drop more.

He sipped, his hand clenching hard to keep from dumping it all down his throat.

He sipped again.

Then he made himself march into the kitchen and put the bottle in the fridge.

The buzzing was more distant. The headache slipped from around his skull, leaving him reasonably all right again.

He got dressed and headed to Ray's.

Ray walked out of the bathroom with a cigarette hanging between his lips. "How much you got left?"

Dan held up his thumb and forefinger, spread a little ways apart.

"How're you doing?"

"All right."

Ray held his gaze. "Straight up?"

"Yeah. I mean it. I'm good for now." Barely. For now. The cat, though—he'd dreamed about that fucking cat last night. Dreamed it was sitting in his closet, watching him from the dark shadows. Twitching its tail every time his dreaming self tried to settle back into sleep. "Got anything promising yet?" he asked, following Ray into the living room, where Ray's laptop rested on one of the easy chair's flat arms. Ray steadied it with two fingers as he sat.

"I've got two possibilities, one maybe we can chase up as early as tomorrow. Tonight if I can talk them into it."

"What about Moss?"

Ray squinted at the screen as he scrolled the browser. After a few seconds, Dan gave up on an answer. He set a cardboard tray of coffees on a battered paperback on quantum physics. "Do you actually read this stuff?"

"Hmm?"

He dropped the bag of Egg McMuffins beside the coffees, opened the top, and pulled one out for himself. He had to move a book on changing reality out of his way to sit on the couch. "So where are these possibilities?"

"Boston, both of them. B.U. kids, I think."

"Do they know each other?"

"If they do, they haven't said anything. And I haven't mentioned I'm talking to someone else in the same area. One I'm not sure is gonna pan out. He keeps asking if he's going to become a vampire."

"Yeah, 'cause that's such a great fucking deal." Dan tore off a piece of the breakfast sandwich.

"Now, he don't know no better," Ray said. "Toss me one of those."

"Do you think I could pass it on to people?" Dan asked.

"Like a cold?"

"I mean, you don't have it, so it's not air- or saliva-borne."

"I guess we have yet to see if Esmy gets it from your other bodily fluids."

"We used a condom."

"Very smart."

"Mostly because I don't want to have a kid on top of being a blood-drinking freak."

"Right," Ray said. He sat back, unwrapping his sandwich.

Dan said, "Esmerelda wanted to taste my blood."

Ray's attention flicked up from the sandwich.

"I said I didn't think it was a good idea," Dan said.

Processing this latest bit of info, Ray nodded slowly.

"It was the first time I thought to wonder if my blood might be infected," Dan said.

Ray gave it some thought before shrugging and taking another bite of the McMuffin.

"What about the other possibility?" Dan nodded at the computer.

"Uh, sleep deprived at this point. I've had them both up all night, emailing back and forth. I really want to do it tonight if I can talk them into it. On the other hand, you have to watch yourself. These guys can get you in a position of spending hours convincing them you're what you say you are, only to decide you're full of shit anyway. Waste of fucking time. You've gotta avoid that whole trap. Not to mention the complete fuckheads like the guy in Brattleboro."

Dan watched him eat.

Eventually he launched into questions again—starting with the one that was most bugging him: "What about Moss? He's not going to want to go out again already."

"We'll talk to him," Ray said without looking. "I have an idea to solve that problem too."

"I actually don't *want* to keep taking him away from his family. We do that enough as it is." Moss didn't come with them overseas—they had a guy in Europe who jumped on the tour to replace him—but even just the North America dates took him away from home for big jumps of time.

He stood, wadding the sandwich wrapper in his fist, and went to the kitchen to throw it away—more to work off his nervousness than anything else. They weren't going to get Moss. Moss was going to sit them down and go, "Look, guys, I hate to do this to you, but..." And who could blame him?

Back in the living room, he fetched one of Ray's guitars and sat, checking the tuning, strumming it a bit, then picking out bits of the melody he'd had in his head all night.

"Something new?"

"Yeah. It's all I've got of it so far."

"I like it. Kind of melancholy, though."

"I'm thinking of building it to chaos and then just—you know, done. Silence."

"This guy's not getting back to me any too quickly," Ray said. "Fuck it." He flipped the laptop shut and lifted his Gibson from beside the chair. "Run through that again?"

Head down, Dan nodded and started to play.

They spent two hours at it till Dan got up to take a leak and Ray sat back to enjoy a cigarette and check his messages.

"Bingo!" Dan heard him call.

"What?" he asked as he walked back in. "We're on for tonight?"

"Ah, no. I don't think that's gonna work out." As Ray scratched the back of his head, Dan found it a wonder he didn't singe his hair with the lit end of the butt. Ray said, "But the other one's definite for tomorrow. Guy calls himself deathly_black."

"At least it's not deathly_black76923."

Ray wheezed out a laugh with a lungful of smoke.

"Tomorrow night," Dan said. "Boston?"

"Yeah."

"And Moss?"

"Gonna call him right now." He stubbed his cigarette and got up to find his phone.

Dan settled back on the couch. Moss was going to say no. You could only push someone's hospitality so far. Moss was going to say no, and he couldn't blame him.

But man did that fuck them. *Him.*

Ray walked by, punching up Moss's number. He was in the kitchen when he started talking. The back door rattled open, swung shut.

Dan slumped lower and said, "Fuck," under his breath. Did they know anyone else who could do it?

Did they know another *way* they could do it?

He itched to jump up and use Ray's laptop to look up...what? Blood Drawing for Dummies?

They could break into a blood bank.

Right.

The door opened. Ray headed for the bathroom instead of the living room. Fucker. Time crawled. The toilet flushed, and eventually Ray appeared in the doorway, towel-drying his hands.

"Well?" Dan asked.

Ray picked up what was left of his coffee. "He's gonna come over in a bit for a half-hour or so."

"For?"

Ray drank. Then he set the cup back down. Then he searched out his pack of cigarettes and found one still in it. He put it between his teeth and lit it.

Dan followed his every move, impatient. Wanting to say *For?* again, louder. *For? For?!*

Finally Ray exhaled a cloud of smoke. "He's gonna teach me how to do it."

Dan watched him, open-mouthed. "Can you?"

"Can we use your arm? He also said we should get some oranges to practice on before we move on to fucking up your arm."

Dan continued to stare.

"He said he's not letting me anywhere near *his* arm, so it's gotta be yours or mine," Ray said. "And mine might be awkward. Plus we might need to use me, so I don't want to fuck up my veins practicing."

"Yeah, that's fine." Maybe. He looked at the coffee cups on the table, at the physics book—*Taking the Quantum Leap*. At envelopes full of bills, at picks and a machine head and a harmonica with a dent in it. "You think it'll be okay?"

"You can chug it when we're done. I know it's not as good as outsourcing..."

"Right."

Ray held the cigarette filter in front of his mouth as he watched Dan. Squinting through the smoke. "If you need more, I'll donate," he said.

It had been, what, five days since his last donation? The glow of the laptop screen wasn't the only thing making him look pale and worn down.

Dan said, "Don't worry about it. I still have Esmy's at my place. And drinking my own's not for nothing."

"How're you feeling?"

"How many times are you going to ask?"

"Hey, I'm just checking." He closed the laptop. "Pass me that guitar. I think I got another idea. And you should run out and get some oranges."

WITH A mesh bag of fruit sitting on the front seat, Dan pulled up behind a dispiritingly familiar car. It wasn't Moss's. He let out a long sigh before collecting the bag and heading upstairs.

They were in the living room, Ray in his chair with the laptop shut, Jamie on the couch.

"Hey," Dan said. "Rehab over?"

"Over for me," Jamie said.

Dan set the oranges on the coffee table and dropped onto the couch.

Jamie pushed his hair back from his eyes. "They got me all hyped up to do rehab while I was at detox, like that was gonna be the icing on the cake, but it's— It didn't do it for me."

"So you left," Dan said.

"What I needed was to get clean. I got clean. I'm still clean. How've you been?"

"Shit." Dan leaned back. "I don't even know where to start."

"He's been having a health problem," Ray said.

Dan wasn't sure he wanted Jamie to know—but of course he had to know. He was the other third of the band.

Jamie turned, bringing his knee up on the couch. "Seriously? What's wrong?"

He pinched the bridge of his nose. "Um, you remember when I was attacked in North Carolina?"

Jamie said nothing.

Ray said, "The bat."

"Oh yeah. Shit. What happened?"

"I've been having some issues. Audio hallucinations, headaches, vision problems…"

"Have you been to a doctor?"

Ray said, "We've figured out how to fix it. For a while at least."

Jamie looked from Dan to Ray to Dan again, and Ray said, "Never mind. Don't worry about it."

Dan let out a breath, but it left a tightness in his chest. On the one hand, he didn't want to deal with Jamie knowing the truth of it. On the other—drug money for blood, right? But he did look clean: bright-eyed, fleshed out. "Where're you staying now?" he asked.

"My parents," Jamie said. "They're cool with it as long as I'm clean."

"Sounds fair."

"What's up with you anyway?" Jamie said to Ray. "How come you look like shit if he's the one who's sick?"

"Too much tobacco, too little sleep, too much worry." He glanced at his fingers as he got ready to fire his lighter up again. "My nails are so chewed-down, I can't get the tab on a can of soda up without using a butter knife."

"Take better care of yourself, Ray-Ray. You're supposed to be on break." Jamie slouched lower on the couch, yawning. "Got any idea when we're getting back to work?"

"It'll be a little while yet."

Jamie hung his head back and let out a sigh.

CHAPTER TWENTY-THREE

HE DREAMED the sky was black and undulating. Buzzing came from loudspeakers, black boxes mounted high on thick black poles. Everyone was running.

It colored his mood when he got into Ray's car, that and the steel-gray clouds crowding the sky. One of the Bostons canceled at the last minute, rescheduling for tonight, leaving Ray more time to practice on the oranges, on Dan. On himself, with Dan pacing restlessly, eyeing the measuring cup he was bleeding into, saying, "That's enough. You just need to get the hang of it, not feed me." Saying, "I'm good, you know. I'm fine for now. Eat a steak or something. Please."

They didn't talk much on the trip down—what was there to say that hadn't been said already, outside of *I hope you can do this*? On a real person. On a stranger.

As they drove through Medford, Dan did think of one thing to say. "I can't tell you how grateful I am you've stuck with me through this."

"What else was I supposed to do? Lose the band?"

Dan laughed. "Shit. You're officially the only member of the band without serious substance abuse problems."

Ray smiled. "I guess I am."

They headed to Cambridge, where deathly_black's street was crowded with huge Georgian and Federal multi-family buildings and suffered from a distinct lack of on-street parking.

"Is that a cemetery?" Dan said as Ray slowed, looking for a side street with parking.

"Wouldn't be surprised if that had been a selling point for our guy. He's a little morbid."

They got out of the car. Ray said, "Up here," as he grabbed a railing. Dan looked across to the cemetery while Ray rapped on the door.

When it opened, Dan turned to see a guy in a red polo shirt with a Staples logo on it. He was probably twenty four and already starting to lose his sandy-brown hair.

"Dude. Hey. I *just* got off work." He held the door wide. "Just ignore the mess."

The place was a single room, the décor schizophrenic: a quilt that looked like a hand-me-down from Mom covered the bed, a chunky computer desk took up most of one end of the room. An iron pentagram thumped lightly on the back of the door as deathly shut it behind them. Satanic posters—goat-headed men, naked women on stone slabs—papered the walls. Black candles beside Mountain Dew bottles and a Kleenex box had been burned down to mounds of wax.

"So you're the vampires," deathly said.

"He's the vampire," Ray said. "I'm the nurse." He brandished the orange bag.

Dan wondered if he could get in trouble for claiming to be a nurse.

"How'd you get to be a vampire?"

"Bad luck," Dan said.

"I've drunk blood before. Mostly goat, but I was involved in a ritual using human blood once."

"How was that?" Dan asked. Because...what else did you say to that?

"Powerful as fuck."

"Why didn't you think of goat blood?" Ray asked Dan as he set the bag on the bed and unzipped it.

"Missed opportunity there." Dan stepped away from the poster of the woman being sacrificed, where the huge shadow of the knife on the chamber wall was more ominous than the knife itself.

"So how this works is just like the Red Cross." Ray worked his hand into a latex glove.

"So you said."

"All right, so have a seat, roll up your sleeve. Let's get started."

"I'm gonna get some air," Dan said.

The guy looked at Ray and said, "You have a squeamish vampire?"

"It takes all kinds," Ray was saying as Dan let himself out. He stuffed his fists in his pockets and stared at the dark cemetery again, waiting. Twenty minutes later, the door opened. Ray came out with Moss's bag and a bottle of Mountain Dew.

"Want some?" He held it out.

"I'll take the blood instead."

"We're good on that." He passed Dan the bag, and Dan waited till their car was headed up 16E before getting the bottle out and uncapping it.

"So that was an experience." He screwed the cap back on.

"It takes all kinds," Ray said.

CHAPTER TWENTY-FOUR

"WHERE are we meeting this one?" Dan asked. After a week, donors were getting hard to come by. The news reports weren't helping—the random attacks by others infected the same way he was. He nudged an empty Filet O'Fish container and some Coke bottles out of the way with his toe so he could slouch down.

"We're gonna do the actual draw at her place, but she wants to meet us at a bus stop first, make sure we're okay."

"Fair enough."

"She has roommates, but she's not telling them what's going on. We're just going to head straight to her room."

"I don't think I'd tell my friends if I was giving blood to a vampire either," Dan said. "You'd think I'd lost my fucking mind."

Ray laughed.

Tonight's stop was Danbury, Connecticut. Ray was hoping to get another donor lined up for tomorrow, thinking New York City should have at least one—at *least*.

"You know, if this band thing doesn't work out," Ray said, "I might go for a phlebotomy certification." He flashed his teeth.

"Right."

When they got to the bus stop, Dan was glad for the chance to stretch his legs. The weather had warmed up—still chilly, but more seasonably chilly than "Holy shit it's fucking cold out for November." Ray leaned against the stop's three-sided shelter, watching traffic.

A bus came by, unloaded people, moved on.

"It's easier without Moss, isn't it?" Ray said.

"How so?"

"I don't know. It's like we've lost our babysitter, no one standing behind us worrying about everything."

"*I'm* worrying about everything," Dan said.

"Me too, but that's not what I mean. I don't know. It's just easier, you and me. More maneuverable. If an opportunity comes up, we just go, you know?"

Dan nodded at the sidewalk.

Ray checked his phone for the third time, put it back in his pocket.

They gave it a half-hour before they started talking about what they should do.

"Fuck it," Ray said, stubbing out his latest cigarette. "We're here, let's find someone else." When they were back in the car, he dug out his laptop. "Take this. Give me a shout when an unlocked Wi-Fi connection pops up."

They didn't have to go far, and Ray took the laptop back, checking messages, contacting the girl who'd been planning to meet up with them, reaching out to a few others to try to line something up.

The lights went out in the coffee shop they were parked alongside. People walked up the sidewalk, alone and together. He had maybe a third of a cup left in the bottle, and he itched to drink it. He wasn't even hearing buzzing anymore these days, had no problems with his vision. The headaches came, though—like the one leaning against his skull now—and with them a hunger that felt a lot like he imagined Jamie's need to use felt. It took you over. It made all other thought impossible. A soft huff of air jumped from his throat at the thought that he finally understood their drummer. Ray, focused on the laptop, didn't look up. Dan chewed his thumbnail. He couldn't live like this. How could anyone live like this?

They sat in front of that dark coffee shop for three hours before Ray slapped the laptop shut and started the car. Buildings slid by Dan's window. He said nothing as they pulled into the parking lot of a Super 8. He stayed in the car while Ray went to get a room key. Closed his eyes. Tried to believe there was an end to this, somewhere down the line.

"I DIDN'T want to tell you this," Ray said when they were sitting on their beds in the motel room, "but there was another attack, this one in Virginia."

Dan pulled the bag toward him. He needed a drink. Just a sip, even.

"This woman jumped another woman in the middle of a grocery store. She'd stalked her. Followed her around the freezer section, staring at her the whole time, like nothing else existed, and then she just went nuts. They brought her to the hospital, and people online are petitioning to have her—have anyone who's been bitten—put to sleep."

He'd lost count of how many reports Ray'd brought to him now. Strangers attacking strangers, roommates attacking roommates, an employee attacking a coworker. The bottle was empty, the taste of blood on his tongue only making him want more. He hated to let on how much his head was pounding again. Quietly, he said, "We need to find someone."

Just as quietly, Ray said, "I know." He grabbed the medic kit on his way to the bathroom. He shut the door, and Dan put his head in his hands. The *him* inside of him wanted to go after Ray and talk him out of doing it. The hunger in him kept him right the fuck where he was. He imagined the needle going in, blood rushing down the tube. He curled his fingers in his hair, gripping hard to distract himself from the war inside him.

CHAPTER TWENTY-FIVE

THE latest was a two-day trip—drive all the way out to the Philly suburbs, get the blood (they hoped they got the blood), and drive all the way back. The drive down went fine. They got a room at a dump in Trevose, and Dan took a moment to splash his face and steady himself before they headed out. They hadn't thought fifteen miles was all that far from the meet point, but they'd forgotten what traffic was like in southeastern Pennsylvania. Dan's teeth were on edge by the twentieth light.

"The way back," Ray said, "we should hop over to Route 1 and come back down that way."

Whatever.

He pressed his head against the glovebox and gripped his shins.

"We're going to the guy's house. It's not like he's not gonna show," Ray said.

When they finally got there, Dan sat up, then grabbed for the dashboard again.

Ray rubbed his back. "You gonna make it?"

Dan gritted his teeth. The headache was so bad it made him sick to his stomach. If he could puke one good time, he might be okay.

"Hang here. If the guy needs to see the vampire, he can come to you." After a few seconds, Ray said, "Okay?"

"Yeah." His gut hurt, like a cramp, but a cramp that wasn't letting up. The door opened and shut. Ray's footsteps faded away. In a moment, the sound of voices carried from the porch, then they stopped.

Dan pushed himself up. They were in the middle of everywhere—a street crowded with generic houses. He fumbled for the seat lever, put the seat back, and tried lying still, his hands resting lightly on his stomach. He was going to need to go to the hospital. They couldn't keep this up. Whatever he had, it was winning.

And Ray's latest news played in his mind: a six year old biting another kid in a school restroom—this one in Virginia like the last. Biting until the tile floor was smeared with blood. They had both kids in the hospital.

He should have Ray drive him to that hospital in Virginia—should just walk in and say, "Whatever it is, I have it too."

He. Needed. Blood. And if he didn't get it, he was going to be like that. *He* was going to hurt people.

He used the console to haul himself up, just so he could fold himself over, head against the dash, the smell of grit and rubber in the floor mat making him green all over again.

If the headache got any worse, his skull was going to crack open.

Which, at this point, sounded like a good thing.

The *click* of the door handle made him jerk. And wince.

Ray slid in. He hadn't even put the bottle in the bag. "Here." He even uncapped it for him. Oh thank fucking god.

He was downing it as they backed out of the driveway.

The bottle was empty by the time they pulled up to the stop sign at the corner. He wiped his mouth with the back of his hand.

"Better?" Ray asked.

"Yeah." The headache was, at least. His stomach still cramped. He still felt green. But the headache was gone—so maybe he had food poisoning or something on top of the bullshit he already had. Wouldn't that be a laugh?

The last place he wanted to have food poisoning was a shitty motel in southeastern Pennsylvania. "Yeah," he said again. "How about let's fuck the shitty motel. I can drive back. You sleep. We'll be home by morning, crash in our own fucking beds."

"I was hoping to scare up another donor or two before we left, but if you want to stay on the road, I'm okay with that," Ray said. "I don't mind driving either. You're the one who should rest."

Dan laughed without humor. "All I fucking do is rest."

"All right. When we get to the interstate, we'll swap. Are you feeling like you could eat something now?" He hadn't managed more than a corner of toast since the morning before. At the mention of eating, his stomach knotted. Saliva rushed his mouth. He thought it was going to be another wave of nausea, but his throat muscles clenched. His guts bucked. Instead of answering, he scrabbled for the door handle.

Ray hit the brakes and swung them toward the sidewalk.

He got his head out the door in time for the pint of blood to come pouring back out, splattering the concrete, looking like a crime scene under the streetlamp's shine.

He hung out the door for thirty seconds, forty, panting, waiting to see if there was more.

Then he pulled himself back inside, Ray tugging him back into his seat.

After another stretch of seconds, Ray said, "Maybe we shouldn't drive back tonight."

And all Dan could think was, *We lost all that goddamned blood.* He wanted to cry.

THEY WOUND up back at the shitty motel.

The first thing Dan did when he got in the room—where they didn't even need to turn on a light because a security light blasted right in their window—was drop to his knees on the bathroom floor and heave up blood-stained stomach acids.

The headache was back.

The cramp would not let the fuck up.

He hauled himself to his feet using the sink and splashed his face, catching sight of someone who looked like he'd had his blood drained out of him. A hollow-eyed stranger in the mirror. His forehead shone with sweat, his jacket unbearable, and he shrugged out of it as he staggered back into the room. The breeze coming through the window Ray had left cracked earlier felt good, but he still didn't.

Ray looked up, lines creasing his brow, his laptop casting a sick glow under his chin. "Should I take you to the hospital?"

Dan shook his head. He *should* be in a hospital, but he couldn't think of a place he'd rather be less right then, feeling like he did. Answering their questions. Being prodded. The stink of disinfectant. Explaining why he was puking blood. He reached for the bed, patting his hand out till it found it, and then he sank to his knees, clutching the bedspread. "It's just food poisoning," he managed, wincing. "I lost all that blood, though. *Fuck.*"

He started to heave again, right on the floor. There was no way he could get back to the bathroom. His body weighed two tons, and he couldn't lift it. The carpet was rough and waxy at the same time. He could smell it, too, the synthetic fibers, the acrid scent of a vacuum cleaner that was about to burn out its belt. The dirt tracked in on guests' shoes.

Ray put a hand on his back, crouching behind him. The lamp by the bed cast his shadow over the grimy carpet.

The cramp clamped his stomach like a metal band, and Dan's jaws opened wide as his muscles heaved his guts up.

Only it wasn't guts. And it wasn't blood. And wasn't that corner of toast he'd nibbled at yesterday.

Something dark and wet flopped to the floor, like a fat leech.

He had no chance to make out what it was before his stomach bucked again, a choked sound coming from his throat. Another leech worked its way up—his ribs heaving, his breaths coming harsh and heavy. He gagged as it reached the back of his throat. Gagged again, watching through a film of tears as the slimy black creature fell from his mouth. A taste like soil and mildew and old, thick blood clung to his tongue.

"God," he croaked.

Ray moved closer. "What the fuck?"

Another came up, his body forcing him to open his throat and let it through. It filled his mouth and slid along his tongue, hot and thick with slime, before it dropped with a *thump* next to the others.

He blinked tears out of his eyes, his face hot and clammy.

"Shit," Ray whispered.

The tears were fucking with his vision, because it looked like—

Shit.

The things wriggled. Their shiny black bodies plumped, puffing up like bread dough.

Ray gripped his shoulder.

And another one was crawling up his throat already, choking off his voice. He retched, his sides convulsing, fingers digging into the grime of the carpet while the first of them pried its rubbery wings free from its body with a sound like tape peeling off a roll.

"Shit," Ray said, his boots thudding.

The thing filling his mouth oozed over his lips and hit the floor with a wet *thump*. Dan caught a flash of Ray's laptop swinging at the flying leech thing before he doubled over again, bringing up another. It landed in the space the first one had been. Panic grabbed Dan, like sharp skeleton fingers around his ribcage. He lifted his head at the flapping of wings.

Saw Ray swinging his laptop at that first fat fucker as it swooped into the corner of the ceiling.

The second one stretched its wings. The third peeled its open—that tape-ripping sound again, making a desperate noise choke in Dan's throat.

The first dove toward the lamp, smacking into its shade. Ray cursed, his boots shuffling across the carpet, the laptop arcing through the air. Light flickered on the carpet as the lamp tilted and swayed. Dan squeezed his eyes shut. A hot tear welled free.

Another heave grabbed him. Something fat came up, blocking his throat, cutting off his air. He fought to get it out, spots skimming across his vision, his headache like the edge of an axe against his forehead. Ray yelled at the things, boots thudding on the floor, and Dan had to get the fucking thing *out* of him. Tears wet on the carpet. Another fat fucker opened its wings. The things already in flight bumped the walls and ceiling. His vision went dark red. His head hurt so much he could hear his pulse thumping in his temples.

The thing in his throat undulated, its fat body drawing itself up into the back of his mouth. It shifted forward, then a little more, then it came sliding out, sluggish and thick, stretching his mouth open as far as it would go. It hung there for long seconds, scraping the edges of his teeth until it finally squeezed free, landing with a *smack* on the carpet.

Dan heaved in air, wanting to throw up for real, except there wasn't anything left in him.

Ray grabbed him under the arm. "Come on."

Dan shook his head. Another cramp slammed him. *Fuck.* He couldn't go through it again. What if this one was even bigger than the last?

A black shadow dove from the ceiling. Ray slammed it with his laptop—hitting it against the wall. It dropped to the floor. He stomped it, hard, twisted his heel.

The things were all over the place, bumping into the TV screen, thumping against the curtains. One glanced off Ray's thigh, and Dan croaked around the fucker climbing his throat. He gripped the grimy carpet, eyes bulging—helpless. His stomach cramped hard. The things were flying, all the things. *Fast.* He couldn't take his eyes off them. Two swooped into the lampshade, making it totter, making light paint the walls.

His muscles cramped again. Saliva flooded his mouth. One of the things flew straight toward Ray, who grabbed Dan's shirt, trying to pull him up.

With the last strength Dan had, he shoved Ray onto his ass, out of the path of the flying leech. It skimmed right over his head. "*Get out*," Dan forced out, tightening his stomach muscles to give the words sound.

Ray, wide-eyed and open-mouthed, scrambled toward the bathroom with one of those things swooping down on him. The door banged shut.

Dan's throat opened. He gripped the thin carpet, holding on for dear life as another fucker worked its way out of him.

CHAPTER TWENTY-SIX

His arms shook under his weight. The leeches batted walls. There was a crash—the lamp falling over—and then the only light was that stupid security lamp outside.

One of the things found the window, started smacking itself against it, fiercely, like a moth trying to get to light.

He wanted to get to the bathroom, get in there with Ray and shut the door and climb in the shower and hug himself.

He wanted to *kill* the fucking things.

If he could get a moment to recover. He sagged onto his side, panting, his cheek flat against the waxy, gritty carpet. He clenched his fists. His stomach ached. Two of the things banged the window.

Three.

He clamped his eyes shut. His body trembled.

At least they didn't seem interested in *him*—because he was in no shape to fend them off.

Another found the window.

He wanted to pull his eyes open and watch, but it took too much energy.

Ray said, "Dan?" from inside the bathroom.

One of the things found the opening in the window, squeezed itself through. Its wings flapped like leaves of paper as it took off into the night.

Through slit eyes, Dan watched the sway of the curtain. Another one found its way to the opening.

"Dan!"

He closed his eyes, listening to the others follow. Until the room was silent.

"Dan, fucking talk to me out there. Fucking say something. Let me know you're alive."

He cracked his eyes open. His gaze found a black stain on the carpet, the thing Ray had crushed with his boot. At first he thought his vision was fucked up, but the stain was actually moving. It twitched. It grew. With a sound like packing tape ripping from its roll, it unstuck its wings from its body.

"Dan, what's going on out there? Is it safe?"

It shook itself off. Flitted into the air with that papery noise that made the back of Dan's neck tingle sickly. It made a quick circle, then dove for the open window.

"I'm coming out unless you tell me otherwise in three…"

Dan rolled a little, one hand against the carpet. The thought of pushing himself up was too much.

"Two."

The doorknob turned in its socket.

"One." The bathroom door swung open. He felt Ray's quick steps across the motel room floor.

"Dan?"

"It's okay," he tried to say. His lips moved like they were made of molasses. He tried again, pushing his voice up his aching throat: "It's okay. They're gone." He dug into the carpet.

Ray put his hands on his side, his shoulder.

The cold air made him shiver. His teeth chattered. "Window," he managed to get out, hugging himself.

"Hold on," Ray said. He hauled the window shut. The curtain went still.

He'd meant they'd *gone out* the window, but this was good too. His fingers twitched. He was covered with sweat. He shuddered. His stomach felt empty. The pain in his gut, at least, was receding.

And no headache. Thank god for that.

"How are you doing?" Ray asked, dropping to one knee.

"F-f-f-fine. B-b-better." His teeth clicked.

"Yeah, you totally look it. Are you cold?"

"C-c-can you t-t-tell?" He shuddered. God, he felt even *more* exhausted, if that was possible.

"Hold on," Ray said, and Dan clamped his eyes shut. The weight of blankets settled on him. He balled up under them, shivering.

"Shit." Dan could picture him dragging his hand through his hair. "Shit, that was fucked up. How are you feeling now?"

He pulled himself into a tighter ball, pushing his face under the blankets. His breath was hot and moist under the covers. The carpet smelled foul as hell.

"Shh," Ray said, a hand on his back. "Shh. It's gonna be okay."

A laugh hitched from his throat, all he had the energy for. His whole body tremored. He wanted to make a joke about how they wouldn't need a quarter to make one of the beds vibrate, but it was too much effort to say it.

"Shh. It's gonna be okay."

It took forever for his muscles to start to relax. For his jaw to ease up. For the shudders to die off. Finally he was breathing easier, but he was still either too tired or too scared to move.

"What the fuck happened out here?" Ray asked.

"Found the window…" He hugged himself tighter, fingers shoved under his arms. "Started hitting at it till they found the opening."

"Did they pay you any attention?"

"N-n-no. They just w-wanted out." Out of him, out of the room. "Th-think it was the light they were after." Or the fresh air. Or…who knew. His muscles tightened like he was going to shiver again, but it faded away. Jesus, this sucked. "They b-broke the lamp."

"Small favors," Ray said.

"The one you s-stomped g-got up and f-flew away."

"Fuck—seriously?"

"M-maybe they're gone. I mean, y-you know. In m-me." His body gave one more shake. A laugh pulled through him, as bad as a shake. "Th-this was not how I was planning on suh-spending my n-night."

"Me neither. Feeling a little better?"

"Fucking starving." That's what the pain in his stomach was now: hunger. Like his stomach had eaten his insides and was clamoring for more.

"Starving we can fix. You want a burger? Tacos? I'll go get 'em for you."

"Get something from the vending machine." Those things were out there somewhere. And maybe they'd ignore Ray right now—they'd ignored *him*—or maybe they wouldn't. It wasn't a chance he wanted to take.

"You want to head back tonight? A couple cups of coffee along the way and I'll be good to drive. I don't think I could sleep anytime soon after that anyway," Ray said.

Dan shook his head, gripped by the image of those things chasing the car all the way home, dark wings swooping through the night. "Let's hole up till daylight."

"It's a plan then. I'll grab some chips and Cokes from the vending machine."

Dan's stomach growled. *Starving*. He stretched his legs out and tugged the blankets closer as Ray got to his feet. Man, but he'd lucked out—because who the fuck else would have put up with all this shit and still been around to get him junk food from the vending machine? While Ray left the room, he hauled himself to his knees, taking the blankets with him. He just wanted to get on the bed, away from the fucking smell of the carpet. He got as far as kneeling at the edge before he had to rest. His muscles ached like he'd spent a long day pushing boulders.

Ray returned as quickly as he'd promised, with Snickers bars and Doritos bags clutched to his chest. Dan dragged himself onto the bed. His legs were heavy—his *shoulders* were heavy. As Ray scooped a candy bar off the floor—*Snickers Really Satisfies You*—a wave of impatience barreled through Dan. Fuck but he was starving.

"Here." Ray unwrapped the bar for him, then tore open a bag of chips.

Dan ripped a chunk off, teeth sinking into thick nougat and caramel.

A soft drink hissed as Ray opened it. He sat by Dan, making the mattress dip.

"See anything out there?" Dan pushed the empty wrapper off the side of the bed.

"Not a thing, thank God. Have the chips. I got them for you. And a couple more candy bars too." He stretched a leg out to dig in his pocket for them.

"What about you?"

"I ate dinner already. I'm good with this." He held up the Coke.

"Thanks."

"Do you think it's over?" Ray said when Dan had emptied the chip bag.

Jesus. They'd flown right out the window. All of them, right out in the world. His appetite slipped away. "I think they'll get someone else, and it'll happen all over again, only there's more of them flying around now."

Ray was quiet.

Dan didn't feel like eating another candy bar. He folded the wrapper over the one he'd started.

Ray said, "I meant for you."

He pulled himself up so he was slouched against the headboard. "I hope so." He straightened his legs. He hated this fucking shitty room. "If it's not, I don't know what I'm gonna do. Check in to that hospital in Virginia, I guess?"

Ray put an arm around him, pulling his shoulders sideways till he leaned against his side. Dan let his head settle. He was so fucking tired. His stomach gurgled like it needed more food, but he couldn't face eating now.

"You want to head back home as soon as it's light?" Ray said.

"Fuck *yes*. What time is it?"

"Early enough for you to get some rest before then."

He closed his eyes. He looked forward to being dead to the world for eight or nine hours solid. He hoped his body could follow through on that promise.

WHEN HE woke, he was alone on the bed.

"Ray?"

Water pattered on the other side of the wall.

A half-eaten candy bar lay on the floor, and now it looked really fucking good. He finished it off and washed it down it with warm Coke.

Ray came out of the bathroom, toweling his hair. "How do you feel?" was the first thing he said.

"Tired. Sore. Hungry. A little sick—I think I ate too much sugar. I feel like we've gone back to touring in a van and staying in hotel rooms with not enough beds."

"Just like the good old days," Ray said.

Daylight splashed through the window. He thought of those things flying out it last night.

"I feel like myself." He rolled over, laying his face on his arm. "It's not as good as how I felt after drinking blood, but it's not as shitty as I felt when I hadn't drunk any, and it's kind of good to feel like myself again."

Ray stood by the bed, watching, jeans hanging off his hips, water droplets on his shoulders. "Good. I'm looking forward to being a musician again. This phlebotomy shit is for the birds."

Dan smiled. "When do you want to start working on the album?"

Ray dragged in a breath, lines digging into his face.

"If I'm really okay, when can we start working on it?" Dan said. "I'm going nuts with all this getting nothing done"—like their next album. Or anything fucking else in his life.

He had to take a leak. And a shower. And get the fuck *out* of this place, back to normal life.

"Well, whenever you're ready," Ray said, "I'm ready. But let's give it a few days at least to make sure you're ready? I want to fire another letter off in the meantime, about these fucking things coming out of you. For all the good that'll do."

Dan pushed up. He didn't want to think about those fucking things anymore. Just wanted to get the fuck on with his life. "Call Sound Block when we get back and see how soon we can get rehearsal space. We can at least move our shit in."

"You got it."

On his feet, he felt free for the first time since they'd entered that fucking alley. The bathroom was still steamy from Ray's shower. Once he was standing under a stream of hot water himself, his brain started to work, asking questions he didn't want to deal with—like, what had he just let loose on the world?

PART THREE

CHAPTER TWENTY-SEVEN

Dan's sleep was infested with fat black bodies whipping through in the night, but when he woke up, he had no headache, no buzzing. His body was his own—worn out, a little battered, but his own.

Ray called to say Sound Block had space for them. They just had to get their equipment out of his mom's barn, and for that they needed Ray's brother's truck. While they waited for Buddy to have a chance to lend it to them, they hung out, playing—not necessarily writing, just playing. And not talking about what happened—not with words at least. It was there, though, in the way they caught each other's eye, in the way one or the other looked away—to light a cigarette, to tune a string, to twist the cap off a bottle that *didn't* contain blood.

Ray looked better. His face had some flesh back. His skin had color again. He'd gone back to shaving, taking a few years off with the swipe of a blade.

Hanging out made Dan think of high school, of summer vacations, when they did nothing *but* hang out, fretting strings until their fingers were peeling, deeper skin hardened underneath. Those thoughts found their way to his last trip to the

Dunkin' Donuts on the corner, and the classmate who'd recognized him. What a freak he must have seemed, running out of the store like that. Or an asshole.

She deserved something nice coming her way.

The day Ray could get the truck, Dan walked down to the doughnut shop at about the same time he'd shown up before. The place was as slow as last time. He leaned on the counter, waiting as the same woman he'd talked to before finished putting coffee in the Bunn.

When she saw him, her face flashed into a smile. "Hey!"

"Hey yourself. How's things?"

"Not bad." She closed the lid on the coffee machine. "What can I get you?"

"Large, regular. And…I really want to apologize about the last time I was in."

She waved him off with the towel she was using to wipe her hands. "Don't worry about it. Hey, I looked up Ray Ford online. You know, just to see. And *you*"—she leveled a finger at him—"left out some info."

"Yeah, I…really wasn't in the frame of mind to get into it. But maybe this will make up for it?" He drew their first CD from his pocket—*Regrets Are for the Dead*—signed by all three of them, a giveaway that hadn't managed to get given away.

"For serious?" She picked it up, beaming, then looked at him. "I looked up some of your stuff on YouTube. You guys are good. How did I not know about you?"

He shrugged a little bashfully.

"I'm so freakin' out of the loop on everything. Now I'd be even more afraid to talk to Ray."

"Uh, well, I hope not."

"What? *What?* What did you do?"

He glanced toward the windows. "He should be here any minute. He's picking me up."

"Oh no! And I look like this? With this stupid visor on? All I did this morning was pull my hair back in an elastic!"

"Shh. You look fine. Really."

"Oh God. He doesn't remember me, does he?"

"I don't know. I didn't mention you. I figured that would take the pressure off. What's your name?"

"Patricia. Patty Donnelly it would have been then. It's Griggs now, but only because I've been too lazy to change my I.D. and bank accounts all again."

"Nice to meet you, Patricia." He offered his hand. When she took it in her warm fingers, he heard nothing but silence inside his skull. His smile broadened. He almost laughed.

She looked over his shoulder, to the plate glass. "Oh no," she said. "Oh no. It would have been hard enough if he weren't famous and all."

Dan laughed. "I don't know about famous. He'll be thrilled you've heard of us." He thought of Esmy's shop, and the Dead Weather confusion.

The door swept open. Ray strolled in.

"Hey," Dan said. "You want a coffee or something?"

Patricia fidgeted with the displays at the cash register, almost knocking one over. He wanted to laugh again.

"I could use a coffee."

"Sure. Hey, do you remember Patricia? Patty. She went to Central with us."

"Hi," she said, her cheeks as red as the insides of a raspberry doughnut. She clutched her towel like she was ready to crawl under the counter.

"How've you been?" Ray said.

"Good! Well, you know, except I'm working here, and I'm twenty-eight and divorced with two kids and all, but other than that."

"Gotta make a living, right? Gimme a large black."

"Coming right up!"

Dan, leaning against the counter, watched Ray—completely oblivious to Patricia's startled, bird-like movements. She yelped and said, "Shoot," as she knocked a half-full coffee over with the edge of the carafe, and Dan pressed his lips together.

"What are you grinning at?" Ray asked.

He lifted his eyebrows and shook his head.

"Here you go. Sorry about the delay." She set both their coffees down as Dan slipped his wallet out of his pocket. "Oh, no," she said. "On the house."

"You gave me a whole bag of coffee on the house already." He held the card out. "You keep giving stuff away, they're not going to be able to afford to keep you in a job. Go on, ring it up."

Ray sipped off his coffee.

"Come on," Dan said. "I don't want people to start thinking I'm that guy who thinks so much of himself he expects people to give him shit."

"Charge him so we can get out of here. Otherwise we're never going to get this next record going."

"You're working on a new record?" She punched their drinks in the register.

"Yep."

"That's wicked cool. I don't even have any idea how that works. I mean, I guess you go into a studio and all."

"Eventually," Ray said.

"We're in the writing phase now," Dan said.

"This is, what, your eighth?"

"Counting the live one, yeah," Ray said.

"Well, good luck on it," she said. "Or am I supposed to say 'break a leg'?"

"You know, I have no idea," Ray said. "You take care of yourself." He gave her a wink before he turned for the doors. Dan stuffed his wallet back in his pocket and grabbed his own coffee. He gave her a wink and smile of his own.

Oh my God, she mouthed, and Dan laughed as he headed out the door.

Out in the sunshine, he hooked an arm around Ray's neck, walking side by side with him toward Buddy's beat-up F-350.

Ray said, "What was that about?"

Smiling, Dan said, "Just returning a favor."

They had a twenty-minute drive out to his mom's. She was at work, so they skipped stopping by the house and backed straight up to the barn, Ray letting the tailgate down as Dan popped the padlock on the doors. As he swung them wide, sunlight fell in, making dust dance in its light. He always liked the look of their equipment sitting there in the shadows, stacked up in cases. Waiting for them to come and pull it back out.

They stripped out of their jackets and got to work, hauling speakers and amp heads and Jamie's drum kit onto the bed. A cigarette jutted from Ray's pursed lips. Sunshine warmed the browns in his hair as he hoisted himself into the bed to haul stuff toward the front and make room for more in the back.

"I could get used to this." Dan put a crate of cables on the truck.

"It's nice, isn't it?" Ray looked up at the blue sky. "You know what else is nice?" He put a hand on the side of the truck and jumped down.

"What?"

"Not looking at the fucking internet twenty-three hours a day. I haven't opened my computer since we got back."

"So you don't know if there's any news?"

"Nope. And I don't want to. It can fucking wait." He clapped Dan on the shoulder on the way back into the barn. "Maybe tomorrow, maybe next week, but right now, I don't want to know shit. Is that everything?"

"Everything that's going, I think."

They drove their gear back to town and hauled it into their new practice space at Sound Block. The funky smell of the carpet remnants tacked to three of the walls was almost good to come back to. The room they'd got thrown in this time even came with a swaybacked couch shoved up a cinderblock wall. They'd hang moving blankets over the bricks before they got down to serious work.

Instead of working, they fooled around, loosening up, enjoying the sound of their amps, the noise they could make, even with it bouncing off the far wall.

Eventually the door opened and Jamie sauntered in, a take-out cup in hand. "Like what you did with the place."

"Hey," Ray said.

"How's it going?" Dan asked.

"Crazy." He examined his drum kit before wheeling his stool over.

"How so?" Ray asked.

"Did you hear the shit that's going on down south?"

Dan, staring at his tuning pedal while he tweaked one of the pegs on his bass, felt a silent yell rising. *Don't go there. Do not tell us about it.* Ray hadn't been the only one avoiding the news, and he wanted to hang on to his ignorance just a little longer.

But Ray said, "Unh-uh."

"Man, it's fucked up. There was this mob. They beat the shit out of someone. Like, beat him to fucking *death*."

Stop now. Stop now. Stop now.

"What was that about?" Ray said.

"They thought the guy was one of the suckers."

"The what?"

"The people who attack people for their blood."

Dan walked toward the back wall, his fingers pushed into his hair, the bass bumping his hip.

"Was he?" Ray asked.

"Dunno. It just happened."

Shit. They needed to write another letter. Send it to the news outlets. He and Ray had been avoiding posting online, even anonymously—just in case. But maybe that's what they had to do if these people weren't listening. Hit up Reddit. "I am a reformed sucker. Ask me anything."

"They had an attack in Pennsylvania too," Jamie said. "It's fucking moving north. I mean, the National Guard is out and all, but what are they supposed to do?"

Dan unslung the bass. He wanted to throw it. Because Pennsylvania was *his*. That was *his* fault.

Ray had his phone out, scrolling. Checking the news.

Dan dropped on the couch, all the energy he'd had playing gone. Fucking vanished. "I should have killed them before they got out the window."

"Like you were in any condition," Ray said without looking up.

"What happened?" Jamie looked from one to the other.

"*I* should have killed them," Ray said.

"So you could have gotten bitten yourself, and we could have kept going on blood drives?" Dan asked.

"I should have killed them as you puked them up."

"What the fuck?" Jamie's head whipped back and forth.

"*It didn't fucking die*," Dan said. "It got up off the fucking floor and flew out the fucking window."

Jamie's jaw dropped halfway to his snare.

Finally, Ray said, "Fuck shit we can't do anything about. Let's get this song figured out." He turned up his amp.

CHAPTER TWENTY-EIGHT

JAMIE SHOWED up for most of the first week, sometimes late, sometimes taking off after only an hour. Then he didn't show up at all. Ray checked on him, making sure he hadn't been bitten. The things had made it to New York, but so far no reports of attacks in New England.

Doctors had discovered parasites in people's spines. Surgery was their first step, but it turned out opening up a patient's neck caused the parasites to burrow deeper. The patients they tried it on were dead within hours. At least they were able to collect the parasites, keeping them alive in blood baths so they could study them. Dan had hope for that. They'd figure it out.

Meanwhile, for the infected, they were moving on to radiation, chemo drugs. Anyone who was attacked—by anything, even if they woke up with a spider bite—was told to report to their nearest hospital, where they were then being transferred to Virginia, to the same hospital that had received the six-year-old girls, one infected, the other just brutally attacked.

The infected one was dead now. That news crawled over Dan's skin. That could have been *him*. He could have gone to the hospital and died.

The regular patients had been transferred out, the place designated infection central. Armed guards patrolled the building, the parking lot.

In the quiet rehearsal room, Ray lit a cigarette, pushed back his hair, and clicked another YouTube video on his phone.

Reports of parasite sightings, the black creatures swooping through the night sky, increased daily, some from as far as Korea. How much of it was real and how much of it panic, there was no way of telling.

Outside Atlanta, a man shot his family and himself, leaving a note that said they were all infected, though the autopsy didn't find any sign of it.

Homeless were beaten and killed, everyone assuming any unwashed person shuffling toward them must be a sucker. A terrifying video from a nightclub in Moscow, where three suckers had lost their shit all at once, had brought some of YouTube's servers down under the traffic. If the video wasn't a hoax, two uninfected were killed and eighteen were injured in the melee. One frame zoomed in on a sucker feasting on a young woman's neck, her eyes open, her empty gaze looking beyond the camera.

Most of the commenters seemed to think getting bitten by a sucker made you a sucker, but Ray, sitting on the edge of the couch as the video played out on his phone, was proof that didn't happen. When the video ended, he clenched the phone in his hand and reached for another cigarette.

Half the news reports were about the importance of staying calm, of leaving any area where you suspected someone might be infected. Call the authorities to handle it, they urged.

And stay in at night.

Dan rubbed his face, his elbows digging into his knees.

Jamie was using again, but they'd known that even before he stopped showing up. The fidgeting, the eye-contact avoidance, the inability to answer any question without fading into a mumble.

They kept going to their windowless room at Sound Block, where musicians milled in the halls, talking about the attacks. The two of them shut themselves in their carpet-walled room and wrote like their lives depended on it.

CHAPTER TWENTY-NINE

THREE weeks in, they actually had an album's worth of songs, between what they'd written on the road and what they'd added at Sound Block. *Bad Blood*, Ray said they should call it. Dan, seated behind Jamie's drum kit, clutching Jamie's sticks, nodded.

Ray unslung his guitar. "I think this deserves a drink." They had about a gigabyte worth of rough sounds and a pile of scrawled notes to sort through. The tracks needed titles—most were still named after the moods they were in when they got started, like "Fuck That Guy at Quiznos." Some of the lyrics needed work, and they needed to get Jamie in, bring him up to speed so he could lay down the drum tracks once they got studio time organized. But, yeah, where they were at now—that deserved a fucking drink.

"What time is it?" Dan dropped the sticks in a bucket.

"Ten."

"Night or morning?"

"We ain't been here *that* long," Ray said.

They'd arrived around one in the afternoon, after having been there till seven in the morning. It kind of blurred together.

Dan stretched, his back popping. “Check the news.” Because he wasn’t going out there at night if those fuckers had made it near New Hampshire.

“South Carolina’s fucking nuts.” Ray, scrolling through his phone, whistled. “Guy in Tennessee shot his wife after she got bit by a dog.”

“Shot her?”

“He says these things are either’s Satan’s work or God’s punishment. I think he’s leaning toward ‘God’s punishment’ because he hinted she’s been sleeping around on him.”

“Some people will look for any excuse.” There’d been a lot of the God’s punishment talk: God’s punishment for letting gay people marry, for electing the antichrist to the White House, for our slothfulness, soullessness, and loose morals.

“The only shit going on our way is people overreacting,” Ray said. “So. Drink? ’Cause I could really use it now.”

Dan slipped into his jacket and put the collar up. “Drink.”

They went outside with their shoulders hunched, the late-November wind whistling down their collars. Dan glanced toward the sky. Lights blinked across it, a flight circling the airport. He was glad they didn’t have to fly right now. The security checks after 9/11 were nothing compared to passenger fear of being stuck in a can with someone who might attack at any moment.

“‘Out the Other Side,’” Ray said as he shoved his key in the Fury’s ignition. “What do you think? For the ‘eight-days-straight-of-rain’ song.”

“Sounds more hopeful than ‘Fuck This Fucking Shit We’re All Gonna Die.’”

“That one had a ring to it, though,” Ray said with a smile.

There was less traffic than usual—Elm Street was dead—but when they walked into McGarvey’s, the narrow bar was packed like a Japanese subway car. They eased through the throng, Ray pushing in toward the bar to order a couple beers. The televisions on the wall were tuned to news instead of ESPN. The one at the end had its volume up, but the voices around Dan overpowered it.

From the visuals, it looked like the National Guard in the streets of Atlanta. He recognized the Olympic torch near the Varsity.

A woman bumped into him, apologizing before squeezing past. A guy easing his jacket back as he put his hand on his hip revealed the butt of a pistol. Ray held two beers above his shoulders as he made his way over. He lowered one to Dan, saying, "Jesus, don't they know they're all going to have to go out in the dark when they leave here?" He tried to make enough room for his elbow so he could take a drink.

"I guess they're as dumb as us." There were a lot of scarves and turtlenecks in the crowd, not just because winter was on its way. Dan wondered if they'd do any good. He figured he was kidding himself if he thought turning up his jacket collar was going to do much. But no confirmed sightings in New Hampshire, just panicked reports that turned out to be bats, stray cats, and, in one case, a homeless man rummaging through a trashcan.

The crowd shoved them together.

"It's like being at a show." Ray had to raise his voice to be heard. Someone else's show, Dan took him to mean, since there was plenty of room up on stage at their own. Jesus, when was the last time they'd been to someone else's show? If they got out of this, if things went back to normal, he'd make it a point to get to more shows.

The heat and tension made the beer taste extra good. He downed it in long swallows. Someone with a bellowing voice talked about holing up in a cabin up in Colebrook, bring his shotguns, his rifle, put up plenty of food. Sit this thing out. "Alaska," someone else said, and the bellower's response was, "No, you need to get closer to the equator. More sunlight. Fewer dark hours." As if Colebrook was all that much closer to the equator.

He thought of Moss's exit strategy and wondered how he, Deb, and the baby were doing.

Someone bumped him. He glanced back, caught sight of one of the TVs again, where draped bodies were being wheeled out on stretchers. The caption said something about a shooting.

It looked like NYC. Maybe it could be a nice, normal gang shooting for a change.

"Jesus Christ," Ray said. "What is wrong with people?"

"Let's get out of here," Dan said.

"I'm with you. We can get a six at the gas station."

"I mean out of the city. Let's just move the fuck in with my mom." She lived in the middle of nowhere. And hey, it was farther south than Colebrook even.

"Faye probably wouldn't mind," Ray said, and he had a point there. Dan knew it was hard on her that he was hardly ever around. She wouldn't mind seeing more of him. And she liked Ray. She even liked Jamie—more, sometimes, than he liked him.

"So let's do it," Dan said.

"You go ahead."

"And leave you here?" Manchester wasn't a big city, but even before this fucking parasite thing it could be a sketchy place to live—where they were at least. The gas station across from the Dunkin' Donuts on Dan's corner was knocked over every few months. It wasn't unusual to wake up to flashing lights outside his windows. Sometimes he'd come across a news item about a murder, only to discover it was within a few blocks of him. Once it had been attempted murder, right below him, where Janice and Lily lived now—attempted murder with a screwdriver, a drunken domestic dispute.

Ray's section of town was better, but not a lot.

"I might move in with Buddy," Ray said—which would be a move of all of a hundred yards. "They could use an extra guy around during this shit. Did I tell you Sarah's pregnant?"

"No. Shit. Awesome. You know, except for the end of the world and all."

"Right?"

His mother was going to kill him for this, but: "So bring them too."

"Just what Faye needs," Ray said. "A house full of people."

"Come on, she loves Buddy and Sarah, and Jane's the closest she's ever getting to a grandkid."

"Never say never." Ray took another swig of beer.

"Not likely. Bring them to Deerfield."

A guy knocked into Ray's elbow, making him spill beer down his chin. He wiped it with the back of his hand. "I'll think about it."

"That's a start."

"In the meantime, can we get the fuck out of here?"

Dan set his bottle on the corner of someone's table on the way out. He turned his collar up before they hit the sidewalk. Ray's car was up the street, the two of them striding toward it, eying the sky. They stopped at the gas station across from Dunkin', where the teenager behind the counter tugged his lip while he watched a video of what sounded like people yelling on his phone. Ray interrupted long enough to pay for a six-pack, then they were on their way again, winding up at Dan's, hanging out in his living room, where they were insulated from the news, speculation, and panic.

The beer still tasted pretty good.

Ray sat on the floor, where the TV would be if Dan had one. In the apartment, life seemed like it could almost be normal. The guy next door was playing what sounded like a first-person-shooter, traffic was going by down on the street, Janice and Lily were probably asleep. If they were even there. He'd been around so little lately that they might have picked up and left, and he'd have had no idea.

Left for where, though? The way this thing was spreading—flying through Asia, making its way through the South and up the East Coast—it didn't look out-runnable, not in the long run.

Ray said, "If I'd known the world was coming to an end, I'd have maybe tried to get laid first."

Dan smiled a little, reminded of the last time he did get laid. "I wonder what Esmerelda thinks now? I've gone from being kind of a cool and mysterious vampire to just infested with fucking parasites."

"She probably appreciates how civilly you went about taking care of your situation, instead of, you know, biting people's faces off." He tipped his beer up.

Hospitals had the infected on blood. The Red Cross was begging for donations. Dan considered giving himself—he probably owed that much—but did having the parasites out of your system mean you were actually clean? And could he give without having to admit that he'd been infected? What if they tested for it? *Could* they test for it? He didn't have a whole lot of motivation to Google that. "You talk to anybody lately?" he asked. "Stick and them?"

"Had a talk with Moss just the other day," Ray said.

"Is he heading up north?"

"Nope. Sandwich, Mass. Taking the baby to his parents' house so he can try to look after everyone. He was glad to hear you're better. Said it gave him some hope."

Dan was tempted to push the issue of moving out of the city again, but he knew Ray. Give him another day or two to mull it over. He changed the topic to what they could do for the deluxe package they'd offer on the website. Red vinyl, obviously.

"You think?" Ray said. "I mean, what with all the panic?"

"Do you want to change the name then?" Dan said, because if red was too far, *Bad Blood* wasn't going to sit well in a world where your neighbor might rip your face open with no warning.

"I don't know." Ray sat back. "I like the idea of white vinyl. You know, purity and hope and a new start."

Dan smiled. Smiled and picked at the label on his beer.

"What?" Ray said.

"What about *Come Through It All?* You could read it as getting through all this shit, or you could read it as...you know. Either hopeful or dirty, later, when this shit is over. We should put a rosary on the label, make the beads look like those fucking parasites."

"We always wanted to do cover art with a dug grave," Ray said.

"That's fucking morbid given the situation," Dan said. It'd be a black-and-white photo. Dirt, hole, shovel. "We should go for it. Two Tons of Dirt: *Come Through It All.*"

"Well that was easy. I'm gonna go sneak a smoke."

Dan had to get rid of some beer. They went through the doors at the same time—Ray to the back porch, Dan to the bathroom. He was just putting himself away when the kitchen door banged hard enough to rattle dishes on the counter. The lights in the kitchen went out.

Dan booked around the corner, his belt buckle swinging loose. A chill ran through his veins.

Ray had the kitchen blinds pinched open, his nose pressed to them.

"What's going on?"

Ray ducked a little, like something was coming at him. "Put the lights out."

Dan shut off the bathroom light, the lamp in the living room. He came up beside Ray in the dark, fingers thrumming. "What's going on?"

"One of those things is out there."

"*Shit.*"

He pinched the blinds open and took a look, breathing the sharp tang of smoke that came off Ray's hair. All he saw was the darkness, the gray shape of a building beyond his apartment's parking area. His breath hit the vinyl slats, his heart like a time bomb. "Did it get you?"

"No. *There.*"

He followed Ray's finger.

Something dark batted a lit window down the street.

"Shit," Dan said.

Ray pushed away to dig his phone out. He reported the sighting while Dan gave him updates: "Still going after that window... They turned their lights out... It just flew toward a streetlight... Coming back this way." But it went right past the building. Dan shoved his shoulder against the door and tried to follow it with his eyes. He lost sight of it at the corner.

Ray was already heading to the windows in the first bedroom, already updating the operator he had on the line.

"I don't see it." Ray pulled back a curtain to peer out. Dan crossed into the other bedroom. "It's over here, smacking a window on Granite."

A car drove by, oblivious, a heavy bass beat thumping from it.

Shit. They were fucking here. He scrubbed sweat from his forehead. They were fucking *here*.

Lights across the street went out, one by one.

The thing took off again. Dan jogged to the living room. Ray's boots clacked after him. He lost sight of it as it swooped behind a house, heading toward Second Street.

Ray stayed on the line, giving an update every thirty seconds or so—not that there was anything to update. The bat was gone.

Dan paced the living room, rubbing his palms on his jeans.

After a bit, the operator let Ray go. He stared at his phone. And Dan said, "You can't go out there."

Ray didn't say anything.

"Use the couch tonight."

He nodded. His hand shook as he tapped the screen. He put the phone to his ear, his face pinched, waiting. "Everyone okay over there…? Yeah, we saw one of those fucking things over here by Dan's. Just turn out the lights and stay in till morning. Yeah, I knew you would, but just in case. Don't decide to drag the trash out to the fucking sidewalk or anything. Okay. Yeah, I'm staying here. I'll stop by in the morning." When he hung up, he said, "Jane's asleep. Buddy and Sarah were getting ready for bed."

"We can't stay in Manchester," Dan said. "The fucking parasites are only half the problem. This is going to be on the news in no time, if it's not fucking already. People are going to go nuts. People had *guns* at McGarvey's, Ray."

"I know."

"People are going to get infected."

"I know."

"Come to my mom's. Bring Buddy and Sarah and Jane. You know she's got the room for it." His old bedroom, a guest room, a finished family room in the basement with a pullout couch. She had plenty of space, and not a lot in the way of neighbors. "I'm calling her now." He needed to make sure she was okay anyway. Needed to let her know *he* was okay before the breaking news aired. He could see her sitting in bed in the dark, watching the television on her dresser. A news report was probably interrupting her show right the fuck now—or would be soon.

As the line rang, he said, "We'll bring all my food, all your food, all Buddy and Sarah's food. We'll throw a fridge on the back of his fucking truck if we have to. Hey, Mom."

"Dan. Did you hear Richmond and Philly have instituted curfews?"

"I guess they're getting hit pretty bad." At least she hadn't heard yet.

"But how do they enforce it? What police officer in his right mind is going to get out of his patrol car to shoo someone into a building after dark?"

The problem with her not hearing yet was that it left it up to him to say it. He pressed his hand to his forehead. "Mom. They're here."

"Who's there?"

"The parasites. They're in Manchester."

The line went quiet.

THE DOOR between the bedroom and living room was open. It felt like it *needed* to be, an open-air link to Ray out on the couch. In the darkness.

A drop of water fell from the faucet in the kitchen every five minutes.

Occasionally a car crept past the building.

At four a.m. a shot rang out, hollow and echoing. Off toward Goffstown, it sounded like. Dan hoped they were shooting the fucking bats. People had been doing that in other places—people and authorities, though the authorities were telling people to stop shooting off guns in populated areas, even if it *was* the fucking bats they were trying to shoot.

It hadn't been helping anyway—or if it had, it hadn't been helping enough.

Talk was they were trying to find a biochemical agent that wiped out the parasites without killing everything around them. Trouble was, the parasites didn't need oxygen. They didn't need water. And once they "hatched"—if you wanted to call climbing out of someone's throat hatching—they didn't need blood. They just had to live long enough to lay more eggs.

They *could* be killed, though—cutting them up did a good job. Buddy'd told him and Ray about a story he'd seen online, how a few groups were trying to work out a way to lure and trap the fuckers. If they couldn't find a better way to bait them, they planned on putting out a call. The terminally ill and the elderly, they'd said, might consider volunteering, maybe death row inmates. Compensation could be made to the families. They were collecting donations.

The couch creaked.

Ray left the living room. When he returned from the bathroom, the roll-spark of his lighter came, the soft scrape of the beer bottle he was using for an ashtray as he dragged it near the couch again.

Dawn took forever to get there.

CHAPTER THIRTY

DAN PULLED in behind Buddy's truck with the late-morning sun glinting off the hood of his car. He wished he felt more certain about this. While he knew going to Deerfield was a better idea than staying in the city, he was less confident everyone would agree.

He had his shit packed in his trunk, because he was going to Deerfield whether the Ford clan went or not. Or at least that was the impression he planned to give. Another thing he wasn't certain about was whether he'd go through with it if Ray didn't come. He liked the idea of being out where it was less populated—and a group could take care of itself better than individuals off on their own. But he couldn't imagine sitting in the middle of nowhere with his mom, wondering what Ray was doing back in town.

Ray, though, wouldn't go if Buddy didn't go, because there was no way Ray was leaving them to deal with this themselves, not with his niece in the equation. Maybe Dan could move his mom out *here*. If Ray moved across the driveway to Buddy's house, Dan and his mom could move into Ray's place. They'd be half a yard away from each other—close enough to have each other's backs.

But Jesus, they'd all seen the news footage. Deerfield would be better.

The walk up the driveway was like going to a funeral, the day unseasonably warm, like early fall instead of a week past Thanksgiving, the neighborhood eerie quiet. He fisted his hands in his jacket pockets. As he put his foot on the first step of the porch, the storm door opened, Ray standing there.

He let the door fall shut behind him.

"Well?" Dan said.

"They're still discussing it."

"My mom's cool with it. She's out shopping for a big dinner to celebrate. No pressure or anything."

Ray smiled. "No pressure."

"Does everything seem weird now that they're here?"

"I stopped by Pigeon's for some smokes on the way home," Ray said. "Place was crazy. You know, a little market. I can't imagine the grocery stores. I hope Faye gets out alive."

"Yeah."

The door swung open, Buddy stepping out, squinting and lifting a hand over his eyes to shield the sun. "Saw one of those things at your place last night, huh?"

"Yep. So let's get the fuck out of here."

"It's fucking tempting."

"It's fucking a good idea," Dan said.

"I've got work. If power lines go down in the middle of all this, and there's no one to fix them…"

"It's *thirty minutes* away."

Buddy rubbed his tongue along the inside of his cheek, watching the road.

Ray tapped a cigarette out of his pack.

Buddy said, "I can't impose on Faye."

"Now that she knows you might come, she'll be disappointed if you didn't show up."

"She's shopping for a welcome-to-your-temporary-home dinner," Ray said.

"Shit."

"No pressure." Ray pushed his lighter back in his pocket.

"She's got that old above-ground pool that needs clearing away," Dan said. "If we happen to tear that down and haul it to the dump while we're there, I doubt she'll think we're much of an intrusion."

"I can tear down a pool," Buddy said. "How's she getting along since your dad anyway?"

"She's okay." The cancer'd been six years ago, life as they'd known it dragging them all down a path they hadn't set a course for: symptoms to diagnosis, chemo to hospice, leaving them a family of two at the end of it. He'd worried about her alone that house in the middle of nowhere—and now here they were, running to it themselves. He hoped.

"Fucking outer space." Buddy scuffed his boots on the porch. "We've been thinking of aliens as being these things with eyes and hands and intelligence and shit, and they turn out to be flying fucking leeches."

"They don't drink blood once they're out in the wild," Ray said. "Just lay, you know, impregnate you."

Dan shuddered inwardly. That wasn't exactly the way he wanted to think of what'd happened to him.

"They've gotta live on something," Buddy said. "You know what I heard?"

"Unh-uh," Ray said.

"They're some kind of biological weapon sent by intelligent aliens."

"Been hanging out on the crackpot forums?"

"It's not even on the crackpot forums. People are actually talking about this, saying it could be their way of colonizing this place. I mean, how else do you explain why they only bother with humans?"

"Parasitoid wasps," Ray said. Cigarette paper hissed as he took a drag. "They lay their eggs in caterpillars. Not earthworms or beetles, just caterpillars. So it's not unheard of."

"Yeah, but wasps and caterpillars are both from Earth," Buddy said. "They evolved together. What the fuck is this?"

"Are you guys coming or not?" Dan said. "We're wasting daylight hours."

"Sarah's not sure," Buddy said. "She'd have to take Janie out of school. It'll be a longer commute to the surgical center. She's worried about being farther away from cops and hospitals. She's in there right now Google-mapping the distance from your mom's to everything."

"Taking Janie out of school's a no-fucking-brainer," Ray said. Cigarette paper crackled as he took a drag.

"We don't know what to do, to tell you the truth," Buddy said. "Everything's such a fucking unknown."

"Daylight." Dan pushed past Buddy to open the door. "Slipping right through our fingers." After the sharp sunlight, the hallway was dim. He aimed himself toward the kitchen at the far end, giving a glance into the two bedrooms as he passed. Jane sat on the floor in one, snapping Duplos on top of each other. Sarah was at the kitchen table, a coffee cup by her hand, the other massaging her shoulder.

"Congratulations," he said, coming into the room.

"Oh, hey."

"Guess it's too early to ask if it's a boy or a girl."

Her smile was a little strained, her hair not brushed yet. Without makeup, her eyes looked small, startled. "Way too early. Want some?" She lifted her mug.

"Nah." He drew out a chair and sat. Leaned back. Waited for her to take another look at him. Her eyebrows came up a little.

He said, "This school in Virginia. A little girl attacked another one. Put her in the hospital."

"Dan—"

"We heard gunshots last night." He sat forward. "People at McGarvey's were packing. Lots of people. And that was even before anyone saw one of those things here. Come on. Let's get out of here. You know you're not really worried about fucking commute times and how far the grocery store is."

"Dan..."

Feet pattered toward them. Ray's niece grinned, hugging a yarn-headed rag doll to her chest.

"Hey there," Dan said.

She thrust the doll toward him, clutched in her hands. "Say hi to Maisie."

"Did you say Daisy?"

"Maisie!"

"Now, I don't think she'd appreciate you calling her crazy."

The doll shook as a laugh rippled through the girl. "I said *MMMMaisie*!"

"*Ah.* Good. I wouldn't want you calling her lazy."

Jane giggled again.

"Hello, Ms. Maisie," he said to the doll. "It's nice to meet you." As he reached for one of the stuffed hands, Jane spun the doll around and clutched it to the crook of her neck. "She's shy," she said.

Smiling, Dan sat back. Sarah was watching Jane. He watched Sarah. Finally he said, "That school in Virginia. They were *six*."

IT FELT like a convoy. In his rearview mirror, he had Ray's dusty black Fury, and beyond that the white tower of a refrigerator rising above the cab of Buddy's truck. A couple mattresses leaned against it—Jane's, and a spare in case the fold-out couch wasn't comfortable.

It was temporary, though. This thing would blow over. A lot of sharp minds were working on the problem.

A parasite that hitched a ride on a space mission wasn't going to be humanity's downfall. He hoped.

Dan put on his blinker and banked off the main road, turning up the steep hill that took him home.

CHAPTER THIRTY-ONE

THE NEXT issue was whether to move Dan's great aunt in with them. They weren't equipped to deal with a ninety-year-old, but neither could they justify hunkering down to protect their families if they were leaving their weakest member out. Fate and pneumonia made the decision for them, and the funeral was held on a Thursday. Sarah's father, her only relative in the area, insisted he was just fine in Seabrook, that this was all a panic that would blow over. The Fords...well, they were all accounted for in the house in Deerfield.

Weeks passed. Buddy, Sarah, and Faye went to work during the day, calling to check in regularly. Dan and Ray kept an eye on Jane, since no one could make a case for sending her off to pre-school. Evenings were big family meals, not unlike the breakfasts his mom made when the band and the crew pulled up with all their equipment at the end of the tour.

The neighborhood had nine houses, big yards near the bottom of the hill, wooded properties at the top. The road ended just one house past Faye's, where the forest took over completely. It felt safe. It felt like a refuge. At moments—when Sarah ribbed

Buddy, when Jane giggled, when his mom shooed his feet off the coffee table—it even felt normal.

Saturday morning, the doorbell rang. Dan eased back the curtain on his bedroom window, the t-shirt he'd been about to put on hanging from his hand. The shape of the house gave him a view of the front steps but not the concrete porch itself. Voices carried from down the hall: Faye, Sarah, and Buddy discussing what they should do. When he came out from his room, pulling his shirt on, Faye was heading down the stairs, Buddy right behind with a wooden rolling pin gripped in his fist.

"Oh, it's just Bethany," Faye said as she threw the lock back. "From up the road." Buddy had the rolling pin ready all the same. Dan leaned against the wall at the top of the stairs, and Ray joined him to watch Bethany ask if they might be able to spare an egg so she could make a cake for her husband's birthday.

"Alex said he'd check the stores on his way home, and if he finds some, I'll bring you two to replace it, but I'd hate to wait till it was almost dark to find out he couldn't find them, you know?" With her ponytail and loose flannel shirt, Bethany made him think of Patricia from Dunkin' Donuts. He wondered what had become of her in all this. Was she still pouring coffee, or was she hunkered down at her parents' with her kids? He hoped for the latter.

Faye had Bethany come in while she went to check, though she was sure they didn't have any eggs. Applesauce, though—applesauce could be substituted for egg, she said. "Comes out just as good. How are you two holding up otherwise?" she asked as she opened the pantry.

"Three," Bethany said with a bashful expression that brightened to a smile as she put a hand to her belly.

"Oh my goodness!" Faye said as she put a snack pack of applesauce in Bethany's hand. "How wonderful!"

Bethany's eyes darkened. "It *would* be. I'm just so scared now, you know? What happens if it's still like this when the time comes?"

"You come see us," Faye said, clasping her wrist. "Whatever help you need, you come see us."

"We should have some practice delivering babies by then," Dan said—and saying it, it hit him that if this went on another six months, they would actually be delivering one right there. And their only medical expert would be the one yelling and pushing. He needed coffee. And fresh air.

"Hold on," Faye said to Bethany. "I think...yes, here it is. Give Alex this, from us." She passed her one of the Hershey bars she'd tucked away behind the oatmeal.

That night, they had their first snowfall. The next morning they dug the Christmas decorations out of the attic. It was the first time Faye had put up anything more than a wreath on the door in years. Jane ran through the living room with bits of tinsel stuck to the sleeves of her fuzzy pajamas as they watched the white lights in the branches sparkle. She was in a panic about Santa: how would he deliver presents if no one was supposed to be out at night?

"He's changed to daylight hours," Buddy said.

"But then kids would *see* him!"

"Nope. He's delivering the presents to your mom's work."

"But then *I* won't get to *see* him!"

Their equipment was still at Sound Block; all they had was a couple of acoustic guitars, which they pulled out at night when the curtains had been pinned shut and the lights turned low, filling the room with music before Jane was carried off to bed and they could turn on the TV. They'd already come to dread the screen popping to life, the images flashing across it.

A crisp, clear Saturday came, a promise of snow in the air again, and the three men pulled the pool down and piled it in Buddy's truck, their jackets hanging over the deck railing, their cheeks ruddy with cold and the flush of physical labor. Sarah brought them coffee, Jane yelled out the back door when it was time for lunch.

Jamie didn't check in, and Ray couldn't reach him. Stick was in Nevada, which surprised no one. Greg had gone to Canada to stay with family. Carey was on his way to Florida. And Josh was just voicemail, unanswered emails. All they could do was hope he was on the road to someplace safe.

Monday came. The sun sparkled off a dusting of snow. Bare trees gave the woods an empty, open feeling, and the three of them—Dan, Ray, and Jane—needed to get out of the house, breathe fresh air. Ray bundled her up, and they tromped through dead leaves, throwing sticks, spotting squirrels.

"We have to be back before dark," Jane said, for the tenth time since they'd left.

"We certainly will, shortcake." Ray squeezed her small hand.

"We have to be back before it even *starts* to get dark," she said.

"We'll be back way before dark," Dan said. "Uncle Ray said he's cooking dinner tonight, and you know how long that takes him."

"Are you making burgers?" She picked her way up the hill in her pink corduroys and bulky blue coat. She was buried in it, a wisp of dark hair poking from under the furred hood.

"Chili," Ray said.

She wrinkled her nose. "I don't like chili."

"I'm making a special chili on the side, just for you. I promise you'll like it."

"Can you make a face on it, like you do with burgers?" She liked the pickle-chip eyes and a ketchup smile...then she'd take off the pickles and give them to Ray.

"I'll see what I can do." They crested the hill, coming to a flattened area, the spot where they'd lit campfires as teenagers, coming out there with beer they shouldn't have had, Ray's endless cigarettes, and all their plans for their future. They'd wanted to make music on their terms—*Fuck it if it doesn't make us rich*, Ray'd said. It hadn't done them too bad. If they'd cared, they could have bought houses by now, reliable cars. They didn't even chase after equipment much these days; they liked what they had. They knew how to get the sounds they were after out of it.

"What's for dessert?" Jane asked. Faye'd made the mistake of bringing pies home the first week or two—until the grocery store got ugly. No attacks, just a lot of fear and mistrust. Now one of the guys went to the store with her, and it was in and out, fast as possible. Dan couldn't tell if the half-stocked shelves made that easier or slowed the process down with Faye and Sarah's frustration.

Ray said, "A magnificent, tasty apple."

Jane sighed. "Can it be a candy apple?" She stooped for a stick, her big blue coat canting out in the back.

"Do you want to have any teeth left when you grow up?" Ray asked.

Dan leaned against a tree, looking off into the distance, his hands stuffed in his pockets. Trying to empty his head, clear out the images that had plagued his sleep—gunfire and panic and the night sky full of black creatures.

When Ray walked up, Dan said, "When this is over, you should find someone who can put up with you and have kids."

"Nah. I'm good with being Uncle Ray."

"Danny," Jane said, drawing in the dirt with her stick, "you should tell him you want a candy apple for dessert."

"Nope. I'm holding on to my teeth as long as I can."

She hummed. After a while, she started gathering sticks, piling them around her drawing.

More memories of being in these woods came as shadows moved to the other side of the trees. Kindling popping in fire. Ray telling him about the day he'd come home from school—sixth grade—and his mother didn't exist anymore. Buddy'd found her when he'd snuck back to the apartment that morning, playing hooky from high school. By the time Ray'd walked in the apartment with his book bag, the body and the rope she'd used were gone.

He'd tossed a pinecone in the fire that night and said to Dan, "We're gonna do this."

"Don't go out of sight," Ray said to Jane. "Otherwise we won't be able to find you when it's time to go back."

"Before *dark*," she said.

"Well before dark."

When she was out of earshot, Dan said, "What if they don't figure it out?" Because he'd checked the news while Ray was getting her ready. Because it didn't look good. Because there were curfews along the entire East Coast, and Congress was talking about a national curfew, and people were attacking each other—either because they were infected or because they were afraid the other person was. Hospitals were jammed with people who'd been attacked, people who thought they'd been attacked, and people who were in such a panic they were breaking down in other ways. The Red Cross pleaded for donations. People on the internet wondered how long it'd be before donations were mandatory, like the draft. The infected being treated by whatever means doctors could come up with were dying, and some morons were going out at night on purpose, *trying* to get attacked—people believing they were voluntarily becoming a part of the aliens. Or joining God's Army. Or who the fuck knew what.

He and Ray watched bare treetops sway against the flat steel sky until it was time to gather Jane and head back.

"SORRY," SARAH said as she eased herself into her chair at the dining table.

"Look." Jane pointed with her spoon. "My chili has a face."

"When I was pregnant with Dan," Faye said, "I couldn't go ten feet from the bathroom the first few months."

Buddy shook hot sauce over his chili as he said, "Yeah, and he's been making girls sick ever since. Also, ketchup on kidney beans, Ray?"

Ray shrugged. "She likes it."

"I *like* it," Jane said. "Can I sing the first song tonight?"

"Is it going to be the spider song again?" Dan asked.

"Yes!"

"Lauren didn't show up for work today," Faye said as she spooned chili onto a slice of bread. "Harry called her and she said she was packing up for California."

"Does she have family out there?" Sarah asked.

"She must," Faye said. "I wouldn't want to drive three thousand miles with those things out there. What if her car breaks down in the middle of Nebraska? I think her feeling is that they're not out *there* yet. But she's always been flighty."

"We're having problem keeping staff too." Sarah nudged her bowl of chili away with the back of her hand. "Two nurses called in sick today, but three patients didn't show for their appointments anyway. I'm glad it's a surgical center and not a hospital. We'd really be hurting. At least no one we know's been affected yet. Just a lot of panic and circle-running."

"You should eat some bread at least," Faye said. "Before you start feeling nauseous from *not* eating."

"Do you think it's true about those things breaking through windows?" Buddy said.

Ray looked up.

Sarah said, "Please don't tell me that's true."

"I heard it on the radio on the way home. There's so much being reported, you can't even tell what's true and what's panic anymore."

They had the curtains pulled shut throughout the house, the lights off in any room they weren't in. Those things were out there, smacking the windows all night long.

"I hate this," Sarah said quietly.

"I think we have some plywood in the garage," Faye said. "Leaned up against the front wall. Paul was planning to do something with it, I don't remember what. We can use that."

DAN LAY in the pitch black of his bedroom, plywood nailed over both windows. The sweet smell of fresh-cut wood lingered. The house was quiet, everyone in bed, lying awake, thinking about the latest news reports.

CHAPTER THIRTY-TWO

Christmas Eve, the federal government put everyone back on daylight saving time. More day to the day, supposedly, though really it was the same amount of daylight, just shuffled around. Dan guessed they had to look like they were doing *something*.

For Christmas they had a ham—Faye'd thought ahead during one of those early trips to the grocery store. With that and Jane's excitement, they were able to pretend—for a few hours—they were together that day on purpose, even if gifts were sparse: a mended shirt, a door rehung so it would stay open, some old Matchbox cars Faye had dug out of the attic. Dan spent half the morning building a car wash and garage to go with them, hanging tinsel in the car wash bay to mimic the mitter curtain of a real car wash. Jane drove cars in and out all afternoon, collecting a penny for each wash, and taking the job very seriously.

By Christmas night, the boards were back on the living-room windows. The limbs on the tree drooped. Crumpled bits of tinsel gave the place the look of a strip club after the girls had gone home.

The next night, Sarah's cellphone rang while she carried a fresh pitcher of water to the table. They all looked up in surprise. Sometimes the cell towers were so jammed up all you got was a fast busy signal—they'd halfway started to think of that as the norm.

She dragged the phone out of the pocket of her sweater. "Hey, Dad. Everything all right?"

Ray handed the bag of corn chips across to Buddy.

Jane scooped up the second-to-last bite of hot dogs and beans and shoved it in her mouth, the backs of her legs swinging against the chair.

Dan refilled his mom's glass, and Sarah sat suddenly, the phone to her face. She clutched the edge of the table. "What? Dad, slow down."

Everyone looked in her direction.

"Is that Grandpa?" Jane said.

"Are you sure? When did it happen?"

Buddy clenched his spoon, watching her.

"Are you okay? Besides that, I mean. Did you get hurt?" Her fingers moved to her sweater as she listened, tugging at a button. "I don't know. I don't know if you should go now or wait till morning. What does the news say to do?"

"Has he been bitten?" Ray said.

"Jane." Dan's mom took her hand. "Janie, why don't we go pick out something to watch tonight?"

"All right," Sarah said. "Which hospital are you going to?"

Dan shot his chair back, flattening his hand on the table. "Tell him not to go to the hospital."

Buddy and Ray's heads swiveled.

"Yes…I…Dad, I really don't know. If you don't feel well, you should definitely go once it gets light."

"*Don't go to the hospital*," Dan said.

Sarah raised her eyes. The tinny, faraway sound of her dad's voice came through the speaker.

"Don't let him go to the hospital."

"Dad, hold on." She put her hand over the phone.

"We can take care of him here," Dan said. "Better than they can." They'd brought the needles, the tubing. Alcohol, swabs, Band-Aids. They hadn't even asked each other if they should. *Of course* they should have that stuff on hand.

"What are you talking about?" Buddy said.

"Tell him to come here. We have enough people. We can get him through this."

His mom had come to the doorway, her fingers at her throat. "Dan, what are talking about?"

He glanced her way before looking back to Sarah. They hadn't said a word about what they'd been through—why worry them? Save that card till they needed it.

They needed it now. He said, "Ray and I can do it. We've been through it already. I got bit at the end of our tour. I'm fine now."

"You were attacked?" his mother said.

"We know how to deal with it," he said to Sarah.

"Dad, let me call you back. Don't go anywhere until you hear back from me, okay? Keep your phone close. Love you too." She clutched the phone between her hands like a pocket Bible and looked at Dan.

His mom said, "You were attacked and you didn't say a word?"

"It was kinda—"

"You were attacked and you didn't say a word, and you let me worry my head off about you being sick? That time you came over here for dinner and you could barely walk a straight line—was that this?"

She was exaggerating—or he thought she was exaggerating. It wasn't the time to argue it either way. "What was I supposed to say? 'Hey, Mom, I've kinda started drinking blood, and I just look like shit because I'm running a little low right now?'"

"You could have said something!"

With one hand on her belly, Sarah leaned forward. "Tell me what you can do for him that the hospital can't." Her eyes searched his.

He wasn't sure they *could* do anything the hospital couldn't; all he could promise was that here her father wouldn't run the risk of being a guinea pig—and he'd have blood. With five adults, they should be able to get him through this. "We have the supplies, and Ray can draw blood."

"Since when do you know how to draw blood?" Buddy asked.

"Since my crash course after our tour." Ray slipped Jane's plate onto his, started gathering silverware.

"Moss taught him," Dan said. "Ray did most of the blood drawing when we went around getting donations."

"Sarah can draw the blood," Buddy said.

"Now hold on," Sarah said. "We need to think this through." But her eyes went right back to Dan's, looking for something there. Something that could assure her that this was the better choice.

"Who did the blood screening?" Dan's mom asked. "What if those people had HIV or hepatitis?"

"I wasn't really in the position to be picky," Dan said.

"What about Jane?" Sarah asked. "Those people who've been bitten have *attacked* people. What's to keep Janie safe if we bring him here?"

"Those people weren't getting blood," Dan said.

"I don't think Dan should donate," Buddy said. "No offense, but if you've been getting blood from strangers..."

"*Drinking* it," Ray said. "Not mainlining it in his arm."

"I still wouldn't want to take the chance."

Sarah shook her head slowly. "No, me neither."

"Plus he's been infected by these things," Buddy said. "Who knows what that does to you?"

Faye hugged herself.

"That still leaves four adults," Dan said. "Four's enough." He hoped. If they alternated. If he gave up his share of food with iron in it.

"What do *you* think?" Sarah said to Buddy.

"My better sense says he should go to the hospital, but if it were me... I mean, you've seen the news. Maybe it's not happening in New Hampshire yet, but people are dying in hospitals. Shit, they're killing each other in hospitals."

"And I'm still here," Dan said. That's what he thought every time they stared at the news: *People went to hospitals and died, but I'm still here.* "They're out of my system. It wasn't fun. He's not going to have a great time over the next couple months. But we can get him through it."

"It's not really our call, though," Buddy said. "It's Faye's house."

"Well of course bring him here," Faye said.

"The Red Cross is hurting for blood," Ray said.

"I know." Sarah didn't take her eyes from Buddy, as if she was trying to suss out what he'd *really* do. If it were him. "We donated at the center today."

"When there's not enough to go around," Ray said, "who are they going to give priority to? You think old guys are going to top the list? And how safe is he in a hospital? They're quarantining the infected—together."

"You just said they weren't violent if they were getting blood!"

"And I said what happens when they don't have enough blood to go around?" Ray said.

Buddy sat back, tapping his spoon against the table. He and Sarah had one of those wordless conversations couples had, studying each other's eyes.

"We're already imposing," she started to say to him.

"You call your dad," Faye said. She put a hand on Sarah's shoulder. "Tell him to come out here. We have to stick together. We're all we've got."

Buddy gave a nod finally, and Sarah picked up the phone.

Ray got up with the plates and silverware.

"Hi, Dad," Sarah said. "First thing in the morning, head out here, okay? I'll give you directions. We've got people here who can help you."

Faye told Buddy she thought she had some camping mattresses in the attic, maybe an old Army surplus cot. It wouldn't be Serta Sleeper comfortable, but they'd find a way to make him feel at home. "Will Sarah's mother be coming too, do you think?" she asked.

"She passed when Sarah was a teenager," Buddy said.

"Oh. I'm sorry."

"Thanks for letting us all invade your space," he said.

"Don't even think of it. And *you.*" She jabbed Ray as he passed with the baked beans pot. "You didn't say a word either!"

"Sorry, Faye."

"'Sorry, Faye.'" She sighed.

"Isn't it way better knowing it happened and I came through fine than worrying the whole time what would happen to me?" Dan said.

"What if you hadn't come through fine? You'd have been dead, and I wouldn't have had a chance to hold your hand and be there with you."

He kissed the top of her head. "I came through fine."

CHAPTER THIRTY-THREE

"How long do you think this will work?" Ray asked, catching the hammer as its handle slid through his grip. He sat on the old Army cot they'd set up in the walk-up attic after they'd cleared out enough space to make a room out of one half of it. Despite the crispness of the air outside, upstairs was stuffy. It would have been nice to have the window open, but the first thing they'd done after they'd moved boxes to make a path to it was board it shut. They didn't know Sarah's father well, and they couldn't take the risk that he'd open the window in the morning and forget about it as the day grew dark.

"What do you mean 'how long'?" Dan dropped a box of books at the foot of the cot, old paperbacks of his dad's. Horror, mostly—unfortunately, considering the situation. Richard Matheson, Robert Bloch, some creased old Stephen Kings. It was something to read when the nights got tedious at least, and with the sun setting so early, they got tedious fast. He fished out a few non-horror paperbacks, dropping them on the bed for Sarah's dad. The rest he'd bring down to the living room. "We should have enough people to get him all the way through it."

"That's not what I meant."

When Dan didn't answer, Ray said, "Hiding. How long do you think we can hide out here?"

Dan still didn't say anything. Until they couldn't scrounge up any food? Until the National Guard came and forced them into some sort of camp? Until everyone was dead? He tossed *The Sound and the Fury* on the cot and picked up the box. "I guess we'll hide out here as long as we need to. You got anything more pressing at the moment?"

"Fuck you," Ray said without any rancor.

"Let's go listen to the radio," Dan said. That's what they did after Jane went to bed. Sat around the living room with all the windows blocked, listening to bad news and thin hope while trying to ignore the patter of black bodies against the glass behind the boards. The TV wasn't good anymore—none of them wanted to watch it play out. They just wanted to know how bad it was getting. If there was any hope on the horizon.

"I'm gonna have a cigarette," Ray said.

"Okay."

The cot creaked as Ray pushed himself up. When they got to the main floor, Ray turned the corner and kept going, heading to the garage.

CHAPTER THIRTY-FOUR

"YOU'RE home early," Ray said as Sarah came in. It was barely ten in the morning. Ray'd been reading to Jane on the living room floor while Dan tried to concentrate on Richard Matheson's *I Am Legend*, a story about the survivor of a pandemic that turned people into vampires. Like maybe he could get something useful out of it. All he got was that it was easier to be in fiction. At least someone knew what was going on then, even if it was only the author.

"I gave my notice," Sarah said.

"How much notice?"

"About thirty minutes." She dropped her bag on the end of the couch. "No sign of my dad yet?"

"How long's the drive from Seabrook?" Ray asked.

"Two hours, a little less."

"He would have had to pack too," Dan said. "There might be traffic." People out trying to get food. National Guard and police out, trying to keep things from getting out of hand.

"Relax. Have a glass of wine," Ray said.

"Do we have any?"

"Nope."

"Good. I shouldn't be drinking it anyway." She sat beside her bag to take off her shoes.

"So why'd you quit?" Dan asked.

"This man," she said. She set her shoes aside and sat up, pushing a lock of hair behind her ear. "I was stopped at a light, and he came out of nowhere and started pounding on my windshield. I had the doors locked, and it was bright as day, and he scared the—" She glanced at Jane. "He scared me. The rest of the way to work, I was shaking. All I could think about was Jane out here alone—I mean, with you guys, but not with me. And the baby." She put her hand to her belly. "I thought, is it really worth it? Showing up for work every day? There's talk they're going to move the infected in, use the surgical center as a quarantine. No more surgeries, just—I should be there, but I can't do it. Not with…" She hugged Jane's dark head to her stomach.

"Yeah," Ray said.

"I'm an awful person. But the minute I decided *the hell with this*, I felt so much better."

"You're not an awful person," Ray said.

Her phone went off. She fished it from her purse.

Ray looked at Dan. They had one of those silent couple's conversations themselves, one where Ray asked, again, *How long can we do this?* and Dan still didn't have an answer.

"Oh good!" Sarah said. "Good, now get off the phone before you get in a wreck." When she hung up, she said, "He's stuck in traffic on I-93."

"That sounds about right," Dan said. "Even without an alien parasite invasion."

"Some things never change," Ray said. "Hey, I'm glad you're going to be home. We've probably done enough damage to your kid."

Dan was glad she was home because it meant maybe one or both of them could get the fuck out of the house more often—without a four year old in tow. Even romps in the woods were off limits now, after gunshots had echoed through the dead trees. Hunters, they'd guessed, feeding their families—but a brown-haired little girl running through the trees could be easily mistaken for game by someone already on edge. Even a little girl in a fluffy blue coat.

CHAPTER THIRTY-FIVE

RICHARD MILLER was fine with the attic bedroom, and a little ashamed he'd gotten himself attacked by one of those flying whatsits. His arrival didn't quite free Dan and Ray up—someone strong enough to wrestle him to the ground if something went wrong had to be around. It was still a help, though. A new person for Jane to pester with questions, an extra set of hands when things needed to be done.

They'd started blood donations the night he arrived. He'd curled his lip at the first taste they offered, and the touch of the warm blood on his tongue made him retch, but they put the rest in the fridge—he'd feel differently soon enough. Or, Sarah said, he wouldn't—maybe he wasn't infected after all. Dan and Ray stayed silent. Tense.

Curfew closed retail stores and any other nonemergency business an hour before sunset. Medical workers, cops, emergency crews, and the National Guard were the only ones out at night, and they stayed inside—hospitals, nursing homes, armored vehicles.

THREE NIGHTS after arriving, Rich had a headache. Dan touched his arm, asked if he heard buzzing. And Rich, staring at Dan's fingers on him, nodded. Dan looked up, but Ray was already in the kitchen, bottles rattling in the fridge door.

The blood did its thing. Sarah looked away, her face tight. Her throat moved as she swallowed the reality of the situation.

They kept extra in the fridge at all times. They might have a thin night of canned soup beefed up with bullion cubes and water, pieces of old bread to dip in it, but they never had a thin night when it came to blood for Rich.

Sarah started baking, flour being easier to get their hands on than convenience foods. Faye made stock from whatever they had—bones or the odds and ends of vegetables. Soup became a staple. Anything that could be stored in the cool garage for later—dried beans, rice, potatoes, whatever the guys could get their hands on—was dumped into garbage bags and stuffed into tubs that Dan had first emptied of old blankets, unalbumed photos, knick-knacks he remembered knocking over when he was a kid.

It was night—Jane in bed, Sarah in the kitchen getting bread dough set to rise overnight so they'd have fresh first thing in the morning. She had flour up to her elbows, asking Dan if he could get her a little water, when the yell cut through the boarded-up windows.

Her hands stopped moving. "Was that an animal?"

Dan turned his eyes toward the front of the house.

It came again, closer. His breath stalled. His scalp prickled.

"That's not an animal," Sarah said. "*Buddy!*"

Feet pounded up the stairs already.

He burst into the kitchen. "Did you hear that?"

"Mommy, what's going on?"

Dan was already moving toward the front of the house. Ray came down the hallway from his room. Buddy came with them.

This time, it was clear: "*Help me!*" A woman's voice. Buddy pushed past them, into the living room. He yanked one of the loose boards down. One of the parasites slammed into the window, as big as a pigeon. Buddy jerked back.

"*Help!*"

They crowded the window, peering into the darkness encroaching at the edges of the outside security light.

"There." Ray pointed toward the tree line at the edge of the yard.

A woman ran over that bit of lawn, her head cranked back to watch the trees behind her. No coat, just what looked like slippers on her feet. Her ponytail jumped as she ran, and Dan's thoughts went first to Patricia at Dunkin' Donuts before he realized it was Bethany from up the street.

"Shit." Ray put a hand against the window. Creatures circled over her head. One broke free, swooping down as she reached the driveway. She flailed an arm, but her immediate concern seemed to be what was behind her. Her feet pounded toward the house. Her eyes turned their way. Caught theirs through the glass. She yelled, "Help!" as another of the parasites dove into her, knocking her to her knees.

A bulky shape burst from the trees a hundred feet behind her. Lumbering with a hitch, almost dragging its leg.

"What is it?" Sarah asked from the doorway.

"Get downstairs with Jane," Buddy said.

Another parasite dove, and Bethany spilled over again, coming down hard on her hands—yelling. Her eyes circled with white as she tipped her head to their window again.

"What are you going to do?" Sarah asked.

"I don't know. Get downstairs."

Bethany's husband limped onto the driveway, teeth gritted, hands clenched. Eyes pinned on her. One leg of his trousers was soaked a deep black in the light cast from the security lamp.

"We have to let her in," Faye said.

Bethany scrambled up their front steps. The storm door rattled with pounding. The attic door opened, Rich tentatively sticking his head out. "What's going on?"

"HELP!"

"*We have to let her in,*" Faye said.

Bethany's husband reached the walkway, dragging that leg.

"Jesus," Buddy said. "We can't—"

"He's got her," Ray said. "He's fucking got her."

Dan put a hand on the window. Bethany's screams vibrated the glass.

The man had her turned around. She hit him with her fists, yelling in his face.

"That's Alex," Faye said. "We can't let this happen. We cannot let this happen on my front steps."

"Where are you going?" Buddy said sharply as she bustled out of the living room.

Dan started away from the window quickly, heading for the hall.

Rich was already halfway down the steps to the front door. No coat, no shoes.

"Don't open that fucking door!" Buddy yelled.

Dan took the stairs in two jumps, grabbing the edge of the door as Rich pulled it open. "I've got it," he said, his heart pounding. Bethany's screams turned to shrieks. "Make it quick."

Then Ray was there, and Buddy.

Bethany's shrieks drove into Dan's head like nails. He gripped the door tighter. He couldn't see around it. Was not sure he wanted to. The noise—it wasn't of someone fighting someone off anymore. It was agony.

Faye clutched his shoulder, put her forehead against his back.

Two thick smacks shook the glass in the storm door. A choked sound jumped from his mom's throat. She held on to him harder.

Bethany's screams became gurgles, wet and airy.

"He's got her," Rich said, frozen with his hand on the latch.

Another creature crashed into the door.

Dan jerked his head aside, trying to get away from the wet grunting and sucking noises coming from just outside. He squeezed his eyes shut. Tried to swallow and couldn't.

That could have been him. That could have fucking been him.

Buddy put a hand on Rich's shoulder. Drawing him back gently, he closed the front door. The latch clicked quietly into place. Buddy braced a hand against the wood, his head bent.

Dan thought of Janice, from the apartment below his. Lily. His throat was a hard ache. *That could have been me.* His mother's tears soaked through his shirt, her body shaking. He reached under Buddy's arm and snapped the deadbolt into place, reached his other hand into his pocket and drew out his phone.

Eight rings went by before the 911 dispatcher answered. He told her what happened. She wanted to know where the sucker was now.

A low-pitched moan came from the other side of the door—endless. It hurt more even than Bethany's cries had: the pain of a man who'd just realized what he'd done to his own wife.

"He's still there," Dan said. Aching.

"It'll be morning before we can send anybody out."

"He just killed his fucking wife." He strode across the landing, shoving a hand into his hair. "He's right outside the fucking door. He just *killed* someone."

"Your doors are locked?"

"Yes."

"Windows boarded?"

"*Yes.*"

"Sit tight. We'll be able to get someone out at sunup."

They spent the night in the living room, all of them, listening to Bethany's husband sob below their windows. Buddy held his daughter, his wife against his side. Faye cried silent tears, and Rich eased her under his arm, rubbing her shoulder, whispering that he was sorry.

It went quiet around four a.m. When they looked out, Bethany's body was alone, her hands folded over her chest, her eyes drawn closed. Before sunup, a single shot echoed through the dead woods.

CHAPTER THIRTY-SIX

WHAT they'd seen ate at all of them, but it seemed to be eating Ray almost literally. Rather than waste a plate of food he didn't have the stomach for, he spent mealtimes in the garage, living on cigarette exhaust. More restless every time he came out.

Dan was moving laundry from the washer to the dryer when he heard Ray's phone go off on the other side of the wall. Something about it stilled his hands. Buddy was at work. If he'd needed to contact them, he'd have used the house number—unless it was something Buddy didn't want Sarah or Faye hearing, and if it was that, it could only be bad.

The wall muted Ray's words.

Dan shoved the wet clothes in the dryer and left the door hanging open as he headed for the garage. When he stepped inside, Ray was saying, "Where are you right now?" And he knew, by those words, by the tone of voice that carried them, that Jamie was on the phone.

He walked up by Ray, and Ray pressed his fingers to his forehead, a half-smoked cigarette clamped between them. "Okay, yeah, I know where that is. I can be there in—" He glanced toward the windows, as if they could tell him the time. They'd been covered with blue paint Faye had bought for the guest room a few years ago. "Yeah, like thirty minutes, forty tops. Stay put, all right?"

Dan picked at a sliver of wood at the edge of his dad's old workbench, his back stiff across the shoulders, his jaw tight.

He waited for Ray to hang up before saying, "Was he bit?" Because that would be the worst situation: four people supporting two infected. They'd have to make it five at that point—either Rich or Jamie was going to have to deal with getting his blood. There was no other way to make it work.

"No," Ray said. "He just doesn't know where to go."

"Where is he?"

"Manchester."

"What about home?" Dan said. "Merrimack's gotta be better than Manchester. Surely his parents have figured something out."

"That's where he was. He couldn't take it." Ray dragged his hair back. "We gotta do it."

"I know." After what they'd seen, he knew. If it was possible to pick up Jamie in the daytime and get him to safety...

"He can't use if he's here," Ray said. "There's nothing *to* use."

Dan nodded.

The wood he'd been picking slipped, jabbing under his fingernail. He shoved his finger in his mouth.

"I'm gonna go get him." Ray grabbed the jacket he'd hung over the vise mounted to Dan's dad's old workbench.

"What time is it?"

"Early enough that I can make it there and back," Ray said.

"I should come too."

"Nope. You're on Rich duty. Like I told Jamie," Ray said, "I'm gonna pull up and honk. I'm not even getting out of the car."

"I wish it was earlier. You could combine it with a supply run. It's stupid to waste the gas without getting anything for it. Where will we put him?"

"Dunno."

He followed Ray out.

"I guess he'll have to room with you or me," Ray said.

"I'm not rooming with Jamie. Not unless Rich is interested in licking blood off the walls." Same house he could handle. Same room? Jesus Christ. An irrational objection to the idea of Jamie bunking with Ray bobbed up too. After everything he and Ray had been through, he couldn't take lying there at night feeling like the third wheel. And he kind of hated himself at that moment: with all that was going on, he was concerned with feeling jealous? "How about you bunk with me? Let Jamie have his own room where he can't annoy the shit out of anyone."

"It's all the same to me. I spend most of the night sitting in the garage anyway."

"You're in a world of hurt when you run out of cigarettes."

"I might have to see if I can get some while I'm out."

"Don't push your luck." He stopped in the doorway of the guest room Ray'd been living in. Clothes lay strewn on the floor. Ray's laptop was open on his bed, its screen black. "Before dusk comes on, get your ass out of there," Dan said. "Anyone looking for trouble comes walking down the road, get your ass out of there. Call me a piece of shit if you want, but if we lose Jamie, we lose Jamie. If we lose you..." He clenched his fists in his pockets. "We'd have to tell Jane she doesn't have an uncle anymore." A tight ache swelled in his throat. He was manipulating Ray; he knew that. He just hadn't realized how hard it would hit him to speak the words. "So keep your eyes on shit, and if there's anything sketchy, get the fuck out of there." His voice came out coarser than he'd intended.

"Yep." Ray's keys jingled as he shoved them in his jacket pocket.

Dan followed him down the hall. Jane's voice coming from the kitchen, asking questions as Sarah kneaded bread. Rich answered them patiently.

"I'll be back," Ray said.

"Promise?" Dan said.

"Scout's honor."

"You were never a Scout." Dan went down the steps with him, held the door open at the bottom. When Ray got in his car, Dan pulled himself back into the house.

"Where's Ray off to?" his mom said when he got to the top of the stairs.

"Picking up Jamie. Set an extra place for dinner." He hoped they wouldn't wind up with two plates too many.

CHAPTER THIRTY-SEVEN

THE boards for the living-room windows stood propped against the fireplace, giving them access to sunlight, if just for a little while. Dan stared out at the road.

"Did your dad fish?" Rich asked, studying the selection of books on the built-in shelves that flanked the windows.

"Yeah." Treetops twitched across the yard as squirrels darted across the branches. Did it look darker out already?

Rich tipped a book from the row, opened it, started flipping pages. The clock on the mantel ticked quietly.

Rich said, "Do you still have his gear?"

"Out in the barn somewhere I think."

"I could get up early and go fishing. I hope he made some of these." He lifted the book—one on tying flies. "Because I'm not sure my fingers were ever that agile."

Dan rubbed his phone, resisting the urge to check the time again.

His ears pinged on road noise, tires on gravel. He put a knee on the window seat and pressed his forehead to the glass. The pickup came bumping into view.

"That Buddy?" Sarah called from the kitchen, an edge to her voice. She wasn't happy about Jamie, not after what they'd witnessed with Bethany. What if Jamie'd been bitten, she'd wanted to know. What if they were letting a time bomb into the house? What if he'd been bitten and he wasn't telling them? Dan told her he and Ray would be able to spot the symptoms before it got too far. He hoped he was right.

Dan said, "Yeah," watching Buddy hop out of the truck.

"I'm gonna show Daddy my bunny bread!" Jane said.

Buddy'd notice they were a car short—and it was the first thing he said as he tromped up the stairs: "Who's out?"

"Ray," Sarah said.

"I'm thinking of going fishing in the morning," Rich held up the fly-tying book for Buddy to see.

"Can I go?" Jane asked. She had her bunny bread clutched in two hands like a doll. One of the ears was ready to fall off.

Dan's stomach churned. He looked back out the window.

"How was work?" Sarah asked.

"Only three of us there today. I knew Bobby was taking off with his family, but Pat didn't call in or nothing."

"I hope he's okay."

Dan listened to him kiss the top of Jane's head and Jane exclaim, "Look at the bunny I made!"

Dan clutched his phone. "I'm gonna get some air."

"Don't stay out too long," Sarah said.

"You all right?" Buddy asked.

"Yeah. Just getting a headache from being cooped up."

Buddy's eyes stayed right on him.

"It's just a headache," Dan said. "People get headaches." Especially when their muscles were tensed up and they had a litany of curses going through their head, all ending with the word "Jamie."

He let himself out the front door and breathed deeply. Crisp clumps of snow clung to the dead grass in the yard. The concrete steps were chilly, and he sat on them, hugging his knees. Watching the road. Checking the position of the sun in the sky.

The door opened behind him.

"Don't mean to disturb," Rich said.

"It's okay. I'm just anxious."

"They don't have a lot of time to beat the dark, do they?"

Dan shook his head.

"I thought maybe you could show me the fishing gear. It'd be better than dragging you out of bed at the crack of dawn."

"Sure." He patted his pockets, found his keys.

When he swung open the barn doors, it hurt to see their equipment, the gear they hadn't taken to Sound Block sitting in shadows, layered with dust.

"Better stand back," Rich said. "In case one of those things is taking a nap in there."

"Light switch is just inside the door."

The bulb snapped on. Nothing stirred.

"It's probably in the back." Dan came in, brushing a speaker cabinet with his fingertips. They should move some of this to the garage. The acoustics sucked, but it'd be fun to play plugged in again. Maybe tomorrow, when it was light out long enough to do it.

Dry paper sounded, like pages turning, and Dan's first thought was that Rich was flipping through the fly-fishing book again.

It came faster.

"*Down,*" Rich said, his hand slamming between Dan's shoulders.

Rich's weight knocked him into a wheelbarrow. The two of them stumbled over it together. Dan grabbed for the rough wooden wall to catch himself. His palm caught a nail, skin tearing open.

The wings—the sound they made as the thing flapped through the barn—turned him cold from the inside.

Rich's body on his back made it hard to breathe. Saliva flooded his mouth. He brought his bloody hand under his shoulder, protecting it from Rich, remembering what it felt like to smell blood.

Wings flapped, frantic, the parasite's fat body bumping the walls like a moth trying to get out a window.

He clenched his hand into a fist, hiding the tear in his skin like a secret, and dug his forehead against the floorboards. All of this going wrong—at *home*. A hard noise broke from his chest as he thought of Ray—God knew what was happening to him. God knew what was happening to any of them.

The weight came off. Rich dragged him to his feet by the back of his collar. "Get to the house."

He aimed himself toward the doors, his boots slipping on the floor, his hand still curled in a fist, held against his stomach. He stumbled when he made it to the dirt, caught himself, kept going. Rich wasn't following. He spun, stepping backward fast, heart pounding. "What about you?"

"After I get the rod and tackle and lock this place back up."

He slowed, clutching his injured hand.

"Go on, I'll be fine. What's the worst that can happen? I get another set of eggs laid in me? Big whoop! Get the hell out of here."

Dan hauled himself around and jogged to the house.

Jesus. Jesus Jesus Jesus.

He yanked the door open. When he got to the top of the stairs, Sarah was setting plates on the table. She glanced over her shoulder. "Where's Dad?" Then she looked again. The plate in her hand crashed to the floor.

"I'M FINE. I just cut it on a nail," he said as his mom dragged him to the sink by his wrist.

"How could you leave him out there?" Sarah said. She stuffed her foot in a boot.

The front door swept open.

"Dad!"

"I'm fine. Everything's fine." He came up the steps with two fishing rods and a plastic tackle box. "It didn't bother with me. It was too busy trying to get out of the sunlight we'd let in."

"What happened to it?" Buddy said.

"It found its way up to the loft, where I guess it found a dark corner to hide in."

"Well fuck. Let's go kill it then."

"You stay right here," Sarah said, adding in a sharp whisper, "And watch your language." Jane sat on a chair, out of the way of where the plate had broken, walking the one-eared bunny bread across her placemat. Humming to herself.

Dan's mom sat him at the table and went to find a bandage. Rich, he noticed, had a hard time not looking at the blood that seeped through the paper towel. Dan clasped his other hand over it, but he knew the scent lingered, knew it cut right through the stewing beans and baking bread and woke things inside of Rich.

Rich said, "I think I'll go upstairs for a bit. See what we've got in this box." He brandished the tackle box as he turned away.

"Can I come?" Jane asked.

"Not this time, honey." He stiff-legged it out of the room.

"How'd it get in the barn?" Buddy wanted to know. "We've gotta tighten this place up. How are the attic vents?"

"There's a screen over them," Dan said.

"That might not be good enough. Where else can they get through? We need to do a walk-through of this whole damned house. Sorry, Faye—I'm not saying anything against your house. They're all like that."

"All houses have their crannies and crevices," she said, "and I probably know where most of this one's are." She handed the bandages and antiseptic off to Sarah. "I'll come with you."

Dan put his elbow on the table and leaned his eyes against the heel of his hand, the one that wasn't injured. He clenched his teeth when Sarah splashed the gouge with alcohol, but didn't mind the pain. It took some of the ache out of the rest of the situation: bat things in the barn, Ray who-the-fuck-knew where.

His phone rang as she wrapped his hand. He dug it from his pocket. "Jesus, where are you?"

"Still in Manchester. Jamie wasn't at the address he gave me."

"So come the fuck back."

"I've got another place I'm gonna try."

Goddamnit. "One place. *One* place, and then get the fuck back here."

DARKNESS CREPT from the trees, reaching like fingers across the driveway. Dan stepped back to let Buddy set the boards against the windows.

He pulled his phone out and tried Ray again. It rang and rang and went to voicemail. Again.

He sat on the couch and put his face in his hands.

After a while, his mom sat next to him, rubbing his back. He silently thanked her for not going on about how it was going to be all right, how Ray was smart and if he had to, he'd hunker down till morning. He was and he would—Dan just hoped nothing happened to him in the meantime.

He pulled his phone out to check the time, not that the numbers mattered anymore. It was how the sky looked beyond the boards, that's all that counted.

"I'm going to feed Jane," Sarah said.

Faye nodded.

Buddy, fresh from a shower, took a seat. "He'll be fine."

"Yeah."

From the kitchen came, "I'm *tired* of beans. Can we have noodles tomorrow? Not with beans!"

The mantel clock ticked.

Dan's chest tightened. The bottoms of his feet itched. He got up, got moving. Needed to burn off a little nervous energy. Halfway down the hall, he dragged out his phone again.

And got the familiar fast-busy signal of the network not being able to keep up.

He ended the call and kept trying, but even when it rang, no one picked up. The first time, he hung up as soon as Ray's voicemail answered. The second time, he let it play for a second. By the fifth time, he put his head against the wall, closed his eyes, and listened to Ray's voice telling him his phone was probably in the other room, buried under a pile of stuff, and he'd return your call as soon as he found it again.

Ray sounding normal.

The *world* sounding normal, if only for twenty seconds.

"Maybe we should eat, honey," his mom said from the mouth of the hall. "We can save plates for them."

He doubted anyone was all that hungry—for beans and bread again—but it was part of the routine, something to look forward to through the long day. All of them sitting down together for a meal.

Ray's empty chair stood out like a casket in the kitchen. They passed the breadbasket in front of it.

It was a physical manifestation of the hole eating through Dan. Buddy went to work every day, came back fine. Faye still insisted on going in three days a week for a couple hours, just to keep what little there was to do going, though he suspected it was more to get out of the house. She came back fine. But Buddy and Faye didn't have Jamie in the equation. And they weren't as hell-fucking-bent on saving people from themselves as Ray. Not being able to save his mother had given him a lifetime complex that annoyed Dan on the best days, and right now it scared the shit out of him.

He told himself to relax, that Ray was smart, that he wouldn't take chances if he didn't have to.

Which only made it worse: Ray *was* smart. He'd have come home by now, if he could.

He couldn't stop picturing some infected lumbering after Ray, dragging him out of his car—leaving him bloody in the street.

"Excuse me." He pushed his chair back, taking his plate to the counter to wrap it and put it in the fridge. He unplugged the radio in the living room and carried it to his room, knocking the door closed behind him with his heel.

He turned the volume low, so Jane wouldn't hear what it had to say, and so he could listen over it—for the sound of tires on gravel, the rumble of an engine. He tuned to a Manchester station, hoping for a news report.

Ad buyers weren't showing up for work, advertising funds weren't getting released, and in the hour he lay on his back on the bed, keenly aware of the empty mattress on the floor that might now never be used, he didn't hear a single commercial. Instead, the music was cut every fifteen minutes for recorded public announcements—about the curfew, about food pick-up points, about medical care. Anyone bitten should proceed immediately to the nearest hospital. If you suspect someone of having been infected with the parasite, contact the police. Do not try to handle the situation yourself. If you need shelter…

Seven o'clock came without a live news broadcast, the station's scheduling on autopilot. Seven thirty. Eight o'clock.

A soft knock came at his door. He sat up. "Yeah."

His mom peeked in. "Jane's going down for bed. Do you want to bring that out to the living room?"

He nodded, his head feeling like it weighed forty pounds. He dropped his feet on the floor and pushed himself up. He knew his mom was biting back an *It's going to be okay.*

He clutched the radio and cord in one hand and started for the door.

And stopped, turning his ear toward the boarded window.

His mother picked it up too, tilting her head.

The swish of tires grew louder.

His heart kicked. He dropped the radio on his bed and pushed past her.

The others were in the living room, Rich about to settle in the rocking chair.

"He back?" Buddy asked.

"Yeah. Gonna unlock the garage."

"Is that a good idea?" Rich said.

Buddy said, "We just sealed the place up so those fucking things wouldn't get in here. Now you're gonna throw open a door."

Shit. Dan called Ray's number. While it rang, his heart thudded—he realized he had no idea who'd actually pulled up outside. He'd just assumed.

Buddy was up and moving around, heading for his coat.

Dan chewed his lip.

Ray picked up halfway through the third ring.

"Are you okay?" Dan asked.

"Yeah, we're fine." *We*. Well, at least the trip was a success, he thought sourly.

Buddy flipped up his collar. "What's his plan?"

"Got any ideas on how to get into the house without letting bats in?" Dan asked.

"We were thinking of camping out in the car. At least we *made it* to the house."

"I'll take that." Dan's fingertips vibrated with the flood of relief. "What happened?"

"It just took a while to get Jamie and get out of there. Wish I'd brought a bottle of water or something with me. All I've got is cigarettes, and they're not helping my thirst."

In the car, Jamie said something about having to take a piss, and Ray, his voice turned from the phone said, "Use a soda cup."

Over the line came the *thud* of a fat body against a car window. He pushed his hand over his face, trying not to picture what that was like, being surrounded on four sides by glass. "Are you going to be okay out there all night?"

"Ain't got no choice, do we?"

"Yeah. Well. We'll see if we can come up with an alternative here. Hang tight." He turned off the phone, everyone watching him.

"So he's just gonna stay out there?" Buddy said, still with his coat on.

"Have they eaten?" Faye asked.

"I don't think so."

"I could get stuff out *to* them—" Rich started.

"Dad!"

"—but I don't know how we get it into the car without one of those things getting in, and I can't guarantee any wouldn't get into the garage when I opened the door to go out myself."

"They got blankets or anything?" Buddy asked. "They can't sit in the car like that, those things banging at the windows all night, the two of them exposed on all sides."

Dan paced, trying to think of any kind of workable plan. The only things Ray was likely to have in the Fury were fast food trash and junk mail.

"Maybe blankets could get them in here," Rich said.

"They don't have blankets," Dan said absentmindedly.

"*We* do," Rich said.

"Dad..." Sarah pulled forward on the couch.

"Shh. I've already been bitten. I can get them out to them. I'm thinking two layers of blankets each. Tell them to get that car as close to the garage door as possible. They just have to crack a window enough for me to feed the blankets through one by one. Once they're bundled up, I'll run them each to the house—"

"That's crazy!" Sarah said.

"And let those fucking things get in the garage," Buddy said. "And then what? The three of you are stuck there with 'em in there."

Dan chewed his cheek. There had to be something. There *had* to be.

"Don't get me wrong," Buddy said. "That's my brother out there, and I want him the fuck in here. But we've gotta be smart about this."

Dan was still half lost in his own thoughts. "We can't handle three infected people. There's not enough of us." He was still hoping there were enough of them to take care of just the one. So far so good, but...

Faye looked up. Looked at each one of them. "We could distract them."

"What?" Sarah said.

"We can uncover the windows in my bedroom, turn on the lights, turn on the TV. We can shut the bedroom door in case anything breaks through. They might be drawn to it." She at looked each of them again. "It's worth a try, isn't it?"

Her bedroom, like Dan's, was right above the garage. It might work.

"No," Sarah said. "No, we can't do this." She looked at her dad. "*You* can't do this."

"Who else then?" he said. "We've got two people out there, and we need to get them in here. And I'm already infected."

"I'll get blankets," Faye said.

"We can use some from my room." Dan went after her, leaving Rich and Sarah to hash it out. Hoping like fuck this worked, and that they weren't just about to fuck themselves in the ass with this stupid plan.

Outside the door to the garage, he pulled up Ray's number again.

"Are you sure about this?" Buddy asked, piling the blankets into Rich's arms.

Rich said, "As sure as I am about anything anymore."

"If any of those things get in the garage…"

"We're screwed pooches." He clutched the blankets to his chest.

Ray answered, and Dan told him the plan. Ray only had two comments: "Seriously?" and a quiet "Okay." Ray wanted to be out of the car as much as Dan wanted him out of there.

Dan nodded at the others.

"Jesus," Buddy said. "We're out of our fucking minds." He stepped to the bottom of the stairs, cupped his hands to his mouth, and yelled up for Faye to go ahead.

Feet bounced on the floor above. The murmur of the TV sifted down. The bedroom door banged shut.

"Well then," Rich said.

Buddy clapped him on the arm. "Take care, man."

Rich gave a nod, and Buddy swept the door open for him.

The garage lights came on.

Buddy shut the door and leaned against it with his eyes closed. "You think this'll work?"

"I sure as fuck hope so."

"We could be making the biggest strategic mistake possible. We could be a house full of suckers by morning, eating each other's faces off."

"Do you want to call it off?" Dan asked.

"No. I want my fucking brother in here where it's safe."

"Me too." *Me fucking too.*

In the garage, the lights clicked back off. The door to the outside opened, then closed quickly. It was out of their hands now.

Dan strained for any sign one of those things had slipped in while it'd had a chance.

The waiting took forever. He leaned on the wall, his legs shaky with adrenaline.

In the finished part of the basement, on the other side of a closed door, Jane's voice asked a question. They couldn't hear Sarah's response, but Dan pictured her smoothing the girl's hair in the dark and whispering, "Shh, it's all right."

He said to Buddy, in that little hallway between the garage, laundry room, and family room, "Do you believe in God?"

"*Now?*"

"Yeah."

He faced the door. "Jesus, what's taking them so long?"

Dan checked his phone. He itched to call Ray, ask the status. Itched to be up in his mom's room, where he could look out the window and see what was going on. She was being quiet up there. Probably standing in the hall, waiting for the go-ahead to reach in and flick the light back off. He and Buddy would take care of putting the boards back when they got upstairs.

A noise came from the far side of the garage. Dan pushed off the wall and stood at the door with Buddy, who rubbed his thumbs across his fingers, ready to do something—anything.

Stepping closer, putting his ear to the door, Buddy said, "I think they're inside."

The crack underneath was still dark. Dan heard soft sounds—it irritated him that he couldn't tell if they were the sounds of people moving under blankets or one of those things flapping its wings.

The end of the house shook as the door to outside thudded closed. Muffled voices came through. Footsteps. After a long moment, the crack under the door lit up.

"Everything okay out there?" Dan bumped against Buddy.

"I think we're good," Rich said. "Just making sure nothing hitched a ride in the blankets."

"Go tell your mom to turn the light off," Buddy said.

Dan took the stairs two at a time, rounding the corner when he got to the top.

The hallway was empty.

"Mom?"

The TV blared through her bedroom door. He stuck his head in his own room, then the guest room. "Mom?"

Jesus, don't tell me… He stopped in front of her door. "Mom, are you in there?"

The TV clicked off. The light under the door went out. He stepped back as the doorknob turned.

"Are they in?" She slipped through the doorway, pulling the door shut behind her.

"What the hell were you doing?"

"They didn't seem interested enough in the lights and TV. I stood in the window."

"*Mom.*"

"Don't tell me I risked my life for nothing. Did they—"

At the sound of feet, they looked toward the steps. Ray emerged first, gave a nod. Dan had never been so happy to see someone in his life.

Jamie was behind him, followed by Buddy and Rich, Buddy's hand on Rich's shoulder, Rich looking a little out of breath. Jamie's eyes, big and dark, engulfed his face. His blankets were wadded in his hands.

Faye headed past Dan, saying, "We saved dinner for you. Let me heat it up."

While they gathered in the kitchen, the sound of small feet came up the steps.

"Janie," Buddy said, his voice a warning before the girl even appeared in the doorway.

"Uncle Ray?" She was in her pajamas. Maisie the doll hung from her hand.

"Jane-Jane. You're supposed to be in bed."

"You're not supposed to be out at night."

He slid from his chair to give her a hug. "Won't happen again."

"Better not or you're grounded."

Smiling, he ruffled her hair.

The fact that they were actually there, and in one piece—and not bitten—started to sink in for Dan. Ray turned Jane around and nudged her back toward the stairs. Sarah appeared in the doorway, hugging herself.

"You want to let her sleep up here till we go back down?" Buddy asked.

"No, I'm going back down with her. I just wanted to see everyone for myself." She looked like she hadn't slept for a week, as if the night had taken its toll on her all at once. She dragged a lock of hair behind her ear and touched Jane's shoulder to get her attention.

"Do you need any help with anything?" Faye said.

"It'd be a big help if you could put everything back to normal."

Faye smiled and went over to hug her.

Dan turned to Jamie. "So what's the story?"

"I had to get out of Merrimack, you know? My parents were driving me toward suicide."

"That's where you've been through all of this?"

He gave half a shrug.

"You weren't bit, were you?" Dan asked.

"No."

As if Jamie would tell him if he were.

Rich said, "No shame in it if you were. These guys could take care of it. They've been doing a good job for me."

"Yeah," Dan said. "It'd be pretty tight, five people feeding two, but we'd find a way to make it work."

"Four, isn't it?" Rich said.

"I'll be donating if we have to support two people."

"Yeah?" Jamie said. He cocked his chin. "What's stopping you from doing it now?"

The explanation caught in his throat. Ray came in for him with a quick rundown, and Dan watched him talk—never so happy to see someone in the flesh in his *life*.

"We didn't want to take chances he'd caught something," Ray finished.

"Oh good," Jamie said, "I'd get to get the tainted blood. Good thing I *wasn't* bitten."

The microwave was going, a dinner plate turning inside.

Faye kissed the top of Ray's head. "Don't do that to us again."

"Yes, Mom."

And all was right with the world, Dan thought, clutching one of the blankets they'd discarded in his lap.

Ray caught his gaze and looked away.

Dan couldn't help but think there was something hollow in the back of his eyes.

"THE NATIONAL Guard and local law enforcement are overtaxed with the responsibility of protecting a panicked public. We ask everyone to..."

Ray, sitting on the living-room floor, pushed to his feet. "Cigarette."

"Me too," Jamie said.

"Anyone want tea?" Faye asked.

Dan, gnawing the side of his thumb, shook his head. Sarah's needles made quick, nervous clicks, a baby blanket slowly emerging from yarn Faye had dug from the back of the guest-room closet. At one point during the litany of recorded announcements, Buddy grumbled, "No fucking shit," his hand gripping a glass of water, because that was mostly what they were down to for beverages now.

Just another big family night at home, except that Ray had something he wasn't telling Dan, and Dan couldn't get him alone for a moment to pin him on it.

Long minutes passed.

Ray and Jamie didn't come back up.

The house was thick with stale air. Too many people, too few open doors—too few cracks for the fresh air outside to get in.

Hemmed in by the boards over the windows, Dan was about to climb out of his skull.

And Ray's behavior was gnawing at his guts.

He got to his feet.

"Are you all right, honey?" his mom asked.

"Yeah. I'm gonna grab some ibuprofen and go to bed." Under the blankets, he could pretend it was just really dark outside instead of going all to hell. He gave her a peck.

He had no intention of sleeping, though. He stepped over Ray's mattress on his way to his bed.

Ray had to turn in eventually.

He hoped.

He stripped down to his shorts and slipped between the sheets, half worried he'd get up in the morning and find Ray'd spent the night on the couch, avoiding him. Avoiding telling him what he was pretty sure he already knew. He just wanted Ray to tell him was overthinking things, that there was nothing to fucking worry about. Scout's honor.

He felt like he could still hear the click-clicking of the knitting needles from down the hall. He crossed his arms over his eyes. Waiting.

The floor creaked outside his door, but the footsteps headed across the hall.

A toilet flushed.

Dishes rattled in the kitchen.

After a while, the house went silent.

When he woke, he was on his stomach, hugging his pillow. He moved his eyes toward the door just as it eased open a crack—something he sensed more than saw moved in the pitch-blackness.

A body bumped the doorjamb, and he pictured Ray misjudging the distance as he tried to slip through in the dark.

The door clicked softly shut. A belt buckle jingled quickly, the soft sweep of leather sliding over denim.

"Hey," Dan whispered.

"Sorry. I was trying to not to wake you."

He pushed onto his elbows. "I was awake anyway."

The sounds were so familiar—Ray toe-heeling a boot off, then nudging it out of the way. He sat on the mattress on the floor to pull the other one off. Cigarette smoke wafted off his clothes.

"What happened when you went to get Jamie?" Dan asked.

"I had to do a little running around to find him."

"Let me guess: it wasn't the good part of town you found him in."

"Is there a good part of town? Jesus, I'm bushed. I was gonna take a shower, but I don't think I can stay up that long."

Dan stretched on his side, his cheek against the pillow.

The blankets on the floor rustled as Ray got under them.

"Feel better?" Dan asked.

"Being in bed? Fuck yeah."

"I mean after getting Jamie."

It took a little time, but a "Yeah" finally came. Another stretch of minutes passed, Dan listening to Ray breathe. Listening to his hand scrub his face.

"We've been through a lot together," Ray said finally, and Dan didn't know if he meant the two of them or if he was talking about Jamie—or all of them. "I've always been glad I met you, you know," he said.

"Yeah, me too."

"Who knew freshman football would have paid off?"

Dan smiled.

"Man, I was shit at it," Ray said. "I hated getting fucking tackled, everyone piling on me over a ball."

"I know. Everyone could see the whites in your eyes when you were running up the field."

After a moment of quiet, Ray said, "We had a good run."

"I don't hear the fat lady singing yet."

Ray rolled over. When he said, "'Night," his voice was pointing toward the bookshelf.

Dan closed his thumb in his fist to keep from chewing the nail down to bleeding. At least his headache was backing off.

See? People get headaches. It hadn't come with any buzzing or crazy thoughts. He was just worried as shit about the possibility that everything had suddenly taken a sharp turn for the worse. "You'd tell me if you got bit, right?" he said.

Ray mumbled something and pulled the blanket over his shoulder.

Dan thought about the zombie apocalypse. And how at first light he'd slip out to Ray's car to make sure buying a gun hadn't been part of what had taken him so long to get back.

Just in case.

CHAPTER THIRTY-EIGHT

DAN STARTLED awake. A thin crack of light crept along the edge of the plywood nailed over his window. When the engine outside cranked to life, he realized what had woken him: the shutting of a car door.

"Shit."

His feet thumped the floor. He struggled into his jeans as the car backed up.

That he couldn't even look out the fucking window drove him crazy.

Barefoot, he pounded down the stairs and out the front door in time to catch the glint of Ray's bumper as it disappeared around the curve.

"*Fuck.*"

Back inside, Jane swung her heel against the leg of a kitchen chair, scooping an oversized spoonful of Cheerios into her mouth.

"Ray gone?" his mom asked, pouring a cup of coffee.

"Did he say where he was going?" Dan asked.

"To pick up supplies."

"Did anyone go with him?" He hoped Ray had taken Rich. Heck, he even hoped he'd taken Jamie. Taking *anyone* meant he wasn't doing what Dan thought he was doing.

"Rich headed out fishing. Buddy's getting ready for work. And Jamie, I believe, is still sleeping. Coffee?"

"No. I'm gonna see if I can catch up to him."

"Honey, if he'd wanted you to go…"

"No shit, but I'm going anyway. How'd he seem this morning?"

Her spoon clinked the side of her mug as she stirred. "He seemed all right. Gave me a nice hug before he left."

"Shit, Mom." He jogged down the hallway. Yesterday's t-shirt, boots yanked over bare feet. His keys confounded him. Not in his pocket, not in his jacket, not on the nightstand. He checked his dresser, the kitchen counter, even the workbench in the garage in case he'd set them down on his way in last time he'd gone anywhere.

Sarah and Buddy were upstairs by the time he accepted the fact that Ray had taken his goddamned keys with him. "Mom, can I borrow your car?"

"Something wrong with yours?" Buddy asked.

"Honey, you don't even know where he was going."

"Who?" Buddy asked. "Jamie?"

"Ray."

Faye said, "He told me he saw a place while he was out yesterday that might have some food. But that could be anywhere."

"*He's not going to get fucking food.*"

The room went silent.

He wished everyone staring at him looked more like they got it and less like he'd lost it.

"What's going on?" said a lazy voice from behind him.

Dan spun.

Jamie, scratching his rumpled hair, yawned in the doorway.

"What happened yesterday?" Dan said. "When did Ray finally meet up with you?"

It took forever for that fucking yawn to pass. When it did, Jamie's voice was still thick from sleep. "I don't know. I wasn't looking at the clock."

Dan grabbed him by the shoulders and shoved him out of the doorway. Tempting as it was to keep shoving until he tripped down the stairs, he made a sharp turn with him instead, slamming his shoulders against the wall. "Was it after fucking *dark*?"

"It was starting to get dark maybe, yeah."

"Did you see any bats?"

"No. But I was trying to get in the car. He'd pulled right up to the steps."

"He didn't get out?"

Jamie shook his head.

"Okay, good." He kept hold of Jamie's shoulders, staring down at nothing while he thought. When he looked back up, he said, "How long had it been getting dark?"

Before Jamie could give him another line of bullshit about clocks, he cut him off with, "How long had it been since you felt like, 'Shit, I need to get inside?'"

Jamie's eyes cut away.

"*How fucking dark was it?*"

Dan shoved him. The pictures on the wall jumped—third-grade class portrait, a photo of his dad grinning in wading boots, Dan in his marching band uniform with the hat's strap digging under his chin. He let go of Jamie and stalked into the kitchen. "I need your keys, Mom."

"I'll need to move the truck," Buddy said as Faye pushed back her chair.

"I really don't care if I have to drive across the fucking yard to get out."

"You think he's been bitten?" Buddy said.

"I just about *know* he's been bitten."

"Stupid fucking asshole. Come on." Buddy hauled his coat on. "We'll take the truck."

CHAPTER THIRTY-NINE

Buddy slowed. The neighborhood was dead, everyone huddled in their apartments or long gone for points west. A soccer ball lay abandoned in the dirt at the edge of a sidewalk. Curtains rippled in a window, someone clutching them back to watch the truck creep by. The corner of Ray's driveway appeared beyond Buddy's weather-beaten fence. Buddy turned in, tires crunching loose pebbles. After ten feet, the asphalt fell apart. Dan held his breath as Buddy pulled around the corner of the building to the parking area.

But he knew even before they rounded it that Ray's car wouldn't be there.

"He might have broke down somewhere and walked," Buddy said.

The Ford's engine rumbled.

A shopping bag kicked up from the dirt and swept across to catch in the straggle of dead weeds between the parking area and Buddy's back yard.

"Maybe he's getting supplies like he said," Buddy offered.

Dan shook his head. "Go to Sound Block." It was the one other place he knew Ray had a key to.

Buddy put the truck in reverse and did a three-point turn. "All right. Where's it at?"

"Out by the airport."

The truck spit pebbles as Buddy gunned it out of the driveway.

At a traffic light on South Willow, Dan stared at the BatteriesPlus building. Sun glinted off the windows, save one that looked like a missing tooth—black with jagged edges around it. A man appeared, framed in it, the collar of his hunting jacket turned up. He threw a few stuffed shopping bags out before he hauled himself through, white clouds of breath leading the way in the cold.

Buddy punched it, and they sped through the intersection.

When they came around the corner for Sound Block, the site of the Fury made Dan go rubbery inside. Had they found him too late?

Buddy cranked the truck into the lot and braked sharply. It was still rocking back when Dan threw open the door and jumped out. He grabbed the door handle and jerked. Pain shot up his arm. *Shit.* He reached for his keys—and stopped, swearing, when he remembered he didn't *have* them.

"What's up?" Buddy asked.

Dan kicked the door—not that Ray would hear, tucked deep in the building. "God*damn*it."

None of the rehearsal rooms had windows. The only two on the building were the grimed-over pair at the office.

"Just a sec." Buddy climbed over the tailgate, his boots thunking on the bed. The slam of the toolbox lid hitting the back of the cab echoed in the empty lot. He jumped down with a hammer, stuffing a pair of leather work gloves in his back pocket. Dan followed him to the corner of the building.

"Cover your eyes."

Dan turned and crouched, his arm across his face.

Glass shattered. He spun back around. The jagged hole wasn't big enough to climb through. Buddy pulled the gloves on and started yanking shards from the frame. They cracked as he tossed them on the ground, the sounds thin and sharp.

"Step up." Buddy locked his fingers at knee level. Dan put one foot in there, the toe of the other against the wall, and pulled himself through as Buddy boosted him.

He tumbled the last bit, landing folded between a desk chair and a trashcan. He picked himself up and headed for the door as Buddy's boots scrabbled against the side of the building. The door came open easier than he was expecting, banging him in the shoulder. He took off through the hall, footfalls echoing the length of it.

If Ray didn't open the heavy wood door for him when he got to it, this whole plan was fucked.

He grabbed the handle to stop his momentum, and to verify that, yeah, it was fucking locked. He slapped the door with the palm of his hand. "Ray! Open up. It's me."

In the corner of his eye, he caught Buddy coming up the hall.

He pounded the door with the side of his fist. As Buddy neared, Dan put his mouth right up to it. "If you don't open up, I'm going to bang on it till my fucking knuckles break."

"Ray," Buddy called, "stop playing around. Open the fucking door."

Please don't be dead in there already. A tight, hot sensation pulled through him, making his eyes squeeze shut. *Please do not be fucking* dead *already.* "You can't leave us like this," he said, his voice thick in his throat.

Buddy jerked a look toward him.

"You didn't even fucking say *goodbye*!" He grasped the handle and tried to force the lock.

"Ray, open the fuck up," Buddy said. "I don't have time for this shit."

"Open the fucking door, Ray. It's me and Buddy. We're the only ones out here. Open the goddamned door." He smelled cigarette smoke. Fresh, or not? "I know you're in there, you asshole. Don't tell me you're gonna off yourself with me standing right here."

"Don't even fucking talk like that," Buddy said lowly—and louder: "Ray, goddamnit!"

Dan pushed his forehead against it. "What if you fuck it up? How'm I gonna finish it for you if I'm locked out here?"

"Jesus," Buddy said. "You fucking talk about that shit? You talk about killing yourselves after what happened to our mom?"

The knob shifted. Dan let go like it was on fire. The door opened inward. A cigarette jutted from Ray's mouth. His tired eyes squinted through smoke.

"I know you've been bit," Dan said.

"Can't put nothin' over on you."

"Yeah, well, stealing my car keys was a pretty big clue."

Ray gave a forced smile as he turned away. "Shoulda known better than to think that'd stop you."

"What I want to know," Buddy said, "is why the fuck you're here, when we have everything we need to take care of you back *there*."

Ray dragged a hand through his hair. Surreal. They'd been here—Dan didn't know how many times they'd been here, under these fluorescent lights, this shitty drop ceiling, even at this same time of the morning. They'd stagger into the daylight, blinking, debating whether they wanted eggs or burgers. *Damn him.*

Ray's fingers were like sticks, pinching the cigarette. His hair stayed stuck up where his hand had run through it.

Dan dropped beside him on the couch, the cushions giving under his weight, hard springs underneath jarring him to a stop. He pressed the heels of his hands against his eyes. "So what was he doing when he wasn't where he was supposed to be? Looking for one last fix?"

With a sigh, Ray said, "Probably."

Anger pounded in him. This was Jamie's fucking fault. He made a call, he said he'd be somewhere, and fucking *lives* depended on his fucking being there. One. Simple. Fucking. Thing. "You never should have fucking went after him."

"If it'd been me that called, you'd have come got me."

"If it'd been you, I wouldn't have had to, and if you were *him*, no I fucking wouldn't have. I'd have told you to find a fucking ride. Or at least I'd have turned around and come back when it started getting late."

"Yeah, that's on me," Ray said.

"You're a fucking idiot," Dan said.

"Believe me, I've been telling myself that all night." His hand trembled as he tapped off an ash.

"You can't save your mom, you know," Dan said.

Ray jolted, leaned forward to crush his cigarette in the ashtray to cover it. Buddy braced a hand against a wall, rubbed his forehead against his outstretched arm as he muttered, "Fuck."

Ray'd never had closure on his mom, just twenty years of what-ifs. What if he'd stayed home sick that day? What if he'd acted like he'd needed her more? What if he'd done a better job taking care of her?

"The Jamie Martins and the Cassandra Fords of the world either get serious about saving themselves, or they self-destruct," Dan said. "We've had this fucking conversation. The key fucking word there is 'self.' It's all on them. You couldn't save her, and you didn't do Jamie any fucking favors getting yourself bitten. Give him two, three days, maybe a whole fucking week before he runs out of whatever stash he's got, then he's gonna find someone to come out to Mom's and take him somewhere the fuck else." The stiffness of Ray's shoulders said he wasn't helping matters, but his mouth didn't want to shut up. He was pissed off. Not at Ray, though Ray's never being able to say no to helping Jamie did piss him off, but mostly he was pissed off at *Jamie.*

Only Jamie wasn't around to punch in the face.

"How'd you get bit?" Buddy asked quietly.

Ray rubbed his lighter with his thumb, then clutched it. "When I couldn't get hold of Jamie, I thought maybe he'd come here. He'd moved in before, right? And this place's got no windows, good locks on the doors… So I pulled up just as it was starting to get dark, and I went inside. The place was dead, empty. I probably took too long making sure of that. When I came out, it was darker, and my car was *right fucking there* at the front door—but not close enough. I fought two of those fucking things off, got in the car, and beat the shit out of the steering wheel for a few minutes. Then, fuck." He dropped his lighter on the table. "I figured I had nothing to fucking lose, right? Might as well find his ass." He closed his eyes and rubbed them. "I should have given up before it got late."

Dan tipped his head back. "So what was your plan now?"

"I was gonna fuck around here for a bit, one last time." Enough of their gear was there for that. He could turn the speakers all the way up, not bother a soul.

"And then?" Dan asked.

"And then go home."

"Home my mom's place, or home—"

"Home-home."

Buddy stepped away from the wall, crossing his arms. "And then?"

"And then wait. I'm gonna wait this shit out."

"Wait?" Dan said.

"The fuck are you gonna wait for?"

"Either those things it put in me will kill me or they won't," Ray said. "No matter which way it goes, though, it's gonna kill *them*."

"Okay, while that's noble and all…" Dan said.

"Yeah," Buddy cut in. "Whatever. We need you both back home, and we'll fucking take care of it like we're doing for Rich, so stop fucking around and come on."

"No." Ray shook a fresh smoke out of his pack. Dan wondered how long till he ran out entirely.

"Yes." Buddy grabbed him by the elbow. "I don't have time for this. I've gotta get to work." He hauled Ray off the couch, and Ray jerked free.

"So go to work. No one's stopping you."

"Get in the truck. I want to make sure your ass is settled at Faye's first."

"No." He jerked out of Buddy's grip again.

Buddy bent and grabbed him around the waist, shoulder to stomach, like he planned to haul Ray out like a sack of potatoes.

Ray's heel knocked the coffee table over. He lost his cigarette. Buddy's work boot flattened it. Ray flung his elbow sharply, knocking Buddy's chin aside, giving himself the chance to squirm free. Buddy came at him again, and Ray took a swing, his eyes wide. His knuckles connected with Buddy's lip.

He stepped back, his chest heaving, his eyes pinned to the shine of blood seeping from Buddy's mouth.

Buddy touched it. "Fuckhead." His fingers came away with blood. He tongued the split and said, "Stubborn fucking asshole." He ran at Ray again, grappling him before he could get away. Ray's breaths came short and quick, from high in his chest. Buddy's blood smeared along Ray's hand as he tried to push his brother away. Buddy snagged his shirt from the back, rucking it up as Ray's boots slipped and slid on the floor.

Blood stained the corner of Buddy's mouth like the Joker's smile, Buddy gritting his teeth, peeling his lips back, dodging Ray's elbow as it flew again.

Shit. Dan got himself moving, his shin knocking the coffee table out. He grabbed Buddy's jacket at the arm, shoved a hand between the two of them, pushed his body between them, backing up, moving Ray back, against the wall.

Buddy came with them, his chest to Dan's. His finger pointing past Dan's shoulder. "This isn't fucking over."

"Not now." Dan held him back.

"You're not fucking staying here," Buddy said to his brother.

"The blood," Dan said. "You've got blood on you."

Buddy swiped at his mouth. His eyes had too much white around them, the way the Fords' eyes got when they were fighting to get their way.

"We can argue about this tonight," Buddy said. "It won't kill you to wait a little fucking while."

"I'll talk to him," Dan said. Ray's frantic breaths came right behind him. The tip of Buddy's tongue touched where his lip was swelling. And Dan said, "Wait outside for a few, okay? Let him calm down."

Buddy gave his brother one last stare before turning away. On the way to the door, he looked at the red on his hand, brought his fingers to his lip again. "Shit."

"I'll talk to him." Dan followed, closing the door behind Buddy. Finally he turned.

By the far wall, Ray opened his fingers. His hand shook as he looked at Buddy's blood. He twitched his head to the side, gaze searching, stopping on a ragged towel lying over a guitar stand. He snatched it free and clutched it over his knuckles. Without lifting his head, he said, "I don't want them to get any."

"What?"

"I don't want to fucking feed them. They don't get *any*." He scrubbed his knuckles with the towel before wadding it, searching the room for someplace to put it. He strode back to the couch, toed a cushion up, and shoved it underneath, kicking it back in place with the heel of his boot.

"It's gonna be okay," Dan said.

"We're fucked."

"We're not. We have five—"

"I've gotta get out of here. All I can smell is the fucking blood." His shoulder banged Dan's, half turning him around. He yanked open the door.

Dan followed him into the hallway.

Buddy pushed off a wall. "Are you going back?"

Ray put a hand up, heading for the front door, for the sunshine and the parking lot, the fresh air.

Buddy cocked his head at Dan, mouth open, wanting answers.

"Just give me some time," Dan said.

Outside, Ray dropped into a crouch on the pavement, head bent, fingers tented against the ground.

"Go on," Dan said to Buddy. "I'll get it straightened out."

"I'm sorry," Buddy said. "I fucking—"

Dan shook his head. Shit happened.

He dug his keys out of his pocket. "Call me if you need anything."

"Yeah."

"Call me if anything happens." On his way by Ray, he said, "If you're not fucking home tonight, I'm coming to fucking get you, if I have to bring a straitjacket to do it."

As the truck pulled out, Dan said to Ray, "All right. Thanks to you, I don't have a car, so you're my ride."

Ray didn't move.

Dan rubbed his arms through the sleeves of his jacket. After a moment of staring at their rehearsal building, he said, "I'm surprised no one's moved in. It's got almost no windows, lots of locks…"

Ray still didn't answer, giving him time to think of the ways it might not be such a good place to hide out—lots of people with keys, lots of dead ends with no way out. And now one of the windows was smashed in.

"Let's go to my place," Ray said, looking at the pavement, like he was thinking of getting up but wasn't ready to do it yet. "You can take my car home from there."

Dan opened his mouth—then shut it. No point in arguing out in the cold. Best to give Ray time to think things over. "I need the keys," he said.

"Shyeah." Ray took another glance at the faded stain of blood on his hand before getting up. "I'll drive to my place."

CHAPTER FORTY

THEY argued up the back steps—not over Ray going back to Deerfield, but over Dan's *not* going to Deerfield immediately. Plenty of daylight left, he insisted.

"I'm showering." Ray dropped the keys on the kitchen table. "I can still smell that blood."

"Okay." Dan grabbed a guitar on his way into the living room, made himself comfortable on the couch. It was in every way pandering when he started playing some of Ray's favorite stuff—delta blues, Blind Willie Johnson's "Dark Was the Night." Ray sang it better than he could, but he gave it his best. A weight lodged in his chest as he worked the strings. He had to push it aside to get the words out, closing his eyes under the heft of it between verses.

He was working his way through Robert Johnson's "Cross Road Blues" when Ray came into the room, wet hair dripping on a clean t-shirt.

He dropped into his usual chair, a bottle of Jack in hand. Dan finished the song and let the last notes fade. "What are you going to do? Really?"

Ray unscrewed the cap. "Wait it out."

"You can't… People *die* not getting blood."

"Those people did get blood. At least once."

"What?"

"As far as we know, everyone who's been bitten has either reported to the hospital, where they're given blood, or attacked someone and got blood. Or hell, maybe some of them did what you did: cut themselves and got a taste of their own. Whatever way, as far as I can tell, no one's *not* had blood."

"And your theory is what?"

"That these things are weak if they don't get any blood. That they can be beat."

Dan dropped back. He stared at Ray. "We don't even know if it's true, that everyone who's died from these things tasted blood first. It's a pretty big assumption."

"We don't know it's false either. I'm not feeding these fuckers." He tipped the whiskey up, swallowing hard and long. When he finished, he held it out. And that was an idea: get drunk, have an excuse not to leave. He leaned across and took it. At least he could drink to the fact that Ray wasn't planning on shooting himself in the head. So far.

The liquor's heat worked its way down his throat. He closed his eyes to savor it. "So that's your plan?"

"Yep."

Dan put a foot against the coffee table, nudging a book on metaphysics out of the way. It kept going. He leaned forward to catch it and caught sight of another. "*Parasite Rex*?" He cocked an eyebrow.

Ray stuck out his arm, wanting the bottle back. "I had to start researching somewhere."

"What are you thinking?" Dan asked. "Seriously."

"I'm thinking I haven't given them any blood, *won't* give them any blood, and we'll see who outlasts who. At any rate, you need to get out of here before it gets dark. They need you back there, and I don't need you here when the blood urge starts up."

"Are you feeling it yet?"

"No. I'm just freaked the fuck out about it."

"Okay then." Dan pulled the guitar back into his lap.

SHADOWS STRETCHED along the floor. The toilet flushed. Dan studied the ceiling, waiting.

Ray stepped into the doorway with a beer. "You need to book if you're gonna get there tonight."

"I'm not going anywhere."

"Fuck you aren't."

"I'm not." He pulled off his boots while Ray watched, dropped his feet on the table. Bare, because he'd never gotten around to socks before leaving that morning.

The whiskey bottle was a lot lighter than it had been.

"Fine," Ray sighed, turning away from the doorway. "Help me pull the shades and get some blankets over the windows."

WHEN IT got dark out—when the city was unsettlingly silent—Ray came out of his bedroom, pulling on his jacket.

"Where're you going?"

"Out."

"Out where?"

"Out not here."

Dan shoved his feet in his boots. The door shuddered closed when he was two steps away. He grabbed the handle and yanked it open. The latch on the storm door was cold against his hand. His breath fogged the glass. Night lay on the other side—night and those things.

Ray swung around the landing, starting down the steps.

Dan pushed the door open and stepped out.

The cold hit him full-on. No time to get a jacket. "Wait up."

The footfalls stopped, started coming back up. Dan crossed the landing, giving a nervous glance to the sky beyond the porch's overhang.

"Get the fuck back inside," Ray said.

"Where you go, I go."

Ray looked up and ducked a little. "Shit." He came pounding back up the last few steps, grabbing Dan.

Wings flapped. Dan ducked, bringing a hand over his head. This could have been a really stupid idea.

Ray dragged him—"Come on"—and kept going, right back into the warm apartment. Once Dan was in, he slammed the door behind them.

"What the fuck are you doing?" Ray asked.

Dan rubbed his arms. It must have been fifteen degrees out there. "Sticking with you."

"Don't make this harder than it is."

"You're the one making it fucking harder than it is. We have everything back in Deerfield. Tubes, needles. We can fucking take care of this."

"And then what?" Ray said.

"And then we keep fucking going!"

Ray pushed off the door.

If *he* wasn't taking his coat off, Dan was putting his on. He was cold anyway. Christ, he was going to have to stay awake all night to make sure Ray didn't slip out. "We keep fucking going." He followed Ray into the living room.

"Call your mom," Ray said. "Let her know you'll be back tomorrow."

"Are you coming?"

He dropped into his chair, fishing for his cigarettes. "Nope."

"Why? What the fuck are you accomplishing here?"

"Listen, you fucking get it or you don't. Call Faye. She'll be worried out of her skull."

"I *want* to get it," Dan said. "Help me fucking get it."

Ray pointed the remote at the TV. A riot in New York flashed onto the screen.

Fuck him then. Dan dragged his phone out. Listened to it ring. When his mom answered, he said, "Hey—yeah, I'm fine. We're fine. No, I'm not gonna be back tonight. I'm gonna stay at Ray's awhile. Yeah, as long as it takes." Watching Ray the whole time, Ray shaking his head, lighting his cigarette. "No, we're good. We'll be fine. How's everything there?" He listened for a while, catching up. When he hung up, he said, "They could really use us there."

"They could really use *you* there."

"Jamie's grudgingly willing to donate, but they're worried about the drug use."

Ray dragged on his cigarette, his face turned away.

Dan sat on the edge of the coffee table. "There's seven donors to two infected, you know. You and Rich can still donate. He needs blood that isn't his, you need blood that isn't yours."

"I don't need any fucking blood. I told you."

"Yeah. It's a great plan. I'm fucking applauding you inside."

Ray gave him the finger.

CHAPTER FORTY-ONE

THE phone jarred him from the uncomfortable armchair he'd parked in front of Ray's bedroom door. As the ringtone played, Ray rolled over in bed. Dan fumbled it, trying to cut off the sound, and brought it to his ear. "Yeah."

"How're things going?" Buddy asked.

"Uneventful."

"He coming back here?"

Dan scrubbed the sleep out of an eye. "Not yet." He had to take a piss, and his neck sent a jolt of pain to his skull when he glanced toward the kitchen window. Early morning sunlight brightened the place at least, making the empty can of Spaghetti-Os on the counter look almost festive.

"Are you at Ray's? Should I come by?"

"I am, and no." He fought a yawn and lost to it.

"Tell him to get over himself and have some sense. We all came out here for safety in numbers, and two of our numbers aren't fucking here anymore."

"Will do." He passed the message along when he hung up. Ray grunted. Dan unfolded himself, nudging the chair with his knee so he could get to the bathroom. He kept an ear out while he was pissing, just in case.

Once Ray was up and in the shower again, Dan turned on the TV, checking the news.

Ray came out, toweling his hair. "Anything new?"

"Nothing you'd want to hear about. What do you want to do today? We should find some food. You've got shit in your cabinets."

"Yeah, I brought most of it to your mom's."

"You're gonna need food to fight this off," Dan said. "Keep your strength up if you're going to outlast them."

"You're humoring me, aren't you?"

"Yeah, well. What else can I do?" He dragged his coat back on. He hadn't bothered taking the boots off, just in case. He wished he'd fucking worn socks.

THEY SCOUTED everywhere they could think of in Ray's car, managed to scrounge up a few grocery bags of stuff they could use. It meant breaking into a Market Basket, but they hadn't been the first—all they had to do was step through smashed glass. They'd picked through what was left on the shelves, Dan asking, "How do you feel about beets?" Ray'd made a face. Dan put them in the sack anyway.

"Let's hit the Vista on Main," Dan said.

"You want to go by your place?"

"Nah." He wanted to go by Dunkin' Donuts, which was no doubt shuttered like everything else. But still…he wanted to go by, see for himself. Patricia clung to his thoughts, all mixed up with what'd happened to Bethany that night her husband had gone nuts.

"How are you holding up?" Dan said.

"Neck's a little itchy," Ray said.

"Yeah, I picked up on that."

"Headache's there too. I threw some aspirin in the bag."

"That won't help much," Dan said.

"I like to feel like I'm doing something proactive."

"Like reading a kid's book about parasites?"

"You should try it. It was interesting. I wanted *The Behavioral Ecology of Parasites* too, but I guess UPS stopped delivering to residences around the time I was expecting it to show up."

"Slow up," Dan said, putting a hand on the dash, looking past Ray to the brick-and-beige coffee shop on the corner. Parking lot empty. Lights off. Two windows smashed, glass glittering on the pavement in the sunlight. He dropped back into his seat, his insides feeling like they'd been dragged through that glass.

"You all right?"

"Yeah." He stared at the other side of the street, across to the mill buildings on the river. Nothing was going to be all right.

They brought the groceries up in a single trip while a man in another yard crossed his arms and watched them make the trek up the stairs. Dan hoped the guy wasn't thinking about their food. He broadened his shoulders, tried to make them look less worth coming after. Of course, if the guy had a gun…

When they were locked back in Ray's kitchen, Ray said, "Will you please just leave? Take care of Jane for me. Help Buddy and Sarah out. Take care of your fucking mom. You left her with Jamie, of all people."

Dan pulled a few dented boxes of rice from the bag and headed for a cabinet.

"They need you," Ray said. "And I need you the fuck out of here."

"Mmhm."

He called his mom enough ahead of dinnertime to tell her not to set plates for them.

At two in the morning, when Dan had his eyes closed, fabric brushed his knee. He peeled his eyes open.

Ray was dressed—boots, coat, ready to go. He crept across the dark kitchen. A floorboard creaked.

Dan grasped the doorframe and pulled himself up from the chair. "Where are we going?"

"Nowhere if you're smart."

"Are you trying the leave-in-the-middle-of-the-night-so-Dan-won't-follow thing again?"

"Yep."

Dan shrugged into his coat. "I'm following."

"Do whatever the fuck you want." Ray jerked the door open. The windowpanes rattled.

"When we get back," Dan said, "can I borrow some socks?" His toes squished in his boots. He must have been sweating while he slept.

"You could go home and get yourself some socks." Ray crossed the landing in quick strides, hands shoved in his pockets. Turning the corner, he started down the stairs, the heels of his boots giving a sharp *rat-a-tat.*

Dan flipped the collar up on his jacket, pushed his hands in his own pockets, and hunched in as he followed, one eye on the night sky.

His breath streamed out white in the cold.

The neighborhood was so silent it seemed breakable, like a sheet of ice.

Ray got to the bottom of the two flights, stopped, swore, and started marching back up, barreling right into Dan, who grabbed the railing and turned to let him by.

He gave another quick glance toward the sky—things flying in the moonlight—before hurrying up after Ray.

Wings flapped like sheaves of paper, fast.

His boot caught the edge of the stair tread. He shot his hands out, touching wood with his fingertips long enough to right himself. When he hit the landing, the thing slammed into his shoulder. He threw a hand against the wall to stay on his feet and covered the back of his neck with his other hand.

Ray held the door open, an arm outstretched, his gaze darting to the sky, where a mass of parasites circled and dove.

A fat, black body banged into the wall ahead of Dan. He drew back, then rushed by before it could pick itself up. He ducked through the door. Ray jumped in behind, yanking it shut.

The thing slammed the storm door's glass, making them jump. Ray threw the heavier door shut. "You're a fucking idiot," he whispered.

"It takes one to know one."

Ray jerked out of his jacket, his lips pressed together, his cheeks ruddy from the cold.

"About those socks..." Dan said.

"How about a shower while you're at it?" Ray shot back.

"You're either going to have to put up with the stink or come to Deerfield, 'cause I'm not letting you slip away while I clean up."

Ray went into his bedroom. A drawer rattled open, slammed shut. He threw a pair of socks onto the chair in the doorway. A moment later, a t-shirt and a pair of sweats followed.

Dan smiled.

IN THE early morning, the apartment's windows rattled with an explosion. Dan pulled the shades and looked out, but the window facing where the sound had come from had another building fifteen feet in front of it. He could barely see the edge of the sky over it.

"The world is going to shit," Ray said.

Dan made coffee—weak so their stash would last—and took his out on the porch, which faced the wrong way to see anything. A few of the neighbors had gathered in the middle of the street, their hair sticking up every which way, eyes bleary, one of them with a blanket tugged around her shoulders.

"What happened?" he called down.

No one knew.

CHAPTER FORTY-TWO

ELLIOT HOSPITAL was on WMUR, half of it a heap of smoking rubble, emergency crews carrying bodies out of the part that was still standing. The fourth floor had been a quarantine unit for suckers; someone must have decided to get rid of them in one swoop.

Dan searched the faces of rescue workers, looking for anyone he knew.

Ray sat on the other end of the couch, his forehead braced on tented fingers.

"Bad, huh?" Dan asked, meaning the headache.

Ray's eyelids creased. His teeth clenched. "I wish you'd go the fuck away. You're making it worse."

"Probably." He popped a handful of popcorn in his mouth. It was a little singed—he hadn't shaken the pan enough—but it'd been one of the few snack foods left at the grocery store; he wasn't about to waste it.

"Can you turn it the fuck off? I don't want to hear this shit anymore."

Dan pointed the remote, then dropped back on the couch. "You want me to put on some music?"

"I want you to fucking leave." He propped his elbows on his knees and rubbed his skull with both hands.

"Buzzing bad?"

"You know what's going to fucking happen. Is that what you want? I attack you, get a taste of blood, fuck up my entire plan, and you think I'll go back to Deerfield with you?"

Dan tossed another kernel in his mouth. "I don't care whether you do or don't go to Deerfield. I just care that I'm with you whatever you do. You and me, baby. 'Cause Two Tons of Dirt is nothing without both of us. I wish one of us had brought a laptop. We could watch Netflix."

Ray's phone rang. Ray didn't move. Dan picked it up. "Hey."

"Hey," Buddy said. "Ray around?"

Dan turned a little on the couch. "You want to talk to your brother?"

Ray shook his head.

"He's not feeling well," Dan told him. "Headache." He listened to Buddy describe the ways he was going to strangle Ray, then asked a few questions about the state of things out there. When he hung up, he set the phone down saying, "Jane wants to know when she's going to see her Uncle Ray again. She's having nightmares, thinking you're dead already."

"Yeah, and she doesn't need to watch that happen firsthand."

"Wouldn't have to if you'd give up your martyrdom and go back."

"I'm gonna go lie down."

He waited till Ray was out of the room before dropping back on the couch and pressing his hands against his eyes. He could find rope—tie him up, put him in the trunk, haul him back. At the same time, he wanted to be *here*. Maybe as much as Ray did. He just didn't want Ray killing himself in the process.

He made Hamburger Helper without hamburger, brought a plate to Ray in the dark bedroom.

"Beets for dessert if you finish that," he said.

"Fuck off." Ray rolled over, shoving his head under a pillow. Muffled, he said, "I can't even fucking hit you. I want to beat the shit out of you right now, and I can't even fucking hit you because it might draw blood."

"Good thing I haven't been shaving," Dan said on his way back to the kitchen. "A razor nick could be your undoing."

"I should just fucking leave," Ray called. "Fuck worrying about you getting bitten if you're dumb enough to follow."

His phone rang while he was picking up his plate from the counter. His mom's number. He knew he'd have to talk to her again, knew she wouldn't be happy.

Instead, Buddy's voice said, "Jesus, I've been trying to get through for hours."

Blood ran cold down Dan's scalp.

"I was just putting my boots on to come see you in person. First things first: we've got it under control."

He lowered his voice. "What happened?" Leaving the plate. Opening the back door. Getting out onto the landing, where Ray wouldn't hear.

"Your mom's been bitten, but we've got it under control. She's not hurt."

He felt like he was trapped in rock, weight and silence pressing on every inch of him. Leadenly he pushed the storm door shut till it latched. "What happened?"

"One got in the garage somehow. She went down to scoop some rice out of the tub, and it got her while she was bent over."

He paced, heat rushing over his skin, making him clammy. Making him sick. Two infected, and only three uninfected to take care of them. And no way Ray would go back there now, add to the load. No way was Ray *not* going to insist he went back. Three for two—it wouldn't be enough.

Fuck.

"We're thinking of moving," Buddy said.

"What? Where?" The WMUR newscast flared into his head, smoking rubble. "They blew up a fucking hospital today." Dan had no idea who 'they' actually were, but it was someone willing to sacrifice the uninfected to get rid of the infected.

"Yeah, we heard it on the news," Buddy said.

"Where are you gonna go?" Where *could* they go? "You're not thinking of the shelters. They'll separate you guys—you, Sarah, and Jane one way, Mom and Rich the other."

"There's a place that's not doing that. They're doing what we're doing. Up in Vermont."

"Vermont?"

"It used to be a school, a little south of Burlington. It's probably mobbed to hell by now, but we're going to try it. Listen, I'll tell you more when I get there."

"No, don't come." Dan looked toward the bedroom.

"Dan, come on. He's my fucking *brother*."

Dan pushed his hand into his hair, pulling till it hurt. With his eyes closed, he said, "If you're leaving in the morning, you guys have a lot to do. And you don't—man, you don't fucking need to come out to Manchester and maybe get yourself killed when they need you. The *hospital*, Bud. They blew up the fucking *hospital*. That's not even a mile from here."

He could almost hear Buddy's jaw grinding through the phone. Finally, Buddy said, "Talk to Ray. We're leaving in the morning. Talk him into coming. It's his kind of shit, everyone banding together to help each other."

CHAPTER FORTY-THREE

"VERMONT," Ray said, wrapped in a quilt, perched on the edge of the couch. The blankets were back over the windows. The only light was the glow of the TV.

The Hamburger Helper had no charm without the beef in it, especially when it was half cold. Especially when his brain kept replaying the scene of his mom's garage: the blue Rubbermaid tub they were storing the rice in, its lid resting against its side while his mom scooped a measuring cup through the grains. The quick beat of wings, the lights flickering over the walls as the thing swooped toward her stooped shape.

He set his plate on the coffee table.

"What happens when they get there and it's not that?" Ray asked. "When it's been overrun or shut down, or it never was to begin with?"

Dan washed what he'd had of dinner down with a glass of water.

"It's out of control." Ray pulled the blanket tighter.

Dan rubbed his eyes. He hated to admit it, but this was a weight off—their families would go, and maybe they'd do all right. But he'd never know, not unless this whole shit fiasco got resolved. And until then, he could imagine them on their way to Vermont, Buddy's truck, Rich's car, everyone nervous and hopeful. His mom on the passenger side, smiling a little, maybe, as she slipped her hand into Rich's. She deserved that, right? Not to be alone at the end?

"This just makes me more fucking convinced," Ray said.

"Of?"

"That I'm not fucking giving in to these things. And that you need to go the fuck home." He rose and walked out of the room, the blanket hugged around him like a shroud.

Dan slept with his neck at an odd angle again, a stab of pain going up behind his ear when he jerked upright, confused in the pitch blackness of drawn shades. The claws of sleep gripped him. His ears strained for what had woken him.

Something moved in the dark. Bare feet on bare wood. The thump of a nightstand against a wall.

He got his limbs moving, scrambling over the top of the chair, toppling it, nearly landing on his chin on the linoleum. Crouching on the balls of his feet, he shoved the chair between them, keeping low, ready to dart in whichever direction he could. His breath hit the back of the chair as he peered over the top.

"*Ray*," he whispered quickly.

A heel came down in the dark in front of the chair, hard and unsteady, making the floor vibrate under Dan's boots.

"*Ray.*"

Ray lumbered into the doorway, face like a sliver of moon in what light the kitchen offered. His shin banged the front of the chair, jolting in Dan's hands. He clutched it harder, his muscles cocked, ready to jump. Ray moaned. His hands reached in the air like a blind man's.

His shin knocked the chair again. Dan did the only thing he could think of, jerking the chair back, then shoving it forward, hard. The shove sent Ray stumbling backward. He tripped over his own foot, landed hard on the wood floor. Dan reflexively thought of the downstairs neighbors—but he hadn't heard anyone else in the building since he'd arrived.

He jerked the chair out of the way and lunged for the door, stretching inside of the bedroom, right over Ray, to grasp the knob.

Ray gripped his calf, his thin fingers digging into his leg. He hung on to the knob and the doorjamb, shaking his foot, trying to get free.

Ray's fingers dragged at him. His mouth opened, his teeth flashing in what little light the room held.

Dan kicked out, knocking Ray in the chest, jarring his teeth shut with a *click*. Ray's mouth popped right back open, lunging for him.

With a grunt, Dan kicked, swift and sharp, then yanked his leg back, wrenching it free of Ray's grip.

Ray's teeth snapped together.

"*Fuck.*" He needed to get Ray out of the way of the fucking door. He searched the darkness, keeping one eye toward Ray while he tried to think, *fast*. The closest thing at hand was the chair. With one last kick at Ray, he scrambled back, grabbed the chair, and put it between them. Digging his boots against the floor, he steamrolled Ray backward with the chair. Ray's sweatpants slid over the hardwood. His fingers clawed at the chair's seat cushion.

There was a *snap*—Ray's fingernail breaking as he tried to haul himself up by the chair's wooden arm.

Dan braced his feet and gave one more heave, cramming Ray between the chair and the bed. He backpedaled, boot heels clicking. He grasped the knob and hauled the door shut with a sharp *clap*.

He sank to the floor with his back against the door, clutching the knob.

The legs of the chair slid behind the door.

Hard knocks came across the floor, like knees hitting it.

Ray's fingernails scraped wood just behind Dan's head.

The knob jiggled.

Dan gripped harder.

Ray made a croaking noise that drew the skin behind Dan's ears tight. Ray's palms made the door bounce against Dan's skull.

His heart thudded into his breastbone, like one of the fucking things out there throwing itself against a window.

A parasite smacked the kitchen window like a rotten pumpkin, rattling the glass, making Dan push his back against the door and grip the knob tighter.

Something pushed under the door, poking him. He slid sideways enough to put a hand on it. The tips of Ray's fingers. Then they were gone. Ray hit the door again, higher, then higher, getting back to his feet. The doorknob twisted. Dan held on with both hands, hanging his weight off it.

It went on for long minutes—Ray, not even really *Ray*, on the other side of the door. Dan's temples ached from gritting his teeth. His thigh muscles screamed from holding his crouch. His knuckles felt like they'd locked up, gripping the doorknob so long.

A *thud* shook the floor.

He held his breath, listening in the silence, mind racing. He could grab a knife from the drawer, make one small fucking cut in his own skin, and end the whole thing. Force Ray to give up and go to Vermont.

He pressed his forehead against his fists, still clutching the knob. Ray would never forgive him. Maybe if this whole problem got sorted out and things got back to normal, he'd get over it. But would he ever trust him again? Deep down? Or would he go to his grave resenting him for not letting him play his conviction out?

However much he *wanted* to make Ray do what they knew worked, he couldn't, not without his consent, because however much Ray might have wanted to take *him* to the hospital, he never had—not as long as Dan was saying he didn't want to go. Even when Dan had been ready to give up and go in, Ray had kept his eye on the ball, come up with another plan. Got him through the fucking thing.

He owed him that.

His knees creaked as he pulled to his feet. There had to be something in the drawers. He *hoped* there was something in the drawers, because if he wasn't going to go against Ray's wishes, and if he wasn't going to leave and let Ray deal with it by himself, then he had to do his part to make it work.

CHAPTER FORTY-FOUR

Ray came to violently, teeth snapping, body jerking. Dan backed away from the end of the bed, wrapping his hand around the broomstick he'd armed himself with.

The electrical cords held.

Dan rubbed his jaw with the side of his arm, the bruise from the flying elbow he'd caught tingling. At least he hadn't fucking gotten bit.

Ray's arms were above his head, wrists tied together to the headboard. Dan wasn't sure whether he'd needed to tie Ray's ankles to the footboard, but better safe than sorry.

He took a few slow steps around the bed, watching his best friend snap and growl like something from a horror movie. He clutched the edge of the dresser, something solid to hold on to while his palm throbbed around the broom's handle. Is this what it had been like when their places had been reversed, when Dan had been the one attacking? Or was it worse now because they knew what was fucking going on.

He wondered if this was all he had left of Ray now. If Ray wasn't going to take any blood, was it just going to be *this*, until it was over?

If it gets worse—if he starts to look like it's killing him… Fuck consent. Ray would hate him, but he'd be alive to do it.

Ray lost consciousness again.

Dan turned on the overhead light long enough to make sure Ray's stomach still dipped and rose with short, shallow breaths, then turned it back off.

The chair was uncomfortable as ever.

Dan laid the broomstick across his lap and got no sleep.

CHAPTER FORTY-FIVE

He heard the footsteps long before they got to the door. He stopped stirring the full-strength cup of coffee he'd just poured. The windows were still covered, sunlight peeking weakly around the edges of the blankets.

The storm door creaked open. Knuckles tapped the door.

He let the spoon drop against the side of the mug and dragged a hand through his hair as he headed across the room, not looking forward to the confrontation with Buddy he knew was coming.

He recognized his mom's hair through the window before anything else. Putting a hand against the door, he peered out at her.

"Danny," she said.

"Mom. What are you doing here?"

"I needed to see you."

"Mom, I heard. I'm so sorry."

"We're leaving," she said. "Can you let me in?"

He glanced toward the bedroom. Turned back to her. Infected or not, she was still at risk from Ray. He had faith in the electrical cords, but not a lot. Who knew how hard Ray'd fight with two bags of blood in the apartment. He said, "Ray's in a pretty bad way. I don't want to risk it. Is anyone with you?"

"Rich is down in the car. Buddy's going through their place for anything that might be useful to bring."

The glass made her look watery. Faded. He pressed his fingers to it. "Where's Jamie?"

"He hopped out the back of the truck when we pulled up and headed on his own way. He doesn't want to go to Vermont. I think after—I think after the thing got in the house, he gave up."

He was probably looking to get wasted, take himself to where it didn't matter what happened outside of his high. He thought of trying to catch up with him—Ray might actually like to see him there. It'd make him feel like everything was the way he always thought it should be, the whole band together. But he couldn't risk leaving Ray just to drag Jamie up to the apartment. What if Ray got free while he was gone? What if the place got torched? What if…Jesus, who knew? Anything could go wrong.

"You look bedraggled," his mom said.

"It's been a rough night."

"There's still time to come with us. I wish you were coming with us." She pressed her hand to the glass, on the other side of his.

"Ray's not in any condition to travel."

Tears brimmed, but she gave a sniff and straightened her back. "Maybe you can come later. When he's better." But they both knew she was saying *when he's gone*, or at least he knew it.

He pressed the heel of his hand to the corner of his eye. "Yeah, we'll do that."

"I love you, Dan."

"I love you too. Drive safe. Don't take any wooden nickels." He gave her a crooked smile that she matched with one of her own. She dabbed her eyes as she turned away. "You call me," she said, stopping halfway across the landing. "Keep trying till you get through."

"You too."

She rounded the landing. He pressed his forehead against the door, eyes squeezed shut, something trying to break free from his chest and follow her, be there to take care of her. But he had other things to see to.

When he came back to the bedroom, Ray said, "Were you talking to someone?" his voice scratchy and soft.

Dan hadn't bothered raising the shades when he'd gotten up; the room was dim and gloomy. Ray was a lump on the bed, his dark eyes feverish, his face drained.

Dan didn't want to get too close and set off another attack—lose Ray to another bout of unconsciousness. "It was my mom, checking up on us."

"Right."

Ray tugged at the cords. "Nice idea," he said. "Wish I'd thought of it." He tried to pull an ankle up the bed. The cords held it back. He lowered his head to the pillow. "This fucking headache, though. You have no idea."

No, he probably didn't. "Other than that, how're you feeling?"

"On the edge of losing it." He wrapped his fingers around a bar in the headboard, tilting his chin up. When he settled back down he said, "I didn't get you, did I?"

"You sure tried."

"I guess I'd feel a whole lot better right now if I had, right?"

"Anything I can get you?"

"A bucket to piss in and a glass of water?"

"How about a bottle of water? I found one in the trash and washed it out. I figured it'd be easier to handle than a glass. Straws would be even better, but you're apparently not a fan."

Ray laughed, a soft *chh* that ended with a grimace.

"I don't know what we're gonna do about the other situation." He hated to tell him he was probably going to have to piss the bed.

He almost made it with the water before the whites of Ray's eyes teemed with squirming darkness, and Ray's body fought the cords with everything it had. His neck corded as it strained.

His teeth snapped. Dan set the bottle between the pillow and headboard and walked out of the room. Walked all the way to the back door and put his hand against it, head bent, heart thudding like a drum.

THE BACK room was silent when heavy footsteps trudged up the steps. Dan held his breath, hoping they'd stop at the apartment next door. Their storm door rattled open. A sharp rap came. He pushed up from the chair.

"Can I see him?" Buddy held a hand above his eyes to shield the glare of the sun from the windowpanes on the kitchen door.

Dan shook his head.

"Danny, it's my fucking brother. We're *leaving*." He glanced toward the street, as if speaking the word had reminded him his wife and daughter were down there, out of sight.

"He's not good, Buddy. He's dangerous right now."

"*You're* in there with him."

"I don't have Jane and another kid on the way."

Buddy rattled the doorknob. The deadbolt was set: he'd have to break in to get in. Dan stepped closer. "As soon as he's better, we'll come up there. As soon as he can make the trip."

"Fuck. Is he taking blood yet?"

"No."

"Jesus. Give him some fucking blood. Do you want Sarah to draw some? Just fucking force it on him. This is stupid."

"I can handle it," Dan said, not wanting to leave Ray so he could get his blood drawn, not wanting to let anyone in there to do it. Not wanting to accept a container of anyone else's blood either—they'd need that themselves, with two of them infected.

"Give him fucking blood," Buddy said again.

Dan nodded.

Buddy looked like he had a hundred things to say. Finally he shook his head, looked off toward the street again. "This is some shit, isn't it? Fuck." He clenched his hands. Turned his back and swore again. Without turning to look at Dan, he said, "You guys take care of yourselves. We'll be looking for you." He glanced back. "If we get up there and find out it's not what we thought, we'll try to get a call through, or you'll see us back here in a few days."

"You guys be careful."

Buddy shook his head again, rueful. Started to walk away. Pulled himself back for one more thing, his fingertips pressed to the window in the door: "Tell that asshole I love him, okay?"

Hours passed. Dan puttered in the kitchen, watched a silent TV, strummed one of Ray's guitars.

As it got late, he stared out the window, until it was time to pull the shades again.

Unplugging the TV, he carried it into the bedroom, where he skirted the edge of the room, making Ray twitch and jerk but not come back to consciousness. He plugged it in and turned it on, volume off. Turned on a portable CD player because music was less horrible to fill his ears with than the news reports. He sat in the uncomfortable chair watching the world fall apart while Black Pistol Fire provided the soundtrack.

Doctors in lab coats got him to unmute the TV. He sat forward with the remote dangling in his fingers, hoping for hope.

All he got was, "They're more virulent than we at first thought," and before the doctor could explain why, he had the sound off again, preferring Kevin McKeown singing about getting his wheel greased to more shitty news.

Ray's breathing had a wheeze to it, a soft, high whistle. He lifted his head slowly to see what the glow was.

"There should be water in reach," Dan said.

Ray let his head drop back down. In the flickering of the TV, he licked his lips. "What're they saying?"

"Nothing good."

"Figured."

"How are you doing?" Dan asked.

"Feel like there's a tractor trailer driving inside my skull. How are *we* doing?"

"We've got this," Dan said. "We'll get through this. You let me know if you change your mind about feeding them, though. Say the fucking word and I'll do it." He thumbed the corner of his eye, flicking away a hot tear he hadn't expected. His throat hurt, like something sharp had gone sideways down it and gotten stuck. He stared hard at the TV, not seeing a thing.

"Fuck those fuckers," Ray whispered.

Dan told him the others were on their way. Left out what Buddy'd told him to say because his throat clamped hot around it when it tried to get it out. He left the room on the pretense of having to piss and squeezed silent tears from his eyes while he gripped the porcelain sink.

RAY FELL asleep on his own, no fit.

The things outside hit the windows, and Dan turned the music up, one eye on Ray's face to make sure it didn't flinch with discomfort. Blues were out of the question. He pulled up stuff they'd listened to in high school—the Violent Femmes, Man Made Murder. He found an old NIN CD half lodged behind the dresser—his, probably, from forever ago—and put that on for a while.

Then he just wanted silence.

He took himself to the bathroom. As he pissed, he realized he could shower now too. Ray wasn't going to be sneaking out, even if he got untied.

Voices jerked his head toward the kitchen door.

The storm door creaked open.

He zipped up and crept across the room.

The doorknob rattled.

Something scraped the wood on the other side of the door.

He backed up a few steps and reached through the bedroom doorway for the broomstick. Lot of fucking help that was going to be. Part of him wanted to announce there was someone infected in here—maybe that'd scare them off. But the bomb at the hospital… A sucker in here might scare them in all the wrong way. And Jesus, it was dark out. Whoever was out there was infected too.

What if it's Jamie?

Hushed voices exchanged quick words. Dan pushed up beside the door, just out of sight.

Metal scraped the metal of the lock.

"Hey," he said, sharp and low at the crack at the edge of the door, keenly aware that strangers were six inches from his face, separated by a few inches of wood.

The sounds stopped.

He closed his eyes for a second, praying this was all it would take. If Jamie were out there, he'd say something. He wouldn't just keep trying to break in. "We've got people in here and we're about out of food, but we've got plenty of bullets. You open that door, we'll fire first, ask questions later." What he wouldn't give for a gun to loudly cock right now.

The scuffling of boots sounded. The storm door fell shut.

He lowered the broomstick and sagged against the wall. He had no idea what he'd have done if they'd called his bluff with Ray in the other room the way he was. Dragging a dining chair over, he propped its back underneath the doorknob. It wasn't any more secure than the deadbolt, but at least he felt he'd done something.

When he went back to his seat in the bedroom, he set the broomstick across his lap and listened to Ray's slow, wheezy breaths in the darkness.

This couldn't go on like this. What if Ray was wrong? What if the things fucking killed him? He rummaged in a kitchen drawer for a knife with a sharp edge. On his way into the bedroom, he turned on the overhead light—the last thing he needed was to accidentally cut an artery in the dark and bleed out just five feet from Ray.

Ray looked like shit, his hair matted, circles like bruises under his eyes.

The knife's wooden handle was worn soft, its blade heavy, a good six inches long. He pressed the edge against his palm and took another step.

Ray didn't move. Maybe there was a point where the things got too weak to spaz him out—maybe he'd reached that point. The blade made his hand itch. He took another step. They could go to Vermont after this. Get out of this stale, dark box. Ride with the windows open, the Fury's engine roaring up I-89.

Ray's eyelids creased. His fingers twitched.

Holding his breath, Dan waited.

When Ray was still again, Dan set a knee on the edge of the bed. He looked down so he could watch the blade make a dent in his palm. He clenched his teeth and pressed harder.

The bats batted the windows with their fat bodies. More tonight than last night. More last night than the night before. More tomorrow probably than tonight. Gestation cycle speeding up, especially in the re-infected. Suckers were sneaking of out hospitals, driven by the things to hatch in private. One hospital had been quietly putting the infected to sleep, and when word got out, people were torn over whether that was the right thing to do—for the rest of us—or the wrong thing to do because they could be fed and cured…only to hide in the dark with everyone else, waiting for food to run out, for the next bat or sucker to get them. On the street it was every man for himself as suckers who'd escaped and suckers who hadn't gone in to begin with went after blood.

Dan's arm dropped like a lead weight.

And the shit that was in Ray woke up. It woke up and snapped and bit, twisting and straining Ray's body. His limbs yanked the electrical cords. Snarls and growls came husky from Ray's throat. His eyes were black as marbles. Moving. Swirling. The things still small, unfed. Fucking starving, Dan hoped.

Wood cracked.

Dan pedaled backward, holding the knife in front of him.

Ray's ankle came free. He twisted his body, trying to crawl across the bed, his other limbs still attached to it. The broken post his ankle was tied to bumped along the blankets as he dug his foot into the mattress, trying to get to Dan.

Dan strode around the bed and out the bedroom door. Through the kitchen. Into the living room, clutching his hands into fists, clutching the knife in his fist. It took fucking forever for the bed in the other room to stop creaking.

He sat on the couch, the knife still in his hand, his other hand dented from the edge of the blade. He clutched the hilt against his forehead, squeezed his eyes shut. After a long minute where he couldn't move at all, his hand finally opened and let the knife clatter to the floor.

CHAPTER FORTY-SIX

DAN TUGGED at the shade. It flew up with a rattle. He squinted in the brightness of the morning sun. The room needed airing out. With Ray tied to the bed for days, the room was in a state worse than stale. He flipped the latches and worked the old wood frames up. One of them needed a book lodged underneath to keep it open.

Brisk air swept in. That was an improvement too, though he couldn't let it go on too long. Ray was a bundle of sticks, his wrists just thin bones. He'd be able to slip free of the cords if this went on much longer. But would he have the energy to do anything once he was free? The bottle of water was untouched. He hadn't had food. His chest went long seconds without moving. Dan hadn't even bothered retying his leg. He didn't want to set another fit off, use up what energy Ray still had.

Come on, come on.

He edged toward the bed. Ray made a better vampire than he ever had—dark hair, skin gone so pale the thin blue veins underneath showed, lips a dusky purple. His breathing was faint and hitching.

Beat those fuckers already.

As Dan picked up a blanket and spread it over him, Ray's fingers twitched. His jaws moved weakly. A noise came from his throat. But he didn't wake up.

Dan pulled the chair close and sat watching him, elbows digging into his knees, chin braced in his hands. Ray'd only been sick once since he'd known him—colds yeah, tour crud yeah, but not *sick* sick, except that time he'd had food poisoning and couldn't even get out of bed. Telling him he'd go to the doctor once he felt better. *Then* Dan hadn't been worried, because Sarah, with her nursing efficiency, hadn't been worried. If Sarah could see him now...

"Hey, Ray?" he said.

Ray's chest went up a little, then sank.

Dan bent his head and pulled at his hair.

LUNCH WAS Rice-A-Roni that stuck in his throat until he gave up spooning it into his mouth. The TV was full of riot gear. In real life, gunshots echoed somewhere to the north.

Dan closed the windows and pulled the shades.

Yelling came from the street. The clang of metal hitting metal. He went into the bathroom, shut the door, and sat on the floor, his back against the wall, his face in his hands.

IT WAS dark again. Ray stirred without waking. A keening came from his throat, ending as quickly as it started.

The things batted the windows.

He scooped a shirt off the floor and lobbed it at the shade. It didn't do any good, but it made him feel better. He wanted to throw bigger things, heavier things. He wanted to destroy everything.

Ray moaned—sudden and sharp. In the flickering light of the TV, Dan went to the bedside.

Ray shivered under the blanket.

Dan sank to his knees and put a hand on Ray's stomach, his chin on the blankets. The things inside Ray spazzed—they were still there, still winning. Ray's lips pulled back, showing pale gums. His teeth snapped without any ferocity. His eyes rolled back. What had started as an urge to attack became a convulsion, Ray's body shuddering, teeth clattering, bedposts banging the wall.

Dan held him with that one hand, head bent. *We can do this. We'll get through this.*

Thinking of those campfires in the woods behind his mom's, firelight flickering across Ray's face—Ray smiling, saying yeah, that's what we'll call ourselves. *I like that.*

He watched the silent TV, his cheek on the blankets. The epidemic flashing soundlessly on the screen. A mother running with a child on her hip and another pulled along by her hand. Smoke billowing behind them. The inside of a school gym, row upon row of blankets—people's lives reduced to the size of coffins laid out across a basketball court. The camera panned over two dark bodies on the floor of the emptied gym, like footage from a war in the Middle East, only the caption said East Orange.

He thought about the others. They'd be where they were going by now, unless they'd run into roadblocks. Unless they'd run into trouble. He passed a hand over his face, not wanting to imagine that. He just wanted to think of them stepping cautiously out of their cars. Wondering if what they'd heard was true. And then a door would open, people would come out, asking how many of them there were, if anyone was infected, if anyone needed care. If they needed food, a place to stay.

He wanted to remember it *that* way.

Ray's body shook under his hand. His teeth rattled.

The TV cut to the White House, footage from earlier in the day, sun in the windows. No one was out at night anymore, except the suckers, who could go anywhere anytime while the rest of them huddled behind drawn curtains, planks of wood, and whatever weapons they had.

A movement to the left caught Dan's attention, dragging it to the shadows beyond the half-open door of Ray's closet. His chest tightened. He blinked, hard, adjusting his eyes from staring at the lit-up television screen. While his eyes were closed, he could see it. That fucking *cat.*

But when he opened them, there was nothing there.

Under his hand, Ray went still.

DAN WAS alone.

A white coat was on the television, the creases in her face saying what Dan didn't need words to hear.

Hot tears washed his eyes.

He hauled the TV off the dresser, its screen hot against his chest. He turned to the window, hefted it up, and threw it at the window.

The shade fell off its bracket with a clatter. Glass exploded. Cold air whipped in—welcome. Real. Smelling of January, bringing wet flakes of snow with it. The papery flutter of wings sounded. A heavy body landed on the sill. He crawled up the bed, over the top of the blankets, Ray's leg unmoving under him, Ray's chest still beneath his palm. More wings, more creatures gathering on the sill, watching. He wrapped an arm around Ray and buried his face in Ray's neck, smelling sweat, smelling the faintest trace of cigarette. A sour laugh rose like bile in his throat: *Hey, you kicked those finally. I've only been after you about it for years.*

At the edge of his vision, the light rippled with shadows. Parasites careened into walls, their wings dry and beating fast, whispers like pages riffling. One of the fat bodies thudded into the lamp.

A crash, a shatter of glass, and the room was plunged into darkness.

EPILOGUE

I REMEMBER Faye's house in the woods. I remember the woods. The boarded-up windows, the short days and the endless nights without stars. I remember Dan and Uncle Ray and their guitars.

"Are you going to make us do the spider song again?"

We left without them. The trip was a blur of color—pines rushing by the truck's windows, abandoned gas stations, a tricycle on its side. I don't remember Dan arriving, though you'd think I would. The memory I have is one I could only have formed later, when I had a better understanding. In this memory, it's a ghost that arrives. Someone hollow and half gone, which is how I think of him still. I can conjure him, in that chair on the porch at the end of the day, watching the shadows grow like tendrils across the grass. Sometimes Uncle Ray was in his eyes. Other times I could see the road there, stretching to someplace in the past.

By then it had ended, like a fever breaking, and there was no reason to fear the shadow, though it took years before I stopped.

When Faye was gone, I remember Dan getting on a motorcycle while the dug-into dishes of macaroni and cheese and plates of cake sat in the chapel. I remember him sliding his sunglasses on, cranking the throttle. The bike's engine cut through the quiet. He looked at me, and the late-afternoon sun shot off his lenses. That was when I was seventeen. I remember because that was my birthday cake in there, laid out with the funeral food.

I remember his scars from the cruor worms. He wasn't alone; near the end, the cruors crawled over people like maggots, overloading them with larvae, causing far more damage than the first attacks had. In the boarded-up dorms at Northlands—in the basements, with rows of shower stalls and washing machines and the earth's cold fingers reaching through the concrete floor—we were mostly protected, but you still see some survivors now with their bodies marked by circles that stayed pale even in the summer. Dan had one in particular, I remember, at the corner of his lip. So many more when he worked in the summer sun with his shirt draped over a fencepost.

There are so few of us.

I often wonder how far he had to ride to find anyone else, or if he ever even bothered to stop.

"Can we sing the spider song?" my son asks, his fist clutching my skirt. I take the beat-up acoustic that belonged to his great-uncle off the shelf, with the neck that Dan glued back on when I was ten, and I lead him into the sunshine, where we can sing while his father chops wood for the winter that will be here again all too soon.

—Jane Ford Cole

Acknowledgements

I need to thank Mr. Rider, first, for giving me some of the most important gifts: space, understanding, and patience. Also, it turns out he missed his calling: developmental editing.

My good friend Nick also helped a great deal in getting the story as good as it could be before it went to editing.

My Dirty Birds, Kate Lowell and Ana J. Phoenix, provided help for this book even when we weren't at all talking *about* this book.

I also need to thank my mom, Mary Ann Wells. I don't know that I wouldn't have reached this point without the care package she sent to me in Okinawa back in 1992, but I like to think the message of "I believe in you" that those two books carried, at a time when writing was the farthest thing from my mind, was one of the flutters of butterfly wings that eventually got me here.

My editor, Ashley Davis, was a great help. Damon Za designed a gorgeous cover that was miles better than anything I could have imagined on my own. Illustrator Nate Olson made my creature "real" with his talent.

Thank you to my awesome Kickstarter backers, who made possible things that would not have been otherwise:

Sue Bibeault • Maria J. Blakely • Elizabeth Broderick• Matt Butler • Michael Cammarata • Rhel ná DecVandé • Duke • Skeet Dupree • Fred • Lia hmq • Richard Kashinski • Kelpie • George Lee • Amy Linsamouth • Ron Locke • Bridget Loo • Peter McQuilian • James Moss • Ashley Oswald • Chan Ka Chun Patrick • Wit Phelps • Ana J. Phoenix • Jake Pierson • Megan Reed • Adriane Ruzak • Jeri-Lyn Thomas • Uncle Howard and Aunt Judi • Christinna Viruet • Collin Wells • Mark W. Wells • Mary Ann Wells • Jay Wells • Peter Wells • Ron & Aggie Wells • and Cheri Woods

You guys are the best!

Thanks for the Music

A number of actual bands/musicians were mentioned in *Suckers.*

Dead Confederate (*www.deadconfederate.com)* played over the P.A. in the first chapter.

Dan mentions Jimi Hendrix (*www.jimihendrix.com*) & Greg Ginn (*gregginn.com*) as influences on Ray's early playing.

Dan puts Bass Drum of Death (*www.bassdrumofdeath.com*) on in his bus bunk.

On the way back from taking Jamie to detox, Dan plays Louisiana Red (*http://youtu.be/BtwPgpK1Wmg*).

Leaving town, Dan starts up "The Likes of You" by Black Rebel Motorcycle Club (*blackrebelmotorcycleclub.com*).

One of the girls in Esmy's shop tells Ray he looks like "that guy from The Dead Weather." (*www.thedeadweather.com*)

On the way to the donation that goes bad, Dan's got METZ's "Negative Space" stuck in his head. (*www.metzztem.com*)

Dan plays Blind Willie Johnson's "Dark Was the Night, Cold Was the Ground," (*http://youtu.be/BNj2BXW852g*) and Robert Johnson's "Cross Road Blues" (*http://youtu.be/Yd60nI4sa9A*) on Ray's guitar after he gets Ray home from Sound Block.

While watching the news with the sound off, Dan listens to Black Pistol Fire's *Hush or Howl.* (*www.blackpistolfire.com*) Later that night, Dan plays a some stuff he and Ray listened to in high school: The Violent Femmes (*www.vfemmes.com*) and Nine Inch Nails (*www.nineinchnails.com*).

None of these bands were in involved with or endorse *Suckers.* They're simply a few of the (many) musicians who've given me great music to listen to over the years.

Z. Rider

www.zriderwriter.com
twitter.com/ZRiderHorror
facebook.com/zoexriderfiction

Join the mailing list to be notified of upcoming releases:
http://eepurl.com/ZbGGP

Z. grew up in New Hampshire and lives in the mountains of northeast Tennessee, where she spends most of her time in a windowless basement basking in the glow of computer screens, except when she's out on the deck swing reading a book, or running off to catch a concert somewhere. SUCKERS is her first horror novel. Her second, MAN MADE MURDER, will be released October 13, 2015.

More from Dark Ride

www.darkridepublishing.com

Man Made Murder by Z. Rider

Book One of the Blood Road Trilogy

Guitarist Dean Thibodeaux leaves a radio station after an interview and crosses the street to a biker bar, hoping to score some weed the night before Man Made Murder embarks on what he's worried could be their last tour, at least under the High Class Records label. The next morning, he wakes in his pickup truck, his shirt stiff with blood.

Twenty-year-old Carl Delacroix has driven two thousand miles to confront the knife-toting biker who killed his sister. He arrives at the bar across from the radio station just in time to lose him again.

One man is hunting evil; the other is becoming it. Salvation lies in the crossing of their paths.

Coming October 2015 from Dark Ride Publishing

More Indie Reading

Not from Dark Ride Publishing, but Dark-Ride-recommended:

MOVERS by Evan Clark

They exist in every big city and small town. They are scattered across the world. Always small. Always inviting. Always friendly. Shopfronts with handwritten signs in the windows, shelves stacked with baubles and cheap antiques. Little treasures. Precious things.

The places that most walk by without a second look. They open. They close. They move in the night. These are the rules.

Jamie Christop is a professional. He's a man without a past or future. During the day, he goes unnoticed, a face that fades into the crowd. At night, he's a veteran of a thousand bars, parking lot fights, and one night stands. He's the empty corner table, the sucker punch in the dark, the shadow that slips away.

He is a mover.

CONSUMPTION (a short story) by Michael Patrick Hicks

You Are... Reclusive chef Heinrich Schauer has invited six guests to a blind twelve-course tasting menu.

What You Eat... While snow blankets the isolated Swiss valley surrounding his estate, the guests feast eagerly, challenging one another to guess at the secret tastes plated before them.

Meat Is Murder... As they eat, each guest is overtaken by carnal appetites, unaware of their host's savage plans... or of the creature lurking below.

One thing is clear: There is more on the menu than any of them have bargained for.